SPARTAN KRYPTEA

PRESS

14172 E Carlson Rd. • Brule, WI 54820
(218) 391-3070 • www.savpress.com

SPΛRTΛN KRYPTEΛ

John F. Saunders

First Edition

Cover Design: Dezime Graphics

ISBN: 978-1-937706-17-3

Library of Congress Catalog Number: 2017946555

Published by:
    Savage Press
    14172 E Carlson Rd.
    Brule, WI 54820
    Email: mail@savpress.com
    Website: www.savpress.com
    Printed in the United States of America

To
Emily

Keeper of Secrets,
Speaker of truth.
The best of us.

Enjoy

And let a man throw his javelin for the last time as he dies. For it is honorable and glorious for a man to fight…against his foes.

Kallinos of Ephesus (650 BC)

1

Frank Kane moved with a singleness of purpose. His eyes were locked like lasers on a target. His movements were quick and controlled as he stalked his prey. Huge muscled shoulders transferred their power through steel strong arms. Just as his hand reached the target the thick wrist turned the fist over.

"Pop. Pop. Pop."

Three quick explosive jabs.

"Boom!"

The big right hand followed as the left withdrew. It was lights out. It was a fight ender. It was a man killer. Robert Chapman smiled.

"Good. Now do it faster. Push it. Push it. Slip. Slip."

The thick leather boxing mitts moved quicker and Frank matched their speed, dodging the teacher's own lightning fast counter punches.

"Pop. Pop. Pop. Boom."

"Now step back and repeat it."

"Pop. Pop. Pop. Boom. Pop. Pop. Pop. Boom!"

"Again," Chapman shouted. "Faster. Faster."

The strikes of the sixteen ounce gloves on the boxing mitts were the sound of war. It was a machine gun staccato repeated over and over. Pop. Pop. Pop. Boom.

"Now the hook. Harder. Again. Again. Snap it. Push. Push."

A bell clanged outside the ring. "Thirty seconds," Chapman said. "You're behind. You got to take this round. Ten seconds. Take it. Take it."

Frank hit harder, faster. His hands were a blur and Chapman struggled to stay ahead of the strikes. Pop. Pop. Boom. Pop. Pop. Boom. The bell sounded.

"Time," Chapman said.

Frank's arms fell to his sides. He was drenched in sweat. His Fallen Kings tee shirt clung to his massive heaving chest. His legs ached. His arms throbbed. The muscles in his back clenched in spasms of overexertion. He smiled too. This was what he had wanted. This was what he had needed. A few months earlier Frank had nearly lost a fight in Fort Worth to a big Russian brawler. It was not in a boxing ring, but in a lamp store. There had been no bells. No referee. It had been life and death.

Frank Kane had once been the chief enforcer for the Spartans motorcycle club. It was an outlaw group, one per-centers, that had grown to immense size and power on the East Coast. He was retired now. He had survived an assassination attempt by his closest friend. He had reinvented himself. He had gone straight. He had tried to do the right things. The right things had included taking in a couple of girls who were caught up in the sex trade in Atlanta. The right things had included a trip to Fort Worth to rescue a friend's brother from some Russians. And now the right thing meant boxing lessons.

Frank needed to refine his technique. Training at home on a heavy bag was different from training in a gym with a former professional boxer as your coach. Robert Chapman was a renowned professional boxer known for his hand speed and counter punching prowess. Chapman worked as the principal coach at the Al Lowe Boxing Club in Greensboro. Frank had come by and introduced himself and arranged for after hours lessons two days a week.

"You sure you never boxed pro?" Chapman asked.

"Yeah."

"You got the power and you got the fastest hands I've ever worked with. And I have worked with some really fast cats. I enjoyed it."

"You tried to kill me."

"That's what you pay me for. To push you."

"How do you know how hard you can push?"

"I know. I watch you. Feel your punch strength. Watch you breathing. I haven't found your breaking point. Yet."

Frank noticed another guy in the gym. He was in his fifties, tall and thin. He was working the same routine Frank did. Double-ended bag, upper cut bag, heavy bag, speed bag, and mitts. Sweat streamed from his bald head. He seemed to be talking to himself.

Frank nodded toward the other man. "I thought the gym was closed."

"It is."

"Who's that guy? He looks like a cop."

"No. He ain't a cop. That's just Doc. Everybody loves Doc. He's up here a lot."

"How did he get in if the gym is closed?"

"Doc's got his own key. Don't know where he got it, but he does. Doc is resourceful. You want to meet him. You'd like him. Hey, Doc, this is Frank. He wants to know if you want to spar a little."

Doc looked up and smiled. "I don't think so."

"Come on three rounds. Give the big guy a work out."

"It wouldn't be three rounds. More like one."

"Why one?"

"I would knock your boy out in the first round. Trust me, he doesn't want any of this." Doc tapped his gloves together for emphasis.

Chapman laughed. "He's funny for a dentist."

The bell sounded. Frank looked at Chapman.

"You got another one in you big man? That would be twelve."

Frank tapped his own gloves together. "I'll be gone on vacation next week. Let's go."

Chapman smiled. His teeth were perfect, Frank thought. Chapman was either super quick or Doc really was a good dentist.

"Pop. Pop. Pop. Pop. Boom. Boom. Boom."

2

There was no wind. No clouds. There was only the thick wet heat of the Caribbean night. The night birds sang a melancholy song in the still darkness. The moon hung, a silent witness to the earthly preparations below. A moth flitted in, drawn by the flickering lamp light.

The man was stretched spread eagle on the ground. His wrists and ankles were secured by leather thongs to wooden stakes pounded into the soft ground with a wooden mallet made from the stump of a lightning struck oak tree. The man was nude. His clothes had been carefully cut away and left folded into a neat pile beside him. His shoes had been unlaced and left on the mound of his discarded clothes. Strange glyphs in indigo and crimson had been painted all over his exposed flesh. The man glistened in a fine sheen of sweat that was not caused by the heat. Tears leaked from his eyes.

The man made no sound. He could not. His lips had been sewn together using a bone from a black cock as a needle and special yarn woven from a dead witch's hair. The yarn was thick and black and left the man with the appearance of a ragged gibbous smile.

Four people crouched near the body and observed it quietly. Three were men, One was a woman. Each head was shaven. Each wore a necklace made from the finger bones of previous sacrifices. Each wore a white tee shirt with a red handprint on the front.

A fifth figure approached slowly up the path. This person's shoes crunched the rocks like distant gunfire. This figure was a scarecrow of a man. He wore a white hoodie sweatshirt with the same red hand emblazoned on the front. The new man was tall and gangly, and moved with an awkward gait like the offspring of a man and a stork.

The man pushed his hoodie back, revealing that he too had a shaved head. He twisted his head at different angles as he watched the bound man. He smiled at his acolytes. He smiled at the weeping man. He knelt beside the man and wiped the moisture from his eyes. He smelled it, then touched it to his tongue. He smiled again.

"Cry, Babylon. Cry."

The tears continued to pour from the man's eyes.

"You tears naa baddaa I, Babylon. De dark one welcomes dem in his place in de blood fire. De place of lost hope."

The man tried to struggle against his bonds. The stork-man patted him reassuringly.

"Rest now, Babylon. Rest. You baited up for de young hotsa girls. De Prophet have you now. I and I naa let you free. All is given. All is forfeit to Lord Tosh. None can escape I power."

The Prophet turned to the others and spoke for their ears. "De daemon, Dreadmon, call to I across I dreams. He say five tosand souls he need to break free and come from blood fire to dis wurl. Five tosand. Wid each I gain power. Wid each de peoples of dis wurl turn to I for protection. Jah is weak. Jesus Christ is weak. Allah is weak. De fat Buddha is weak. Only Dreadmon be strong. Only Dreadmon can free dis wicked wicked wurl."

The four acolytes murmured their awe and agreement.

"De rude boys fear de five. De hard men put de fear in the belly. Dey come to I and I for helps. 'Catch de D. E. A. mon,' dey beg. Money dey send. Tribute dey give. Only Lord Tosh can help dem. Only Lord Tosh can save dem."

The woman rose and approached the Prophet. She knelt at his feet and placed a small leather packet on the ground. She unrolled it without looking up into the Prophet's face. Inside was a fat ganja spliff. She raised it in offering. Lord Tosh took the spliff and lit it with a gold lighter. He breathed in the bittersweet smoke and held it in his lungs for a few seconds before exhaling. He nodded his approval.

"Share dis herb wit you brothers, Little Bird." Lord Tosh spoke to his acolyte. "Let de divine herb calm you for de task ahead. Let it make de will strong."

The four acolytes smoked in silence. Occasionally they would nod to each other. When the spliff was burnt to a small stub, the last one chewed it and ate it. That man rose and approached the Prophet. He too carried a leather packet. He unrolled it. Inside was a brown glass vial the size of a man's hand, and a thin white straw carved from the bone of a dead child. He lifted the items to Lord Tosh.

Lord Tosh unscrewed the vile and dipped the straw inside. He placed one long finger over the other end as he packed the straw. He knelt beside the captive D.E.A. agent.

"Dreadmon waits for you soul. But de takin be long. Much pain. Sometimes de dying too quick. Dis will help."

He removed the straw. A sickly yellow powder clung to one end. He placed it into the man's nostril and blew hard. The man thrashed wildly. Lord Tosh repeated his actions, blowing the powder into the other nostril. The man shook, then calmed.

"Dis will not ease de pain. Noting will ease de pain. Dis will make your heart strong so you not die too soon."

The man's eyes were wild with terror. Lord Tosh patted him on the head like a man pats a favorite pet. "When you see de Dreadmon whisper our names." He nodded first toward the girl, Little Bird, then to the man who had brought the yellow powder, Roach, then to a man with a thick tangled beard whose name was Dawg, and lastly to Bat, a small, thin man. "Dreadmon will know I name. Tis de time of offering."

The man called Dawg moved toward the Prophet with his parcel. He unrolled it. Inside were six knives. Their blades were long and thin like fisherman's filleting knives. Their handles were wooden and carved with bizarre markings. Four of the knives were the same, but the fifth knife was different. Its blade was longer and thicker. Where the other blades glistened silver steel, this blade shone onyx black. The handle was thicker, and a tangle of beads and feather fetish hung from it. Lord Tosh nodded, and Dawg handed him the black bladed knife. Dawg then rose and passed a knife to each of the other three.

"I children will remove you flesh to free you soul for Dreadmon. He will drink de pain you offer. Den I will cut out de wicked heart, Babylon, and send you to meet de father of daemons."

The last acolyte rose and lifted a backpacker's day pack. He knelt in front of Lord Tosh and removed its contents. It was a large ancient boom box. He checked to be sure the batteries were in place, and passed it up to Lord Tosh. The Prophet carried it a few feet away and sat it gently on the ground. He smiled at his children.

"Take you places," he commanded, and each of the four moved to a different arm or leg. They placed their knives lightly against the man's flesh. Each turned toward Lord Tosh and waited.

Lord Tosh turned on the CD player. Creedence Clearwater Revival began to sing about a bad moon on the rise. John Fogerty's creaky voice rose and fell with a distinctive Cajun lilt. Lord Tosh swayed from side to side. Then like a scarecrow released from its perch, he began to dance. He swirled and dipped like a bird on unseen wind currents. The four turned back to the body. They each locked eyes with the others and then they began to skin the D.E.A. agent alive. Dreadmon drank in his pain.

3

Claudia Murphy scanned the departure lounge. She checked her Cartier watch. Her respectable two-inch high heels clacked as she walked a few steps and then stopped to check her watch again. She wore a tasteful black double breasted suit with a white blouse and a small elegant string of pearls. She looked exactly like what she was, a successful business woman.

She was the president of VIP Travel in Charlotte, North Carolina. She organized conventional trips and specialty travel for her elite clients. She had not always been so legitimate. Long ago, she had worked for the notorious Spartans motorcycle club. She had run one of their most profitable strip clubs. When the local Spartan Captain had tried to force her into the rotation of call girls they ran, there had been trouble. Frank Kane had been called. Frank Kane was one of the founders of the Spartans. Why he had decided to involve himself in such a petty dispute, she never knew. But he did. He met with her, and when he learned of her background in travel, he had seen a unique opportunity for the Spartans. Thus, they had created VIP travel as both a legitimate travel agency and as a cover for less legal transportation needs. She had arranged numerous trips for Frank over the years. She even thought that at some level they had become friends. If one can truly say a wild lion is their friend.

The Spartans had grown incredibly large and powerful, drawing the intense interest of every law enforcement agency with a handful of initials . Eventually, they had fallen. The leaders had been killed, arrested, or simply had disappeared. She had not heard from Frank Kane in half a dozen years since the Spartans fell. That was until a few months ago.

Frank had contacted her and had her arrange a private trip to the Bahamas for him and a small group of friends. He had called it a vacation, but she doubted it. If Frank Kane was involved, it was never what it appeared. She wondered what he was really up to. She knew she had to find out.

But now where was he? He was late, and Frank Kane was never late. What if he had changed his mind? What if he wasn't coming? It didn't matter and she knew it. She would wait. She would wait all day and all night and all day again. She would not leave.

If Frank did show, he might consider her absence a sign of disrespect. She knew she didn't want him mad at her. Those people had a nasty habit of disappearing.

She watched an Eagle taxi work its way up the long drive toward the small private plane departure area. It was a local cab. The cab pulled to a stop. Claudia quickly memorized the cab number. It would be good to know where Frank had come from.

The driver got out and hurried to the trunk. He removed a backpack. It was a dull green. It looked like military surplus. The back door of the cab opened and a giant emerged. Frank Kane was six feet four inches tall and a little over two hundred and thirty pounds. He moved with the easy grace of an elite athlete, a professional dancer, or a lion. He radiated danger. His hair had been cut away to a buzz cut and the thick beard he had once sported was gone, but he was still the same man. He glanced around the area. His eyes swept over Claudia, but made no reaction. He turned to the cab driver and paid him. The man thanked him and drove away.

Frank lifted his bag and walked toward Claudia. Then he did something few people had ever seen him do. He smiled. It was a pretty good smile, she thought. Her heart raced a little.

"Frank," she said extending her hand.

Frank took her hand gently. "Claudia. It has been a long time."

"Yes, it has. What have you been up to?"

"I've been around. Trying to stay out of trouble."

"I was worried that when the Spartans went down that something might have happened to you."

The smile again. More genuine, she thought. He seemed almost human.

"They can't kill me, Claudia. You know that. I'm glad you agreed to help me."

She blushed a little. She felt nervous, like a teenager on a date.

"Who could say no to you? Did you have a long ride?"

Frank stared at her, calculating something.

"Not too bad."

"I could have arranged a limo."

"I know, Claudia. But it is better if you don't know where I am. You understand. I still have enemies."

"Of course. Of course, Frank. I just meant..."

"I know what you meant. Did you make the arrangements I asked for?"

"Absolutely. No passports, no customs inspections, off the books, good hotel, nice beach, blue Caribbean waters, not too touristy all included. Did I forget anything?"

"No. That sounds about right."

He handed her a fat envelope filled with cash. She slipped it into her purse without looking inside. Counting it in front of Frank would be disrespectful.

"One small change in plans. I know we talked about Eleuthera..."

"It is Greek for freedom."

Claudia paused. Where did he get this stuff from, she thought. "I didn't know that. Anyway, after they caught that barefoot criminal guy, the island has become a lot more security conscious."

"So where?"

"There is a nearby island called Cat Island. Named after a pirate. Less people. Less crowded. Just as beautiful."

"Cops?"

"They have a dinky saltbox jail and a handful of cops, three or four, to look after the drunks. A couple more customs agents that stick to the airport."

"Sounds right. Who did you get to pilot?"

"Phil. You said you wanted Phil Bullington, so I got him. I didn't think it was negotiable."

"It wasn't. We got some history."

"Do you know how hard it is keeping him clean enough to fly? He is into the coke pretty hard. Almost got shot down over Cuba."

"I like him."

Claudia held up her hands in the universal gesture for don't be mad at me.

"I know. I know. He's on board. But I thought there were supposed to be four of you."

Frank placed two fingers in his mouth and whistled. Three people came out of the airport lounge. Claudia had seen them, but dismissed them as kids going on a Thanksgiving vacation trip. They weren't the kind of hard men that usually accompanied Frank.

DC was wearing a faded tee shirt with the logo for some obscure metal band called DOPE. He stopped to pull up his pair of baggy cargo shorts. Jenny and Caron were both wearing thin sun dresses and oversized sunglasses. They were pretty in the way young girls are all pretty, with perfect skin, soft hair and unselfconscious smiles. They could have been sisters. The three had been invisible to her. She rearranged her previous scenarios about Frank Kane's trip.

"I see why you and Phil get along so well. He likes them very young too."

"It's not what you think."

"You don't know what I'm thinking."

Claudia was smiling.

"Yes, I do, Claudia. I know exactly what you are thinking all the time."

"Well, you have to admit that she is a little young for you."

"Thanks, Mom."

Claudia turned from Frank and walked toward the three approaching. She extended her hand.

"Hi. I'm Claudia."

DC shook her hand and started to speak. Frank cut him off.

"She doesn't need to know your names."

DC nodded. "Right. Sorry. Nice to meet you."

The girls followed suit shaking her hand but not introducing themselves either. Claudia turned back toward Frank.

"You are so paranoid."

"Old habits. That's why I'm still here. Remember I know how you think."

"And how is that?"

"Just like me. That's why I like you."

Claudia shook her head at Frank. She wasn't sure if that was a great compliment or an insult.

"Come on everyone, I'll walk you to the plane."

Everyone carried their own small bag. The girls were laughing and pushing each other like puppies.

Bullington met them at the passenger door of the plane. It was a twin turboprop called the Queen Air. It was made by Beechcraft in the 1960s and 70s. It had a distinctive straight-up tail. The Queen Air was the workhorse for drug smugglers everywhere. Frank remembered that it cruised at something like 160 knots, but you could push the maximum speed up to 215 knots if you had to. He had flown in the Queen Air too many times to count. Bullington was wearing navy shorts, a white short sleeve shirt with worn navy and red epaulets on the shoulders and slides on his feet.

"Big man," Bullington said. "It's good to see you up and kicking again."

"Good to be alive."

"I heard that. Every day is a good day."

"You know the plan?"

"Claudia, briefed me. Just like the old days."

"Just like."

"Don't worry about a thing. I got everything wired to go. I got a cooler with some water and beers for the flight and a paper bag back there with some snacks if you get hungry."

"Thanks."

"Alrighty, everybody grab a seat and buckle up."

Claudia smiled. "It is like old times isn't it?"

"Sort of. Take care of yourself."

"Phil will pick you up at the airport at eight on Sunday. Thanksgiving makes it a little easier to pull off. Lots of travel. Lots of borders to watch. Lots of people to watch. You will be fine."

"I know. And Claudia..."

"What?"

"In case you plan on calling the cab company and finding out where he picked me up... well he picked me up at the Sheraton where another cab dropped me, that picked me up from another hotel and so on. You won't find my ride so don't waste your Thanksgiving weekend trying. They are all dead ends."

"Frank, I wasn't planning anything like that."

"Of course you were. It's what I would do. Knowledge is power. Look after yourself."

"You too. And stay out of trouble."

"I always do."

John F. Saunders

4

Helen stood with her arms crossed. She was angry and she wasn't hiding it. She glared at her husband Cyrus.

"You do understand why I have to do it, don't you, Helen?" Cyrus asked.

"You do what you think is best," she answered and turned away to stare around the master bedroom of the mansion. It was a move perfected by women all over the world. She seemed to be studying the sofa as if she had never seen it before. She drew a long, perfectly manicured hand along the fabric.

"Helen."

She didn't respond. She sighed just deeply enough for an observant man to notice. She had never been angry. Not really angry. But for her plan to work she needed to seem to have been. She let her head tilt just a fraction as a sign of resignation. When she turned back toward Cyrus she wore a small thin smile.

"Helen, you understand why I'm sending Ronnie? Why I have to."

"Darling, I understand you completely."

"I have enemies. You do too. It wouldn't be prudent..."

"I know," Helen said taking his hand. "You are only trying to protect me like you always do. I am being selfish and silly."

Cyrus smiled. He was handsome. He was strong. He was brilliant. He was a wealthy businessman. He was also the past president of the Spartans motorcycle club in his former life. The Spartans had assigned the name of a god to each of their founders. Cyrus was Zeus. He was the first among equals. He was cautious, paranoid and ruthless with his enemies. The Spartans were all gone now. Betrayed, persecuted, infiltrated, and ultimately attacked. Cyrus had disappeared after the assault on his compound in Asheville, North Carolina. He had reemerged with Helen by his side. Without his leadership, what was left of the organization had deteriorated to anarchy and eventually disappeared. They had too many enemies. He had seen that coming. He had prepared for it. He had taken precautions. He had helped to orchestrate it. It was better this way. Fame had a price.

Helen leaned forward and kissed him on his cheek. "It is almost three. The girls will be here soon. I better go down to meet them."

She reached to pick up her Louis Vuitton suitcase. Cyrus took it from her.

"Let me get that for you."

"Thank you."

She followed Cyrus down the stairs. She studied his back. Despite the change in his appearance, he was still the same man. That man inside did not change. She knew him so well. Knew his secrets. Knew his passions. Knew his fear. His only fear was Frank Kane.

Helen and Frank had been lovers a lifetime ago. She had given herself to Cyrus in an effort to save them both. It had succeeded, but it had killed something inside her. She had loved Frank with all of her heart, but it wasn't enough in the end. That was not why he feared Frank. Cyrus was a practical man. He feared Frank because he believed one day Frank would come for him. He believed in the truth of his darkest fear, that somehow Frank would discover his treachery and seek retribution.

Cyrus had molded Frank into a remorseless, unstoppable, killing machine. He had mixed Frank's rage, and power with a heady brew of Greek honor. If Frank turned his mind toward Cyrus, he would not be stopped. Helen cringed slightly. Frank might come for her as well. He might seek justice from her as well. Love would not sway him. Nothing swayed the Spartans' chief enforcer. Maybe not even death if the legends about him were true. Many whispered that he couldn't be killed. God knew how many had tried and suffered for it.

Cyrus carried the bag and placed it gently by the oak front doors. He turned to Helen.

"Would you like a glass of wine while you wait?"

"That would be splendid. The Shiraz I think."

Cyrus walked into the kitchen and opened the door to the walk-in wine refrigerator. It was a G. E. Monogram, the finest walk in cooler in the world. The nearly one thousand bottles were held gently in the redwood racks. The digital temperature gauge on the wall registered 55 degrees, the ideal temperature to preserve wine. Most people did not keep their reds chilled, under the mistaken impression that reds were served at room temperature. They were idiots. Cyrus hated stupid people.

He took out a bottle and carried it to the counter. He used a silver monogrammed cork cutter to remove the covering and opened the bottle. Cyrus took a pair of wide lipped wine glasses from the hanging holder. He poured them both a glass and carried it to her. Helen took the glass and tasted the wine.

"Perfect."

Cyrus raised his glass in toast. "To victory in the Holiday Tennis Tournament."

Helen smiled. "Now, it isn't always about winning."

"Yes, it is."

"Not this time. Meredith invited me for a girls' weekend. Not to go all Chrissie Evert on everyone. I want to have fun."

"Doesn't mean you have to loose to have fun."

"No, it doesn't. But she's not that good a player and I doubt I can carry her to the finals."

"But you will try."

"Of course I will. I like to win as much as you do. Well, maybe not quite as much." She lifted the glass to her pink lips and drank. The front door bell chimed. Helen looked at her Couture watch. "Right on time."

Helen opened the door to three women. Johanna was a natural redhead. She was tall and beautiful, with full lips and flawless pale skin. Ashley was shorter and athletically trim. She had wide inquisitive brown eyes and a small perfect nose. Meredith was the last. She looked like a living Barbie doll. She was statuesque and blonde with a bombshell figure. She was married to a cosmetic surgeon. He had improved her natural beauty in his office, tweaking the shape of her nose, the size of her cheek bones, the shape of her breasts, the lift of her butt, the fullness of her lips. In fact, if there was a cosmetic surgery, Meredith had tried it. She had definitely been on the family plan.

The women all hugged Helen.

"Honey, you know the girls, right?"

"Of course. It's nice to see you again. Can I get you a glass of wine before you leave?"

"Have we got time, Helen?" Johanna asked.

"It's my plane. I think the pilot will wait," Cyrus answered.

"I would love a glass," Meredith cooed.

"Me too," Ashley said.

"I guess it's unanimous," Johanna said.

Cyrus got three more glasses and poured each of the ladies a glass. He carried the glasses to them on a silver butler's tray.

"I'll have Ronnie bring the Bentley around. Enjoy."

Cyrus walked toward the back of his house where his office was.

"This is so awesome," Johanna said.

"First class," Meredith answered. "I love traveiing first class."

"Which one is Ronnie?" Ashley asked.

Cyrus had a number of men that worked for him. Some were former Spartan loyalists. Some were former military special forces that had to find other employment. Some were only gun thugs. Ronnie was a gun thug.

Helen laughed. "You know which one, Ash. The guido. The one you think is so hot."

Ashley blushed. "I don't know which one."

"Yes, you do," Meredith said. "He's the one that keeps an eye on Helen sometimes when we are playing tennis. The security guy with the big muscles and all the thick black hair. The one who gets your panties so wet."

"That is so gross. And only half true anyway. So is he really coming with us?"

"Wipe that smile off your face, Ash," Johanna said. "This is a girls' trip, not a hook up."

"You are so mean."

"I can read you like a book," Johanna said. "A dirty book. Fifty Shades of Ash."

The girls all laughed. It was good to laugh, Helen thought. Innocent girl fun.

Cyrus returned. "He's just pulling up out front."

The women all grabbed their bags, and this time Cyrus let Helen carry her own.

Outside, the dark sapphire blue Bentley Mulsanne eased to a stop. Ronnie jumped out of the driver's seat. He was about six feet tall and weighed a good two hundred pounds. He quickly loaded their bags into the trunk. The girls all climbed inside, still carrying their wine glasses.

"I will sit in the front," Ashley said.

"That is so thoughtful of you, Ash." Johanna mocked.

"A word," Cyrus called out.

Ronnie hurried over to him. "Yes, sir."

"I am trusting you. Don't fuck this up."

"I won't."

"Keep your eyes open. And your ears too. I want a detailed daily report about everything they do."

"Yes, sir."

"Everywhere she goes. Everyone she speaks to. Everything she says. Everything the other women say. Do you understand?"

"Yes, sir."

"This isn't a vacation for you."

"Yes, sir."

"Stay in the background. Try to fit in. Keep a low profile."

"Yes, sir."

"Good. I am counting on you. You do good, I'll have a bonus for you. You fuck this up..."

"Yes, sir. I know. I won't."

Cyrus turned toward the car and waved. Helen and her friends waved back.

"See you Sunday," Helen called. "Don't miss me too much."

"Every day will be agony," Cyrus answered clutching melodramatically at his heart. The other women laughed. "Have fun."

Ronnie got into the driver's seat and pulled away. Cyrus returned to the house. Inside, a lone man with sunglasses waited. The man was six feet tall, but lean as a panther. His dark hair was combed back and he wore a small trim soul patch beneath his lower lip. He was very handsome.

"Don't start with me, Spanish Johnny."

"I prefer John these days, Cyrus."

"Like I give a fuck what you prefer, Johnny. If you had done your job right the first time, Frank Kane would be dead."

"He caught two to the chest. And I cut him in half. He should have died."

"You and fucking blades. You should have put two more into the back of his head. Or fifteen if he was still up."

"He should have been dead. I paid for my mistake didn't I?"

Cyrus face softened. When Spanish Johnny had stabbed Frank, but failed to kill him, Frank had issued two savage head butts to Johnny's face. It had shattered his skull and should have killed him. But, like Frank, Johnny was tough. He had recovered.

"Raise your sunglasses."

"I don't..." Johnny hesitated, then raised the dark sunglasses.

His face looked normal. Repeated surgeries had corrected and replaced the shattered bone. Even the eye socket looked normal now. Cyrus ran a hand over Johnny's face. Johnny tensed but held still.

"Still have the light sensitivity?"

"Yeah. It's not so bad now."

"And the migraines?"

"Not as often. Nothing I can't handle."

"The sudden explosions of pain?"

"Rarely."

"Good. Sorry about the attitude, John. These are stressful times."

Johnny lowered his sunglasses back into place. "For all of us. Now that we know he's alive, it's just a matter of time before he puts it all together and comes knocking."

"Maybe."

"Maybe. Hell. You know how he is."

"I know exactly how he is. I have made arrangements to help resolve the issue."

"I hope sending Helen off to the Bahamas is part of those plans."

"It isn't."

"What if she is meeting Frank?"

"I will know. That's why I sent Ronnie."

"He's an idiot. I should have gone."

Cyrus laughed. "A wolf to watch the sheep. You are like catnip to women, brother. They would be all over you before the plane landed."

"I could resist," Johnny said with a smile.

"No, you couldn't. You never could. Hell, I've never seen anything like it. I don't think I would like the idea of Helen being alone with you."

Johnny did not answer the dig.

"Ronnie doesn't even know who he is looking for."

"Exactly. But Helen knows Ronnie. She knows he is an idiot. She will ignore him. He has a better chance of seeing something."

"And then?"

"Whatever is necessary for my protection, Johnny."

5

The inside of the small Beechcraft was sweltering. It was as hot as Hades, Frank thought, and the thought made him remember the Spartans. It was in the early days. A half dozen of the founders had gone to Virginia Beach to expand their territories. They had set up temporary headquarters at a small biker bar called Choppers. Bikers were not renowned for their clever use of language.

Back then they had all been brothers; Apollo, Frank, Spanish Johnny, Hendo, Carpenter, and Cyrus. They had taken a table in the back of the bar. Carpenter had his laptop out. He was a wizard with it, searching the web for information. Spanish Johnny had a pretty runaway sitting on his lap. She wanted a ride out of town. Spanish was offering a different kind of ride. Hendo was watching the door like he always did. Hendo always worried about trouble catching him unprepared. His Glock was in his lap. Apollo and Frank laughed over their beers. They seemed above fear. And Cyrus. Cyrus just watched and made his silent spider plans.

Two men sat sipping beers in a corner booth. They wore collared pullover shirts tucked into neatly pressed jeans. They whispered to each other, but did not approach.

"That the guys?"

Cyrus nodded. "Third time they've showed. You check out their rides?"

"Two big Harley Fat Bobs."

Cyrus smiled. "At least they aren't riding bitch. You run the tags?"

"Cops. What do you want to do?" Carpenter said.

"Nothing. Just wait 'til they show their hand."

"We should bury them," Hendo said. "Put them in the fucking dirt."

"Plenty of time for that, brother."

The door to the bar opened and a man walked in. He was nearly seven feet tall and weighed in the neighborhood of two hundred and ninety pounds. His back and shoulders were huge. His head seemed tiny in comparison. Behind him walked a smaller man who looked like a hippie college professor. He was skinny with long salt and pepper chin whiskers, like some kind of Chinaman and long, thinning hair. A third man rose from his seat at the bar and followed them over. He had been waiting too. This man was young and a little soft around the middle. He had long brown hair parted down the middle. He wore old jeans and a biker vest.

The three men stood in front of Cyrus. The Spartans looked up.

"Can we help you gentlemen with something?"

The giant spoke first. "We heard you are starting an MC. I don't know about these other pussies, but I want in."

"What's your name?"

"Name's Antonovich Strehl."

"What do you do Mr. Strehl?"

"I am dock manager in Norfolk."

"Where are you from?" Cyrus asked.

"Georgia."

"Not the GA I know."

"Soviet, Georgia."

"And you," to the third man, "Who are you?"

"Bill Johnson. I'm an out of work welder. Just looking for some fun. I love to ride."

The little guy spoke up without being asked. "Name's Neil Lutins. I'm a cook."

"Like short order?"

"Like meth."

"Are you any good?"

"I never got blown up yet. Must be doing something right."

"Hand over your driver's licenses."

Carpenter spread them in front of his laptop and started typing. He turned the screen so that Cyrus could see it. Bill had no police record. Strehl had been arrested twice for assault. Neil had a long sheet.

"You did time for meth."

"I said I was good. Not that I never got popped."

Cyrus templed his fingers before his face. He thought carefully about what he was going to say.

"This is not a game gentlemen. This is serious business. The Spartans are only interested in those who can commit. We want warriors."

The three men looked at each other and nodded.

"The Spartans will take everything from you. You will become part of us. We will be your family. We will give you wealth and power and prestige. People will fear and respect you because you are Spartans. You will become the tip of a spear we are forging. This opportunity will not be made to everyone who comes. We offer you the world, but we demand complete loyalty. Are you sure you can promise that?"

The three answered in unison. "Yes."

"Good. Russian, what kind of bike do you ride?"

"I have no bike. I drive a Chevrolet Tacoma."

"A cage. That's fine. You don't have to have a bike. We can always get you a bike. But you can't wear your colors when you drive the truck. What about you Bad Billy?"

"Got a Harley Street Bob. Mini ape hanger handle bars. Fully blacked out. It's a sweet ride."

"I got an Indian," Neil said.

"You like it?" Frank asked.

"So far. I picked it up in Pennsylvania outside a biker bar. Still getting use to it."

"Today is the first step as a prospect. If you are still committed, there is a seventy page background questionnaire for you to fill out. But that's later. We don't bless members in. We jump you in. Forty seconds. Forty seconds for the chance to become my brother. Are you ready?"

Strehl smiled a wolf's grin. He looked at Apollo. "I am ready. But I did not think the Spartans allowed niggers as members."

Apollo made no reaction to the words. Frank smiled. So did Spanish Johnny. Hendo took the Glock 19 from his lap and laid it on the table before him.

"Membership is open to anyone who earns it. Niggers, spics, hebs, slants, towel heads, chinks, even fags. Isn't that right Spanish?"

"Fuck you."

"We might even have room for a Russian bull. Why don't you go first to show the others how to do it."

"Can I fight back?" Strehl asked.

Cyrus smiled. "Oh, yes. I expect you to. The Spartans need men who can fight. Warriors. Men of bronze."

"Blonde men? Why do the Spartans need blonde men?"

"Not blonde you Russian idiot, bronze. Men of bronze."

"I do not understand."

Cyrus sighed. "Never mind. Do you understand the word fight?"

Strehl smiled and cracked the knuckles on his huge right hand. "Good. This word I do understand. I will try not to hurt him too badly."

Frank got up and started pulling on a pair of four ounce fingerless gloves like MMA fighters wear.

Strehl was sneering. "I thought I would be fighting the nigger."

"No," Frank answered. "The jump in is my job."

"You do not need to worry about hurting me," Strehl said. "The gloves are not necessary."

"They aren't for you, fucktard," Frank said. "It protects my hands while I kick your ass. I got to do this all day, my hands get sore."

"Lock the door, Apollo. We don't want to be disturbed," Cyrus said.

Apollo went to the bar's front door and locked it. Frank pushed a table back out of the way. Glasses wobbled and almost fell. He followed the table with the old wooden chairs that had circled it. No other Spartan moved. The girl in Spanish Johnny's lap snuggled in tighter. Her eyes were on fire with excitement. Frank waved the Russian over.

Strehl moved forward slowly on small steps. He was slow, but he kept good balance. When he got in range, he looked back at Apollo and smiled. He threw the sweeping right sucker punch as he turned. Frank knew it was coming. He was already moving to the side. Frank struck him with two savage jabs that broke his nose. Strehl stumbled backward. He blew the blood from his nose and wiped it on the back of a scarred hand the size of a ham. Strehl stepped in and threw a hard left hook. Frank rolled beneath it and hit him three times to the body. Strehl stumbled and Frank followed with a right hand uppercut and a short left hook. Strehl fell to the floor. He lay sprawled on the sawdust. He did not move.

"Ten seconds," Carpenter called.

Strehl rose slowly to his feet and charged like a bull hoping to tackle Frank and take the fight to the ground. Frank stepped back and caught him with a knee and then flattened him with two elbow drops to his back. Strehl reached a hand up as if he wanted to pull himself up on Frank. Frank kicked him in the chest. When he went down, Frank kicked him twice in the ribs, breaking them.

"Twenty seconds," Carpenter called.

"Do you want to be a Spartan? This is what it takes," Cyrus said. "Get up. Don't quit."

Strehl rose to his knees. He stared hard at Frank. His hand went behind his back, under his shirt. The black knife was barely out before Frank moved. Frank crow hopped a step and a half and struck him with a leaping superman punch. Strehl fell unconscious. The knife skittered away. Frank walked over and retrieved it.

"Toss that here, brother," Spanish Johnny said. "Let me have a look at it."

Frank tossed the knife to Spanish Johnny, who snatched it out of the air. He rolled it around in his hands. He was the knife expert. He was lethal with a blade.

Spanish Johnny examined the blade. It was very distinctive. The diamond cross-shaped blade was seven inches long before joining the metal handle for another five inches of length. Double wide serrations marked the blade on each side near the hilt.

"This is a nice tactical blade. It's a Gerber Mark II."

Spanish Johnny turned the handle toward Frank where the word GERBER was stamped on one side. Frank nodded. He knelt beside Strehl and removed the sheath from the back of his pants and tossed it to Spanish Johnny.

"Spoils of war."

Spanish Johnny sheathed the knife and slipped it behind his own back under his shirt.

Strehl moaned on the floor. Frank pulled his head up and looked into his swimming eyes.

"Do you still want to be a Spartan?"

Strehl took a feeble backhand swipe at Frank. Frank hit him beneath his left eye. Strehl tried to rise but couldn't. Only his head and shoulders came up from the floor. Frank leaned in close.

"This is for Apollo," he whispered and punched him on the chin.

Strehl fell unconscious again.

"Forty seconds, more or less," Cyrus said.

"More like twenty five," Frank added.

He grabbed Strehl by his shirt collar and dragged the big man to the corner. He knelt and felt for a pulse on his neck. It was there. It was thready and weak, but it was there.

Cyrus smiled. "He did well. Better than most. Alright Bad Billy. It's your turn."

Bill looked nervous. He looked at Strehl and back at Frank. Then again at Strehl's bloody broken face.

"Listen, maybe I was wrong. Maybe I'm not right for this life. I think I should just leave."

Cyrus looked untroubled. "That is your choice Bad Billy. The Spartans are not for everyone."

Bill turned to leave when Cyrus continued. "Just leave the keys to your bike on the table."

"My keys? What do you mean?"

"Your bike is forfeit. Leave the keys and walk out."

"But that's my ride. I got no way home."

"Try to leave with those keys and you won't need to worry about going home. Count yourself lucky that I am feeling so generous for you wasting my time."

Bill took the keys from his pocket and separated the motorcycle key from it. He placed it gently on the table in front of Cyrus. "Thank you. I am sorry I wasted your time."

"Let him out."

Hendo got up and walked him to the door and Apollo unlocked it. Bill Johnson walked outside. He already had his cell phone out calling for a ride. The Spartans returned to their drinks. The girl in Spanish Johnny's lap licked his ear. Frank dumped a pitcher of beer on Strehl to rouse him. The Russian moaned.

"What about me?" Neil asked.

Cyrus turned to the little man. "Just walk away, friend. You can keep your bike."

"Fuck that. I came to be a Spartan."

"You saw what happens. Are you sure you truly wish to be one of us?"

"I ain't no pussy like that guy or a slow ass dumb ox like the other one. I'll take mine like any other swinging dick. On my mother fucking feet."

"Frank," Cyrus said. "Jump him in. Be quick, we have business to discuss."

Neil spit on the floor and came forward on spindly legs. His eyes were locked on Frank. Frank smiled. He liked the little guy's spirit. Heart was important.

Neil threw a hard right that Frank stepped away from. Neil pressed onward and threw a pathetic one two combination. Frank hit him under his right eye. The skin split and blood started flowing. Neil didn't give up. He moved in again and threw right, left, right. Frank slipped all three and punched him about quarter strength to the solar plexus. The air went out of Neil's lungs. He tumbled to his knees gasping for breath. Frank gave him time. Neil regained his legs and came on hard. Frank threw a left that was intentionally slow. Neil ducked it. Frank threw another punch dipped in molasses and Neil avoided it as well. He danced around Frank trying to hit him. Neil threw a looping overhead punch, and Frank tagged him to the kidneys, staggering him. Neil didn't falter. He came on. He got his hands back up. His skinny arms started throwing windmill punches like they could actually hurt a man like Frank Kane. Kane danced away, deflecting them.

"Knock him out," Spanish Johnny shouted.

Frank gave him a short punch to his head and then missed on purpose again with a slow right.

"Come on, Frank. Bust the old dude's ass," Johnny shouted.

Carpenter was laughing. Apollo was too. The girl in Johnny's lap looked confused. Cyrus said nothing. Hendo looked away bored.

Neil waded in, throwing one punch after another that Frank easily avoided.

Cyrus whispered to Carpenter.

"Time," Carpenter called.

Neil looked stunned. He was still alive. He turned to Frank.

"You're too fast, brother," Frank said. "I couldn't get a clear shot at you."

Neil ran up to Frank and hugged him. "Thank you. Thank you. You won't regret it."

"Hell, I didn't do anything. You made it on your own."

"Congratulations," Cyrus said without emotion. "You are now a prospect. In the weeks ahead, you will look back on today as an important day. It is. Now, your first duty is to load Strehl into his truck and take him to a hospital. Put Billy's Street Bob in the back. Strehl earned it. Johnny, go with them. See that they take care of him."

"What about me?" the girl pouted.

"Wait for me darling. I will be back before you know it. Maybe I will find a pretty nurse to bring back for us to play with." Johnny said and gave her a chaste kiss on the cheek. "Come on, little brother, we have a bull to take to the vet."

Spanish Johnny and Neil helped Strehl out the door to his truck. Cyrus turned to Frank who had taken his seat beside Apollo.

"What was that?"

"What?"

"That was pathetic. He's got no business being a Spartan. He isn't hard enough."

"It was my call. I like something about him. He'll do us proud. You'll see."

"He's your responsibility. See that you train him right. He fucks up, you got to make it right."

Frank saluted Cyrus with his glass of beer.

"Here they come," Carpenter said, indicating the two policemen that had been watching the whole show.

"Let's see what's what," Cyrus said. "Blaze up a joint."

Carpenter did and started smoking it.

The two guys came over and stood in front of Cyrus.

"You the big dog?" one asked.

Cyrus smiled. "No dogs here. I am Cyrus."

"I'm Van Horn and this is Yarber."

"What can we do for you? Want to join our social club?"

Van Horn laughed. "I don't think so. We had another arrangement in mind. We're cops. We think you guys are the real deal."

Cyrus shrugged and took the joint from Carpenter. He took a deep drag. "So?"

He offered it to Van Horn. Van Horn smiled and took the joint and took a hit. He passed it to Yarber who did the same. "So, maybe we can help each other out from time to time."

"In what way?"

"Say we exchange information for certain considerations."

"Money, women, drugs? Those kind of considerations?"

"Sometimes. Sometimes favors. We cover your backs, let you know who is moving into your territory, what the word is downtown... the usual stuff. We get into a jam, you help us out."

"Remove snitches, keep the streets quiet...the usual stuff?"

"Yeah. We can work out the details. Just wanted to let you know we were on board if you want us to be."

Cyrus stood and extended his hand. "Welcome aboard, officers. Have a seat and a drink if you like."

"No, we got to roll. We go on duty at six. But we'll be back."

"Thanks for taking the time. We value friendship very highly. Treachery is another matter altogether."

Hendo put his hand on the Glock 19, and turned it toward the policemen. The message was clear.

The two policemen left the bar.

That was the first time Frank had met Neil. If he had known then what was ahead, he would have beaten the little man to death in that bar. Hell, he would have beaten them both to death.

6

The Gulfstream G650 sat like a winged cheetah on the tarmac. It was flawlessly white. The G650 was the gold standard in business aviation. It was the fastest, most comfortable, most technologically advanced business aircraft in the sky. The four man crew consisted of a pilot, co-pilot, and two flight attendants. The entire crew stood beside the ladder waiting for the passengers. The captain wore a uniform complete with navy jacket and captain's hat. He was smiling.

The Bentley pulled to a stop near the tail of the airplane. Ronnie scrambled out and held the door open for the women inside.

"Helen, I like your style, girl," Meredith said.

"Thank you," Helen replied.

"I've never flown in a Lear jet before," Johanna said. "Is it okay if I have an orgasm from excitement?"

"You are allowed," Helen said. "But just one."

"You'll love it," Meredith said. "It is so so so first class."

"Nothing is too good for my girls," Helen added.

Ronnie popped the Bentley's trunk and removed the bags. He carried them to the storage compartment near the tail of the plane. He carefully placed the bags inside. Ashley watched him with a wistful gaze.

"Don't let him see you drool," Johanna said.

"What do you mean? I was looking at the jet."

"Of course you were," Johanna teased. "If it's the jet in Ronnie's pants."

"I bet it's a 747 wide-body," Meredith said.

"I hope it's not one of those Concorde jets. They have that funky looking bent nose. And they say the ride is over really fast."

"You are both so bad," Ashley said and laughed.

"As bad as we can be," Meredith said.

'Help me out, Helen," Ashley begged.

Helen just smiled. "I want no part of this. It's your vacation too."

"Yeah, have a good time. No one will tell. What happens in the Bahamas stays in the Bahamas."

"At least for nine months," Johanna said.

Ashley punched her good naturedly in the arm. "Be quiet or he'll hear."

Ronnie walked back smiling. "What are you ladies talking about?"

"The plane," Ashley said.

The other women laughed.

The pilot approached with his hand out. "Good afternoon, ladies. I'm Captain Steve. I'll be your pilot."

They each shook his hand and introduced themselves, except Helen.

"It is good to see you again, Helen. Are you ready to go?"

"Yes, thank you, Steve. Will it be a long flight?"

"Not in this baby. She will do an easy mach .85. I'll have you there in a couple of hours."

"That would be great."

"Don't worry about a thing, ladies. I have our flight plan approved, and here is a copy of your reservations for the Caribbean Dream hotel. You are booked into the presidential suite. It is magnificent. Or so I have been told. Two large bedrooms, a servants' quarters and a private deck with its own pool.

"That sounds wonderful," Ashley said.

"I am sure it is," Meredith added.

"Ronnie, if you would park the car, we will be ready to go. Cyrus will send someone for it."

Ronnie nodded and got back into the Bentley and drove it a short distance to a private VIP parking area. He jogged back, aware that Ashley was watching him. He wore a smile the entire time.

Helen's cell phone chirped.

She checked the screen. "Excuse me for a moment. I need to take this."

She walked a few feet further from the group as she answered the phone.

"Yes?"

"This is Claudia. Frank's party left this morning. There are four people including Frank. His group consists of a young man in his twenties and two girls who look to be a little younger. Frank looks different. He's cut his hair short and shaved his beard. But it's the same old Frank. He covered his trail. No way to back track where he came from."

"That's fine."

"We'll be set up for the return. You can count on me."

"I know I can, Claudia. You have always been a good friend to me."

"I try. They have three rooms booked at the Falcon's Nest. It's a small hotel north of your hotel, but still on the five mile beach. Do you want room numbers?"

"No. I don't think that will be necessary."

"Do you have any idea what he is up to?"

"No. With Frank it's never what it seems. Thank you again, Claudia. I will call you when I can."

"Good luck and one more thing. It's kind of weird."

"What?"

"He seems almost happy."

Helen disconnected and called Cyrus on speed dial. He picked up on the second ring.

"Is everything alright?"

"Everything is perfect, darling. I just wanted to call you before we left to thank you again. The plane is wonderful. The girls are thrilled."

"Good. You know I would do anything for you. Have a great trip and get home soon. I already miss you."

"I miss you too. See you soon."

She disconnected again and returned to the group.

"Who was that?" Ronnie asked.

"Cyrus, just saying good bye."

Captain Steve indicated the plane with a sweep of his hand.

"Welcome, aboard."

Amidst giggles and shoves, the four women climbed into the plane, followed by Ronnie. They all took seats. The interior of the Gulfstream was as impressive as the exterior. Behind the cockpit was a full galley. The body of the Gulfstream had been designed with a large table, sofa, and comfortable leather chairs. The full bathroom in the rear of the plane was outfitted in chrome and steel like a yacht.

Captain Steve followed them inside and the co-pilot pulled the ladder up, securing the door from the inside. Captain Steve turned back to the women.

"Excuse me one final time. There is a well stocked bar on board as well as WiFi connections. Cyrus suggested that, since you will probably be drinking tropical drinks like Pina Coladas, Mai Tais, and Bahama Mamas once we reach our destination, I should prepare some different travel drinks for you. There is a pitcher of gin and tonics in the refrigerator. I also took the liberty of placing some snacks for you. There are cucumber sandwiches, and an assortment of fruit and cheeses."

"Thank you, Steve," Helen said. "That was very thoughtful. I will be sure to tell Cyrus when we return."

Steve beamed his gratitude. "Thank you very much. If there is anything you need, don't hesitate to tell me or the crew during the flight. I want this to be a nice trip for you."

"I am sure it will be perfect, Captain."

"I'll get on our clearance from the tower and we should be on our way in a few minutes."

The air was cool and clean as the air conditioner hummed quietly in the background. One of the flight attendants poured the women their gin and tonics. The ladies took their seats. No one buckled in. Johanna nibbled on a cucumber sandwich. Meredith looked out of the window and sipped her drink. Ashley took Ronnie a drink. He hesitated and then took it from her with a thank you.

Helen took out a copy of *Full Throttle*, a biker magazine, and started to thumb through the pages. It reminded her of her former life with the Spartans. Helen closed her eyes. She felt the jet move effortlessly down the runway and lift off. She could feel the cool air on her skin. She heard the others chatting about tennis and travel. She thought about what lay ahead for her. She tried to form a plan. Who were the people with Frank? Why were they here? How could she talk to Frank with Ronnie watching her? What would she say to him? How would he react?

There were a lot of questions. Her head started to hurt.

There was an old Spartan MC saying, "SFFS". Spartans Forever Forever Spartans. Frank even had the letters tattooed on his side. Spartans were realists. She would play it as it came. That had always been her strength. She was great at spinning situations to her advantage. After all she had once been a goddess. They had called her Aphrodite. There was nothing she could not do.

7

"Almost there," Bullington shouted over his shoulder over the booming drone of the props. "We are coming up on Cat Island."

Jenny, Caron and DC all pressed their faces to windows to watch the approach.

"You guys know the story of Cat Island, right?"

"No, man. What's the down low?" DC shouted back.

"You should dig this, Frank. It was named after Captain William Catt. He was a famous pirate in these waters. He hung out with Captain Morgan and Blackbeard. Although there are stories that he and old Teach had some kind of beef. Cat used this island as his base because of its natural harbor. Take a look."

Frank moved up to the cockpit and took the co-pilot's vacant seat. He moved the seat back as far as it would go, but it was still a cramped fit.

"The island is only twelve miles long and one to three miles wide and shaped like a fishing hook at the southern end. See?"

The plane banked to the right.

"It's the marina now. They call it the Yacht Club. Very fancy in some ways, very laid back in others. Most of the good hotels are on Five Mile Beach. It gives you a nice breeze and funky pink sand."

"Why is the sand pink?" Jenny asked.

"This island is volcanic in origin. As the lava rock is eroded, it turns into a fine pink sand. It is something to see. The island is still pockmarked with lava tubes and blue holes from when it was formed. Really cool geography. There is even an abandoned monastery on the highest hill. If you get a chance you should check it out. Rent some quad bikes and do a little tour. It is very spooky. They say the lava tubes up there lead straight to Hell."

Everyone laughed.

"The airport is at the northern end of the island. That's where my guy is."

Bullington banked the plane farther to the right.

"Where are you taking us now?" Frank asked.

"Got something to show you first. You are going to love this. You got to see it from the air to appreciate it."

The plane buzzed through the clear blue sky like a giant dragonfly. Eight and a half miles offshore on the leeward side of the island was a pinnacle of rock rising like an angry fist.

"That's Falcon's Aerie. Most people don't know, but Captain Catt had a sister ship that he used during his hunts. The captain of the second ship was a dude named James Falcon. When he retired as a privateer, as they called themselves, he set up on that rock."

"You got to be kidding, man," DC shouted, "There's nothing there."

"Wasn't always like that. Back in the day, Falcon had a floating bridge constructed out to the rock. It was an incredible engineering feat. It was anchored on a line of small skiffs linked together. It was kind of like some bridge a Persian dude made to cross the Black Sea. Falcon had everything he wanted brought out to him on that bridge. He set up a huge garden for food, devised a funky watering system to funnel rainwater from cisterns to keep it going. He built a mansion on the peak. He brought up a battery of cannons for protection. He even had a small zoo. The monkeys are still on the island today. And he did the craziest thing at the time. He petitioned and purchased the island. His heirs still own it. It is private property and no one is allowed to go there."

"What happened to Falcon?" Jenny asked.

"That's cool too. Once Falcon had everything the way he wanted for him and his woman he had the bridge destroyed. Then the only way to reach the island was by boat. The rip currents make swimming it suicide. There is only one good anchorage for a boat. It is a huge flat rock that extends out from the pinnacle."

"So how did he resupply?"

"When he needed something he just sailed back to the main island in his twelve footer. He would load up and then he would sail back. Sometimes he would send word that he needed something from town and a boat would bring it out and leave it on the dock."

"What about his pirate ship?"

"He used the lumber from his pirate ship in the mansion he built. He was an interesting dude. He was supposed to be a scientist or scholar or something like that. Maybe an architect. Some people claim he was a fag, but I don't believe it. I mean he had a woman with him. Really hot looking in her picture. They were suppose to have pagan orgies on the pinnacle."

"Why do they think he was gay?" Caron asked.

"I forgot. You haven't seen his flag. It is crazy. It has a falcon carrying a skull with a rainbow in the background."

"Rainbow? You mean the rainbow symbol that gay pride uses now was used back then?" DC said.

"No. It is just that now it is associated with gay people so they sort of adopted him. You know a semi-famous gay pirate is pretty cool."

"What about his woman or girlfriend or whatever?" Jenny asked.

"The rumor is she was a she-male. One of those cross dressers. A heshe, or shemale, or whatever. Who knows? The flag is some trippy shit. There are pictures of him all over town as well as Cat."

"That's a good story, but what happened to him?" Frank asked.

"Oh, yeah. After his woman died, he went all hermit. No one ever saw him. People started wondering about his treasure. What had happened to it? Where was it? Shit like that. On a couple of occasions other cutthroats came to steal it. He blew them out of the water with his cannons."

"Until..." Frank said.

"One night, a bunch of other pirates got the bright idea to come in under disguise. They fitted their boat with supplies he was waiting for, and hid around the cargo. When they landed, there was a great battle as they tried to work their way up toward his mansion. Their plan had been to capture Falcon alive and torture him to tell where his treasure was."

"Did he tell?"

"No, when the surviving pirates reached the summit, Falcon was gone."

"Did they find his treasure? No. They tore his house apart looking for it. When they couldn't find it they burned it down. If you look, you can see the remains. Not much but chimneys and old lumber."

"Did they look in the garden?" Jenny said.

Frank smiled. She was clever.

"Dug it up. And the zoo too. Set the monkeys free to see if it was under their cages."

"But they got nothing?" DC asked.

"They got stuff. Weapons and silverware, but if you mean treasure, no. Sometimes locals still sneak out there to look for it and to party."

"Cool," Caron said.

"Falcon did leave one clue as to the treasure's whereabouts. He was drinking in one of the pubs on Cat Island one night and someone straight up asked him where it was."

"What did he say?"

"Legend says he looked the man in the eye and said, 'if anything ere happen to me, Giby show where the treasure be."

"Awesome. Did this cat ever lead them to the treasure?"

"No. He was never found. Might have been a code of some kind. They say Falcon liked codes and puzzles and riddles and shit."

Bullington banked the plane back toward the main island. Something below caught Frank's eye.

"What's that?" he asked, pointing.

Bullington swung the plane in closer. On the west face of the rock tower was a natural indentation in the cliff face. The water was shallower here, and the wind driven waves had piled up to form a nice clean surf break. The waves looked to be about six feet tall, and there was someone surfing the waves. The man moved up and down the face and spun off the lip. Frank watched him work the wave front with the casual ease of a lifetime spent in the water. The surfer launched a 360 off a wave and fell from his board.

Bullington banked the plane back around.

"Wow. I didn't know there was even any surf here. Must be a local. No one else would know about a break like that. Now buckle in. Touch down in like five minutes."

The plane touched down and Bullington taxied it to an open area off the main runway.

"Sit tight. Let me go see my man. Make sure everything is set."

Frank watched Bullington jog toward the fence nearest to him. A man in a porter's uniform was waiting for him. They hugged a greeting. Bullington handed the man an envelope, and the porter handed Bullington a large box. Bullington jogged back.

"Everything's set. Daniel is with the airport. He's got a guy to drive you to your hotel. You're already registered under the name Kaley."

"The hotel going to be a hassle about IDs?"

"No, it's all taken care of. Come grab your stuff. I'll be back to pick you up Sunday morning at 8:00. The first commercial flight doesn't get in until two, so we can slip in and out with no trouble. But you got to be on time. Customs shows up right after that."

The uniformed man and a second man, the driver, approached the plane, each carrying an identical box to the one Bullington had carried back.

"Working double duty?" Frank asked.

"Just trying to maximize my air time. Fuel is expensive. But, hey, don't mention this to Claudia, okay?"

"I don't know what you are talking about. I didn't see anything."

Bullington shook Frank's hand.

"Thanks, Frank. Sometimes Claudia is a little uptight about side work."

Frank nodded. The girls and DC grabbed their bags and headed toward a gate in the fence where the car was parked. Bullington loaded the three boxes and climbed back inside.

Frank knew if something was going to happen, it would happen now. He was close enough to the two men to take them if something went south. Nothing did. The uniformed man smiled and gave Frank a small salute. The driver hurried over and opened the trunk on his taxi for their luggage. They tossed their bags into the back and climbed inside. Frank sat in the front seat next to the driver.

"Hotel Falcon's Nest," the driver said instead of asked.

Frank nodded. He needed a vacation. It had been a long time. This one seemed to be going well. The taxi was an old KIA. The A had been replaced with a lambda, the Spartan symbol for home. It was a good omen. Frank liked omens.

8

The Falcon's Nest hotel had seen better days. Once the premier hotel on the island, it had started to show its age. The façade was faded and slightly weathered. The landscaping had a dry brittle appearance. But the view across the pink sand to the diamond clear waters was breathtaking. The hotel was only four floors tall and was dwarfed by the other premium hotels farther down the beach.

The lobby was large, with a seating area, coffee kiosk, and a bookshelf stocked with local topic books. A huge portrait of a man and woman decorated one wall. A single black woman stood sentry behind the mahogany reception desk. She was thin, with long dreadlocks. She was wearing a bright yellow YALE tee shirt. She was smiling as they entered. A portrait of Sidney Poitier, Cat Island's most famous person covered a distant wall.

Frank led the way to the desk and the smiling woman.

"Welcome to Falcon's Nest," the smiling woman said. "I am Gabriella Bergeron."

"Thanks. I'm Mark Kaley. I believe you have rooms for us."

The smiling woman punched some keys on her computer. She continued smiling as she nodded at the information on the screen only she could see.

"Here it is. Three rooms."

She turned around and took three keys off a hanger behind him. Old school mail slots were open behind each key for messages. She extended a key to Frank.

"One for the gentleman. An adjacent room for the other gentleman. And last but not least, a room for the young ladies."

Frank took the keys and passed them out. "Did you go to Yale?"

Gabriella hesitated. "No, one of the guests left this. I like the pretty color."

Frank could tell she was lying. Next time she was trying to hide her past it would be wise to ditch the shirt. Frank imagined her as some environmental radical that had fled to the islands ahead of the cops. Probably a tree spiker in Oregon. Or a monkey wrencher in Pennsylvania.

"Thanks," Frank said to the suddenly unsmiling woman. He pointed toward the oil painting. "Is that Captain Falcon?"

"Indeed." She said and the smile returned in earnest. "It is based on descriptions of the original portrait that once stood in his own home."

The painting depicted Captain Falcon just like Bullington had described.

"Hmm," Frank said.

"And they never found his treasure?" Jenny asked.

"No, Miss. It is one of our island's greatest mysteries. Will you be needing a porter?"

"No, we got this," Frank said. "What do you want to do first?"

"I want to go for a swim in the ocean," Jenny said. "I've never seen water like this before."

"Me too," Caron said. "I got a new bikini I'm dying to try."

"Sounds like I'm going swimming too," DC said. "I want to see that bathing suit. What about you?"

"I'm up for a swim, but I would like to take a look at those ruins sometime."

"Me too," Jenny said. "It is early. We can do both today can't we?"

"And jet skis tomorrow," DC said. "We got to do jet skis."

"I can have four wheelers dropped for you if you like," the smiling woman said. "We have maps that show the way. It is really simple."

"Sounds good. We can get something to eat on the way to the ruins. Then take a swim."

"Very good. The rentals run fifty dollars per person."

"Cash?" Frank asked.

"Of course," the smiling woman said.

Frank reached into his pocket and removed a roll of bills. He dealt out two hundred dollar bills and passed them to the smiling woman who slipped them into her pocket.

"I'll have the quad bikes here in an hour. They are yours for the rest of the day. Just stop by the desk for the keys."

Frank nodded his thanks and turned away.

Frank approached the portrait. He studied it more closely. The painting depicted a tall hawk-faced man. He wore a buccaneer's greatcoat crossed with a brace of flintlock pistols. His waist was bounded by a broad red sash. The butts of two more flintlocks protruded from the band. No need to be out-gunned. A thick cutlass hung from his hip. Captain Falcon held a protractor in one hand. Maybe he was some kind of engineer, Frank thought, or a Freemason. There was the hint of a large necklace around his neck. In the center of the ring was a trident. It was a traditional nautical symbol and a good omen for Frank. Captain Falcon's heavy brown pants ended in knee high black boots. His left arm circled the waist of a very tall woman.

The woman was expectantly beautiful, with her thick dark hair swept up on her head in a style probably common to the period. Her eyes were equally dark and showed a hint of Asian ancestry. She was looking adoringly at Captain Falcon. Her wide mouth looked spoiled. He fingers were adorned with rings that sparkled with rubies and diamonds. Her bulky dress disguised any female figure she may have had. She had very long fingers and big hands. Could be a man, Frank thought. Could just be woman with big hands. What did lesbians call that? Well hung?

"What was his woman's name?" Frank asked.

Gabriella smiled. "It was Marlin."

"Really? That is a unique name."

"Yes, very unique. No one knows its origin."

Could be a she-male, Frank thought. But it was only a painting. Someone's interpretation of someone else's memory passed down to someone else. And the subject of portraits were probably very narcissistic in their depictions. Hell, maybe Captain Falcon looked more like Quasimodo than Errol Flynn.

Behind the pair was the stone fortress home of the pirate captain. A white painted mansion adorned the topmost peak. The flag it flew depicted a falcon perched atop a human skull. The background was indeed a rainbow.

Falcon looked a little like a dandy, Frank thought. Those were strange times. Anything was possible. Frank didn't much care one way or the other. He wasn't on a treasure hunt.

They all moved to the elevator and pushed the button for their floor. Frank turned to the others.

"I don't want to spoil anyone's vacation, but remember to keep it low key. We need to stay under the radar."

"Like outlaws," DC said. "Should we use fake names too?"

Frank laughed. "Whatever makes you happy. First rule of travel is everyone makes it home alive."

"What's the second rule?" Jenny asked.

"There isn't a second rule," Frank said. "Just stay safe. Have fun, but stay safe."

"We can do that," Caron said.

Frank opened his door and tossed his bag on his bed. He went to the balcony and stared out at the ocean. He had missed the ocean. He had missed the smell and the feel and the sound. A knock at his door broke his daydream. He went to the door. It was Jenny.

"I hate to bother you, Frank."

"What's the matter? Something wrong with your room?"

"No, it's great. I just…. We just bought you something for the trip that I thought you might need. We talked about it and this is what we decided to get you. Everyone pitched in."

Frank waited. He didn't know what to say. People did not buy Frank Kane gifts. Jenny handed him a bag. Inside was a box. Inside the box was a watch. It was big and black and bulky. It had a very large face like the new style. He held it up.

"I thought you could use a new watch. Your old Casio is beat to Hell. This one has a little more style. Not too much, but a little."

Frank smiled. It was a face splitting grin. "This is badass," he said.

"So you like it?"

"It is awesome. I love the color."

"I knew you liked red, but…well I just thought it was you."

"Thanks, Jenny. It was very sweet."

"It is called a Night Finder. The reviews say it is a good watch. It's waterproof and has one super-cool feature." She pressed a button on the side of the face and a light shone. "It's called a map light. I know you don't read maps, but I figure you might need a light sometime when you are doing what you do and this way you don't have to remember to bring one with you."

Frank took the watch and buckled it on. "That is very cool."

"Caron helped me pick it out. DC gave money. He doesn't know anything about watches."

"Tell her thank you too. You know you guys didn't have to do this."

"We wanted to. You have done so much for us... and well, we just wanted to do something nice for you."

"It might be the nicest gift I ever received."

Jenny leaned over and kissed Frank on his cheek. "We love you," she said, and spun on her heels with a smile of her own.

"Jenny. You did call your grandmother before you left"?"

"Yes. I wanted her to know where we were going and that I was fine."

"Good. I don't like Sybil or Lamar to worry. And she does worry."

Jenny's face took on a strange look. "It was weird when we talked. She was really worried."

"I hope you told her I would keep you safe."

"Sybil wasn't worried about me. She was worried about you. She said she had this bad dream."

"What kind of dream?"

"It is crazy. She said she saw you standing in a wide pool of blood and a blackness was coming for you. It was moving real slow like one of those giant snakes, but you didn't see it creeping up on you. She was afraid you wouldn't escape."

Frank laughed to calm Jenny. "I will watch out for pools of blood and dark clouds."

Jenny laughed too. "I told you it was weird."

She hurried to her room. Frank closed the door behind her. It was an omen. He was sure. Not much he could do about it. He would keep his eyes open.

9

The house rested at the end of a nice paved road. It was a modern colonial style, sixty-five hundred square foot testament to someone's success. The house rested on the ocean behind a savage limestone beach. A large swimming pool filled half of the well landscaped back yard.

The house itself was white with a bright red stone tiled roof. Huge columns marked the front door. The inside was decorated with a pleasing mix of modern and traditional Caribbean styles.

The original owners had fled Jamaica under threats from local gang lords. The house was now the home of the Red Hand. There were no fences. No guard dogs. No armed men patrolling the grounds. The Red Hand needed none of those things. Only a fool would challenge the Prophet in his own home.

The doorbell rang deep in the mansion. Dawg was busy playing FIFA soccer on his Playstation 4. He didn't respond to the bell. Let someone else answer it, he thought. He was driving for the winning score. The bell again.

Dawg paused the game. He lifted up the ganja spliff and sparked it up again. He held the sweet bitter smoke for a second before exhaling. The doorbell again. He rose slowly to his feet and left the room.

Down the hall was the Prophet's bedroom. The door was closed. He could hear music playing. He paused to identify the song. It was something from Three Dog Night. It was a song about a bullfrog named Jeremiah. An odd song, he mused. But Lord Tosh loved 70s music. He was not foolish enough to offer a rebuff to the Prophet's musical tastes. He turned down the long hallway toward the stairs.

Bat lay sprawled unconscious on his bed, his skinny arms and legs spread eagle on the sheets. Dawg could see the remnants of the mushrooms he had been consuming. He knocked on the open door. Bat did not stir. Dawg watched his chest rise and fall. Lost in a psychedelic haze, Bat was of no use. At least he was still alive. That was something.

Dawg started down the curved stairway as the bell chimed again. The sound was beginning to annoy him. At the foot of the long, curved stairs he stopped and looked into the giant living room. Little Bird was naked on her knees. Roach crouched behind her, riding her like a dog. Little Bird smiled an inviting smile.

"Join we, bruder," Little Bird called out.

Dawg hesitated. He ran a long fingered hand through his tangled beard. He was tempted. But he was so close to defeating the thrice cursed all-star team from Brazil. Fucking Pele, he cursed. The bell again.

Damn it, he thought. Mother fuckers had better have a good reason for disturbing him.

Dawg shrugged and walked toward the front door. He peeped out the spy hole in the door. The chief of police stood by the door. Dawg opened the double doors.

Two more Jamaican policemen in full uniform stood beside the police car parked in the driveway. No one spoke.

Dawg took a deep pull on the spliff. He exhaled the smoke into the police chief's face.

"What you be wanting, Babylon?" he asked.

The police chief cleared his throat. He looked over his shoulder as if to reassure himself that his policemen were still behind him. They were. He nodded in their direction.

"I received a report that the D.E.A. lost their senior field agent. The Americans are very upset."

Dawg stared at him with dead eyes. "So."

"His body was found this morning in town. His skin had been removed and he had been disfigured with knives."

"Again, what dat to I?"

"The word is that the Red Hand was involved. The people say it is the work of the Dreadmon."

"I don know dis ting. De followers of Lord Tosh be peaceful. You not be sayin' udur?"

"No. No. Nothing like that. The man's death has brought a lot of pressure on us from his government to find his killers. We are doing that. I just wanted to let Lord Tosh know he is not a suspect. Nor will he ever be implicated in this crime. I will protect him."

Dawg took another hit of the ganja. "Dat why you come den? To tell no worries?"

"Yes. Tell Lord Tosh I am his friend. I brought him a gift."

The police chief signaled one of the officers who opened the back of the police car. He removed a long object in a cloth sack case. He brought it up to the chief and hurried back to the safety of the car. The police chief untied the ends of the cloth and removed a shotgun. The wood was polished to a golden sheen. Gold scrollwork ran in a delicate pattern along its length. The twin barrel's cold silver contrasted with the dark wood. It was beautiful.

"This is a fine gun. It is very expensive. It is made for shooting sporting clay."

"Who is dis, Clay?"

"No. Clay is another name for skeet."

"What are dees skeet?"

"Pigeons. Clay pigeons. You throw them into the air and shoot them. It is a lot of fun."

Dawg took the gun and examined it. He opened the breach and looked inside.

"Der are no bullets."

The chief signaled the officers by the car again. Both men approached this time. One man carried a portable skeet thrower and a box of shotgun shells. The other policeman carried a large box of clay skeet. He sat them down on the ground by

Dawg's feet.

"See," the police chief said putting a skeet into the skeet thrower. "You use it like this."

He hurled the clay pigeon out toward the ocean.

"Then you shoot it."

Dawg grunted and took the box of shells. He removed two shells and popped them into place. He raised the gun to his shoulder. He sighted down the long barrel. He lowered the shotgun and balanced its weight in his big hands. It felt good. He swung the shotgun to his shoulder again and shot the box of clay pigeons. The police chief jumped back. Dawg shot the box again, destroying it.

The police chief's eyes were huge. Dawg broke the gun and ejected the spent shells. He inserted two more.

"Dat was funs. Tanks."

The police chief was nodding fast now.

"And you will tell Lord Tosh that I brought him the gun. Tell him that I am his friend."

"Yeah, yeah," Dawg said and stepped back inside.

He closed the door and propped the shotgun in the corner. He heard the doors slam on the police car. He listened to it speed away. Dawg laughed. He walked back toward the stairs.

Little Bird was now on her back. Roach was pounding away like a black jackhammer. Dawg watched her large breasts bounce with each thrust. She was damp with the sweat of their love making. Her large bright eyes were on him. She smiled again. But he was so close to beating the Brazilians. He could have Little Bird anytime. Something in his pants stirred. The serpent in his pants cast its vote. Dawg watched for a few seconds more. The serpent became insistent. She was incredibly beautiful.

Well, the game was already paused, Dawg thought.

He undid the belt at his waist and his pants fell to the floor. He stepped out of them. Little Bird was smiling. She reached out her hand to him. She started smiling wider as he approached, as she saw what he had for her.

He could beat the Brazilians later.

10

The four wheelers were waiting for them when they got unpacked. They were Polaris Sportsman 550s in a garish orange color. At least they would be easy to spot on the road. Small white plastic crates had been bolted on the rear of each of the ATVs for storage. The hotel manager came outside to see them off. She was carrying four one liter sized bottles of water.

"It can get very hot. Better take some water for the trip. It's complimentary."

"Thanks," they each said, and collected a bottle to put in their crates.

"Any recommendations for lunch?" Frank asked.

"Are you looking for American food or traditional Bahamian fare?"

"Traditional," Jenny said. Then she looked at the others. "We can eat burgers back home."

"A wise choice young Miss. But if you must have a burger, we have a wonderful goat burger and delicious American style fried potatoes. I highly recommend them."

"Eww," Caron said. "That sounds so gross."

"Where's your sense of adventure?" DC kidded her. "Try something new. You might like it."

"That's what you always say. Especially at night," Caron replied with a dirty leer.

"Enough of the sexual innuendo," Jenny said. "I'm starved.'

The manager pointed down the street. "That is the direction to the Hermitage. There is a map in each vehicle. Unfortunately, I only found one of our brochures on the Hermitage. I will have some more sent over."

"Not a problem," Frank said.

"So you go down about a mile and Momma's is on your right." It is a blue and white building with a white fence. She serves authentic Bahamian food. Not too touristy."

"Great," DC said. "Saddle up."

They cach chose an ATV. Frank liked that they each wanted their own ride. No one wanted to ride bitch. He liked independence.

"How do you drive one of these?" Caron asked.

"It is simple. Place it in neutral. Turn the key and you are ready to go. They have power steering so they are easy to drive. Have a good time. Just drop the keys off at the front desk when you return. I'll have someone pick them up."

"Great. Appreciate it," Frank said.

"I'll lead," DC said with a look to Frank.

Frank nodded. "I'll play sweeper and bring up the rear."

They fell into single file and accelerated onto the road. Frank couldn't help but smile. He could sense their excitement. It was one thing to see something like the

Caribbean on television or on a video. It was something else to see it for real. To feel it and taste it and hear it all around you. He was glad he had taken the risk. Vacations were good. It had been a long time.

A few minutes later, DC parked in front of Momma's. They left the quad bikes and went inside. It was a small place. There were a dozen old tables with matching old chairs. Four ceiling fans struggled to stir the thick hot air. The windows were propped open with rods to let in more of the nonexistent breeze. At the back was the kitchen separated by a low wall with a counter on top. Near the door was another small counter. This one held a heavy metal cash register. There was no one else inside.

They took seats at a table near the main door. A fat black woman emerged from the back. She was somewhere between twenty-five and sixty years old. It was hard to tell. She was wearing shorts and a thin tee shirt. Across the front she wore a large dark blue apron covered with flour dust. She walked over to the counter by the door and picked up four menus and brought them to the table.

"Welcome honeybunches. You be wanting something to eat?" she said and laid the menus in front of each of them.

"Could we start with some water?" DC said.

"Sure. Sure," the woman said.

"Are you Momma?" Jenny asked.

The woman smiled. "No, child. I'm Robin. Ain't no Momma Noonkester no more. She was my gran, but she died long time ago."

"I'm sorry," Jenny said.

"Don't need to be. We all die. She had a good life."

Robin turned without another word and went into the kitchen.

"Smooth," Caron said. Now she'll probably spit in our food."

"That's what they call island spice. Supposed to make it taste better," DC kidded.

"You are gross," she said.

Robin lumbered back into the room carrying a pitcher of water and four glasses. She placed glasses before them and carefully filled them. She sat the sweating pitcher on the table.

"Anything else to drink while you look over the menu?"

"Four Kaliks," Frank said.

Robin turned back for the kitchen.

"Kalik? What's that? Jenny asked.

"It's a local beer. The biggest seller in the Bahamas, I think. They also drink Sands and Policemen a lot."

"Policeman? Why do they call a beer a policeman?" DC asked.

"It's Jamaican beer. Red Stripe. It comes in a squat brown bottle with a broad red stripe on it. It is supposed to look like the police uniform in Jamaica. It's not a bad beer if you like lager. I like it better than Becks or Heinekens. In the Bahamas,

Kalik is king."

"I could use a beer," Caron said.

"We all could," DC said. "We are on vacation, man. Time to relax and enjoy."

"What should we order?" Jenny asked.

"Depends," Frank said. "I say we ask Robin what she recommends. That's always a good policy."

"As long as it isn't a goat burger," Caron said. "I couldn't eat that. I would throw up."

"Such a lady," DC said. "That's why I'm crazy about her."

Caron stuck her tongue out at him. "Well, at least you admit you're crazy."

Robin returned with the beers and four coasters. It was a tall clear bottle with a bright yellow brew inside. The label was a brilliant blue like the sea. She set the beers out. They all reached for their beers and took a sip.

"Not bad," DC said. "I like it."

"You like it because it has alcohol, that's all," Caron teased.

"Sound reasoning if I ever heard it. To vacation," DC said and raised his bottle. They all clinked bottles and took another sip.

"Do you need more time or do you know what you want?"

"What do you suggest, Robin?" Frank asked.

Robin thought for a minute and then said, "I tell you. Today's special is fish stew with Johnny cake. We got a nice grouper fish in the back. Just came in. Very fresh."

"What's in the stew?" Caron asked.

"Celery, onions, tomatoes, spices, and fish. It's good, I tell you."

"That sounds great," Frank said. "Four orders."

Robin smiled. "You like it I'm sure. I be right back."

After she had gone Caron asked, "What the devil is a Johnny cake?"

DC shrugged. "Beats me, but I like cake."

"It's bread that's cooked in a pan. It's pretty good. It's a staple in the island," Frank said.

"You know a lot about the Bahamas," Jenny said.

"There was a time I had dealings in the Caribbean. I was here a bunch of times. Never to Cat Island, but other places."

"Cool," DC said.

Jenny took another drink of her beer. "This is really good even if it's got a weird name. What does Kalik mean anyway?"

Frank smiled. "I'm not sure. I was told it was named after the sound cowbells make during the big Junkanoo festival. But I was also told Cat island was named after all the feral cats that use to live here."

"Wow. There are bunch of different stories for stuff," Caron said. "It sounds like they just make it up."

"They probably do," DC added. "Same way in the states. Government makes up shit and tells us and we believe it. Same thing for doctors and scientists, and..."

"Boyfriends," Caron said.

"Ouch," DC said. "But probably just as true."

Caron reached out and squeezed his hand. "I was just teasing."

DC smiled. "I know. Still some truth in it. Everyone lies about something."

Frank raised his bottle in toast. "I heard that."

Jenny tapped bottles with him and smiled. "Everyone has secrets."

Robin returned on cue with a large tray with their food. She placed the food on the table and then, with a flourish, a small bottle of reddish liquid.

"This is Bahamian Hellfire sauce. In case your stew needs some fire. But I warn you, it is very hot. Men go up to the monastery and climb down the hellfire pit to scoop it up."

DC lifted the bottle and studied it. Then he unscrewed the top and dribbled a drop on his hand. He dipped his tongue to eat. He waited a few seconds before his eyes grew wide.

"Shit. She's not kidding." He said downing a huge gulp of beer. "That stuff is like liquid fire." He took another drink that he swished around in his mouth. Then he wiped his tongue on his napkin. "Man, I'm still burning."

"Just my luck," Caron said. "I finally go on vacation with my man and his tongue gets burned off."

Jenny laughed and blew beer out her nose. Frank smiled. DC leered.

Frank looked away. He wasn't comfortable with their sex talk. Kids.

Robin returned to check on her only guests.

"Honeybunches do you have everything you need?"

"We are fine."

"I got a question," DC said. "Your last name is Noonkester. Is that a local name?"

Robin's smiled morphed into an icy glare. "No, it is German. The man that owned my great grandmother was named Noonkester. He gave his last name to all of his slaves. Noonkester is our slave name."

DC didn't reply. There was nothing for him to say. Robin walked away.

"Smooth," Caron said. "Very smooth. At least she can't spit in our food now."

11

Frank, DC, Jenny, and Caron followed their maps to the Hermitage. They parked at the foot of Mount Alveria. Mount Alveria was two hundred and six feet above sea level at its peak. It was the tallest mountain in the Bahamas. The switchback trail took them up to the top where the Hermitage had been built. Frank noticed the small bottles hung from trees. There were also small animal bones tied to trees.

"What's with the bottles?" DC asked.

"Obeah," Frank said. "This island is a hub for it."

"Obeah? What's that?" Caron said.

"Magic. The offerings are for blessings or curses."

"Like Voodoo?" Jenny asked.

"Sort of. It's incorporates a lot of religions. It is all spells and stuff. It is native to the islands."

"Can we take one as a souvenir?" Caron asked.

"If you want to be cursed," DC said.

"I would just leave it alone," Frank added. "The locals must think the Hermitage on top is sacred. They are probably a little afraid of it so this is as close to its power as they come."

"That is wild," Jenny said. "Who believes in that stuff today? I mean it is silly."

"Locals take it seriously," Frank said. "Probably wouldn't admit it to your face, but they do or they wouldn't put the spells up here."

A dozen more steps brought them in sight of the Hermitage. A huge cross loomed over the pathway up. The Hermitage was a collection of buildings centered around an open courtyard. There was a distinctly medieval feel to the buildings. There were Roman arches and a curved tower.

Jenny pulled out her brochure and started reading aloud.

"The Hermitage was built by Monsignor Jerome Hawkes. He was an Anglican priest who later became a Catholic priest. Brother Jerome, as he was called, traveled throughout the Bahamas rebuilding churches that had been destroyed by a hurricane. He settled on Cat Island and constructed four churches. The Hermitage is built out of local Limestone blocks so that it would not rot or decay. Brother Jerome passed away in 1956."

"Damn. This place is like a zoo. You got a famous Cat, a famous Falcon, and now a famous Hawke. What's next, some dude named Shark?'

"Shut up retard. I would have thought this was a lot older than that," Caron said.

They walked amid the ruins scattering the local lizards.

"Dude, check this out," DC yelled.

He had found a deep lava tube that disappeared into the top of the peak just outside the ruins. There was a small wooden sign beside the open pit.

"It says the Gate to Hell," DC said. "This must be where they get that fire sauce."

"That's just for tourists," Caron said.

"I know," DC said. "But what are we? I dig it. It looks like it could drop straight to Hell."

"You know what this reminds me of?" Caron said. "With those little buildings off to the side. It looks like a brothel. You know, a whore house."

Brothel. The word triggered something in Frank and he thought once again of Neil, the little meth cook.

A couple of Guatemalans had set up a brothel in Virginia Beach. Van Horn had heard about it and sent word to Cyrus. It was in Spartan territory. Frank, Spanish Johnny, Hendo, and the two new prospects, Strehl and Neil, had gone to check it out. Five Spartans was considered an appropriate show of force.

The building was a large old stand-alone in a rundown industrial park. There was a McDonald's, a dry cleaners, a Kinko's copy store, a Kangaroo Express self serve gas station, a goddamn Starbucks, and not much else. Across the street was a Lowes and a Taco Bell. The blacktop in front was well kept and clean. Three trucks and a white Ford Fiesta were parked out front.

There was a main set of solid metal double doors. The sign above the doors read Church of Christ. There was no welcome mat.

They backed their bikes in by the front door. Better if you needed to jam out later. Each man wore his Spartan vest with the Lambda on the back. No three-piece patch. No location stenciled on the bottom rocker to let the cops know where you were from. No top rocker with the word Spartan. There was only the Lambda branded into the leather. Permanent. The lambda said it all.

Hendo took up a position on the outside beside the doors. He slipped his Glock 19 out of his holster and held it by his right thigh.

Frank and the others went inside. They looked sufficiently fearsome, Frank thought. Except for Neil. He was wearing his Spartan vest over some kind of long Cowboy style duster. He looked like a mad scientist. Inside Strehl took a position with his back to the front doors as they had instructed him to do. With his back safe by the door and Hendo on the other side, Strehl could watch the wings without worry. He took his Glock out and let it hang by his leg just like Hendo.

Inside, the one-time narthex had been converted back to a large receptionist desk. To each side of the desk were two wide doors that led to the shipping area that had once been the main part of the converted church in the back. There was a computer terminal on the desk behind the counter with a card swipe machine. Odd for a church, Frank thought. Perfect for a brothel.

Two men sat behind the desk. They were both Hispanic. One wore glasses. Both wore their dark hair cut close. Both wore baggy, short-sleeved shirts bloused over cargo pants. Shooters clothes, Frank called them. It made it easy to conceal a pistol. Frank had once worn a similar outfit and on a dare had been able to secret eight guns without detection. He knew they were armed. If you ran a brothel, you better be.

They stood when the Spartans entered. Frank could read the worry in their eyes. Fake smiles covered their faces. Nervous hands fumbled with pencils.

"Can I help you?" Glasses asked.

"Maybe," Spanish Johnny said moving toward the desk.

"Have you been here before? I don't recognize you. Do you recognize them brother?"

The brother shook his head, no. "I am afraid this is a private denominational church. We currently can't handle any more members."

Spanish Johnny grinned. "Church? Church of the hungry pussy is what I hear."

"I don't know what you are talking about," Glasses said. "And that type of gutter talk is not appropriate for a house of God."

"I hear tell you got some fine young Guatemalan pussy in the back. I thought I might try some out. God, willing."

Glasses looked nervous. He was a good judge of character and these were not customers. He knew they were dangerous.

"I apologize again, sir. But you are mistaken. This is a church."

"Can we take a tour of the back?" Spanish Johnny asked.

"I am sorry. That is only allowed for members of the congregation. Now if you don't mind I need you to leave."

"Go get the man," Frank said. "If you're not him, go round him up."

Glasses looked at his brother and nodded. "Go get Mr. Santiago, Hector."

Hector looked to Frank for permission. Frank waved him away. They stood watching Glasses. Spanish Johnny had taken out his knife and was cleaning his fingernails with great showmanship. Strehl didn't blink. Neil glanced around nervously. He stroked his long chin whiskers. Frank regretted not telling him to stash the duster before they came in. He looked like a fool. It lessened the effect he had wanted to impart.

Mr. Santiago burst through one set of doors. Hector was right behind him. He took a position next to his brother. Mr. Santiago walked to the front of the desk and glared at Frank.

"What do you assholes want?" he asked.

"Do you know who we are?" Frank asked.

"What the fuck do I care who you are?"

"I asked if you knew who we were?" Frank repeated.

Mr. Santiago didn't answer. He continued to glare. His face was turning red and a large vein in his forehead pulsed. Finally, he answered.

"Yeah, I know. Bikers. Fucking Spartans."

"Good. Then you know why we've come. You are in our territory. Nothing goes down in our territory we don't control or have a piece of. We are not greedy. But we are businessmen. Just like you. From now on you will pay us a percentage to operate here."

"Do you know who the fuck I am? Do you have any idea who you are trying to fuck with?"

"It doesn't matter. Everybody pays."

"Not me, mother fucker. Not me by a long fucking shot. I'm hooked in with MS-13. They got my back. My brother is a fucking general."

Frank hid the shock from his face. This could change things if the 13 was trying to move into Spartan territory. No retreat.

"That does not concern us, Mr. Santiago."

Mr. Santiago unbuttoned his shirt and showed a light blue tee shirt underneath with a thirteen emblazoned on it. He tapped the number. "That fucking better concern you biker bitches. Now get the fuck out of my place of business before I have you stepped on like the worms you are."

"Settle down. This is Spartan territory. We are Spartans. If you operate here under our protection then..."

"I don't need no fucking Spartan protection. Fuck the Spartans. And fuck you too." Santiago spit at the center of Frank's chest.

Frank didn't react. He was under control. The sound of the shotgun blast startled him. His hand went to the gun under his vest even as he saw Spanish Johnny spin away. Santiago's head exploded. Neil was standing with a sawed off shotgun in his bony hands. It all made sense at that moment. That was the reason he wore a duster, to hide the gun.

Santiago's body stood headless for a second before slumping to the floor like a puppet with the strings cut. Neil swung the barrel toward the two brothers. Their hands went up into the air.

Frank reached out and lowered the barrel. He stared hard at Neil.

"Did I tell you to ice him, Neil?"

"No, Frank, but he disrespected the Spartans. When he disrespected you I snapped. Ain't no mother fucker walks this earth going to do that while I'm alive."

Frank smiled. Neil was a tough little terrier. Frank patted him on the head. "Alright. Go wait by the door with Strehl."

Frank turned to the two brothers, the gun still in his hand. "Put your guns on the counter."

Spanish Johnny had drawn his pistol too.

The brothers did as they were told. There was a 357 revolver and a 9mm Beretta. They didn't speak.

"What are your names?"

"I am Ricardo," Glasses said. "This is my brother, Hector."

"Alright, Ricardo. What's your relationship to Santiago?"

"He was our boss. He brought us up here to help run the business."

"Not family?"

"No. He was an asshole."

"We don't want to go to war with the 13 if we don't have too. What kind of back up did he have with the 13? Was Santiago from El Sal?"

"No. He was from Cuba like we are. He doesn't have family in MS-13 like he said. It was all lies to scare away people trying to cut in on his business."

"You sure about that?'

"We would know. Right, Hector?"

Hector nodded so hard Frank thought his head might shake loose.

Frank thought for a minute. He ran scenarios in his head.

"You fixed for women?"

"Yes. Plenty. And more come looking for work all the time."

"This is the way it is going to be. You can do this the hard way or the easy way."

The brothers stared intently. They didn't want to miss a single word.

"What is the easy way? Ricardo asked.

"From now on this is a Spartan run business. We offer you the same deal we offered Santiago. Or were going to offer. We take a percentage of profits. In turn we keep the cops off your backs. We make sure no gangs come in to hassle you. We make sure no trick tries to rip you off. We make sure no girl gives you trouble. You both become Spartans. Here. Now. Today."

Hector leaned over and whispered to his brother. Ricardo nodded.

"What is the other way?"

"The hard way? You decide you don't need our help. We bring in our own people to run the place and you go out to a landfill with Santiago."

The brother's faces showed their fear. A quick exchange in Spanish. Then Ricardo spoke. "We like the easy way best."

"I thought you would. Johnny, you got the mark?"

Johnny holstered his pistol and dug a small branding loop from his vest. It was shaped like a small lambda, the Spartan symbol.

"Put your right arm out," Frank instructed.

Both men obeyed. Spanish Johnny used his lighter to heat the lambda to a cherry red.

Frank grabbed Ricardo's wrist and held it firm. "Anyone fucks with you, you show them this mark. If you need us, just call. We'll leave you a number."

Ricardo nodded. Tears were in his dark eyes.

"Johnny."

Spanish Johnny moved to Ricardo. He looked him in the eyes.

"Don't take your eyes off me," Johnny said. "The pain doesn't last long."

Ricardo nodded.

Johnny pressed the glowing metal to Ricardo's arm above the wrist. The stench of burnt pork filled the air. The sound of the searing flesh filled the room. And then it was done. Frank released him. They let him stand for a moment to gather himself. When he had regained control, Ricardo turned to his brother and nodded.

Hector stepped up and presented his arm to Frank. Frank took the wrist to steady it. Spanish Johnny reheated the metal and repeated the branding.

"What about him?" Ricardo asked pointing toward Santiago's body.

"We'll take care of that. That's what we do. Does he have a car?"

"The white Fiesta," Hector said, suddenly talkative.

"Give me the keys. We'll get rid of it too. Anyone comes looking for him, tell them he went home to Cuba."

"No one will, believe us. The girls will think we killed him."

"Good. It will help keep them in line. A little street cred is good for business. Word will spread. No one will fuck with you guys."

"I got body bags in my saddle bags," Neil offered. "The good ones. Six hundred gauge. Seventy-five inches long. Long zipper."

Frank was stunned. Who carried body bags, he wondered. "You got latex gloves in there too?"

"No," Neil said.

"I didn't think so," Frank said.

"I'm allergic to latex. Got nitrile gloves though. A whole box of funky blue ones. Powder free."

"Well, don't just stand there. Go get the stuff."

The brothers started whispering in Spanish. Spanish Johnny walked over to Frank. He was smiling.

"Damn, that little fucker is intense."

"You got that right."

"Those guys back there are calling him Pocito muerte."

Frank stared at Spanish Johnny. "What's that mean?"

"Little Death. Talk about some street cred. Little fucker has it now in spades."

"Spades? Is that supposed to be a joke?"

"Lighten up big man. It's funny. We'll dump the body and the car and we're home free."

"Yeah, well those two fuckers can clean up the blood. We're not doing all the heavy lifting for them."

Spanish Johnny started to laugh.

"Frank. Frank. Hello, Frank. Earth to Frank," Jenny said.

Frank snapped back.

"Did you hear what I was saying?"

"Sorry, Jenny, my mind was elsewhere."

"You think? I was saying there is a second brochure here that talks about all the blue holes around here. There's even a saltwater lake that drains through deep underground channels to the ocean. The locals think a monster lives there and eats horses."

Frank looked blankly at her.

"Never mind. I just thought it was interesting."

"It is. It is. That's probably where the witch doctors dump their sacrifices."

Jenny shivered. "Now you are scaring me. That Voodoo stuff gives me the creeps. I don't believe in it, but knowing people do is weird."

"I know what you mean."

"You don't believe in that stuff do you? All that magic mumbo jumbo."

Frank paused. He believed that Sybil, Jenny's grandmother, was probably right when she told him everything happens for a reason. That was fate, right? He believed that there was some reason Sybil was able to revive him when he should have been dead after the ambush. There was some plan for him. He thought there were truly evil people in this world that needed killing. That was good and evil. He had gone to church as a kid so he believed in Jesus and the whole died for our sins thing. That was the basis of Christianity. Sometimes he thought the ocean and the rain and the wind all had sentience. That was paganism wasn't it? He believed in omens more than he should. Believed that maybe the gods or God was giving you a heads up. That was pantheism. He was superstitious. He looked at Jenny and smiled.

"I don't believe any of that stuff. It's all nonsense. It makes people do crazy things."

"That's what I'm talking about," Jenny said.

"I don't like black cats," Caron added. "They give me the heebie jeebies."

"Don't you start," Jenny warned.

12

The Gulfstream G650 landed on the empty tarmac. It taxied up before the small airport terminal. The engine was dialed back, but still idled. The air conditioner hummed. The cockpit door opened and the captain stepped into the main cabin.

The copilot moved behind him and opened the exterior door. He lowered the stairs and went outside to retrieve their luggage.

"Excuse me, just formalities of international travel. If you would pass me your passports and immigration forms, I'll have everything taken care of for you."

"Don't we have to show them at customs?" Ashley asked.

"Not necessary. There are a lot of people here for the tennis tournament. That makes you VIPs. This is one of the courtesies for coming."

"Nice," Johanna said. "I hate standing in lines."

"Me, too," Meredith added. "Especially when it's hot and I'm drunk."

Ashley giggled. "I got a buzz too. Johanna?"

"High as a kite. What about it Helen? Are you feeling it?"

Helen smiled. She knew the power of self control. She had had the glass of wine and then nursed the gin and tonic for the remainder of the flight. She was sober, but she knew how to be a good hostess.

"I'm feeling it too. Thank you, Captain. I will tell my husband of your kindness."

The Captain smiled and collected the documents from the passengers. He hurried out of the plane.

"I think he's got an eye for Helen," Meredith said.

"Who doesn't?" Johanna added. "She is like sugar to a diabetic."

"Nice ass on the Captain, though," Ashley said and giggled. "I wouldn't mind flying those friendly thighs...I mean skies."

Meredith nudged her. "You're drunk."

"Am so," Ashley giggled again.

"I hope we don't have to go far before we can pour her into a cab," Johanna said.

"The boss says a limo is picking us up for the ride to the hotel," Ronnie added.

"We have to take more trips together," Johanna said. "I like this."

"Your husband has style, Helen. Ben would never indulge me like this."

"I am sure he indulges you in lots of ways."

"If you count free plastic surgery. That's just so he can keep banging a Barbie doll."

"It would be neat if Ben's name were Ken," Ashley said and giggled. "Ken and Barbie."

Meredith rolled her eyes. "Lord, help us."

The Captain returned. He gave the ladies back their passports. "If you would follow me ladies. Your luggage is already loaded in the car."

The girls deplaned and followed him to the terminal. Ronnie brought up the rear.

They passed through customs and the lobby to the taxi stand outside. The Captain opened the door for them and they all climbed inside.

"The limo will bring you back Sunday at noon. I'll meet you here to help you through customs again. I hope you have a nice stay."

"I'm sure we will, Captain," Helen said.

"If there is anything you need, the hotel manager has been alerted."

"Thank you again," Helen said. "I will tell my husband of your service."

"I would appreciate that. Tell him I still remember the old days and I am always available if he should need me."

The captain slipped back the sleeve of his jacket to reveal a lambda shaped scar on his forearm. Helen looked at it and then back into the captain's eyes. She smiled her smile that said she understood everything.

"I will tell him. Have a safe trip home, Captain Steve."

The Captain gave her a small salute from the brim of his cap and closed the door.

The drive to the hotel was short. The dusty pitted road gave way to a well-groomed section of paved roadway. The long paved driveway led to immaculately groomed grounds surrounding the tallest hotel on Cat Island, The Royal Caribbean Dream. It was a new hotel, but it dominated Five Mile Beach. It climbed fourteen stories into the clear Caribbean sky. Large private balconies hung like tiny jewels around the hotel.

The front of the hotel was flanked by massive marble columns. The lobby was predictably huge, morphing into a lounge with sofas, thick Persian rugs, and heavy teak tables for waiting guests.

Ronnie led the way to the mahogany front desk. A cute, thin island-girl smiled at their approach. She wore a white blouse, gray slacks, and a gray coat. Her name tag was just large enough to read, but small enough to not be ornate. It said Mandy.

"Welcome to the Royal Dream. My name is Mandy. Do you have reservations?"

Ronnie stepped up past the women. "I'm Ronnie Genest. We're here for the tennis tournament. We're in the Presidential suite."

Mandy's eyes flashed shock for an instant. "Excuse me for a moment. Your room is tagged for the manager. Let me get him for you. She picked up the phone and pressed some numbers. "Mr. Lofton. The party for the Presidential suite is here. Yes, sir."

She cradled the house phone.

"If you would be so kind as to take a seat on one of the sofas, Mr. Lofton will be right down. It will only be a moment I promise you."

They had only just sat down when Mr. Lofton rushed into the lobby. He was in his early fifties. He was balding with neatly trimmed hair. He wore a little thin moustache and thick tortoise rimmed glasses. He wore the same uniform as Mandy, gray slacks, white shirt, and red tie. Only his jacket was a rich burgundy color, signifying his rank in the hotel pecking order. He spotted them and hurried over, nervously combing his thin hair into place with his fingers as he came.

"I am Mr. Lofton, the hotel manager. I apologize for not being down here when you arrived. I was in your suite making sure everything was ready for your arrival."

"That's fine," Helen said. "Are our rooms ready?"

"Yes. Yes indeed. Let me get your steward to bring your bags up." Lofton looked around the hotel and signaled to one of the men at the concierge desk. The man was young and very black. His starched white shirt and brilliant smile accented his blackness. "James, see to their bags."

"Very good, sir," James replied.

"If you would follow me to the elevators, please."

Like a line of geese, they followed Lofton to the bank of elevators. One elevator stood off to the side. The sign above it read, "P. Suite Only". Lofton swiped a key card that was attached to his belt. The elevator opened and they followed him inside. The interior was all dark mahogany wood with a waist high mirror that covered three walls. The door slid closed with barely a whisper. The elevator controls were simple. There was only one button. Lofton pushed it.

"Are we on camera, Mr. Lofton?" Helen asked.

Lofton looked aghast. "Certainly not. That would be an invasion of privacy. Penthouse guests have a right and a desire for complete privacy."

"Excellent. I want to be able to assure my friends that what happens in the Bahamas stays in the Bahamas."

"Of course. I understand. The hotel does employ video security, but not here or in the penthouse."

"Ooh, I like that," Ashley said. "Off the grid." She raised her arms in the air and made a woohoo sound.

"Ssh," Meredith said. "No one wants to see your drunk butt anyway."

The elevator stopped on the top floor and opened onto a wide tiled entrance. There was a single cherry door in front of them.

"The cleaning staff will not enter unless you put the sign on the door requesting service. Additional privacy. Your husband was adamant about that." Lofton motioned with his arm for them to exit the elevator. "If you would allow me."

They waited outside the door.

"The same magnetic keycard also unlocks the front door. I have a card for each of you."

Lofton passed out five identical cards. Ronnie smiled when he received his card and slipped it immediately into his pocket. Lofton swiped his card and the green light signaled that it was open.

"Follow me."

The Presidential Suite was amazing. It occupied the top floor of the hotel. There were two large master bedrooms, each with a pair of king size beds. There was also a separate servant's room for staff or children or guido bodyguards. Past the bedrooms was a large living area complete with sofas and comfortable chairs. There was even a pool table near the full size kitchen. Through this room and out through the wall of glass was a twenty-five hundred square foot deck. The deck was partially covered by a wooden pergola offering some shade to those that sought it. There was another smaller kitchen and bar area with antique wrought iron table and chairs. But what was truly amazing was the private infinite swimming pool that looked out into the diamond clear Bahamian ocean.

James arrived with their luggage on a luggage cart and waited in the hallway. He stood at attention with his hands clasped behind his back. He was smiling.

"There are three phones in the suite. You have your own personal concierge. Press 9 if you need anything, twenty-four hours a day. James is on call from 6 pm to 6 am every night of your stay. Reggie is on the day shift from 6 am until 6 pm. If you need anything at all press 9. Normally James wouldn't be here this early, but he wanted to meet you. Isn't that right, James?"

"Yes, sir. I am the Principle. It is my duty to greet our VIPs. I will be available for anything you need or if you have questions."

"One final point. The hotel provides shuttle bus service to the Yacht Club for the tennis tournament, but your husband indicated that he had arranged limo service to transport you."

"Yes," Helen said.

"Very good. The limo service has informed me they will be waiting for you outside at 7:00 each morning. The first match starts at 8. Is that satisfactory?"

"That should give us plenty of time to warm up," Helen said.

"Excellent. James, see to their bags and then get back to your post."

"Yes, sir. If you ladies would tell me which bags go where."

Helen and Meredith took one room and Johanna and Ashley took the other. Ronnie carried his own bag to his room.

Ashley watched James move around the rooms carrying the bags. She grinned at Meredith. "Nice ass."

Johanna looked shocked. "Ash, he works here."

"He does have a tight little ass," Meredith added. "You got to admit that is a fine ass."

"Meredith," Johanna said.

"You know what they say, 'Once black never back,'" Meredith continued. "You ever have any black snake before Jo?"

"No. I never wanted any. Have you?"

"No. But I always wondered. A girlfriend told me they are like animals in bed. Insatiable."

"I can see you are going to need watching," Johanna said. "And Ash too. You girls are crazy."

"Crazy, crazy, crazy," Ashley started trying to sing like Patsy Cline. She was still drunk.

Ronnie walked back up. "I'm going to change. I'll see you guys in a minute."

"He's got a nice ass too," Ashley said. "I would love to spank it."

"Come on, hot pants, let's get you to your room," Johanna said and took Ashley's arm. She led her to their room and closed the door behind them.

James walked past. "You need anything, Miss, you call."

"Thank you. I will," Helen said and slipped him some folded money. "I would appreciate it if you called me, Helen."

"Thank you very much, Helen," James said, smiled and left the room.

It was always good to tip the staff at the start of a trip. That got people used to the little bribes and hungry for more. It made them easier to manipulate later if she needed to.

Helen walked out onto the deck and then to the rail. She stared out at the water and then down the beach toward the hotel where Frank was staying five miles away. Her heart ached. She wasn't sure what she would do. She wasn't sure what she should do.

Five minutes later, Johanna met Helen on the deck. The blue water stretched out before them. Johanna was smiling.

"I got Ash to take a nap. I thought it might help to sober her up a little."

"Good idea."

"Meredith is probably getting ready to sunbathe. Which could take hours before she comes out to dazzle us with her perfect body. Of course by that time the sun will have gone down."

Helen smiled. "She is pretty spectacular."

"She isn't as pretty as you are. She doesn't look real."

"You're sweet. I will let you in on a little secret. I think most men would prefer your natural beauty over Meredith's."

"You really think so? I thought all men were just idiots when it came to tits and ass."

"Well, your husband seems to prefer your tits and ass."

Johanna smiled. "Lee is pretty special. I am a lucky girl."

"We all are. Let's change into our suits and go for a little swim."

"Sounds good. We can always eat at the hotel tonight."

13

They parked the ATVs at the hotel and went inside. The manager was still at her station.

"Did you see the Hermitage?"

"Yes, it was very impressive."

"I knew you would like it. Are you finished with the quad bikes or will you be needing them longer?"

"We're done," Frank said. "Call the man. What about jet skis? We were thinking about doing something tomorrow morning."

"Excellent. I will make the arrangements. There are several places, but we use Beaman Jet Skis. It is very close. Come by tonight after dinner and I will give you the details."

"Great," DC said. "I always wanted to ride on one of those bad boys."

"Like a motorcycle on water," Jenny said.

"But it doesn't hurt as bad if you fall off," Caron added. "At least it shouldn't."

"Have you ridden one before, Frank?" Jenny asked.

"A few times."

"Hell, the big man has done everything there is to do. We each get our own jet skis, right?" DC said.

"Only way to ride. You got complete control over how fast you go."

"Best way to ride is flat out. Ride it like you stole it," DC said.

"They are easier to control when they are moving fast that's for sure. When you slow down they rock like a duck in a bathtub."

"But they'll give us like instructions tomorrow?"

"Don't worry Caron. It's easy or they wouldn't let tourists do it. Now, let's get that swim in before dinner."

Caron and Jenny made eye contact and ran for the elevator. DC was close behind. Frank followed, allowing them to have their fun. He envied their innocence.

The late afternoon beach was deserted. The four swam in the calm warm water enjoying the solitude. It was perfect. As darkness crept in, they returned to their rooms. Frank ordered wood-cooked pizzas and Kalik beer. They drank and ate in his room, sitting around the bed and the small table. Frank watched Caron's subtle rubbing of DC's hand. She was trying to get his attention. It took a dozen seconds before DC realized it was a hint. They excused themselves and left Frank alone. Frank lay alone in his bed watching the ceiling fan, thinking about Sybil's dream. Blood and danger were nothing new to Frank Kane. But here in this paradise it seemed like a foolish joke.

14

Helen stood on the deck waiting for the other ladies to get ready. Ronnie pulled out his cell phone. She stared at him.

"What are you doing?"

"I was just checking in. Cyrus wanted me to let him know when we got in and got settled."

"I have called my husband. He is aware that we have arrived safely. "

"But Cyrus wanted..."

"Ronnie," Helen smiled. "I agreed to your presence under the assurance that you would not be obvious. You can watch over us, but I will not have you spying on us. I let you come for Cyrus, I will not have you acting like our parent."

"I'm not. It's just I have to do what Cyrus tells me."

Helen turned away. "When you report in, make it clear to my husband that I am not happy about this intrusion."

"Yes, Ma'am." Ronnie answered like a scolded child. He walked away from Helen to complete his call. He never saw her smiling behind his back.

Cyrus answered on the first ring. "Yes."

"This is Ronnie. I'm checking in like you asked."

"Is everything alright, Ronnie. You sound worried."

"Yes, sir. Everything is fine. The plane ride was super smooth and the rooms are fantastic. We are getting ready to go to dinner."

"I sense a but."

"Yes, sir. Helen wanted me to tell you she does not appreciate me spying on her. She said to tell you she isn't happy to have me acting like a babysitter."

"That is a problem," Cyrus replied. "We discussed this before you left. What do you plan to do about it?"

"Sir? I don't understand. What do you want me to do?"

Cyrus smiled to himself. He loved Ronnie. He was a typical muscle-head. He was big as a house and dumb as a post. "I am asking you, Ronnie, what you recommend. This is your assignment."

"I don't know, sir. Do you want me to come home?"

"No, then there would be no one to watch over them."

"So, what do I do?"

Cyrus laughed. "Whatever my wife says. Be discreet. Call me from your room or when they can't see you. Be subtle. Stay in the background. Don't add to their conversations. Don't give advice or set up rules. Just follow them at a respectable distance. Watch for trouble. You know how to do that."

"Yes, sir."

"I am serious, Ronnie. I don't want my wife to return home angry with me. Do what she tells you to do when she tells you to."

"Yes, sir. I will. I'm sorry I messed up."

"Ronnie, you didn't mess up. This is important. It is a delicate business. You are doing fine. Just let me know if you see anything that you think I need to know about. Otherwise, we'll talk in greater depth after you get home."

"Yes, sir. Thank you, sir. I appreciate your faith in me."

"Don't let me down."

"I won't."

Cyrus disconnected. He was smiling.

"What is so funny?" Spanish Johnny snapped.

"What an attitude, John. You are always so quick to anger."

"I got a lot on my mind. What did the gorilla say?"

"Nothing. Just checking in."

"Then why the smiles?"

"It just reconfirms what sets us apart."

"And what is that, Cyrus?"

"Many things of course, but intelligence, creativity, finesse. Most criminals are stupid, brutish, and simple, without vision."

Johnny smiled at the implied compliment. "That was why we rose so quickly. We could be ruthless when necessary, but we were smarter than everyone else. We saw opportunities they didn't."

"Because we weren't caught up with being criminals. It was about money not lifestyle."

"You are right, Johnny. Often, thugs get so caught up trying to be thugs they forget it is about making money. It is about power."

"Ronnie is a perfect thug. He likes being a thug. He likes people knowing he is a thug. That is all he will ever be."

"He is a dog. He has to be trained. He can't think for himself."

"Do you think Helen is really upset?"

"What do you think?"

"No. She is just letting you know that she knows what you are up to. She is controlling Ronnie. She is figuratively sticking her tongue out at you."

"I agree. Helen can be many things. She is not petty. This would not concern her. She is just giving me the finger a little."

Johnny laughed. "Poor, Ronnie. He is so out of his league. But that is why you sent him."

Cyrus smiled. "Like I told you, that is exactly why he might see something. Helen will be lazy. She knows she is smarter than he is."

After dinner at the hotel, the four women congregated on the deck. It was a beautiful, warm night.

Helen went to the bar and started fixing after dinner drinks.

"Everyone want a drink?" she asked.

No one declined. Helen made everyone Gray Goose and cranberry Cosmopolitans. Johanna fixed a platter with almonds and cheese and brought it over. The women drank and ate and laughed. It was good to be away from the men in their lives. Women needed girl trips too. They could be themselves. It gave them a chance to let their guards down, at least as much as women ever allowed themselves to let their guards down.

Helen looked at the bright stars above them. In the clear sky they seemed to glow brighter than anywhere else. She wondered if Frank was looking at the stars tonight. She hoped he thought about her sometimes. She hoped that a part of him still loved her.

15

Frank woke up in the pre-morning darkness. He checked his new watch. He liked how brightly the numbers glowed emerald green. It reminded him of the translucent green of the ocean. He took that to be a good omen. He rolled out of bed and began a series of stretches. It wasn't a set routine. He just stretched each group of muscles to wake himself up. Shaking off the cobwebs, Apollo had called it.

Apollo had been a former Navy SEAL sniper and his best friend. He had taught Frank how to train. Hell, he had taught him almost everything he knew in those early days with the Spartans. He felt a twinge of regret. Apollo was dead now. Assassinated in Costa Rica. His head had been blown off. Frank had been there. He hadn't been able to stop it. He had made sure those responsible all died that same night. Then Frank had fled north to Nicaragua, bribing his way across borders to a small rundown landing strip. It was probably used for drug drops. Or weapons drops. He had called Claudia Murphy at VIP Travel for help then too. She had sent Phil Bullington in a small plane to pick him up and bring him home. That was the last time Frank had left the United States.

Frank shook off his memories. He was turning into an old man with that shit. He dropped and started doing push-ups. He didn't have a set number anymore. He just did them, as many with perfect form as he could. When his speed slowed he kept going. trying to squeeze out all that he could. Once his form started to fall apart, he stopped. It was simple. It allowed his mind to shut down and let his body do its thing. He went through more exercises, sit-ups, squats, dips, all to the point of exhaustion. His muscles sang with blood and pain. It felt good.

He pulled on his board shorts and slipped the room key into the side zippered pocket. He slipped on a black tee shirt with the name of a band he had never heard of, Combichrist. He had gotten it at a Goodwill store back in Greensboro. He left his shoes off. He took the stairs down to the lower level and slipped out unseen to the beach.

There were people already up and moving about. Not many, but a few. Mostly older people, couples with white hair and deep bronze tans. Some held hands as they walked. It was sweet in a Mayberry sort of way. Frank had missed out on that. He still missed Helen sometimes. He missed the future they might have had together. But you move on. You get past it. You heal. You get over it. She was gone. Probably dead in some shallow grave that no one even remembered its location. It was too bad, but then again, a lot of good people died when the Spartans fell. There was a tiny place in his heart that believed she had gotten away when the purge started. He knew it wasn't probable. But that tiny piece of his heart still loved her.

His body brought him back from his melancholy. It knew its job. It knew what he needed. Barefoot, he started to run. It was not a sprint, but a slow jog in the deep sand. He moved along the tide line and through the scattered groups of people. The sea surge nudged his feet with foam and he smiled at the cool touch of the ocean. He ran the five miles past the last hotel until the beach became less pristine. He turned and started back to the hotel.

He felt fantastic. His body felt in perfect sync. He passed the beautiful high rises when the urge took him. He stopped and stripped off his shirt. He turned and ran into the water. He started to swim. The salt water streamed across his flesh as he picked up speed. His body seemed to extend in the water. He felt a peace he had not felt for years. When he at last grew tired, he stopped. He treaded water and enjoyed the view of the pink sand beach from the sea.

Slowly now, he began to swim back to shore. He focused on each stroke. The purity of the motion. When he got to shore, someone had stolen his black tee shirt. He wasn't mad. He laughed. Someone saw it as an opportunity and they took it. Criminals were the same everywhere. Just their crimes varied. He started to turn back up the beach when he felt eyes on him.

It was a sixth sense or maybe a seventh sense. Like an animal does when it is being hunted. You can see it tense. It knows something is there. It doesn't know where, but it is there. The fight or flight reflex kicks in, but it will pause, ready to react, scanning its surroundings. Searching for the source of the threat. Frank did the same. No one seemed to be looking at him. He looked at the hotels. There were lots of lights on, but he couldn't make anyone out. He waited. Nothing happened. The feeling slowly faded and he turned up the beach again for home. Old habits. Old paranoia.

Helen watched Frank run down the beach toward her hotel through her small binoculars. She knew him. She knew his routines. She knew he liked to run every morning before the sun rose. She marveled at how little his body seemed to have changed. He was still thick with muscles. He still moved like a professional football player. No, she thought, that wasn't what Frank reminded her of. He reminded her of a lion running along a beach. She had seen a program once on national Geographic, and that was what he looked like. Proud and strong and fearless. He was a beast as elemental as any lion. He turned and dove into the ocean and swam out. He swam for a long time, and she was worried that he might exhaust himself and be unable to make it back. A flutter of fear seized her, but she quelled it. He was Frank Kane. His will would bring him back safely. He was unstoppable.

When he reached shore he did something she had never seen him do. He laughed. She could see his beautiful white teeth shine in the morning sun. He seemed so happy. She felt an ache of desire for him and an ache of hatred. How could he be so happy without her? How dare he? She saw him freeze and start to scan his surroundings. She had heard stories about his uncanny senses. He was a predator, a hunter, a man killer. She sank down a little lower on the balcony and froze. It was always movement that gives you away. Frank had taught her that. She watched him scan the beach and then the hotels. His eyes seemed to linger on her hotel for a moment longer. She felt his eyes on her. She held her breath. She closed her eyes. It wasn't possible. He turned and ran up the beach at the same pace he had come down.

Her heart was racing. It threatened to burst from her chest. What in the hell was she going to do?

She put the binoculars on the little glass table and went to the coffee pot. She poured herself a cup and returned to the balcony to watch the rest of the sunrise. She was watching the blue water when she heard Ronnie open the sliding doors and come out.

Helen turned. Ronnie looked sheepish.

"Is it okay if I get a cup of coffee?"

Helen smiled. She had dominated him on the first day. He knew his place in the pack. His head was tilted slightly down. His eyes looked up at her.

"Of course, Ronnie. Help yourself."

"Thank you," Ronnie said. He poured a cup and returned back into the suite. "Just knock on my door when you guys are ready to head down to the tournament."

"I will. Thanks. I'll get them up in a few minutes. I so enjoy my private quiet time in the morning."

"Yes, ma'am," he answered

Good dog, Helen thought. Whatever she decided to do, Ronnie wouldn't be a problem.

16

Frank rested when he reached the hotel. Families were already coming down and setting up on the beach for the day. The hotel provided twenty or thirty thatch-roofed sun umbrellas circled with lounge chairs. Tourists were busily claiming their spots for later in the day. They dropped off towels and magazines to imply they were already using the lounges and then hurried back to the hotel to eat, or go back to bed. A few clever travelers had brought a sun tent. It was like the kind they use at parties. They were tying ropes and stretching nylon. Frank wondered if they had brought it with them or had just bought it on the island and were planning to leave it behind. It wouldn't be a bad investment if you were sun sensitive, he thought. The bright colors awoke more memories about the Spartans and the little meth cooker, Neil.

The Spartans were still in the process of claiming Virginia. Their rigid membership requirements had attracted a more hard core biker element, which was what they wanted. As the Spartans grew their Virginia chapter, they began to clash with another OMC, the Chrome Firebirds. The Firebirds considered Virginia their territory. Although they had a few other chapters in other East Coast states, Virginia was home.

The clashes were mostly verbal, a few fights, a couple of stabbings, and a failed attempt to firebomb the Spartans' clubhouse in Virginia Beach. The Spartans slowly expanded, taking over areas that the Firebirds had once controlled. The situation was building toward a confrontation. So the Spartans did what was least expected. They threw a huge party and bike rally.

The Spartans had bought a large dilapidated farm in the middle of Virginia. They brush hogged the brush back. They brought in backhoes to dig a huge garbage pit. They groomed a sprint track for the bikers. They installed a couple of burnout pits. They provided four dozen port-a-johns. They sent out flyers to all the tattoo parlors, bike shops, tee shirt vendors, funnel cake makers, ham biscuit cookers, and any other person that might be interested. Admission was only five dollars. Festivities would begin at 9 a.m. and run through the night, although the vendors would have to leave by midnight. The implication being that things might get a little wilder late at night and John Q. Public should not be around.

The Chrome Firebirds saw this as an opportunity to get rid of the Spartans with a show of force. All the members were contacted. It would be a mandatory ride. When the time was right. When everyone else was gone. The Firebirds would show the Spartans the meaning of tough. Wills were signed. Some of the Firebirds knew they might die. They knew it would be a declaration of war on the Spartans.

There were thousands at the event. A single narrow, two lane, dirt track controlled access to the party. Thick woods surrounded it, preventing unwanted guests. And out here in the country, no one would complain about a little noise. Numerous other motorcycle clubs were there. A few small outlaw one-percenter clubs, but mostly family clubs. There was even a cop bike club, the Iron Hogs. Everything went as planned. The Spartans busied themselves partying, and the Chrome Firebirds watched and waited.

At midnight, the vendors closed and were ushered out of the farm. Shortly after that, two flatbed trucks arrived with stripper poles. A bus full of strippers arrived right behind it. The girls took to the stage and the night got wilder. The Firebirds had to admit the Spartans knew how to throw a party. By two or three o'clock in the morning, all the family bike clubs had left. Most on their own, the rest heeding the quiet suggestions of the Spartans. By four o'clock ,the air reeked of marijuana and meth. A beer truck arrived and unloaded more kegs of beer. By seven in the morning, the party had died down and burned out. The strippers and whores that had lingered were loaded on the bus and left.

To the Firebirds' surprise, most of the Spartan members were gone as well. The little meth cook, Neil, was still there, helping the handful of Spartan prospects left to break down the tents. It was a let down. The Firebirds juiced on meth and beer and rage were ready for a brawl. This would be a massacre. Six - three against six. Almost ten to one. They would make an example of the Spartans who had stayed behind.

The Firebirds instructed the other bike clubs that it would be a good time to go. Now. They knew what was up. They were gone in minutes. The Spartans seemed oblivious to their danger. When the last bike left, it was time to get started. No witnesses.

The Firebirds crossed the field toward the Spartans in mass. The National President, Rory "Cue Ball," Koster led the way. He was tall and lean like a wolf. Word was that he was a former marine. He was called Cue Ball, not because he shaved his head, but because he had once beaten a rival to death with a pool ball, the white cue ball. The club's national enforcer, Big Rusty Garrett was close at hand.

"Spartan," Cue Ball yelled, "where are your friends?"

"How the fuck do I know? They're big boys they can go where they want," Neil said.

"We told you boys that Virginia was our territory. We told you to leave. We warned you."

Neil stopped what he was doing. "No one tells the Spartans what they can and cannot do. You understand me, bitch?"

"Those are bold words for a skinny old man and some pups."

The prospects froze. They looked around scared. Neil was the only true Spartan full-patch in sight. Neil scratched his nuts. Then slapped at his neck.

"Damn, must be mosquitoes around here. I can hear the little fuckers buzzing around. But ain't no one afeared of mosquitoes."

"The Spartans are a bunch of pussies," Big Rusty said.

Neil punched him in the face. Rusty was more shocked than hurt. He hit Neil in the side of the head and the little man flew backward over a table. Neil got to his feet and dove at the bigger man. Rusty caught him and threw him off to the side. Neil struggled to his feet and Rusty struck him again and again with his big rough hands. The little Spartan tried to rise and couldn't. Other Firebirds moved toward him. They carried chains, and bats, and knives, and even a few pistols.

Cue Ball knelt beside him on the ground. "This isn't your lucky day, little man. We need to send a message and you and your boys have to be it."

The roar of motorcycles broke the morning air. Frank and Spanish Johnny rode back into the meadow. The Firebirds took a step backward as the two Spartans approached. They parked their bikes and got off.

Frank walked over to Neil and stood on the left beside him. Johnny stood on the right. Neither Spartan said a word. They stood like pillars as Neil used their blue jean covered legs to hoist himself to his feet. When he finally stood, he turned to Frank.

"I knew you would be back. I got him right where I want him."

Frank smiled. "Thanks for waiting. You alright?"

"Yeah, he hits like a girl."

"You boys picked a bad time to show up."

Frank moved his cut enough to show the butt of his gun in an inside the belt holster under the vest.

Cue Ball was unimpressed. "Not much against sixty guys. Oh, you'll get a couple of us, sure. Even as good as you are, it ain't enough. We got you and you know it."

Frank raised his hands palms outward like he was holding an invisible wall up.

"Everybody stay cool for one minute. I need to show you something before this gets out of hand."

Frank took a whistle out of an outside pocket of his leather vest. "Do you want the honors, Neil?"

"Damn straight," Neil said. He took the whistle from Frank and blew into it hard three times.

The Chrome Firebirds looked around to see what had just happened. The first red laser sight came to rest on the center of Cue Ball's chest. Spartans stepped out of Port-a-Johns that had been labeled 'out of order.' They carried MP5 submachine guns equipped with sound suppressors. More Spartans converged from the thick woods that fringed the meadow. They all carried automatic weapons.

The Firebirds pulled back into a tighter group. Their eyes shifted nervously around. Fear danced on Cue Ball's face, then he saw the police cruiser edge up the driveway and stop. The light bar came on splashing blue lights across the field. Two policemen got out of the cruiser. Each was carrying an M-16 automatic rifle.

Cue Ball smiled. He had just gotten a reprieve.

"Not your lucky day either, Frank," Cue Ball said.

One of the cops shouted. "You got everything covered, Frank?"

"We're good," Frank answered and waved.

"Okay. We'll make sure you aren't disturbed." The policemen got back into their car and backed out of the driveway.

Cue Ball looked like he had been hit with an axe. He knew he was a dead man.

Neil spit a wad of bloody phlegm from his mouth and wiped his split lips. Frank turned to him and whispered.

"Thank you. You see why we had to leave you here. It kept them focused, held them. They had to feel in control for this to work. They needed that emotional blow."

"I know, big man. I know. I agreed didn't I? You ever need me, I'm your man. I got your back."

"And I got yours. Now let's sort this out."

Frank turned back toward the Firebirds. He could tell they were screwing up their courage. They would go down fighting. He smiled. He liked that. Time for another emotional body blow.

Frank walked to the Spartans' camp area and lifted two stools. He carried them back between the two groups and sat them down.

"Let's take a seat, Cue Ball, and see what we can work out. No one has to die today."

Cue Ball looked at his brothers. Some nodded. Some looked to be in shock. Big Rusty was boiling with rage. Cue ball nodded and took a stool.

"I know you think that Virginia can't accommodate two motorcycle clubs with the same intentions."

"Yeah. I guess I was wrong about that. We might be able to work out some kind of truce. Divide territories," Cue Ball said.

"No. No, you were right. There is only room for one. We can do this the easy way or the hard way."

"Let's hear it."

"The Chrome Firebirds are done. This is a patch-over here and now. You drop your colors and join us."

"Fuck that. We ain't patching over shit. You would have to kill us first."

"That's the hard way. We kill every last one of you and bury you in the garbage pit. Did you see how big and deep we dug that bitch? We got you outgunned and surrounded. We put in a little lime to hide the smell and cover you back up."

"You knew we would try something."

"What else could you do? It was a perfect set-up. Only problem was we set the trap."

Cue Ball laughed. "You played us right pretty."

"Do the smart thing, Cue Ball. Together we can do amazing things. We can show you ways to make money that you haven't dreamed of. You agree, your boys will follow."

"What about those that aren't here? What about them?"

"They can patch-over or get out. And I mean out of Virginia. After today there are no more Chrome Firebirds in Virginia, or anywhere."

"Full members? No prospect, bullshit? Equals."

"In every way." Frank leaned in closer and whispered. "There are special rewards for you, Cue Ball. You'll become a First Citizen. That has special meaning to Spartans. Special perks."

Cue ball rubbed a hand over his shaved head.

"Don't look like we got a lot of choice."

"You don't."

"What if some of my boys agree today and then try to bail later?"

Frank said it loud enough for the Firebirds to hear clearly.

"Then wherever they go. Whatever they do. We will green light them. We will hunt them and kill them."

Cue Ball nodded his understanding. He stood and extended his hand to Frank. Frank shook it.

"Brothers in arms," Frank said.

"This is bullshit," Big Rusty screamed.

Cue Ball turned to him. "It's the only way, Rusty."

"They can fucking kill me then. I'm not dropping my colors."

Cue Ball stood and grabbed him by his jacket.

"Get your head right. You'll do what I tell you."

Big Rusty shoved Cue Ball away.

"If they want my colors come and take them."

Laser lights lit up his chest. Big Rusty reached behind his back and pulled a bowie knife. He spread his arms wide.

"See, brothers. They hide behind their guns. They are afraid to face me like men."

He turned to stare at Frank. Frank just shook his head.

"This is foolish. The Spartans would hate to lose a warrior like you. Is there nothing we can offer you?'

"Blood," Big Rusty said with a devil's grin on his face.

Frank looked around at the Spartans. "Johnny, let me have your knife."

Spanish Johnny stepped up close to Frank. "Let me do him, Frank. It will make a better example."

Frank looked into his eyes. "Alright."

Spanish Johnny drew his own knife. It had only a thin six inch blade.

"You are fucked," Big Rusty said looking at his much larger knife. "Biggest dick always wins."

Big Rusty slashed a quick backhand stroke. Spanish Johnny leaped back from the attack. Rusty charged forward and sliced through the air again. Spanish Johnny darted beneath it and opened Big Rusty's leg with a cut down across his thigh. The big man stumbled and rose quickly. He lunged at Spanish Johnny. Johnny moved back out of the way. Rusty moved slower now as the blood loss weakened him. He lunged and stabbed straight at Spanish Johnny. Once more, Spanish Johnny ducked beneath it and connected the first wound with an identical slash going the other direction. It formed a lambda.

Rusty sliced at Spanish Johnny who danced away.

Big Rusty lunged again and Spanish Johnny dipped beneath the blade and opened his other thigh. Rage showed in Big Rusty's face. He redoubled the ferocity of his attacks, but his blade found only air.

"There is still time," Frank said. "Drop your weapon. Join us."

Big Rusty took another slash at Spanish Johnny, who danced back beyond his reach. He slashed again unable to reach the faster Spartan. Spanish Johnny darted in and cut him again, completing the second lambda. Rusty fell to his knees. A thick froth of spit bubbled from his lips. The blood was flowing heavily now. Big Rusty was weakening. His face was wet with sweat.

"I will not submit."

He threw a wild swipe that Spanish Johnny easily avoided. Spanish Johnny looked toward Frank.

"Be quick, Johnny" Frank said.

Spanish Johnny moved forward with a fake attack. When Big Rusty tried a counter stroke, Spanish Johnny pivoted behind him. He paused for an instant so that Big Rusty would know he was dead, and then slit his throat. Spanish Johnny was a master with a blade, but he was also a showman. Big Rusty clutched at his throat with both hands. Thick dark blood spurted from his fingers and then pitched forward onto the ground.

No one spoke as he bled out.

Spanish Johnny wiped his blade on the three piece rocker on Rusty's back and then sheathed his knife.

"Is there anyone else," Frank demanded getting to his feet. "Is there any other mother fucker so stupid he would rather die than ride as a Spartan? If so, come the fuck on. Let's get this over with so the rest of you can start making some real money. So the rest of you can get a seat at the big table. So the rest of you can start to see the respect a Spartan gets. Come on. Who is next? What dumb cock sucker wants to die?"

No one moved. Cue Ball shook his head. He had loved Big Rusty like a brother. Dumb ass, he thought. Cue Ball took off his colors and tossed them on the ground at Frank's feet. Others followed, each pausing to look at the reality of opposing the Spartan will.

The Spartan prospects had the fire burning and the steel with the Spartan brands cooking in the fire. It would take a long time to brand sixty-two new Spartan brothers. As each passed through the ceremony, they were handed a cold beer and their new colors to sew on.

Frank and Neil dragged Big Rusty's body over to the garbage pit and pushed it in. Strehl would bring the backhoe over and cover him up. Frank left Big Rusty's colors on him. Big Rusty had died a Chrome Firebird. He deserved to be buried as one. Frank respected it. It was stupid and arrogant and prideful. And Frank respected it.

"There are only two groups of people," Neil said to Frank.

"What's that?"

"Either you are a Spartan or you're not."

"Makes the world simple doesn't it?"

"It had to be done, Frank. Probably saved a lot of those other guys. You can't tell me you didn't expect it."

Frank looked at the little man. He had expected it. In fact, he had counted on it for exactly the lesson it taught. He and Spanish Johnny had discussed it in great detail. He put a big hand on Neil's shoulder.

"You continue to surprise me, Neil."

The little Spartan smiled. "I want to make you proud of me. You took a chance on me, and I want people to know you were right. I don't want you to ever doubt me."

Frank gave him a friendly shove. "Don't go getting all misty on me you fucking meth head. We got brothers to bond with."

"You going to bring them girls back?"

Frank smiled. "After Strehl gets finished, we'll call the bus. They aren't far from here waiting for the call."

"I like your style. I had my eye on a red head that could touch her legs behind her head."

"Tie something to your scrawny ass. I don't want you to fall in and have to go looking for you."

That had been a time, Frank reminisced. Sixty more bodies, nearly a hundred when you counted the members who couldn't make the ride. The Spartans had jumped up the food chain in Virginia. They had become a force to be reckoned with. The money started to flow. And with the money came the power and influence.

17

The cab was parked at the curb. Frank lounged against the hood, talking with the driver. DC and the girls had not come down yet. They were twenty minutes late. Frank just smiled. He had knocked on their doors as he was heading down and got mumbled responses from each room. Punctuality was not a strong point for young people.

The driver smiled and shrugged his shoulders.

"Island time," he said.

Frank smiled. Damn, he was getting good at smiling. He didn't have to pretend to smile, it just happened. He felt as good as he had felt in a long time. Everything seemed to be going right. Frank heard the girls before he saw them.

"I'm sorry we're late. It's my fault," Caron said. "I couldn't get my hair dry."

"I told her not to worry about it," Jenny added. "It's just going to get wet anyway."

"This coming from the girl who was busy putting on her makeup."

"That's different. I look like hell without a little blush. And everyone wears lipstick. It isn't even considered makeup. It is totally different."

"No, it isn't. Plus if I look like a hag, DC will start eyeing all the hot babes on the island."

"I got news for you, girl. It doesn't matter if you look like Megan Fox, boys will always look."

Caron spun around at DC who was following them out. "Is that true? Do you always check out other girls? Still?"

DC held his hands up in surrender. "I am not in this conversation, ladies. I plead the fifth."

Caron glared at him. "You are such a chicken." She looked over at Frank. "Do guys ever grow up?"

Frank smiled. "I'll let you know when I get there. You guys got all your stuff?"

Jenny started rummaging through her oversized beach bag and calling out the items inside.

"Sunscreen, bug spray, spare hair scrunchy, big ass hat, and towels. Yes, I brought a spare towel for you just in case." She smiled at Frank. "You didn't bring one did you?"

"Guilty," Frank said. "Thank you."

In reality Frank hadn't brought a towel on purpose. He had planned to let the wind dry him off and a towel was just something else to look after.

Jenny snapped her sunglasses down over her dark eyes. "I am ready to depart."

Caron snapped to mock attention. "Me too, sir."

DC rolled his eyes. "Women," he said walking toward the taxi.

DC held the door for the girls and climbed in behind them. Frank got into the front seat beside the driver. He liked riding in the front. It gave him options if there was trouble.

The driver jumped in and took off in a cloud of dust and gravel. The overgrown marsh flats sped past. The windows were down on the cab and Frank could smell the mix of salt, water, and decay that filled the air. He loved it.

It took only a few minutes to reach Beaman Jet Ski Adventures. There was a large sign at the road. The cab turned down the gravel drive and drove a few hundred yards to the beach. There was a Honda Pilot and a worn out old car parked near a large main building. There was a storage area for the jet skis off to the side. There was also a small repair shop near the water. There was a huge pile of gravel in the middle of the road. A shovel rose from the top like a bare flagpole, presumably waiting for someone to grab it and fill in the assorted pot holes. Frank knew those kind of shovel-ready jobs were always last on the to-do list. There just never seemed enough time in a day to break your back in the hot sun shoveling gravel.

A half dozen bright yellow Yamaha VXR jet skis rested on a trailer, and another ten bobbed off the side of the short dock. They would carry one to three passengers each. The VXR was fast and durable. It was a good choice for a jet ski business.

Frank and the others got out and Frank paid the driver. There was a black guy on the dock. When he saw them pull up he came their way. The black man was thin. He was wearing Lost brand boardshorts. He wore his short sleeve button up shirt unbuttoned. He had a bony chest. He wore his hair in dreadlocks that reached past his shoulders. Around his neck was a white shell necklace. He was all smiles and loose limbs.

"Greetings. Greetings. I am Tonello. I work for Mr. Beaman. You are the party from the hotel, yes?"

"Yes," Frank answered. "I'm Frank, this is DC and Jenny and Caron."

Tonello shook each hand in turn. Each time he repeated, "Welcome."

As the last hand was shaken he continued. "We have some good funs today. Special trips. I take you all the spots the tourists don't get to see."

Jenny high fived Caron and then DC. "That's what I'm talking about."

"These jet skis not like other ones they rent on the island. These are very fast. No restrictor."

DC smiled. "I like me some speed."

"You like hearing anybody say the restrictions are off," Caron said.

"I do indeed."

"Where is your boss?" Frank asked.

Tonello pointed to other building. Mr. B-Man finishing some paperwork. He always like to meet the clients. He be right down. But I leading this trip. I got the skis all gassed up and ready to go. Got a cooler strap down on mine full of cold Kalik and some snacks for break time. We take break on secret beach. No one there but us."

"We could go skinny dipping," Caron teased.

"That would be so wicked," Jenny said.

"Hey, I'm game," DC added.

"You think we could, Frank?" Caron asked.

"No, you couldn't," Frank said. "Maybe next time when I'm not around."

"Prude," Jenny teased and she had a sudden flash of sympathy for Frank being forced to act like an adult.

Frank smiled. "I've been called a lot of things before, but that's a first."

Frank heard the dog before he turned. He could hear the distinctive scrabbling sound of claws on the gravel. He turned as the dog reached them. The dog was a classic boxer. A male. His skin was a golden sheen over large muscles. The dog was shaking so hard in excitement Frank thought his head might fall off. It ran from person to person to greet them. Its stub of a tail was twitching wildly. The girls squealed and took turns trying to pet the excited dog. Even DC knelt to get in on the love-fest. The noise and commotion had distracted Frank. He had not heard the man approach.

Frank felt the familiar coldness of metal pressed hard against the back of his neck. "Don't move," the voice whispered behind him, "or you're dead."

Those words have been shouted a million times by policemen around the world. For citizens it is an order that must be obeyed or dire consequences will ensue. To lifelong criminals it is a different directive. If you are ordered to stop, you go. If you are ordered to turn around, you do not. If you are instructed to drop the weapon, you fire.

The order to not move could mean many things. It could mean the man with the gun is not quite in position yet. It could mean he is giving you a chance to surrender since your situation is hopeless. It could mean that the gunman wishes to converse with you. Either a message, or final taunt, or an offer of a deal. It didn't matter. Frank knew what he would do.

As the man leaned in to give his warning, Frank was already spinning away. His outside right arm swept the weapon arm from behind him as he turned. The right hand locked around the wrist. The left leg continued to swing around and swept the legs from the man. Even as the man fell backward, Frank was dropping after him. His left forearm cocked back to deliver a smashing blow to the head like wrestlers do on TV, except this blow would be real. And it would be lethal. Frank's eyes swept the man as he fell on him.

The man was in his late twenties. He was wearing only a pair of surfer boardshorts. He was lean, but very muscular. His hair was buzz-cut short. That's when he saw the tattoo. Two twin tiger sharks decorated his forearm. That was when he recognized the man. Frank had seen the real twins himself in Costa Rica. His old prison cell mate had seen them in Indonesia and commemorated it with these images. Frank shifted his body slightly as he fell and landed hard beside the shocked man. The elbow remained unused.

Frank lay on his back in the dirt beside the stunned man. He got to his feet and extended his hand to the man.

"Bruce, what are you doing here?"

Bruce took his hand and let Frank pull him to his feet. He was shaking. "Damn, man, you could have killed me."

"Could have. You should know better than to stick a gun in my back."

Bruce bent over and picked up the wrench from the ground. "It wasn't a gun. It was a wrench."

"Felt like a gun."

"It was a joke. That's all. Damn." Then he smiled. He gave Frank a huge hug.

"It is good to see you, Frank. When I recognized you outside on the dock, I couldn't believe my eyes. I almost had a heart attack. Frank Kane. After all this time. Man, it is good to see you. I figured I would never run into you again, and then now on this island. Wow. I should have known better than to think I could sneak up on you. Got to be a good omen."

"It's good to see you again too, Bruce. What's with the Beaman. You buy this place?"

"Yeah, yeah. I just decided to call it Beaman because you were always telling me to be a man. And man up. And saying shit about what a man does. I thought instead of trying to be afraid of the man as in authority, I would become the man. Everyone on Cat calls me B Man. As in, 'be a man.' Get it?"

"I get it. Let me introduce you to my friends."

"This is DC and Caron and this is Jenny."

Bruce shook each hand in turn. "Jenny's a little young for you isn't she man? Not that she isn't hot. She is that. I'm just saying."

Jenny smiled at the compliment.

"She's my niece," Frank said

"Oh, sure. Really? Ok, Cool." Bruce smiled at Jenny.

Frank gave him a light slap to his head. "Focus, Bruce. What are you doing here?"

Bruce smiled. "It is a long story."

"Give me the short version."

"I was traveling around after we parted company and I met this kid from here. He told me about a secret break off the island. It's out near the huge pinnacle out there."

"That was you we saw surfing from the plane?"

"Had to be, bro, if the guy you saw was flat shredding. And good looking."

"Must not have been you. This guy was surfing good, but he was dog ugly."

Bruce knelt and put his hands over the dog's ears. "Don't listen to them, Thor boy. Dogs aren't ugly." He nuzzled the dog. "Even when they have a squish face like yours."

"How do you know Frank? Were you a Spartan?"

Bruce smiled and touched his chest. "Only in here, Jenny. We did a little time together. Frank had a short ticket."

"You knew Frank from prison? I use to come visit him all the time."

"That's where I recognized you from. With the older couple. I remember. Like clockwork. Wow. You have grown up into a beautiful woman."

"Thank you," Jenny said as she blushed.

"What happened after I got out?"

Bruce stood up. He smiled. "Just like you planned. The Norse Men protected me. No one messed with me with an army at my back. They told everyone that you had paid for my protection. It gave them new status. They strutted around like the new kings of the walk. The Muslim brotherhood tested it once, but that monster, the one they called the Fenris Wolf, that guy is an animal, he beat the guy nearly to death. After that no one dared."

"Good."

"The Wolf claimed you came to their leader, the guy who calls himself Loki, and begged a favor. They claimed you were a punk. The once great Frank Kane. But I knew they were lying. Everyone else did too."

"That why you named your dog, Thor? In tribute for their protection?"

"Fuck no. My mythology is a little shaky, but if I remember the story right, even though Loki and Thor were brothers they hated each other. It was eventually Thor who destroyed Loki and his children. The Norse Men are assholes. Sweet Thor here just reminds me not to be like those dicks."

"Glad to hear it, Bruce."

"That's not all. Did you check out the new me?" Bruce spread his arms and pivoted in a slow circle. Covering nearly his entire back was a black Spartan lambda. "That's because you, the Spartans, had my back. That reminds me to go straight ahead and not look over my shoulder all the time."

He showed his left arm. He had a three quarter sleeve of tattoos that ran from elbow up onto his left shoulder. The arm tats were all ocean related. On his left shoulder was a surfer entering a tube made by a huge wave.

"That's like your tat, Frank, only it pertains to my life. I got to be who I am. At heart I am only a surfer. That's what I do. That's my soul. But dig this," He lifted his right arm. tattooed on his side near his ribs in Old English script was SFFS. "That is just like the one you have except mine stands for Surfer Forever Forever Surfer. I know I am not a Spartan. I am a surfer. But in my heart, brother. In there I am a Spartan."

"You were as Spartan as anyone I knew, Bruce. But why a jet ski rental place?"

"It's obvious. I came for the wave, but I had to have a way to pay the bills. I didn't want to run weed anymore. I was trying to go straight like you said you were, so I found this business for sale and bought it with my leftover cash. The rest is beautiful history."

Frank patted him on the shoulder. "I'm happy for you, Bruce. I really am. You've done good."

"I couldn't have done it without you, Frank."

"Sure you could have." Frank knelt and rubbed Thor's huge head. "This is a good dog. And I know dogs."

"He's a sweetie. He loves everybody. Don't you, boy?"

The dog jumped up on his chest. Bruce rubbed his head.

"Hey, why don't you come with us?" Jenny asked.

Bruce smiled. "Better than that. Listen, Tonello, I'll take these guys out."

"You sure, Mr. B Man? I don't mind."

"No, I got this."

"Tonello was going to take us on a special run that the tourists don't get," Jenny said.

"And take us to a secret beach," Caron added.

Bruce laughed. "That's what we tell everyone. I'll take you on a real adventure and to a real secluded beach."

Jenny and Caron gave Tonello the stink eye.

Tonello shrugged. "It is my job."

"Don't blame him. I make him do the spiel. The tourists all want to be special. But you guys are special. Tonello, cancel the other rentals for today. We are closing early today."

"But we have made arrangements, Mr. B Man."

"Okay. Take the spare skis. These are booked all week. You guys here all week, right?"

"Until Sunday morning," DC said.

"Until Sunday these are reserved. Now mount up. I always love to say that," Bruce said. "Go pick out a jet ski and I'll be right down to show you the ropes on how they run. I got to get Thor some food and water out if daddy is going to be gone. Isn't that right, Thor boy?"

Tonello followed Bruce up to the office. Thor followed close behind. Bruce got out a big bag of food and filled Thor's bowl and poured some water from a jug into his other bowl.

Tonello kept looking back at Frank's group.

"Don't stare, Tonello. Frank might not like that."

"He is the one? The one you talk about from the prison. Frank Kane?"

"Yes, sir. He's the famous Frank Kane."

"After your stories I looked him up on the computer at the library. There are many many things written about him. His enemies claimed he could not be killed. They call him killer, enforcer, monster, daemon even. The police feared him."

"You say that like it is a bad thing, Tonello. He was all of those things, but he is also my friend. Don't worry about it. Everything happens for a reason."

18

Cyrus sat at his desk waiting. He was wearing tan linen slacks and a white silk shirt. He opened a drawer and removed a dark green felt cloth and a small white towel. He spread it on top of his desk. He withdrew a gun cleaning kit from a leather case. He opened the top drawer of the desk and removed a Night Hawk semiautomatic. It was in the classic 1911 format. He released the magazine and used his thumb to eject the rounds. They were all .45 caliber hollow points. Man killers, he called them, because it didn't matter where you hit a man with one. He would die. It could blow off limbs as easily as it could deliver killing force to a torso. He liked the feel of the Night Hawk. He had been told that it was a company formed by former employees of Kimber. Each gun was handmade. If it was true, they knew guns and top of the line materials.

Cyrus broke the gun down and cleaned each piece. It was amazing to him that a gun was on one level such a simple machine. So few parts. Such a straightforward design. It was perfect. Sure, gun makers could tweak the sights or the trigger pull or the finish or the grip or a thousand other unimportant parts, but the soul of the gun was unchanged. It was a killing machine. It had no other purpose. Self defense, law enforcement, war, crime, it didn't matter. It was meant to kill, or at the very least impart that threat.

He added a drop of Rem Oil to the parts where it could be used. He had always used high performance motor oil, but recently he had changed to Rem Oil. It was made by Remington. He liked the cleanness of the oil. He even liked the slight almond smell.

He rebuilt the Night Hawk. He wiped each round as he replaced them in the magazine. He snapped the magazine back into place. With well practiced movements he worked the slide to load a round. An unloaded gun was of no use. A loaded gun without a round in the chamber was little better. Frank had described such a gun as a hammer.

His cell phone rang. Cyrus placed the gun gently onto the mat. He wiped his hands on the small towel imparting another stain. He flipped up the cover of the protective case and checked the caller's ID.

"Good morning," Cyrus said. "Are we secure?"

The voice laughed. "You are so funny. If we weren't, I wouldn't have called."

Cyrus smiled. "It is a habit for me to ask, nothing more. I did not mean to insult you."

"I fully understand."

"I have been waiting for your call."

"As you said yourself, Cyrus, I had to be sure we were secure."

"You could have come to the house. It is secure."

"I prefer this."

"Are you saying you don't trust me?"

"Of course I don't trust you. I don't trust anyone. That's why I'm still alive. And let's face it, you're not that trusting yourself."

"No, I am not. But I would prefer to talk with you in person."

"And I would prefer to have a really big dick. Oh, wait I have that."

"Fuck you, asshole."

"Now brother, does that kind of prison flirting ever work?"

Cyrus laughed. "You have a wit about you, Helios. I admit that."

"Thank you, Cyrus. You can call me Carpenter. You don't have to flatter me with my Spartan god name. Now what can I do for you?"

"If you are so all knowing as you claim, you tell me. What do I want?"

Helios thought for a few seconds. "It has to be to trace someone or something. I will venture it's a person you want me to find or investigate. Since your own people are pretty good at investigating people, I have to deduce it is to find someone important that has disappeared. Am I right?"

"You are very clever. All the gods were."

"Yet not all of them were clever enough to survive the purge."

"We did. Ultimately I think that is all that is truly important to us."

"True. True. So whom do you want me to find for you?"

"Prometheus."

"Ah, the fire walker. Masnick was a rat, so I hear."

"True. That issue is ancient history. It doesn't concern me. I have other issues with him. Can you find him?"

"He has been underground for a long time. He always liked being off the radar. I don't think he trusted you either."

"Good for him. Can you do it or not?"

"Of course I can. You know that or you wouldn't have sought my help."

"How long will it take?"

"As long as it takes. I guarantee results not timetables. What is the price?"

"You still counting your pennies, Helios?"

Helios laughed. "Cyrus, my brother, you know payment is not always about money. It is about respect and dignity. Turning over rocks can be a dangerous business. Do you know anything about hunting Cape Buffalo?"

"Is this going somewhere?"

"Indulge me."

"Very well."

"When you hunt Cape Buffalo on foot it is a risky business. If you fail to drop the beast with your first shot it will run to deep cover to hide."

"I don't see where..."

"But it doesn't hide, that is the point. It fishhooks around on its own trail and lies waiting for the hunter to follow. If the hunter isn't careful he becomes the victim not the buffalo."

Cyrus sighed. "I see your point. Seeking puts you at some risk. I get it."

"Good. I was going to follow up with an anecdote about a certain giant wasp in South America that hunts spiders by tripping their webs and luring the spider to its death. It's pretty cool if you want to hear it."

"Another time, Helios.'

"You sure? The wasp is badass."

"I'm sure. What is your fee?"

"Well, Masnick was always an arrogant prick anyway so let's say a million."

"Very well. I'll wire transfer to your account in the Caymans."

"The Caymans are not as secure as I like. I have an account in the Seychelles that will serve as first stop for the funds."

"Which you will transfer again anyway."

"Of course. That is obvious. Would anyone do it any other way?'

"I suppose not. One million even? You don't want to send me on a fucking scavenger hunt for something else to sooth your ego?"

"No, the money will be fine. It tells me you are serious about this. That is important to me. If you are half-ass, why should I even waste my time."

"I hear you. I am serious. Find Prometheus for me."

"Consider it done."

"I may have some other less important people for you to locate."

"I will throw them in for free."

"One more thing, Helios."

"Shoot."

Cyrus looked down at the gun on his desk and smiled. The word choice was ironic he thought. "I need you to find a second person. It is very important to me."

"Who?"

"Frank Kane."

19

Helen wiped the beads of sweat from her forehead with a small white cotton towel she had brought from the hotel. The towel was so soft it felt like she was using a cloud.

"It is fucking hot," Meredith said. "What happened to the breeze?"

Helen smiled. She liked it hot. It made other people weak.

"I don't know. Drink some water. Ronnie, bring us some water."

Ronnie grabbed two cold bottles of water from the cooler and rushed over. He passed the water out to the ladies.

"Here you go."

"Thanks."

"How are Ashley and Jo doing?"

Ronnie looked over his shoulder at a distant court. "Last time I checked they were squeaking by."

"We got another match this afternoon after lunch. Better rest while you can."

"Fuck a bunch of tennis," Meredith said. "I say we forfeit and hit the beach."

Helen smiled. "I know how you feel, but I want to play some more tennis and it is single elimination."

Meredith stared at Helen like she was an alien.

"You are a fucking bionic woman. It must be like a thousand degrees out here. I don't know if I can do another doubles match."

Helen smiled. Quitter, she thought. Spoiled bitch, she thought. But she said, "Of course you can Meredith. You are a lot tougher than you make out. You just try to hide it from people."

Meredith looked stunned. "You mean it? You think I'm tough?"

Helen used her own towel to wipe the sweat from Meredith's forehead. It was a very intimate gesture.

"Inside I think you are a fucking she-tiger."

Meredith seemed to gain strength from the words.

"You're right, Helen. I got another match in me. Fuck the heat. Fuck being tired. Fuck these bitches. Let's go kick some ass. I want to win that fucking trophy."

Helen smiled her thousand watt smile.

"That's my girl. Come on. Ronnie, go see if the other girls need anything."

"Yes, ma'am," he said and jogged away.

Good little dog, she thought. Now run, call Cyrus and give him your little report. Every word I said. For an instant her mind flashed to Frank on the beach, but she brushed it away. That would have to wait. She did want to win some more tennis matches. She didn't like to lose. Not at anything.

20

Tonello sat with his legs dangling off the dock. He looked off toward where the jet skis had disappeared. He was afraid. What he was thinking was filled with dangers. If he was right, he would become rich and powerful. He would become respected and feared. If he was wrong, he would be signing his own death notice. He had to risk it. Had to. He opened his cell phone and punched in his cousin's phone number. The phone rang and rang, but no one answered. It switched to voice mail and he hung up. He sat for a few seconds more and dialed again. Once more it rang until it was transferred to voicemail again. Tonello hung up. He was a little afraid of his cousin, but he was committed now. He dialed a third time.

The phone was answered on the second ring.

"Don be actin' da fool. What you want be callin' like dis?"

"It is me, Tonello."

"I know who de fuck dis be. What you be wantin' so bad be callin' like da fool?"

Tonello swallowed hard. "I need to tell you something."

"So tell it."

"I need you to speak to the Prophet for me, Dawg."

Dawg did not answer. "The Prophet only speaks to de disciples."

"You have to get a message to him. It is important. He must hear my message."

"What you need be sayin'?"

"I have a gift for Lord Tosh. A sacrifice here on Cat Island fittin' for the Dreadmon."

"You mad mon. De Prophet na leave de motherland for nothin'"

"This would be worth it. He is here."

"Who is here? What you mean?"

"Frank Kane is here on Cat Island."

"Frank Kane. I don' believe dis name."

"Look him up. He is a powerful man. His soul will have much power. Look him up, Dawg. He is here. Frank Kane is here. The Spartan. The undead man is here."

Dawg could hear the urgency in his cousin's voice. He felt a surge of excitement in the pit of his stomach. Frank Kane. Could it be so? After so many years had the daemon Dreadmon finally sent him to me, he wondered.

"I call you back. You best na be lyin.'"

Dawg hung up. He sat silent for thirty seconds, going back in time.

He went back to Miami and the Rude Boys. Back to a time when Dawg had been called by another name. Back in those glory days of running primo Jamaican ganja. He worked with an all Jamaican crew run by Georgie-boy. Georgie-boy's crew were hard boys. They came to Miami and started taking control of the marijuana business around little Jamaica. The Rude Boys walked loud and tall. They took what they wanted. Other dealers either moved on or disappeared. It didn't matter to Georgie-boy. He was old school gangster. Life was good. There was plenty of money and women and weed. What more could a Rasta child want?

Then the Spartans came. The Rude Boys knew of the Spartans supposed control. They had informants watching for motorcycle riding rednecks. The trouble was Florida was full of them. When the Spartans did come, they did not come on bikes.

Georgie-boy was playing dominos at his club when the Spartans came. Dawg had been on lookout by the front doors when the white van stopped. The door slid open and five men rushed out. The men all carried AK-47 automatic rifles. The AK's were old, the wooden stocks were worn, but the metal glistened in a well-oiled black mat finish. All the men, except the leader, the big man, Frank Kane. He carried a small package.

Before Dawg could cry out a warning they were to the doors. The Asian one turned to watch the street behind. The other three spun Dawg around and marched him inside before them like a human shield.

The club was dark. It wasn't due to open for four more hours. There were nearly a dozen Rude Boys inside. Faces turned to the intruders. A black Spartan moved to one side of the main doors. His weapon swept the room from his hip like a soldier.

The other three moved toward the VIP section where Georgie-boy was playing bones. Georgie-boy glanced up as the men approached. He did not look alarmed. He held a hand up and the Rude Boys seemed to relax, if only a little. Georgie-boy played a double six.

"So the Spartans have come at last."

The biggest one, the leader had stepped up to the table.

"I am Frank Kane."

"I know who you are. Who be your friends, brudder?"

Kane smiled or maybe it was a grimace. Dawg thought it was the worst smile he had ever seen. He nodded. "This is Blanco Grande," he said indicating a man with a white beard and a long scar down the side of his neck. "And this is The Jake." The Jake looked like a child. He was a teenager, but his eyes held a cold fire like a snake's that shook Dawg.

Georgie-boy nodded his head. "So they have sent the Kryptea for poor Georgie-boy. Do you hear that, boys, I tremble."

"I am not here to make threats. Carlo said you have taken over his territory without compensation. Carlo is a Spartan. We have come for resolvement."

"And what dat be?"

"Two ways to do this. Easy way and hard way. Easy way you pay or you go. We set the terms. Hard way only body bags."

Kane laid the package down and unrolled it. The burlap package contained something. Dawg moved closer to see. It was an ordinary hammer, only someone had painted it dark red. Georgie-boy lifted the hammer and turned it over in his hands. There was a letter cut into the handle. It looked like a V. Georgie-boy tossed it onto the table.

"What is dis thing? You want I to build some ting?"

"Build your coffin. You have been warned. The hammer of Sparta has come. You have forty-eight hours, two days…"

"I know what two days are. You think I the fool?"

"I know exactly who and what you are, Georgie-boy. You know we do not play. You have forty-eight hours to fix this."

Kane turned and walked out with his back to the Rude Boys. The other Spartans, however, backed out slowly watching everyone. The young one was smiling. He made a small motion with his head toward Dawg. Dawg didn't understand what the teenager wanted him to do. Dawg could tell the boy wanted to trigger a fight. He wanted to kill. He was smiling like a cobra if a cobra could smile. He was trying to coax a response from Dawg. Dawg did not move.

When they were gone, Georgie-boy signaled Dawg over.

"Find Carlo. I know he has gone to ground, but dig him out. I want his arms and legs cut off and his body dumped on main street. The Spartans want to send a message. We send them a message. You want war? No one presses the Rude Boys. We will kill them all. Jah will protect us in all tings.

The tension was gone. The bartender started pouring them all drinks. Someone lit a spliff and the air reeked of the beautiful scent of the holy ganja. They feared no man. Everyone feared the Rude Boys. This time the Spartans had made a mistake. This time the Spartans would pay.

Two days later they had not found Carlo, but they would. He could not hide forever. Georgie-boy had brought the Rude Boys all together in his mansion. Three men were posted outside. Dawg was one of them. Nothing stirred outside and the reggae had long since died away inside. He felt metal against his head. He had heard nothing. No sound.

The big man, Frank Kane, whispered in his ear.

"Drop your weapon."

He had no choice. He did as he was told. He started to shake a little at the immediacy of his death.

"Stay calm. I will not kill you. You must carry a message for me."

"To Georgie-boy? Sure."

"No. Georgie-boy is gone. Tell your friends in Jamaica that the Spartans run Miami. Tell them what you have seen."

"But I haven't seen anything. What do you mean?"

But Kane was gone. Dawg had spun around, but the man was nowhere to be seen. He reached down for his Mac 10, but it was gone as well. He ran toward the house. Inside was madness. In every room men lay dead. No one had fired a shot. No one had made a sound. Everything was soaked in blood. Upstairs he found Georgie-boy in his bed. The red hammer was clutched in his hands that lay across his chest.

Dawg understood. The warning and been a way to pull all the Rude Boys together into one place. No women, no friends, no innocent bystanders, only the Rude Boys. No witnesses. No survivors. No one would care very much.

Dawg went into the bathroom right then. He took out his knife and cut off his dreadlocks. No more. No more Jah. No more Rasta. Four years later he had met Lord Tosh, the Prophet of the daemon Dreadmon. He had been reborn and renamed Dawg. And Dawg he was now until he drew his last breath. He had not told the other disciples of his humiliation by Kane. He would not.

Dawg rose to his feet. His hands were shaking. He went to talk to the Prophet. His door was closed. Dawg could hear music playing. It was a band called Cream, they were singing about the tales of brave Ulysses. He knocked on the door. He heard movement inside. A deep voice called to him as from the grave.

"Enter my child."

21

The jet skis were pulled up on the beach. The cooler had been unstrapped and nestled into the sand. Frank sat at the water's edge sipping a cold beer. He watched the condensation drip down the sides.

"Really, big man. You got to give me a chance."

"No, I don't."

"I could do it. I swear. Give me one day and I'll have you up on a surfboard. I got a longboard back at my crib. It's a sweet Robert August composite. Nine foot two. Very smooth ride."

"I appreciate it, Bruce. I just don't have the time on this trip."

"Fair enough. But when you come back we carve out some time. Or we could even hook up in CR for a session."

"We'll see."

Bruce turned back toward the water. He watched Jenny splashing around with Caron and DC. Caron had her back to them, but they could tell she flashed DC with her bikini top.

"Jenny has grown up a lot from the little girl who came to see you."

"Yes."

"I don't mean anything creepy by it. Just that she's very pretty."

"I know exactly what you are saying."

"Look, I know my limits. You can trust me."

"Uh huh."

"Seriously, there's a huge Thanksgiving party at the Yacht Club tonight. You guys all come and we will tear it up."

"Sounds good. I know they will want to come."

"You got to come too."

"Are you sure I won't cramp your style?"

"No way. You got to come. I owe you like a million beers or something."

"You don't owe me anything."

Jenny and Caron and DC all headed toward shore. Jenny studied their faces.

"What were you talking about?"

"There's a big Thanksgiving party at the Yacht Club," Frank said.

"Can we go?"

"Of course. Whatever you want to do. It's a vacation."

"I'm trying to get Frank to come. He's trying to beg off going."

"Yeah, you got to come," Jenny said. "It wouldn't seem right."

"She's right, dude. You don't want to ruin our trip on Thanksgiving do you? We are a team."

"You are supposed to spend Thanksgiving with your friends and family."

"Being thankful," Caron added clumsily.

"In a bar?" Frank asked.

"In a fucking bar in the Bahamas, man. That is pretty cool stuff."

"Please," Jenny said.

"Sure. It will be fun," Frank said.

Jenny high fived Bruce.

Hanging around a bunch of rich people Frank didn't know sounded like hell to him. But it wasn't all about him anymore. It was a vacation, he reminded himself again. Everyone's vacation. Go with the flow.

Helen and her friends were all laughing and trying to talk at the same time. The manager saw as they entered the hotel.

"How was the tennis tournament?" he asked with a tone that implied he really cared, which he didn't.

"We all advanced," Johanna said. "We all get to play again tomorrow."

"Lucky us," Meredith said. "I wanted to sit in the sun all day."

"Bad for your skin," Ashley said. "It makes you wrinkle like a prune."

"Just like playing tennis in this damn oven," Meredith said. "And it makes my tan uneven."

"Oh, dear God. Don't let her start laying out nude," Johanna said. "It would give Ronnie a heart attack."

"I could handle it," Ronnie said.

"You only think you could," Meredith said. "It would probably burn your eyes out of their sockets."

"If she goes nude, I will," Ashley said.

"Sounds good to me," Ronnie said.

Ashley actually blushed. She looked away.

"Our matches were pretty easy, but Helen and Meredith beat last year's champions."

"Is that so?" the manager said. "Congratulations."

"They were good, but we were better today."

"We? You. You played like one of the Williams sisters. You must have aced them a dozen times. They couldn't stop your serve."

Helen smiled. "They were so smug when we started. They were so sure they would win. I just wanted to wipe that look off their faces."

"Well, you did that, girl. After the last set they stood around like deer in the headlights. They couldn't believe we won."

"Feels good to win," Helen said.

"Yes it does," Meredith said. "You were spectacular."

"You were pretty good yourself. You worked the net like a pro."

"Why don't you just make out with each other," Ashley said. "All this sisterhood stuff makes my stomach hurt." Helen and Meredith laughed.

Johanna grabbed Ashley and pretended to try to kiss her.

"Give me a little sugar, partner."

"Get away," Ashley said.

"What's for dinner?" Meredith asked. "It's Thanksgiving. We should do something special."

"I would recommend the hotel as a matter of policy, but The Chart House has the best food on the island. It is a little pricey, but excellent."

"That sounds good," Meredith said. "You girls up for that?"

"Sure," Helen said.

Ashley and Johanna exchanged looks and nodded.

"Can you make reservations for us? Say about six. I would like to rest up before dinner."

"The Chart House is usually booked, but for you, I will arrange it. Six o'clock."

"Thank you."

They took the elevator up to their suite and spilled out onto the sun deck. Helen stared out at the blue ocean. She thought about Frank. She thought about Cyrus. She didn't think about tennis.

Johanna joined her.

"It is so beautiful here."

Helen smiled.

"I'm glad we came. It is such a treat to get away from home and all those stresses."

"I know what you mean."

There was a squeal behind them as Meredith jumped into the pool with her tennis dress on. Ashley was laughing. Ronnie was leering like a gorilla. Ronnie's eyes may have been steaming just a little like Meredith had predicted.

The water plastered the white tennis top across Meredith's chest. She was smiling. She waded over to the steps and climbed out. She used both hands to sweep her hair back from her face. She ran her hands down her body as if she were trying to wipe some of the water off and not caress herself. Every eye was glued to her as she stepped from the water. She was beaming.

Helen smiled. Meredith was so predictable.

22

They drove the jet skis back to the dock. Tonello was gone, out with the other group of tourists and had not returned. Bruce jumped off his jet ski first. He grabbed a line and secured it to the dock by the ring on the front. The others all followed his lead, and he grabbed lines to secure each boat with a bowman's hitch. Frank could have tied his own hitch line, but he let Bruce do it. Let him be the expert, he thought.

Thor came racing down the driveway from his bed on the front porch of the office. He splashed into the shallow water and Bruce petted him roughly.

"He's a water dog. Loves it."

Thor went from person to person to reacquaint himself. The girls hugged his big head like a lost friend. The ritual complete, Thor loped out of the water and waited on the shore, shaking the water from his coat.

"What can we do to help you," Frank asked.

"Nothing, man. Nothing at all. I'll run you guys back to the hotel, then I'll come back and clean up the jet skis."

"What do you have to do?" Jenny asked.

"Flush them out with some fresh water, hose them down a little, refuel them. No big deal."

"We could help," Jenny said.

"Sure," DC said, "there are four of us it wouldn't take long."

"No way. I won't hear of it. I'll get them done when I get back. Tonello will be back by then. We got a routine. And it is his job. I pay him to do it."

"If you're sure," Jenny said.

"Positive. Come on. Get your gear and we'll roll. That's my old Honda Pilot over there."

They got into the SUV, Frank taking the front seat. Thor stood outside whimpering.

Bruce popped the trunk and the big dog jumped into the back.

"I hope you don't mind. Thor loves to ride."

Frank smiled. A man and his dog. It was a special bond. The ancient Spartans were renowned breeders of Kastorian hounds. They loved their dogs too. History described an almost supernatural bond between Spartans and dogs.

"It's fine as long as you don't let him drive."

Bruce backed them up and turned the Pilot around. They drove down the long driveway. Instead of turning toward the hotel, he turned the other way.

"Wait," Caron said, "this is the wrong way."

"No. No. I got one stop to make first. You guys will love it."

A short drive took them to a small roadside diner. There were three picnic tables outside. There was an old white garbage can with a black plastic liner. The diner was called the Yellow Dog. The logo bore a faint resemblance to Thor.

"You see, Frank. When I first saw the dog, I knew it was a good omen so I stopped. And it was. They make the best turtle burgers and guava shakes in the world."

"Turtle burgers?" Jenny said. "Are you kidding?"

"No. They're great."

"That is gross. Who eats turtles?" Caron asked.

"Everyone. It is a staple here. The people live off the sea whenever they can.'

"Aren't sea turtles protected or something?" Jenny asked.

"Not here."

"It's still gross," Caron added.

"Not any grosser than eating chickens or cows or snails."

"But turtles are cute," Caron said.

"You ever have veal?" DC said. "Do you know how they make it so tender?"

"Don't start," Caron warned.

"I'm just saying..."

"Keep talking mister. I'll show you someone who isn't getting any on this trip."

DC paused. He stared dumbfounded. He looked to Frank for support, but found none. Bruce smiled.

"Eating turtle is sick," DC said. "I would rather starve."

Caron leaned over and gave him a peck on the cheek. "Good answer."

Frank laughed.

"Pull a goddamn battleship with one," Bruce said.

"What are you talking about? What does that mean?" Jenny said.

"Nothing," Bruce lied.

"I guess the turtle burgers are out," Frank said.

"Thank you," Jenny and Caron said at the same time.

"But you have to try the guava shakes," Bruce pleaded. "They are really awesome and I promise the guavas feel no pain in the process."

Frank opened his door and got out. Bruce opened the trunk and Thor jumped out. It was obvious he had been here before. Everyone followed him up to the counter. The mesh was pockmarked with holes. A fat black Bahamian woman sat on a stool inside fanning herself with a paper fan. The grill behind her was cold. She smiled at Bruce.

"Hey, baby," she said. "You brought friends."

"You know I can't resist you."

"No one can resist Miss Mabel. What you have?"

"Five guava shakes."

"You want them special?'

"You know it, girl. I'm trying to impress them."

She laughed. "That will do it. If they don't like them, they don't have to pay."

She turned to the refrigerator and started removing the ingredients. She sliced the green guava, exposing the bright pink pulp inside.

"What's in a guava shake?" Jenny asked.

"It is simple really. Guava mixed with sugar and a little milk."

"Milkshakes are fattening," Caron whined.

"These are like smoothies," Bruce said. "They are full of vitamins and antioxidants. I have her add a little coconut milk to the mix to make the flavor pop."

The blender produced the first two shakes and the Mabel passed them out to Jenny and Caron. The shakes were a rich milk color. Caron and Jenny exchanged suspicious glances. They raised the cups slowly and took tentative sips. They started to smile.

"This is really good," Jenny said.

"Wow. It's so creamy and just sweet enough without being too sweet."

Bruce did a mock bow.

The woman passed the next two out. Frank and DC took the cups and clicked plastic. They drank without hesitation. Both smiled.

Mabel turned back and made the last of the shakes. She turned to Bruce. He handed her the money.

Frank started to speak, but Bruce cut him off.

"I got this. Five guava shakes," Bruce said as he gave her the money.

Mabel smiled and took the money she got a small bowl from behind the counter and poured some of the leftover shake into the bowl. She passed it out to Bruce who sat it at his feet. Thor stood slobbering as he waited. The spittle fell like a heavy rain. Bruce snapped his fingers, and the dog took to greedily lapping the bowl.

"Thor drink for free," Mabel said. "He is a good boy."

Bruce beamed.

When Thor had cleaned his bowl, Bruce passed it back to Mabel.

They all got back in the Pilot and he drove them to the hotel. The girls were still drinking their shakes.

"Rest up. Take a nap. Catch some late afternoon sun. I'll meet you back here at seven for dinner."

"How do we dress for dinner?" Caron asked.

"In the Bahamas always dress casual."

He dropped them off. Frank watched Bruce pull away.

"What a great guy," DC said.

Frank nodded. "He is that."

"What are you up for, Caron?"

"I think I'm going to crash. I'm worn out," Caron said.

"Me too," Jenny added.

"I think I might catch some rays," DC said. "What about you, Frank?"

"I might read a little. Just chill."

The man from the beach walked up with a big smile. "Smokey time," he said.

Frank smiled. "You got a cutter and lighter like you said?"

"Free with every box of Cohibas."

"Come on up stairs. I'll get you some cash."

"Show me the way."

They all went to the elevator and took it to their rooms.

"See you at dinner," Jenny said.

"See you there," Frank said as he unlocked his door. "Come on in."

The man followed him into the room. Frank went to his dresser and opened it. He took out an envelope. He thumbed through it and took out two one hundred dollar bills.

"Big bills alright?"

"As long as they aren't counterfeit."

"You take them to the bank tomorrow. They give you any trouble, come back and I'll exchange them." Frank smiled and took out an ink pen and wrote the same Greek word on each bill. He handed them back to the man. "Just to be sure they give you back the right bills if they say they aren't real. You can keep the change."

The man smiled. "Thank you. This mark. Clever. What does this word mean?"

"Honor."

The man nodded. He handed the box to Frank and took the money. He fished in his pocket and removed a Bic style lighter. He struck it to show that it still worked. He searched another pocket and found a cheap plastic cigar cutter. He passed them both to Frank.

"Light one now, my friend. See that they are the real thing not a fake. You smoke the Cohiba before?"

Frank nodded. He tore the cellophane seal on the box and removed a cigar. The Cohiba was enclosed in its own cellophane tube. He broke the seal and shook the cigar out. He smelled it.

"This is like I tell you, from Cuba."

Frank clipped the end and wet the cigar with his mouth. He walked to the balcony and opened the sliding glass doors. He stepped outside and the man followed him. Frank lit it and inhaled the smoke, savoring the familiar taste. Frank blew the smoke out and smiled.

"Very nice."

"I told you. Smooth."

"Would you like one?"

"No. No. I do not smoke them anymore," the man said tapping his chest. "My lungs are no longer good." He breathed in deeply. "But I miss the smell of a good cigar."

Frank walked the man back inside.

"Thank you."

When you leave, put them loose in a bag. Without the box, the customs people can't tell where you got them. Tell them they are from Dominican Republic. They won't know the difference."

"Thanks again. I'll remember that."

"I see you again tomorrow. You need anything you ask for me. I get you anything you want. Anything."

Frank closed the door behind the man. He took an empty water glass from the sink and carried out to the balcony. He placed the cigar in it like an ashtray. Frank went back inside and found his book. It was Thucydides' History of the Peloponnesian War. He sat down and found his place.

Thucydides was an Athenian and fought in the Peloponnesian War. He was widely regarded as the first true scientific historian. He tried to report facts that he could corroborate, not myths. He had once said that, in the distant future, if people ever viewed the sparse ruins of Sparta they would believe she was less powerful than she had been, and that Athens would appear more powerful than she ever was. Frank liked Thucydides. He had a handful of famous sayings that spoke to Frank's view of himself. Thucydides wrote, "The bravest are surely those who have the clearest vision of what is before them, glory and danger alike, and yet notwithstanding go out to meet it." He also said, "The strong do what they can and the weak suffer what they must." And finally, "People despise those who treat them well, and look up to those who make no concession."

Frank lifted the Cohiba and took a deep draw. He blew the thick white smoke into the air. It tasted divine. Life was very good. No black clouds were moving in.

23

Tonello and Bruce struggled to load the jet skis onto their trailers. There were four jet skis loaded onto each of the trailers. Four jet skis were left tied to the pier. Bruce backed the Honda Pilot down to the water's edge and hooked up the trailer. He pulled forward and placed the trailer under the metal shed. A second trailer was already parked there cradling four more jet skis. There was an empty third trailer. Bruce unhooked the trailer and pulled away. He got the padlocks out of the front seat of the Pilot and secured the trailer hitches of all three trailers. The padlocks on the trailers and on the chains across the entrance were all the security that was needed. Even if someone did break in and steal a jet ski, he thought, there was no place to take them. They had VIN numbers, and his logo plastered all over them. They would be easy to find.

"That's good, Tonello. You going to the reggae party at the Yacht Club, right."

"Of course. Where else would a Rasta child be this night?"

"And I've never known you to miss any party."

"What else is there in this short life?"

"True enough. Remember we got no clients scheduled until 2 o'clock tomorrow, so you don't need to get here before noon. The skis are all flushed and gassed up. You are set to go."

"And you will not be in at all?"

"No, I'm spending the day with my friends."

"Ire."

Bruce opened the passenger side door and Thor jumped inside, his big tongue lolling out of his mouth. A long spit trail hung from the corner.

"Damn, Thor, you got to work on your hygiene or something. That is nasty."

Bruce closed the door.

"Do you mind closing up, Tonello? I'm supposed to meet my friends."

"No problem."

"We'll see you at the party."

"I be there," Tonello said.

Tonello's cell phone buzzed. He hurried over to the office and picked it up from the front steps where it was kept in his daypack. He looked at the caller ID. Bruce waved at him as he pulled away, and Tonello waved back at him. He slid the lock off on his phone. He took a deep breath.

"Tonello?"

"Dawg."

"I ask you dis one time more, me bruder. You be sure? Dis be Frank Kane his own self?"

"Aye. The boss man talk of no one else but this man, this killer man. He has the marks on his belly and back."

"But are you sure?"

"Me life, Dawg. I swear."

"Dat is what dis will cost if you wrong."

"I am not. It is Frank Kane."

"Tings must be arrange. Much trouble, me bruder, much trouble. If dis no de man, Kane, de Prophet will take your soul in his place."

Tonello shuddered. He knew about the ritual. He could imagine the terror. He could imagine the pain of the long knives. But he was right. He knew it.

"It is him, Dawg."

"Very well. De Prophet is pleased with dis thing, me bruder. Very pleased. He say dis man, Kane, his soul be very powerful. Very old. Very evil. It must be taken very slowly."

"Yes, Dawg. Yes."

"De Prophet say dis man, Kane, his soul worth a tosand other men souls. A tosand, me bruder, a tosand."

"Yes, dis is da man. When will de Prophet come?"

"We make ready now. When dis man leave?"

"Sunday."

"Good. We come on de Saturday. Little Bird say the moon will be right for sacrifice dis night. Very powerful. Is der private place we can perform de ritual?"

Tonello thought for a moment. Falcon's aerie. It was perfect.

"There is a place, Dawg. A big spike of stone that rises from the sea. No one lives there. It is off shore too far to hear a man's screams."

"No mon screams when de Prophet takes his soul," Dawg corrected. "But privacy be good."

"No one will disturb you there."

"Us, me bruder, us."

"I will be allowed to attend? This is a great honor Dawg."

"No attend. Participate, me bruder. De Prophet is most pleased with I and I. Long has he look for de last finger for de Red Hand. Now he find it. You be de last finger of dat hand."

Tonello's legs buckled slightly. He had never hoped for such a thing. He would be part of the Red Hand. Not a follower, but an actual part.

"De power will be in you. All dis world has will be yours. All de next world has will be yours."

"I am honored."

"Yes, you are. After dis ting you will renounce Jah and his weakness. You will shave off you dreads. You will leave you possessions behind and return with us to de motherland. You will be reborn in the blood of the Dreadmon."

"Yes, Dawg."

"All new childs needs a name. De Prophet says your new name will be Crab."

"That is a good name. Thank you."

"We will be comin' on a boat..."

"A boat? That is a long journey, Dawg."

"Not so bad. De hard men will find us one for our journey. Dey will clear a path through the sea for us. We will fly the Red Hand flag. No one will stop us. No one will slow us. No one will interfere. Dey all fear de wrath of de Dreadmon."

"Good. The stone island is not far from where I work. It has a deep water bay. I can tell you where to land and leave my car there. I can draw a map to lead you here and then we can go and get this man Kane."

"I be happy for you, Crab. Dis day will change you life."

With pride Tonello, now called Crab, explained the details Dawg needed. It was a blessed day.

24

Frank, DC, Jenny, and Caron ate at the hotel. The girls hurried to dress for the big Thanksgiving Reggae party at the Yacht Club.

Frank took a long hot shower and brushed his teeth. Frank didn't have a lot of clothes to choose from. He always packed light. He decided on his only pair of blue jeans, his sandals and a loose button-up shirt. It was cut loosely and Frank appreciated that. He made sure to wear the watch they had given him. He kind of hated to part with his old work watch, but he knew it would mean a lot to them that he wore the new one. It was a pretty nice watch, he decided. He tossed his old Casio into the garbage can. It was easier to avoid temptation than to resist it.

It had taken him a good five minutes to dress for the party, so he got out his book and sat on the balcony. He figured he had at least another hour and a half until the girls were ready. There was no hurry. They were all on island time.

Jenny and Caron tried on and discarded everything they had brought. Next they tried on each other's clothes. They modeled the outfits for each other until they finally decided. Both chose summer sun dresses that were short enough to display their long shapely legs, but not too slutty to show their butts. They weren't whores. They chose the only pair of strappy sandals they had with thick, wedged heels. They would make their legs look great and be easy to dance in. Once the attire was decided on, it only took another hour to get their hair right. It took a surprisingly long time to put on makeup so that it accentuated their features but at the same time didn't look like they had spent any time applying it. Being a young girl was a tough job. Being a young girl and feeling pretty and a little sexy was even harder.

Helen and her friends had eaten at the Chart House. They had chosen a table outside on the wide veranda to be able to enjoy the ocean breeze. James met them on their return and escorted them up to their suite. Although the suite had an impressively stocked bar, he had brought a dessert cart complete with after dinner drinks. The Chart House had informed him that the ladies had not stayed for dessert. They all thanked him and felt compelled to sample the desserts.

Afterwards, they all returned to their rooms to prepare. They spent a similar amount of time preparing for the party as Frank's girls had. Helen was sharing her room with Meredith, and she noticed that Meredith never missed an opportunity to run around with her top off. Maybe it was some kind of Alpha she-male thing, Helen thought. Maybe Meredith was intimidated by Helen's beauty and sought to assert that she too was very attractive. Knowing how vain Meredith was, Helen decided it was probably just her ego wanting to display her body to anyone who would look. And God help you if you didn't look. She would insist upon it before she was shocked that you had misunderstood and act innocent and embarrassed. Helen laughed to herself. Bitches be crazy. Eventually, they all met once more outside by the pool, enjoying the reflection of the hotel lights over the Caribbean Sea.

The ladies were dressed in perfect-fitting dresses designed by the icons of fashion; Gucci, Dior, Versace, Couture, and, of course, shoes by Louis Vuitton. Even Ronnie had packed for the occasion with a dark suit by Valentino.

Johanna retrieved a bottle of 2006 Shiraz from Australia and poured each of them a drink. Even Ronnie was included. He looked like he might clap he was so excited. It was very aromatic, and they all tried to detect the taste of mint, tea leaf, and wild blackberry that Shiraz was famous for. They sipped and chatted and stared at the sea some more, each lost in her own thoughts.

Suddenly, Helen, realized the precariousness of her position. She had been a fool not to have seen it sooner. This was the biggest party on the island. If Frank were here with friends or associates, they would surely be at the party. He would be at the party. That would be disastrous. She was not ready to see Frank yet. What would she say? How would he react to seeing her? What was her next step? There were too many unknowns. What she did know was that Ronnie would report it to Cyrus. He would have to. He might not know who Frank was, but he would know enough that Cyrus would know. And that led down a path Helen was not prepared to walk just yet.

A sudden thought struck her. Ronnie might seek to challenge Frank in some way. That would leave Ronnie dead and Helen with an impossible amount of explaining to do. What could she do? They were leaving any minute. She had to think of something. She could not go to that party with Ronnie skulking about.

Helen rubbed her temples. Her head was pounding. Johanna noticed her grimace and came over to her side.

"Are you alright?"

Helen was startled. "Yes. I just have a headache."

"God, I hope it isn't a migraine or something."

"I didn't want to say anything. It has been killing me all afternoon." Helen said seizing the opportunity.

"I hate that for you. Do you have anything you can take?"

"Yes. I have some Relpax. But I just hate to take it. The stuff knocks me out."

"Well, I've only had a couple of migraines, but I'll tell you I wanted to be knocked out. Is there anything I can do?"

Helen reached out and touched her arm. "You are sweet. It just takes time for these things to pass."

"Maybe you should stay here tonight and rest."

Helen smiled her sweetest smile. "You are probably right. I don't want to miss my match tomorrow."

"We'll all stay then. We are a team. If you stay, then I stay."

"What's going on?" Ashley asked.

"Helen has a migraine. She isn't going to the party."

"Oh, no. It would have been so much fun."

"I say we all stay in tonight. It doesn't seem right for us to go if she has to stay."

"I agree," Ashley said.

"No. No. That is not necessary. You girls go and have a good time. There is no reason you have to miss the party. You all look so pretty. It would be a shame for you to stay here. Think of all the hearts that won't be broken if you don't go."

"Helen is right. There is nothing we can do for her if we stay except keep her awake. Isn't that right?"

"Exactly, Meredith. Tell them. Tell them they have to go. I insist."

"She's right. We should go and let her get some rest."

"It doesn't seem fair. I mean, we're your guests and if you can't go, we shouldn't."

"It is alright, Johanna. Really. Go and have fun. And tell me all about it. I mean everything. I want lots of details and juicy gossip."

"If you're sure."

"I am."

"I will stay too," Ronnie added. "Just in case you need anything."

Ashley looked a little crestfallen, but didn't say anything. Meredith smirked like she had somehow cleverly manipulated everyone into doing exactly what she wanted to do. Johanna seemed genuinely disappointed. Ronnie thought he was clever too. He knew that Cyrus didn't care anything about Helen's friends or what happened to them.

"Thanks, Ron. Would you please call the limo service to pick the girls up?"

"Yes, ma'am."

Ronnie hurried off to use the hotel phone. She knew he would be reporting to Cyrus too. But that was fine. What did the police like to say? Oh, yes. "Move along. Nothing to see here. Move along."

Bruce showed up precisely on time. He was wearing cargo shorts and a pullover shirt with a collar. Frank didn't recognize the emblem on the breast. It looked like a penguin.

"Did you hear the news?"

"What news?"

"There is a hurricane coming this way."

"Bull," DC said. "No way."

"For real. It has just started to form off the coast of Africa."

"How big?" Frank asked.

"It's a small one, but on a little island I guess they are all big."

"Do we need to leave sooner than Sunday?" Jenny asked.

"No. It isn't supposed to reach us until like Wednesday. And you know how these things sometimes just turn out to sea."

"Are you going to keep an eye on it?"

"You know it, Jenny. But it isn't anything for you to worry about."

"What about you and your business?"

"I will pull the skis inland, strap everything down, shutter up the buildings and just ride it out like the locals."

"Isn't that scary?"

"I've never been through one before so I can't really say, but it has me kind of jazzed up about the thought of it. Who knows, it might even create a new surf break."

"Or drown you."

"Or that. But what I do know is that the hurricane mojo will jack up the party tonight."

"Then we better roll."

"I heard that."

25

It was Bruce's island so Frank gave him the honor of leading them into the Yacht Club party. They scoped out a table and got comfortable. The Yacht Club had erected massive white tents that covered most of the parking lot and the nearby dock. The place was packed. A huge bar stretched down one entire side of the party area. There were at least thirty servers running drinks back and forth from the bar. The music was loud and scores of people danced together in a writhing mass of suntanned flesh. Frank's eyes swept the area. He was looking for faces. He didn't just look for faces that he recognized, but also for signs that someone recognized him. It was ego. How could anyone here in on a tiny spit of land in the middle of the ocean recognize him? He had walked tall for a decade, but that was all in the past. He looked different. His beard and long hair were gone. He was invisible.

A waiter hurried over and they ordered beers. It was an easy first order. They looked around the room. DC enjoyed the spectacle. Bruce looked for some of his many friends. The girls checked out the competition, and, to be sure, they were properly attired. Frank continued to scan for danger. The waiter rushed back with the beers, and Frank paid him over Bruce's objections.

"Do you want to dance?" DC asked Caron.

Frank smiled to himself. The kid was smooth. He knew she wanted to dance. Girls always wanted to dance. Girls practiced at home in front of mirrors making sure they looked good. They watched videos and learned the steps to certain songs. DC had stolen her thunder. Asking her implied that he wanted to dance as much as she did. Jenny's eyes sparkled in the light.

"Yeah," Caron said and reached out her hand toward him like she was a princess and he was leading her from her carriage to the great ball.

Young love, Frank thought. There was something so innocent and beautiful about it. He thought of Dorian, the girl he had known in Fort Worth. They had shared a special connection. He missed her. She would have loved this.

Caron paused and looked back at the table and then directly at Bruce. Bruce was grinning and drinking his beer. She held her stare on him. Bruce was starting to tell Frank a story about Thor and an iguana when he caught Caron's eye. He stopped the story. Caron nodded her head toward Jenny. He looked confused. She nodded her head again toward Jenny. Bruce nodded and put his beer down.

"Frank, I'll finish the story later. This song is the bomb. I got to do my thing first. Jenny, would you dance with me?"

Jenny smiled as big as she could. "Let's do it."

She jumped up. She turned to Frank. "You going to be okay?"

There was genuine concern in her voice. She was worried that he would be lonely or feel left out. She was a good girl. She had a huge heart. Frank loved her as much as he had probably loved anyone in his life.

"Not a problem. I might just ask some lady to dance myself.'

Jenny and Caron both looked stunned. It was an image so foreign to them that they could not picture it. Frank Kane dancing. Absurd. Frank Kane did not dance. Frank smiled.

He remembered once when the Spartans had a huge party in Asheville at Cyrus' compound. There were hundreds of people there. There were representatives from different crime families that the Spartans did business with. There was a vast array of criminals. There were shooters and stealers and sellers and hiders and traders. He had sat at a table with The Jake and Spanish Johnny and Reaper. Spanish had been the first to bolt for the dance floor. He was a great dancer. He made it look effortless. For some unexplainable reason all women were drawn to him. His dance was a preview of sexuality. He was the best dancer Frank had ever seen.

"You going to get out there, big man?"

"I don't dance."

The Jake had smiled and sipped his drink, black ice coffee. The Jake rarely drank alcohol, but he drank ten cups of coffee a day at least. He swirled the ice cubes around in a circle within the cup. "Why not?"

"I don't like to dance. So, I don't. I'm not like Spanish. It's not something I am good at. I'm not built for it."

The Jake had smiled his knowing smile. "The great Frank Kane afraid to dance. I cannot believe there is anything you are afraid of my friend."

"Just the way it is."

"May I make an observation?"

"Sure."

"It's a test."

"What are you talking about? What's a test?"

"Dancing. Everyone here knows who you are. They fear you. You in your own way are untouchable to them. They know the stories. Even the stories that aren't true. It is good for them. It is good for the Spartans. Good for business."

"Your point?"

"If you do not dance, they will think it is a tell. Something the man killer does not do. They will ask themselves, if he fears embarrassment, what else does he fear? What other weaknesses does the god of death have? What does Poseidon fear? You will become real to them. You will become human. If you dance they will forget you. Good or bad it makes no difference. They will not remember. Who remembers a man dancing anyway?"

Reaper patted the Jake on his shoulder. "The young dude is right, bro. You should listen to him. That's some sage shit."

Frank thought. It was insane, but probably true. The Jake had a way of seeing things Frank did not. He was always watching.

"Fuck," he growled.

"One or two dances. Choose a beautiful woman. She will draw their eyes away from you."

"I suck at this."

"We all do. We'll maybe not Spanish Johnny, but ninety-nine per cent of everyone else. You want to know the secret of dancing?"

"Yeah."

The Jake pointed toward Neil who was spinning around the dance floor like a whirling dervish on crack, which was pretty close to what he was.

"Do the opposite of that."

"No shit."

The Jake laughed.

"Just keep your hands in close. No arm movements. Move your feet, but small steps. A tiny dip now and then and there you have it. Your dancing is neither good nor bad. It is bland, completely forgettable. And you will be invisible."

Frank rose to his feet. His face was set like he was going to war.

"Relax, big man. You might even like it. And try to smile."

Frank forced a smile that was somewhere between a wolf's snarl and a lion's growl.

"On second thought. Don't smile. Just pick a girl. Poker face. What woman here would turn down the chance to dance with Frank Kane?"

Frank had nodded and gone and danced. It hadn't been all that bad. In fact, he had kind of liked it.

Frank smiled at the girls. "I think I will find my own dance partner."

The four young people stood frozen as Frank slipped past them. They looked like deer caught in the headlights of a car.

"Excuse me," Frank said as he passed. He had noticed a group of three women at the bar. They were all beautiful. He estimated their ages to be in the appropriate range to accept a dance from a stranger. He moved closer. Frank knew his look attracted some women and repulsed others. There were a lot of women near the dance floor. One would dance with him he felt sure.

Johanna, Ashley and Meredith sipped their drinks and looked across the dance floor. Meredith played with her swizzle stick and sucked seductively at it. Frank approached from across the room. People parted to let him pass. Meredith felt her pulse quicken. There was some animal instinct at work. She locked eyes with him. She sent him psychic messages of what she wanted to do to him. She flashed mental images of the things she would let him do to her. Frank stopped before the women.

"Excuse me ladies."

They all turned. Meredith jutted her chest out a little farther. Not far enough to knock him over, but far enough that men on the other side of the island could appreciate her cleavage. She licked her plump full lips. She smiled her perfect toothed, bleach enhanced smile.

"Yes," Meredith cooed in a throaty voice that all but dripped sex.

"I was hoping one of you ladies would do me the honor of a dance."

Meredith beamed and started to speak.

Frank extended his hand toward Johanna. "Would you do me the honor? I confess I am not a very good dancer myself."

"I would love to," Johanna said and handed her drink to Ashley. She extended her hand in a formal way. "I'm Johanna."

Frank shook her hand as gently as he could. "I'm Mark. Mark Kaley."

"Nice to meet you, Mark."

Frank led them to the middle of the floor where the press of bodies hid his amateurish dance moves. He glanced at Jenny and Caron who still stood rooted in place watching him. Frank smiled again. Johanna was a very good dancer. She moved with a casual grace. DC and Bruce led the girls onto the dance floor and they all began to dance. It was funny, Frank thought. Here, surrounded by people, you were boxed in. Pinched into place where you could barely move. He flashed on the night he and Neil had been surrounded.

26

The Spartan MC had grown since Strehl and Neil first joined in Virginia. Their contributions had not gone unnoticed. In a move of incredible hubris, Cyrus had taken to giving many of the founders the names of ancient Greek gods. Cyrus said it was because they were no longer bound by the rules of mortal men. They could do whatever they wanted. They answered to no one.

The Spartan ceremony of godhood was a hedonistic week of debauchery. Drugs, alcohol, women, whatever the honoree desired was given. It culminated with a final tattoo on the left shoulder. The tattoo was the Greek letter that represented the god's name. For Strehl it was the Greek letter alpha. Cyrus had given him the new name of Atlas. Atlas had once held the weight of the world on his broad shoulders. Strehl's new name symbolized that ancient strength. For Neil it was an H. His new name was Hades. Hades was a brother to Zeus and a powerful god, but he was an outcast, choosing to live and rule among the dead. As always, Cyrus had chosen a perfect name for its new owner.

The final night of the godhood ceremony for Hades had extended into a tour of strip clubs and dive bars. At last they had left for home. Hades rode shotgun in a silver Toyota Tacoma truck with Frank at the wheel. Hades did a bump of meth from the web of his left hand. He wiped his nose and put the small glass vial back into his shirt pocket. He smiled his ragged-tooth, gum-ravaged smile. Meth took a high toll on your teeth.

He turned toward Frank.

"Best night of my fucking life. Best fucking night."

"It is a big step. A rare honor. Cyrus says we have all the gods we need now."

"It was a good thing I joined up when I did. Call me Lucky."

Frank laughed. "I have heard you called many names, brother. But never Lucky."

Hades looked shocked. "You're kidding, right? I am the luckiest guy you know."

"If you say so."

"Really. Think about it. If I hadn't had the stones to stand up to you in that bar back in the day, I wouldn't be where I am now."

"True. You were straight up badass. I could see that from the jump."

"It is all due to you, Frank. You gave me a chance when the others wouldn't have."

"You earned your chance."

"Cyrus would never have let me in the MC. I know that. The prick thinks he is better than me. What made you different?"

Frank gave the question a tone of dignity like it deserved. "I guess I saw something in you."

"You took a lot of weight on to sponsor me like you did. I won't forget it. Not ever. You hear me? Not ever. Whatever you need. Whenever you need it. You just ask."

"I hear you."

"Do you? Do you hear what I am saying? Anything. We are brothers. I would die for you."

"I hear you, you old dope head."

Hades unscrewed the cap on the bottle of Crown Royal he had resting between his scrawny legs. He took a long pull and sighed, wiping his lips on his sleeve.

"I am now and always will be an alcoholic first. Alcoholic, then drug addict, then sodomite, and finally a psychopath."

Frank reached over and patted his shoulder. "Spartan first. Always a Spartan first. That family above all others."

"FFLA. Family: first, last, always."

Hades took another pull on the Crown. He ran a thin hand through his long chin whiskers. His loopy grin was plastered on his face. He extended the bottle toward Frank.

"Food of the gods."

Frank was only half listening. They were on a four lane road. Two lanes traveled each way. Ahead at the green light, an old Ford LTD sat unmoving. Frank's hyper aware mind scrolled through the options. Broken down? Distracted driver? Heart attack? Dumbass? The light went yellow. Then red. The driver waved an arm outside his window. He seemed to indicate that he had just missed the light. No problem here. Frank slowed his truck down as he approached the rear bumper. There was one of those obnoxious Coexist bumper stickers on the back window. It was made up of all different religious symbols to spell the word coexist. In the side mirror, he caught the image of another car slipping up on his left side. It was three a.m. There was no other traffic.

Why was there traffic here now? Frank's truck stopped. In the rear view mirror, he saw more headlights approaching from behind. Something was not right. He glanced at Hades. The loopy smile was slipping from his face.

Frank glanced as the car on the left crept up.

Pincher, Frank thought.

Everything moved in slow motion. Frank saw the tip of a shotgun barrel through the passenger's window of the car as it slipped past. The passenger was turned away from Frank. It didn't hide his true identity. It screamed hitter. The fast approaching car from the rear was closing the backdoor. The trap was closing quickly. Time was nearly out. They were being boxed in.

Even as Frank threw his truck into reverse his eyes swept over Hades. Hades knew the trap. He knew they were being pinched in place so the hitters could take them out. In the split second his eyes swept over Hades, Frank saw him drop the Crown and reach both hands up onto the dashboard for support. The trail car was almost there. Frank thought he could hear the creak of the trap door closing.

The plan was for the rear car to hit Frank to distract him and push him tightly against the lead car. Locked in place, the hitter could take them easily.

Frank smashed the gas pedal flat. Frank's truck lurched backward as it built speed. There wasn't enough space or time for much speed. The rear of the truck smashed into the front of the car approaching from the rear.

Anyone who ever watched demolition derby races knew that the front of a car was its weak point. Under the hood were all the things that made a car go. Derby racers always smashed into their opponents with the rear of their vehicles to protect their own engines. The impact was massive. Frank's force striking the momentum of the car's. There was no way for that energy to be dispelled. Both vehicles slammed to a stop. The airbags in the car deployed at something like two hundred miles an hour into the faces of the two hitters in the rear car.

Amateurs, Frank thought.

He was out his door before the cars had settled. He was behind the side car, the pincher car. He could see the shotgun man turning at what had just happened. His mind was racing to comprehend. He was too slow.

Frank had the Kimber long-slide out. He fired three rounds through the car's rear window and into the shotgun man's back. He tracked the gun two feet and put three more into the driver. He pivoted and stepped to the rear car. The driver and occupant were groaning. The air bag deployment had broken noses and teeth. The car stunk from the airbags. Frank could see the barrel of an AR 15 jutting up from the floor where it had been thrown. Frank shot the driver in the front of his head. The head disintegrated from the round. Frank put two into the passenger as he tried to unhook his seat belt.

Frank spun and stepped back toward his truck. The blocking car understood the trap was blown and was pulling away. Frank tried to get a clear shot. He heard the staccato sound of Hades' nine millimeter Glock. Fifteen rounds punched tiny spider webs into the back window of the LTD. There was no tight pattern, just a hail of gunfire. Hades made up for his lack of accuracy with volume. His gun went dry just as Frank started firing at the fleeing car with his other pistol. The car slowed and swerved off the road into a telephone pole. Frank didn't know who had hit the driver.

Hades smiled and shook his empty gun at the car. "Fuck you." He turned to Frank and smiled.

"We need to go," Frank said.

"We got to collect our brass like you taught me."

"No time."

Hades climbed back into the truck's cab. The back was bowed in but the truck still ran. Frank slipped it into gear and they drove ahead past the wrecked blocking car. There was blood all over the front windshield.

"I put him down. That's the splatter from a nine, no question," Hades said.

"I think if we stopped you would see it was my .45 that stopped him while you sprayed everything but the driver."

"You're crazy. That's my kill. I don't think you even hit the car."

"What about the other guys."

Hades waved his hand in the air like brushing away a fly. "That. That wasn't shit. Anybody can cap a guy from two feet away. But put one in the back of a man's head in a speeding car, at night. Hell, that's real gun work."

Frank laughed. He pulled out his cell phone and punched in a number. The person answered without speaking.

"We got a problem. Escaped an ambush. You got my phone on GPS. I need closest enclosed garage where I can stash our ride."

There was silence. David Carpenter, also known as Helios, didn't ask were they injured, or what happened, or was the vehicle drivable, or were the cops enroute, or any of a thousand other mundane questions that a normal person would ask. Those questions did not matter. The only thing that mattered was getting the vehicle off the street and into hiding. There would be time for questions later.

The silence stretched on for a minute, then two. "Take Wendover for two miles. Then a right onto Bellmeade. Five miles to Lois Lane. Number 733. Local member's home has a full garage. He will be alerted."

Frank hung up the phone. He looked at Hades. Hades was retrieving the half spilled bottle of Crown from the floorboard. He wiped the opening on his grimy sleeve to get rid of the dirt and fibers from the floor of the car. Hades took a drink and passed the bottle to Frank. Frank wiped the opening a second time. Frank took a drink.

"You, okay?"

"Best day of my fucking life, Frank. The best. I am untouchable. I am a fucking God. I can do anything I want."

That was Hades. Wide open. Flat out. Straight ahead. No concern about fallout or consequences. He lived in the here and now. He was fearless. And yes, Frank thought, he was a fucking psychopath. Frank had read somewhere that the traits that distinguished a psychopath from a normal person were the same traits that separated the most successful CEOs from other businessmen. Damn if Frank didn't like the old bastard. They had made it. Cheated death one more time. The end wouldn't come for years, but the road was already laid out for them. They drove down it unaware.

27

Even as Frank danced, he scanned the people around him. He noticed two women as they turned from the bar. He scrolled through his memories trying to place them. There was something. The older woman was in her early forties with long bleach blonde hair. She was wearing a pair of shorts and a loose white cotton top. She saw him looking and charged straight through the crowd at him. She tapped Johanna on the shoulder.

"Mind if I cut in, sister?"

Johanna looked stunned. "I guess not."

The blonde started dancing in front of Frank.

"I'm April C."

April C did a spin move and slapped the ground.

"I saw you staring at me. I thought if a hot stud like you wanted to dance, I best get to it. Me and Slim can drink later. That's her over there by the bar. We're here playing in the big tennis tournament. We won our division in North Carolina so we got the invite. What do you do?"

"My name's Mark. I work on one of the boats."

"Which one?"

Frank's eyes swept the marina. There was a one hundred ninety foot yacht tied up down the dock. The name on it read Neptune's Dream. It was an omen. Neptune was the Roman god of the sea just like Poseidon was for the Greeks. Fucking Romans couldn't even invent their own gods, Frank thought. They had to steal the Greek gods and rename them. Wow. Very clever. Ruled the world, but never had an original idea. Bunch of fools. Still, all in all, Frank took it as a good omen. This vacation was his dream vacation. Poseidon's Dream, he thought.

Frank pointed down toward the dock. "I mate on Neptune's Dream."

"I just bet you do."

Frank ignored the sexual innuendo. He could tell she was all talk. It was probably part of her persona. What her friends expected. What got a laugh. She was funny.

"I apologize for staring. You looked familiar."

"That's what he said last night."

Frank could not help himself. He laughed. "I am serious. I thought I recognized you. I shouldn't have been staring."

"Really? Who did you think I was, Sharon Stone?" April said again and did another spin move, but added a shimmy to the end of it. She was laughing.

"I wasn't sure. You are a good dancer."

"Thanks. This isn't my first rodeo. I know what I'm doing." April laughed and continued dancing. Frank had been staring at them. But not at April. The woman with her, the one she called Slim, was Trisha Ware.

She was a very pretty brunette. She wore these funky little glasses. That was what had caught Frank's eye. The glasses. He had not seen Trisha Ware in a long, long time. She seemed happy and healthy. He noticed a wedding ring on her left hand, so she had gotten married. Good for her. Whatever tragedies had impacted her life were behind her. She was moving on.

Prometheus, Keith Masnick, had pointed her out to Frank once through high powered binoculars from a distant rooftop. She had struck Frank at the time as being very frail and sad, like she had just lost someone very close to her. Masnick had asked Frank to kill her for him. Masnick claimed it was an honor killing. That she had dishonored him in some unspecified way. Frank had told Masnick if the girl needed to die, he should do it himself. Masnick had said he could not because of some vague reasons he wouldn't elaborate on. Masnick had raged at Frank that he had to kill her. Frank did not like being told what to do. He had grabbed Masnick and held him over the side of the roof. He had calmly explained that the Spartans were not animals. He explained that Frank Kane was not an animal. He explained that Frank Kane would not have hands laid upon him. In recompense for that insult Masnick had two choices. He could forswear any vengeance on the girl or he could learn if he could bounce when Frank dropped him from an eight story building. Easy way or hard way? Wisely, Masnick calmed down and agreed to spare the girl, even vowing to make sure no one else harmed her.

It had been a strange exchange. Masnick and Frank were close friends. They were both Gods within the Spartan system. But something about the request had been wrong. Frank never found what was behind the request. He didn't care. The sight of Trisha made him smile. April saw the smile and misinterpreted it.

"Now you're feeling me, baby. Whoo."

Once more she spun around and slapped the floor. Frank thought she might need medication. To April's right, another blonde woman was moving toward him. She wore a black form-fitting dress that came down over one shoulder. Her blonde hair fell just to her shoulders. She looked a little like Helen had. She was beautiful. She was smiling. She stepped up to Frank and put a hand on his shoulder. She smiled at him and then turned her smile on April. Then back to Frank.

"There you are. A girl can't powder her nose without you trying to pick someone else up."

"Is Mark with you?"

"I am afraid he is. He is being very wicked. But I forgive him. Come on back to our table and let's finish our drink, Mark."

"He's a lot of man for one woman, honey. You need any help you call April. Me and Slim would be glad to help hold him down for you."

"Thanks. I got this."

"I bet you do. That's what he said last night. Wooo." April danced across the floor toward where Trisha was standing. Trisha was smoking one of those electronic cigarettes. It was one of the blue colored ones. Electric cigarettes had gotten cool in the last few years. All the taste of smoking with none of the carcinogens. It seemed like a no brainer if you wanted to be healthy. Frank seemed to remember that Masnick had said she smoked Pall Malls, a menthol cigarette, back in the day.

Frank smiled at the blonde. "Thanks. I didn't need saving."

"I did. Why don't we sit down?"

Helen stood at the balcony staring out at the lights of the party. She sighed. It could have been a disaster. She was unprepared and that wasn't like her. Her desire to see Frank again had made her careless. And seeing him actually alive had nearly exploded her heart. What should she do? What could she do? Some steps were obvious. Better to do those first. Take care of the small stuff she could control. Like Ronnie. She saw him sitting at the outside bar. He was sipping a glass of Scotch. He drank Scotch not because he liked the taste or even the heady aroma. He drank Scotch because he thought it made him look more sophisticated. He was such a fool.

"Ron, would you bring me a drink."

He jumped to his feet. "Absolutely. What would you like?"

"A glass of the 2007 Sassicaia."

Ron found the bottle and poured the Tuscan red into a wine glass and hurried to bring it to her. Helen took a small sip and smiled.

"Thank you," Helen said. "You are very sweet."

Ronnie colored a little. "It's my job."

Helen leaned in a little closer. She smiled her irresistible smile. "And you are very handsome. Do you know that?"

"For a guido, I guess."

"Well, I think you are very handsome." She leaned in a little closer. She could smell the Scotch on his breath. "Do I make you nervous?"

Ronnie held his ground. She leaned in closer. Her soft hair was almost touching his face. He had a smirk on his face.

"No," he said. "I'm not afraid of you."

Helen leaned in until her delicate lips were nearly touching his. "You should be afraid."

Helen kissed Ronnie. It was a delicate kiss. Their lips met and lingered. She parted her perfect mouth slightly. Her pink tongue slipped out slowly and caressed his lips. Ronnie kissed her back. Their tongues fencing. The kiss became more passionate, more forceful. Ronnie moaned his desire and raised a hand to pull her closer. Helen broke their kiss and stepped back. She turned and looked once more out at the lights of the party. She smiled and turned back to Ronnie. He was smiling too. She could imagine the fantasies at play in his small, wicked monkey brain.

"Ron."

"Yes, Helen," he answered.

"I want to make this clear for you. I don't want any misunderstandings between us."

"There won't be."

Idiot, she thought. He still doesn't get it. He still thinks we are going to have some one night stand like in Penthouse magazine. He would keep their secret. He would feel powerful. He already felt powerful. He had kissed Cyrus' woman. He didn't realize he was a dead man.

"Ron, what just happened between us..."

"I know. It just happened."

"No. I made it happen for a reason. Do you understand what that reason is?"

"Does it have something to do with what happens on vacation stays on vacation?"

"No. It has to do with your perception of reality. I own you now. Do you understand? You will do exactly as I say or I will tell Cyrus what you did and he will have you killed."

The shock showed in Ronnie's face. "What are you talking about?"

"The kiss. It was necessary to make the betrayal real. Do you understand? It had to be real."

"What the fuck? You kissed me."

"Yes, I did. But that is not what I will tell Cyrus. I will tell him I stayed behind because of a migraine. That you tried to force yourself on me."

"That's bullshit."

"I know. But Cyrus will believe me. I am an excellent liar."

"I'll tell him the truth."

"Who will he believe? And when he asks you if you kissed me what will you say. Can you hide the truth from him? Cyrus will read it in your eyes and voice and your smell. He will know what you did, what you were planning to do, and he will have you cut into very tiny pieces."

Ronnie spun around trying to think his way out. It was pointless, she knew. But she let him try.

"Bitch," he spat.

"Yes," Helen agreed. "I am. If you want to live you only have one choice."

Ronnie moved toward her. His hands were fists. His rage burned out. "How about I just throw your evil ass off the roof? Huh, how about that?"

Helen smiled. He was such a child.

"Then Cyrus would spend all his wealth and power to find you and still cut you into very tiny pieces over a great long period of time."

"Fuck," Ronnie said. He punched one of the hanging vases. It exploded, spraying dirt, pottery and plants onto the deck. He stomped his feet like he was crushing a man to death beneath them. Helen let him rage for a few seconds. Get it out of his system. Burn it out.

"Are you finished?"

He snarled. Now was the time to show him the life jacket.

"If you do as I ask, Cyrus will never know of your infidelity. I will praise the job you did and he will honor you. Money. Power. Position. But if you ever refuse me, then he will learn my truth of this night. Do you understand?"

Ronnie was breathing hard like a young bull. He wanted to smash something.

"Do you understand?"

"Yes. What do you want me to do?"

"It doesn't matter. When I tell you to do something, you will do it. You will not question me. You will not hesitate. You will not ever speak of it to my husband. Do you understand?"

"I understand."

"I know what you are thinking. You can tell Cyrus. You can turn the tables on me. You are not clever enough. He will not believe you. And even if he does he will still have you killed for you will have forced him to kill me. The only thing he loves. So truly believe me when I tell you, you must do as I say if you wish to live."

Ronnie thought about it. She could see him weighing his options again. His sigh was his answer. He had no choices left. She knew she had him. He was still glaring at her.

"Ronnie. Ronnie. Don't be angry. We can be friends."

"Just tell me what you want me to do."

"When it is time. When it is time. Now go back to your room. I wish to be alone."

"Yes, ma'am," Ronnie said and turned away.

He was such a spoiled little baby, Helen thought. She took a cigarette from her purse. It was a Virginia Slims Super Slim. It looked very girly. She lit the tip and took a deep drag. Phase one of her new plan was complete. She could move freely now. She took a healthy drink of her super red. Another tug on the cigarette. Everything was going to be fine. She could spin this. She could control things.

Of course Helen was wrong. Of course the world did not bend to her will as she thought. Old gods conspired against her. Old weaknesses drifted to the surface. With Frank Kane, nothing was ever certain.

The blonde followed Frank over to the table.

"Have a seat."

"Thank you," she said and sat down.

"What did you need saving from?" Frank asked.

She waved a hand toward the bar where a group of handsome, apparently rich, men stood watching her.

"Men are such liars, Mark."

"We are that. And worse I expect when it comes to attractive women."

She smiled. "I'm Natalie Schorr." She extended her hand and Frank took it.

"I'm Frank."

"That woman said your name was Mark."

"I lied to her."

Natalie laughed. "Why did you lie to her and not to me?"

"She's not as interesting as you are."

"Am I interesting? In what way?"

"Anytime a beautiful woman chooses to talk to me out of all these men, she is interesting or delusional."

DC came over leading Caron. "Everything cool, Frank?"

"Yes. Couldn't be better."

"Just checking." DC went back to the dance floor.

"See. I told you my name was Frank."

"Lucky for you."

A waiter came by with a pad and an empty tray. "Can I get you something cool to drink?"

"I would like a gin and tonic," Natalie said.

"Make that two, with Bombay."

"Very good," the waiter said and hurried off.

"So why me?" Frank asked.

Natalie stared at him for a moment as if considering his question. "I could tell you something cute. Something sexy and vague. I do that really well. Sexy and vague."

"But..."

"But this isn't really about you as much as it is about me." She looked quizzically at Frank to see if he understood.

He didn't but he was smart enough not to try to guess the right response. He sat silent. Natalie laughed at herself.

"I attract a certain type of man. I always have. They tend to be handsome, well educated, wealthy, vain and incredibly shallow. It is almost like they are punched from the same pattern. Do you know what I mean?"

"I've known men like that."

"I married a man like that. His name was Kenneth. Not Ken or Kenny but Kenneth."

"Was?"

"We are divorced. Or at least in the process. I caught him having an affair with his assistant. His male assistant."

"Did that make it easier or harder. That it was with another guy?"

"What do you mean?"

"I mean if he was gay, you can't compete with that. I just wondered if it was easier to get your head around than if it had been another woman."

"What do you think?"

"I don't know. I knew a guy once who kept pressuring his girlfriend to bring her hot girlfriend for a three way. She finally agreed. She found out she liked things better with the girl and switched teams."

"Did your friend think that made it easier?"

"Don't know. He got killed a little time later so I never got to ask him."

"Well. It doesn't make it easier. It's still devastating. It messes with your head. Really fucks..."

Natalie put her hand to her mouth.

"Sorry. I don't say that word."

"Why not. It's a great word. It fits in any sentence. Adjective. Adverb. Noun. Etc."

Natalie slapped him on the arm. "You are a bad man."

"You have no fucking idea how bad."

Natalie laughed again. The waiter showed up and placed their G & T's in front of them. Frank pulled out his roll of cash, but Natalie put her hand on top of his.

"Let me. I've never bought a man a drink."

Frank pocketed his money and tipped his drink in her direction. They clinked glasses.

"So that's why you are on Cat Island. Getting over the divorce?"

"Reevaluating my life choices. That's why I wanted to buy you the drink. It seems in retrospect that all my correct choices have turned out wrong. I followed a set path, did everything I was suppose to do, studied hard, got good grades, went to the right schools, met the right people, married the ideal man and yet here I am. I know how I got here, but I don't know where I want to go from here. So I thought I would start by doing the opposite of what I normally would do."

"Like pick up an ugly man."

"You're not ugly. You have a strong face. A man's face."

"Your husband didn't?"

"He looked like the kind of man who had just put lotion on his hands. Do you know what I mean? He was handsome in a pretty sort of way."

"I don't think I have ever been accused of being pretty."

"I didn't mean it in a bad way. I am tired of pretty. Tired of soft. Look at them," Natalie said nodding toward the group of men at the bar who were still watching her expectantly.

The men were all wearing khaki pants and Top Siders. They wore knit shirts under blazers adorned with emblems and crests and one even had epaulets on the shoulder like he was a general or something. They were all about forty with handsome faces and thick manes of dark hair. The hair worn a little long, but expertly cut. Their teeth were white and straight and veneered to perfection.

"They are all clones. Not just on the outside. On the inside too. Like they have some chip implanted that dictates their view of the world. Now look at yourself."

Frank didn't need to look at himself. He knew what he looked like.

"I like it," Natalie said. She trailed a manicured hand down his tattoos. "I even like these."

"Good. They are hard to wash off."

She punched him in the arm again. "What do you do?"

Frank paused. "I fix things. I work with my hands."

She placed her hand inside of his with the fingers spread. "Your hands are huge and so rough."

"Work does that to you."

She locked her fingers in between his. "I like the way they feel. I'm glad I came over."

"Me too," Frank said.

28

Jenny watched Frank with the blonde woman. She thought she might feel jealous or angry or something. Instead she felt sort of happy for him. The woman was closer to his age and very attractive. Whatever weird shit had been running through her head about Frank must have burned itself out. She was glad. It was getting too weird. She looked over at DC and Caron dancing and then back at Bruce. He was smiling at her. She leaned forward and kissed him. He didn't resist or hesitate. It felt good.

Johanna, Ashley and Meredith hadn't had to wait long before other men rushed to dance with them. Drinks were bought. Promises of midnight cruises were offered. Even trips to other distant isles were dangled for them. The women all flirted shamelessly, knowing that they wouldn't be going home with any of the men.

Tonello danced with a local girl on the beach where he could see Frank sitting. He was happy. Finally, something good was coming to him. Finally, he had seen opportunity and seized it. The girl gyrated her buttocks against his pelvis. Tonello smiled. He took another hit off the ganja spliff in his hand. Life was good. Life was very very good. And it was about to get better.

The musicians took a short break, and Frank's friends all returned to the table. Introductions were made all around. Drinks were ordered. There was a commotion as a new entourage entered. The center of the new group was a black man in his twenties. He was handsome and as black as coal. He wore expensive black slacks and a starched white shirt with the sleeves rolled up. He had one small diamond earring in his left ear. He was smiling and greeting people like he was the mayor. Women hurried to intercept him.

Frank tapped Bruce's arm.

"Who is that guy?"

Bruce turned where Frank was looking.

"That's John Keown. He is the Prime Minister's favorite nephew. He's a douche bag. He thinks the Bahamas are is private playground. Everybody kisses his ass."

"He's a good looking dude," DC said. "Can't blame him for taking advantage. I know I would."

"Is that right?" Caron said. "Exactly what would you take advantage of?"

DC paused. He waved at the waiter.

"More drinks."

Caron broke into a smile. "I was just teasing you."

DC smiled back. "I know."

It was a good night.

Helen was waiting when the girls finally came back to the hotel. They were all tipsy and giddy with excitement. Johanna had asked about Helen's migraine before anyone could start recounting the night's fun. Helen assured her that it had passed and that she was fine. They all laughed and giggled as they recounted the pick-up lines the men had used to try and woo them. They retold the lies they had told to the men and the false promises they had made. Helen enjoyed the girl talk. She kept her smile painted on her perfect face even as Johanna described her dance with Frank and the old bleach blonde bitch that cut in on her. Helen fought to remain placid when Johanna then described the beautiful blonde who had snaked Frank from the woman. Johanna had even described the beautiful blonde as looking a "little like you, Helen." Frank was so close, so very close. She was glad she hadn't gone tonight.

Ronnie stayed in his room doing pushups. Exercise was the best way for him to burn off anger. It always had been. As his energy drained, so did his rage. She was the devil. He had never seen it coming. She had played him, but why? What was the point? Maybe she was just pissed off at being watched like a child. Maybe she was hiding something. What? With his arms relegated to the strength of limp noodles, Ronnie switched to sit ups. He tried to see some way to get out from under Helen's thumb, but she was right. He wasn't smart enough. Every choice seemed to end with his dismembered body in a shallow grave feeding insects. Maybe he could just run. Hide out somewhere. Then what? He was a thug. He would always be a thug. This was the best gig he had ever had. He hated to leave it behind. What if Cyrus came looking for him to find out why he had run? Well, that was the end of the story. Ten minutes later with his abs on fire he lay back onto the cool tile floor. He would just have to do what she said. At least for now.

29

The next morning, Frank and his crew ate a late breakfast outside on the veranda overlooking the ocean.

"This view is amazing," Jenny said. "The water is clear and blue. It doesn't look real."

"And the weather is perfect. The breeze is to die for. It makes the heat bearable," Caron added.

"I dig the air. Man, it is so clear. And that sea smell is so pure. I am hungry all the time."

"Did you say hungry or horny?"

DC laughed.

Frank took a drink of coffee. "I am glad you are all having a good time."

"We are. Thank you so much," Jenny said.

"Yeah, thanks big man, for letting me tag along."

"And me too," Caron said.

"It really is my pleasure."

"And you are sure you don't want to hang with us today? Your boy, Bruce is going to take us on an island tour and then do some serious jet skiing."

"No, I think I will just chill on the beach. Catch some rays."

"What about tonight?" Jenny said. "Bruce is going to grill out at his place and then we are going to hit some hot bar in town."

"Wicked Wanda's," Caron said.

"That's right. Supposed to play local music. Something called scrape and bang."

"No. I have dinner plans."

"With the woman from last night? Nice."

"You have fun. You don't need an old silverback hanging around. I will see you tomorrow. We can all do something tomorrow."

"Okay. If you're sure."

"I'm sure, Jenny. Have a good time. But stay out of trouble."

"Guaranteed, big man. Bruce will keep us straight," DC said.

"And who will keep him straight?"

Jenny started to answer then stopped and started giggling.

"Don't say it, girl. Don't say it. You almost said you would keep him straight didn't you?"

Jenny was still giggling.

DC looked at Frank and shrugged. "Women."

Frank smiled. It was turning into a great vacation. Sybil's dream was forgotten.

Helen had heard about the blonde. She had seen Frank on his morning run and then the bitch had come out onto the beach to greet him as he came in from his swim. Even giving him a light kiss. The whore, Helen thought. She was trim and athletically built like a runner. She had been out there since before sunrise watching and waiting. Waiting to act like she happened on him. She was carrying him some kind of juice, probably orange. Maybe she should have Ronnie pay her a little visit. Nothing too severe. Just slap her around a little. Teach her that the world was a dangerous place. Whore. Slut. Bitch.

Her jealousy had sparked her anger. It seemed to build as she reached the tennis match. The day's first match had been crushed by her will and rage. Then it had burned out. Her energy slipped. Meredith seemed not to care. They were eliminated in the semis.

They had done a quick tour of the island in Bruce's SUV. There wasn't really that much more to see. Then they had taken the jet skis out. Bruce had claimed that they had to ride double because he needed the others for clients. Everyone knew it was a lie. But it was a nice excuse for them to split into couples. Jenny liked the feel of having her arms wrapped around Bruce as they rode. She liked the steady vibration of the jet ski as they skirted around the island. Sometimes she even rested her head against his broad back. They parked the jet skis on a secluded stretch of the island. They ate the lunch Bruce had packed and played in the clear water. Caron and DC went for a walk on the beach. Jenny watched them go. They were holding hands. They looked so happy, and Jenny felt a twinge of jealousy. She wanted what they had.

"Bruce, do you think I'm pretty."

Bruce smiled. "You are very hot. You got to know that."

"But I make you a little uncomfortable don't I? I mean because of Frank?"

Bruce's constant smile had a tiny tremble to it. "I guess. I mean me and Frank go way back. We got history. I really owe the dude my life. I wouldn't want to do anything that would piss him off."

"Do you think kissing me would piss him off?"

"I…I don't really know. Did you tell him we kissed on the dance floor?"

"No."

"Good. I don't know what he would think."

"But you have thought about that kiss haven't you? About what it would feel like to kiss me again."

"Sure. I guess. But I don't want to make waves or anything."

"Would it be bad if I wanted you to kiss me too?"

"Not bad. But we would have to think about where it could lead. What kind of trouble we might get in with Frank."

Jenny leaned in close to Bruce. "You think way too much." She kissed him lightly on his salty lips. "Mmm that was nice."

She leaned in again and this time Bruce met her kiss and returned it. They turned up their kisses and soon were moaning. Finally, Bruce broke their make-out session.

"We just have to know where to draw the line. When to stop."

Jenny smiled. She leaned back and untied her bikini top. She pulled it loose and dropped it beside them in the sand. Her small breasts stood out in pale contrast to her suntanned skin. She took Bruce's hand and placed it on her breast. Bruce began to gently massage it.

"I'll tell you when to stop."

Bruce pulled her on top of himself. They locked their arms together and searched for each others' mouths.

30

Frank was stretched out on the beach enjoying the sun. He loved the ocean. On some elemental level he needed the ocean. He felt the gentle brush of the wind. He smelled the crisp salt in the air. He closed his eyes for a few seconds filling his head with the sounds of the waves. He rose up on his towel and looked around the beach. He had scanned the other guests. No one seemed a threat. There was an older couple sitting under a thatched beach cabana. They were early sixties. Harmless. The woman's iron gray hair seemed so stiff that Frank wondered if she combed it with a magnet.

There was a family near the water. There were four of them. The father was about forty, with a great mustache and light brown hair. He was in good shape, but he seemed to be hitting the bottle of Jack he carried awfully hard this early in the day. The wife was a good bit younger and also pleasant looking. She was trim with age appropriate short brown hair. The wife kept a close watch on her kids, a boy and a girl. The boy was probably ten or eleven, the girl about sixteen. The girl had that tight, toned body that is effortless at sixteen, but almost impossible to acquire at thirty. She had a pair of the longest legs Frank had ever seen. She looked like a budding runway model. She also had the attitude that comes with the age. She seemed to simmer with misplaced anger. Probably something her parents did, or didn't do, or her little brother, or the weather. Frank doubted there was a much harder age for a girl than her teens. With her body maturing and her hormones raging it was a wonder any of them made it through the teen years. Frank had a flash memory that Jenny and Caron were not much older than the girl. They just seemed older because of all the stuff they had already gone through.

There was a group of ten college kids laughing and playing some kind of game with a ball. It looked a lot like tennis, but Frank didn't know its name or the rules. The group was basically four couples and a couple of extra girls. They were all attractive and healthy. They had beer nestled in buckets and were already drinking.

Frank noticed another couple sitting farther to his right. A man and a woman. They were model attractive. Maybe they were famous actors or something. They seemed too attractive to be real people. At first, he thought they might be brother and sister, but judging by the fact that they seemed unable to keep their hands off each other, he doubted it. Of course, the world was a strange place and getting weirder all the time. The couple started kissing. Definitely not brother and sister. Middle age love, he thought.

Frank took out a cigar and tried to light it. The wind was blowing too hard for the cheap lighter to maintain the flame. He took his second towel and wrapped it over his head to provide a windscreen for the lighter. A few tries proved the old trick effective. Frank unwrapped his head and took a deep drag. The Cohiba burned so smooth that it always amazed him. The thick white cigar smoke swirled around his head. He smiled. Life was good.

He watched the people around him. It was almost like being at a party and still outside of it. He noticed a lone man under another thatched cabana. He was about sixty and as pale as fresh milk. His arms and legs were spindly. He had a long set of white chin whiskers without the rest of the beard or mustache. It made him look like a goat. On his head he wore a knit cap. Maybe he was recovering from surgery or cancer or was just frail looking. Frank didn't really care. The sounds and the old man sparked a memory. It reminded him of a party Cyrus had thrown at his estate in Asheville. It was the year before Cyrus took Helen, when they were all still brothers. A long time ago.

Frank could still see it so clear in his memory.

Cyrus threw the best parties. There were always young women at the estate. A dozen lived on site in a sort of dorm. More were brought in as needed. Frank had been walking past the swimming pool that day. The sun was warm on his face. He was heading to the shooting range with The Jake. The Jake was eager to get to the range. Hell, he was always eager to get to the range. The kid loved to shoot. It didn't matter which weapon. He loved them all. Today they were using a .45 cal ACP in the classic 1911 frame.

There was a poker game in progress near the swimming pool. Probably five card draw because that was Cyrus' favorite game and Cyrus always got whatever he wanted. There were four players at the table. Cyrus sat in his chair, dealing. He was dressed like the handsome men from the yacht party last night. He wore silk gray pants with a black short sleeve shirt. He even wore nice Italian loafers without socks. He did not look like the leader of a bike gang.

Spanish Johnny sat opposite Cyrus. He had a smoking hot redhead in his lap. She was only wearing a small bikini bottom without the top. Frank could still remember the light dancing off the nipple ring in her right nipple. Spanish wore his colors without a shirt, a pair of old blue jeans and some ratty sandals. Frank knew Spanish liked to carry his pistol in an ankle holster. He considered it his backup weapon. The sun also glinted off the handle of the blade he wore in a shoulder rig under the vest. Spanish Johnny was a blade man. He loved the damn things.

To Cyrus' left sat another hitter named Reaper. He was young, only a few years older than The Jake who was a damned baby. Hell, they were both teenagers. He wore his hair long and slicked back. He used his sunglasses to hold it in place. He was a good looking kid and wore a small soul patch below his lower lip. He was also wearing his Spartan colors. He was a blade man too, but he wore his knife on his belt. There was some kind of tension between him and Spanish Johnny. Always had been as far as Frank could remember.

To Cyrus' left sat Helios. He was wearing clothes much closer to those of Cyrus. Proper dress pants, silk shirt and loafers. His colors were draped over the back of the chair. He had a short goatee without the mustache part. When Frank had first hooked up with the Spartans, he had hired a detective to investigate his new brothers. Frank did it to be sure none were cops. They weren't. But he had learned some interesting facts. Helios claimed his real name was David Carpenter, but Frank had learned his birth name was actually Jeff Foster. Years later on a whim he had hired a second investigator. This detective had been unable to trace Helios. Helios had by that time perfected his computer skills and wiped his trail clean.

Each man at that table brought something different and special to the Spartans. Helios gathered information. Cyrus was a businessman, and in his own way, a visionary. Spanish Johnny and Reaper were killers. That was the simplest way to describe them. Being a killer did not diminish their importance. It took a special man to be able to take another man's life.

But the man who held his attention was Hades. The little meth cook sat in the hot tub next to the swimming pool. He didn't have a bathing suit, so he was rocking a pair of jorts, jean shorts. He was ghost pale and thin, and wore his beard long in the front like an old goat. Hades was drinking Absinthe from a glass and alternating doing a bump of meth and patting the bottom of one of the two platinum blondes who flanked him. When he saw Frank, he beamed.

"How is the great Frank Kane?" Hades called.

"It's all good. You look like you are being well cared for, Neil."

"I'm on top of the world, my friend. It is good to be a god."

"I would think so, Neil."

"Check out my new teeth." Hades said and displayed a smile of white perfectly shaped teeth.

"Nice.'

"I finally got my old snags fixed. Got these dentures from a top guy. They are snapped in. They look good don't they?"

"Just like the real thing."

"Better. They never hurt, never break. Hell, I can even take the damn things out if I want to be getting something down at the Y if you get my drift."

"I hear you. The ladies seem to like them."

"Bitches have always been easy for me. You know that." He turned toward the blonde on his left. "Give me some sugar, baby."

One of the blondes in the hot tub leaned in and kissed Hades on the cheek. He turned his head and kissed her more passionately. The other blond turned his head toward her and started kissing him. She was stabbing her tongue into his mouth like it was a knife. Hades finally broke the kiss and hooted with joy.

"Wish I had hooked up with you years ago, Frank."

"Better slow down a little on those chems or you might not last another year."

"Fuck it. We all die man. I'm riding this as long and hard as I can."

As long as I can, Frank thought. Hades had been made for the outlaw life. He lacked any moral roadblocks to his desires. If he thought it served the Spartans, he did it. No questions asked. Poor dumb bastard, Frank thought. He was already running out of time.

The scream brought Frank back to reality. The ten year old boy was standing in waist deep water screaming. Frank's first thought was shark. Bull sharks liked the same kind of beaches as people. And they seemed to strike in shallow water. Frank's eyes scanned the water but there was no disturbance in the water. No blood swirl. No fin. No thrashing large body.

Most of the people on the beach heard the scream. They did what people everywhere were trained to do. They stood and stared. They assessed. They filtered the information through their perceptions and fears and balanced that against their own desires and reluctance to get involved with anything that did not involve them. Frank filtered and computed information as well. But there was a distinct difference. Frank was in motion. Frank did not fear danger or risk. He was confident in his ability to handle any situation. He worked without the constraints of society to slow him.

Frank reached the boy before even his sister got there. The boy was limping toward shore.

"What is your name?"

The boy looked startled, but he answered. "Bradley Lamont. Are you the lifeguard?"

In times of trouble people always looked for authority figures to guide them through it. "Something like that," Frank said.

Frank guided the kid into the shallows. He knelt in the water and lifted his foot. There was a puncture wound in the left heel. It was bleeding.

"Something stabbed me. Twice. I think it was a big crab."

Frank was slowly massaging downward on the ankle while he held the leg above it. "It wasn't a crab, Brad. It was a stingray. You felt the barb go in and come out again."

The sixteen year old girl ran up. She looked terrified. "Are you alright?"

"Brad got hit by a stingray," Frank said.

"Am I going to die," Brad asked, "like that crocodile hunter guy?"

"No. What is your name?"

"Neelley," the girl said.

"Cool."

Up close, Frank saw that she was a very pretty girl. She had beautiful teeth. They were so white and straight. It must have cost a fortune. She had fire in her eyes. All the pouting stuff was forgotten with her brother hurt. That was good. Cyrus always said blood tells all. She was going to be okay.

"Here's what you need to do. Run up to the hotel. The lady at the desk is Gabriella. Tell her your brother stepped on a stingray. Tell her you need a pot of really hot water to soak his foot in. As hot as he can stand."

"What are you going to do?"

"Brad and I are going to spend a couple of minutes keeping the toxins from traveling up his leg and then we will be right behind you."

Neelley took off on her long perfect legs. She was fast.

Brad looked scared. "It's starting to hurt."

Frank nodded.

"Is it going to get worse?"

Frank nodded as he massaged the leg. "Yeah. It hurts a lot. It has happened to me too."

"Really?"

Frank nodded. "A couple of times. But once we get your foot into the hot water, you will be fine. The hot water breaks the toxins down and the pain disappears almost like magic."

Brad's lip started quivering. His eyes were welling up with tears.

"I'm scared," he whimpered.

"Pain defines us," Frank grumbled.

Brad stared. "I don't want to hurt."

"No one does. In a few days when you are home you can retell this story over and over. You can talk about the pain and how you handled it. This is a big step toward becoming a man."

"It will make a kick ass story."

"Hell yeah. None of your friends can match it. Now I am going to carry you up to the hotel at a run."

"And it will start hurting?"

"Yep. You ready?"

"Yes." Brad wrapped his arms around Frank's neck.

Frank swept him up and ran. He ran past the sleeping form of Brad's dad. The bottle was half empty in the sand beside him. Frank smiled. The guy might have a problem with the booze, but he still had an awesome mustache. Damn, the world was unfair.

Frank pounded into the hotel and straight through to the kitchen. The chair and pot of water were waiting. He put Brad in the chair. He tested the water with a hand and stuck Brad's foot into the pot. Brad was grimacing.

"Hold on. It takes a couple of minutes." Frank turned to Gabriella. We are going to need more hot water to keep the temperature up. Get some water boiling. And if you have any stingray leaves toss them in."

Gabriella stammered. "Stingray leaves?"

"Leaves shaped like a stingray. Locals use them."

The cook nodded and jogged out the back of the kitchen.

"I don't know if they work or not, but I trust traditional medicine. How you doing, Brad?"

"It is easing off a little."

Frank patted him on the shoulder. "The ancient Greeks used to grind up stingray barbs as anesthetic. Mostly for removing teeth, but for other stuff too."

"What do we do now?" Neelley asked.

"Soak the foot for about an hour or two. Once the pain is gone it won't come back. You got to keep your eye on the puncture wound. He could get an infection. When you get home keep it rinsed out. It takes a while to heal."

"I'll get you some tea tree oil to put on it. It helps speed healing," Gabriella added.

"Thanks," Brad said. "I like your tattoos. Did they hurt?"

"Yeah. They hurt some."

Brad stared for a moment. "I still might get one someday. Neelley has one. It's on her butt. Mom and dad don't know."

"It is always nice when you can hide them."

"It's mistletoe."

"Huh?"

"You know. Kiss my ass."

Frank laughed.

"Don't tell anybody," Brad said.

"I won't. You got this?" Frank asked.

Brad nodded.

Frank turned to Neelley as she came in with the leaves the cook had cut. "This might be a good time to find your parents and let them know what happened."

"Good idea," she said and ran from the kitchen.

Frank headed back to the beach. Gabriella followed him, leaving Brad with the cook, who had returned with more leaves.

"It was lucky you were there," Gabriella said.

Frank shrugged.

"I recognize your tattoos. I remember the Spartans."

Frank didn't respond. He kept walking toward the beach.

"My boyfriend rode for the Black Lions. They worked with the Spartans."

Frank stopped and looked at her, but did not speak.

"I was helping him with a business deal near school. We hit an armored car and it went bad. Everyone was shooting. A civilian, a mother, caught a round and died. That's why I came here ten years ago. To hide."

"The Black Lions were loyal and brave. What happened to your boyfriend?"

"He died. The police shot him."

Frank nodded like he had heard it all before. He had.

"If you keep your head down and stay on the island you should be fine. Pretty good life here I expect."

Gabriella smiled and nodded. "Is that what you do? Hide from your past?"

"No."

"This is still my prison."

"Not a bad prison. You go home, you might get to find out how nice this setup was."

Gabriella looked away. "I miss my family."

Frank smiled. "Look after the kid 'til his mom shows up."

Frank went back to his towel. He saw the mother and Neelley racing back up the beach toward the hotel. He sat down. He found his cigar. It had gone out. He got his lighter and re-blazed the cigar. He took a couple of deep draws and eased back down onto the blanket. He blew the smoke out. He repositioned his sunglasses.

Two of the college girls were approaching him. They were whispering to each other and nudging each other. One had long dark hair drawn back into a ponytail. She wore a yellow bikini that was barely there and yet managed to magically cover all the critical parts. Her friend had short blonde hair cut into some kind of funky dip over one eye. She was wearing an orange bikini of the same cut and style as the dark haired girl. They were both attractive. The blonde was carrying a beer.

"Hi," the dark haired one said. "I'm Melanie and this is Karina. We saw what you did with that little boy. It was awesome. You're a hero."

The blonde handed him the cold beer. "We brought you a beer."

"Thanks."

Frank took a drink. It was very good.

The girls stood looking back and forth between them, trying to figure out what to say next. The blonde, Karina, took the next step.

"We are down here with a bunch of friends from school and we wanted to invite you to hang out with us. You know, party and stuff. Hit some bars tonight."

"That is very nice. And I do appreciate it, but I have to decline."

"It is just that there are more girls than guys and you would even things up a little."

Frank smiled. "I hate it. I really do. I got a date."

"Another time," Melanie said.

The girls smiled. They turned and went back toward their friends. Frank smiled too. It was turning into an interesting day.

Melanie turned back and walked back to where Frank lay.

"But you think we are hot, right?"

"On fire."

"And you are tempted to blow off your date and hang with us?"

"You have no idea."

"If your date turns out dull you can always hook back up with us," Karina added.

"You read my mind exactly."

"Well at least there's that."

The two girls walked off. He could hear them giggling.

31

Dawg stood on the deep-water dock near the mansion. He watched the four drug smugglers busying about the boat. They double checked that the bumpers were all in place. The tie lines were all lashed down snuggly. The boat's captain, a fat white man with even whiter hair, cut the engines. He climbed out of the boat with a joint in his hand. He offered the joint to Dawg. Dawg took a long hit and passed it back to the captain.

"She is a beauty," the captain said. "She is strong and fast."

Dawg nodded.

The boat was beautiful. It was a 32 foot Grady White with a walk around cabin. There was a dark blue hard-top over it to offer protection from the brutal Caribbean sun. It appeared new.

"Do you know much about boats?"

Dawg shook his bald head and reached out for the joint again. He took another long hit and passed it back.

The captain looked surprised. "I thought you knew boats. You got a long journey. You need someone that knows boats."

Dawg drug a long fingered hand through his matted beard. "Not I, me brudder."

The captain fidgeted slightly. "I can get Shorty to go with you. He can captain her for you. I would go myself, but I got business to attend to."

Dawg stared at him with his dark dead eyes. He nodded.

The captain looked around nervously.

"I know dem boats," Little Bird said.

Little Bird was walking down the dock. Roach was beside her with his arm around her waist. Roach was starting to think of Little Bird as his woman, Dawg thought. Maybe she was starting to think of Roach as her man. It was too bad. She had been fun. A lot of fun. But there were other women who would gladly take her place in his bed. Dawg could see the relief on the captain's face.

"Great. That is great."

"What she runnin'?"

"Twin engine Yamaha 250's. Four stroke."

"Nice. How big her tanks?"

"Big. She carries two hundred and eighty gallons. We got a half dozen spare five gallon gas tanks strapped to the inside. Just in case."

"How deep she go?"

"She drafts right at twenty three feet."

Little Bird smiled and nodded as if she had known all of this. "Show her to me."

The captain led Little Bird onto the boat. He gave her a tour of the boat. He pointed out the engine housing beneath the deck. He pointed out the transom door and latch in the rear of the boat. He showed her the scuppers and quick drain.

He led her to the cabin and pointed out the obvious furnishings, the cherry table in the galley, the top of the line microwave, refrigerator and stove. He showed her the full size head. He pointed out the forward berths for sleeping. Little Bird let her fingers drift over everything as if by touch she could remember it better. They went back topside to the cockpit.

The captain showed her the electrical boxes and gear. There was radar, and GPS, and depth finder, and gauges showing fuel, and oil and engine conditions. There was a marine VHF radio. Lastly, he pointed out the throttle and controls. Little Bird was beaming. She trailed her fingers over the chrome throttle, feeling its cold hardness. Her tongue protruded slightly as she touched it like she could feels its power. It was a little too erotic for the captain, who cleared his throat to break the spell.

"Her water tanks are full. The batteries are all fully charged. Do you have any questions?"

Little Bird stared at him with an almost predatory gaze. Then she smiled.

"Where is I hat?"

The captain stammered and retrieved his own captain's hat from the console and offered it to her. He was no fool. She took it and wiggled it to place on her head. She was still smiling.

"You got food and drink on dis ting?" Roach asked.

"Yes. She is fully stocked. The liquor cabinet is full as well."

"Do you have I ganja?"

The captain hurried to one of the storage boxes and opened it. There was a freezer size Ziploc bag packed with marijuana.

"Just like you asked."

Roach did not seem satisfied. Dawg knew he was looking for an excuse to hurt the captain. Roach liked to hurt people.

"Go on now," Dawg said to the captain.

The captain climbed back out of the boat and started down the dock.

"You will tell them I did like they asked? Tell them I brought a good boat?"

"Yah, yah. Hurry now, me brudder. Dis one," Dawg said as he pointed at Roach, "him be wanting harm on you. Hurry on."

The captain slipped past Roach. His three crewmen who had been waiting on the dock followed him. The captain glanced once over his shoulder once to make sure no one was following them.

"Why you do dat?' Roach asked. "Why not kill de white mon?'

"I kill no mon, unless de Prophet say to."

Roach snorted his contempt and climbed on board.

Bat came weaving down the dock. He was carrying the new shotgun. When he reached Dawg, he held it out. Dawg opened it to be sure it was loaded, and handed it back to Bat.

"For protection."

Dawg reached into the cargo pocket of his shorts and pulled out something. Bat stared as he unfolded it. It was a flag with a bright red hand printed on each side.

"Dis be all de protection we need. No ship will dare stop us."

"De Coast Guard might."

"Fuck de US of A. We will be nowheres near dey waters."

Bat passed the shotgun to Dawg and took the flag. He hurried on board to hoist it. Dawg laid the shotgun in the cabin. He looked the ship over. He was satisfied.

"When do we sail?" Bat asked.

"When de Prophet come."

"When will dat be?"

"Who knows. When he comes, he comes."

Roach grinned at Little Bird. "Mayhaps we have time for some fun before Lord Tosh come."

Little Bird leered.

Bat rolled his eyes.

Dawg pointed down the dock. "Cool you selfs. Lord Tosh is coming."

32

Cyrus' private cell phone chirped in his pocket. He took it out. He didn't recognize the number. He knew it was Helios. Helios never kept the same number.

"Carp, what did you find out?"

"Just did the preliminary names on the list for you."

"What you got?"

"Blanco Grande, Robert Ziglar, gets out of jail in about two months. May have been involved with some hits in prison. Doesn't seem to have been in contact with any of the high end members of the old Spartans."

"Hendo?"

"Hendo has been busy. He got in with some Asians. They run some stuff for one of the triads. He's moving up in their organization. No high level contacts."

"Atlas and Apollo?"

"Both still dead as far as I can tell. Ares too."

"The Jake?"

"The Jake was doing some contract work for the Russians, but he's gone off the map. I think they probably did him. He's a ghost."

"Spanish Johnny?"

Helios laughed. "You are a funny man, Cyrus. Spanish is with you. He's had a lot of medical work done, but he seems to be in fine shape. I figured you only included him to see if I was on the up and up."

"I apologize. A man can't be too careful."

"No, he can not. It was refreshing to see that you hadn't gotten soft. If you had, it might have worried me."

"Masnick?"

"I have several leads on Prometheus. But it will take some time. He has a lot of resources at his disposal."

"But you will find him?"

"Of course. But tell Spanish Johnny to back off. He is just driving him farther underground. It makes my work more difficult."

"Will do. And Frank?"

Carpenter paused. "I am working on that one as well." Carpenter gave a little laugh.

"What do you find so funny?"

"Part of this is our own fault you see. When you had me scrub the Spartans from the databases, it erased a lot of the tools I could use to track them back down. Things like finger prints. Past criminal associates. DNA."

"It is only a roadblock, correct? You will be able to find him?"

"I will do my best."

"Good. Call when you know anything new. If you find any evidence the Spartans are rebuilding, I want to know."

"One more thing, Cyrus."

"What is it?"

"Give Helen my love. I was happy to see she is still alive and well."

Cyrus made a harrumphing sound into the phone and disconnected. Arrogant bastard, he thought. But clever that was for sure. Helios was very clever. A part of Cyrus would have felt better if he could have put a bullet into that blonde head and bury him in a shallow grave. Helios was too smart for that. And that was as it should be. The other part of Cyrus, the part he liked to keep hidden, was glad Helios was still alive. They had been friends, more than that, brothers. He liked knowing some of them had survived the purge. He liked knowing they were still alive out in the wide world, working their plots and schemes. Cyrus thought about Helen. They had been together a long time. He loved her. He knew that. He also knew she was a liability. Those worries would have to wait. There were more pressing concerns.

Cyrus opened his desk drawer and withdrew a deck of tarot cards. He shuffled them three times and dealt the cards. Tarot cards were a nuanced fortune teller's trick. There were multiple patterns that could be used. Tarot dealers favored the ten card spread known as the Celtic Cross. Cyrus used the seven card Horseshoe spread. The basics were that you asked the cards a question. The dealt cards represented from left to right: the past, the present, what is helping, the obstacles that must be overcome, the attitudes of others, what the questioner should do, and finally, the outcome. The position of the cards right side up or upside down helped determine what they represented. The cards were divided into Major Arcana or Minor Arcana. The Minor Arcana were basically the four suits.

Cyrus smiled. He turned the cards over slowly. They weren't in perfect order, but all the players were represented. The emperor. The lovers. And in the final position, a skeletal knight on a pale horse bearing a white rose. Death. Interpreting the Tarot cards was an art. In Tarot, Death meant rebirth or transitioning. It urged the questioner to accept change and let go of past issues that were holding you back. Cyrus interpreted the last card to mean the death of Frank Kane. It could have applied to Helen or himself, but he was sure it meant Frank. He reshuffled the cards and replaced them in their pack. Cyrus was the prince of lies. He could even delude himself.

33

Bruce gently turned the grouper on the grill. The day had been perfect. They had returned from the jet ski trip to his house. They had all changed out of their bathing suits, taken naps and showers, and had started dinner. It was a simple meal. It was an island meal. Fresh mango salad. Some local asparagus grilled beside the fish. And the fish. The fish was a twelve pound grouper Bruce had speared free diving just before their return. It couldn't get much fresher than that. Caron and DC were busy mixing mojitos with fresh lime. Jenny was throwing a well-worn tennis ball for Thor.

"He is relentless," Bruce called. "Just so you know. He doesn't get tired of it. Ever. O.C.D. Obsessive Compulsive Dog. "

Jenny laughed. "Sounds like most boys."

"Now that is unfair," Bruce answered. "I have been a perfect gentleman."

Jenny turned back to look at him. She stared for a few seconds and then walked back to the grill.

"You really are a gentleman, Bruce. Do you realize that?"

"Don't go getting all mushy. Just trying to live the life. Follow the code."

"It's good. It suits you."

"Thanks. Mature and surfer don't usually go hand in hand."

"I don't know. It is a nice mix. How is it going? Doing the right thing all the time?"

Bruce laughed. "Seems to be working out pretty well. Good food. Good friends. Great weather. A secret swell. I don't know if it could get any better."

"What about a hot girl? You aren't forgetting about me are you?"

"No one will ever forget about you, Jenny. You are the best part."

Jenny giggled. "Sounds like somebody might get some loving tonight."

Bruce pointed the tongs at himself and looked from side to side and then up at the sky. "Please, God, let her be talking about me."

Jenny giggled and threw the ball again. Thor lopped down the beach again. Even the dog seemed to think it was a great day. DC appeared carrying red Solo cups for everyone.

"Let's get our drinks on. Booze always tastes better out of a red Solo cup."

Caron lifted her cup to the air and started singing. "Red Solo cup. I fill you up. Proceed to party."

The others joined in with the Toby Keith standard. Thor twisted his head from side to side, trying to figure out what in the hell the two-legs were doing. Why had they stopped throwing the ball, he wondered.

"After we eat we'll head out to Wicked Wanda's. You will love it. Local music. Very Bahamian."

"It's better in the Bahamas," Caron said.

"True words. Needs to be on a tee shirt."

"Yeah, like every shirt we see," DC mocked.

"I'm just saying," Bruce said. "Get some plates. We are ready to eat."

Helen knew there was a good probability that Frank would be at Wicked Wanda's tonight. It seemed to be the go to place on Friday night. He might be with his little whore, but she could handle her. Helen was a Spartan. The little whore wouldn't stand a chance. And she had decided what she would say to Frank. She had it all worked out. She would separate from the girls on some pretext and just walk right up to him. He would let her have her say at the very least. He was a gentleman in a lot of ways. What happened next would depend on what Frank said or revealed. She was operating from the dark here. She had no expectations on what was really happening in Frank's world. She would just play it as it lay. She knew he had loved her. She thought he probably still did. She doubted he would kill her. Why would he? How could he know all that had happened? In any case, if Frank wanted her dead, then she was dead. It was just a matter of time. And she needed resolution.

Her only problem was Ronnie. Big, dumb, loyal Ronnie. He would have to be out of the equation. Helen had a plan. She smoked a Virginia Slim Super Slim while looking out at the black ocean. Time to start the ball rolling. She stubbed out the butt and went inside. Her friends were almost ready.

She smiled. They did not do casual well. Their clothes said money and style. And she couldn't blame them. They all looked stunning. Even Meredith had tried to reign in her normal exhibitionism. Although her chest looked like it might jump out of her tight sequenced blouse at any moment. There was only so much you could expect Meredith to do.

Helen walked to Ronnie's door and knocked lightly. It was a nice touch, the knock. Polite. Shy. Like asking him for permission to enter. She smiled. She was so far out of his league. The door opened immediately. Ronnie was dressed for the trip to Wicked Wanda's. He had the requisite guido casual attire, silk short-sleeve shirt, pleated linen slacks.

"Is anything wrong?" Ronnie asked.

"May I come in for a minute?"

"Sure. Yeah. The room is kind of a mess." Ronnie started picking things up off the chair and bed.

"No. Don't worry about that. It is fine. It looks like Cyrus' bedroom. He never picks up anything. Our maids are saints."

She knew invoking Cyrus would get Ronnie's attention. It was an unspoken threat. It was a flash of absolute power.

"Thanks. I will try to keep it neater."

"No, don't worry about it. I have a favor to ask you."

"Sure. Anything you need. You know that."

"Well, I know I was a bit harsh last time we talked. I shouldn't have been. It is just this trip is very important to me."

"I understand."

"I don't get away with the girls very often. It is a time for me to relax without someone watching my every move. It is like I live in a fishbowl."

"Cyrus just wants to keep you safe."

"I know. And I love him for it, but it can be very trying. What I am trying to say is that I would like a little girl-time tonight. Just to hang with my friends."

"I hear you. I will stay way in the background."

Helen reached out and touched his arm. Ronnie gave a little jump.

"No. I don't want you to come with us. I want a night out without you watching me."

"But Cyrus was absolutely clear. I have to go. If something were to happen..."

"Nothing is going to happen. I will fill you in on all the details when we get back so you can make your report to Cyrus. It will be our little secret."

Ronnie shifted from foot to foot. "I don't know. One of your friends might give it away. Cyrus would kill me."

"Yes, he would. But they won't tell. I will tell them you got a stomach bug and I made you stay behind."

"I don't like it. I could get in big, big trouble."

Helen's beautiful, angelic smiled disappeared in a flash. The hard look swept over her face. Her voice grew cold enough to frost the air.

"I have asked you nicely. Do not forget our earlier conversation. You will do as I order. You will keep my secrets. Or you will suffer for it. Is that clear?"

Ronnie nodded.

"I asked is that clear. Say it."

"Yes, ma'am. It is clear."

"Good. I will tell the girls. Just order room service. We won't be out late."

Ronnie nodded and looked down at the floor like a misbehaving dog. He mumbled something under his breath Helen could not make out.

"If you go behind my back to Cyrus, I will kill you myself."

Ronnie met her gaze and nodded.

"Do you believe me?'

Ronnie nodded again. The gentle face returned. Her radiant smile swept the tension from the room.

"Smile, Ronnie. It will be fine. Cyrus will never know."

Helen returned to the main living room. The others were waiting purses in hand.

"Where's Ronnie?" Ashley asked.

"I just went to check on him. He has some kind of stomach bug. I told him to stay in tonight."

"Should I check on him? Ashley asked.

"Check on him or jump in bed with him?" Meredith mocked.

"No. He was going straight to bed. We'll check on him when we get back. But if anyone asks, you have to tell them he was with us. If my husband finds out that he stayed behind, even if he was sick, he will fire him. Or worse."

"What would be worse than losing your job?" Ashley said.

"My husband is very protective of me as you know. And he is very powerful. He could have Ronnie black-balled so he couldn't get any more security work."

"That is so mean."

"My husband can be spiteful. Do I have your promises?"

"Sure," Johanna said. "Who would ask? Who beside your husband would care?"

"As secrets go this is pretty lame. I keep lots more juicy stuff than this from my husband all the time."

"I bet you do, Meredith," Johanna said.

"Ash?"

"Absolutely. I don't want him to get into trouble."

"Good. Now let's get the party started."

In unison the four women all shouted "Woo Hoo!"

34

Lord Tosh rested inside the cabin of the boat. He was playing his boom box. It was playing KC and the Sunshine Band, a disco band from the 70s. The sound washed over the rest of the boat.

"That's the way, a huh, a huh, I like it."

Lord Tosh sang along off key with the lyrics with his eyes closed.

Little Bird was steering. She was watching the blue line of the GPS guide them on their hunt. She was focused. Her eyes swept the console, registering gas and oil pressure. She scanned the dark horizon for other ships. She checked the radar. Then back to the GPS. Her lips were set in a hard line.

Roach stood beside her, singing along with the music too. He was smiling. He was having fun. He liked riding in the boat the way a real dog likes to ride, with its head out the car window. He would alternately steal a glance at Little Bird's breasts as they bounced beneath her thin tee shirt. He liked the way the waves shook her breasts. Her nipples were hard and tight through the material.

Little Bird caught him staring. She smiled and winked at him.

"Stand behind me dat you can help steer de boat."

Roach moved behind her. She pressed her bottom against his crotch. He wrapped his arms around her waist. She reached down and raised his hands up until they rested on her breasts.

"Dat is mo better."

"Yeah, mon," Roach said and could feel his excitement start to grow. He briefly wondered if they could actually do it as she drove the boat.

Bat sat behind them in one of the deck seats and looked at the stars. He had taken a handful of mushrooms and he marveled at the beautiful colors of the night sky. It looked like black velvet. Sometimes Bat felt as if he could reach out and touch the stars. He lifted a hand toward the sky and wrapped a hand around a distant star. He closed his hand and seemed to crush it out. There was a bright flash.

"Woah," he moaned to himself.

Dawg heard the music and grimaced. He hated this lame cracker shit. The lyrics just seemed to repeat over and over until he thought he would scream. He hid any sign of distaste from his face. He felt the knot in his stomach. He stroked his tangled bead. Frank Kane. Frank fucking Kane. Finally, he would have his revenge. Finally, he would carve away his own cowardice and fear. Before Frank Kane died, he would whisper the truth to him. He would tell him how their paths had crossed so long ago. He would watch the great man tremble with fear, with helplessness, with panic. He smiled. He had waited so long, but Dreadmon had delivered his enemy into his hands.

Helen and her friends had taken the limo to a small upscale restaurant near the marina. They ate and talked. Helen feigned interest as she waited. Frank would not be here. He would be at Wicked Wanda's. She picked over her conch salad with Triggerfish. She tried to appear upbeat and excited, but she knew the flutter in her stomach was fear. Tonight might well determine the direction for the rest of her life. It was like looking over a cliff into the water below and trying to get up the courage to jump. When dinner was complete, she steered the conversation to going to the local bar. There was a little snag about desert, but when Helen demurred, the others could hardly indulge. A final glass of Pinot Noir and they returned to the limo and drove downtown. Helen noticed her hand was trembling.

Bruce led his group into Wicked Wanda's. Wicked Wanda's was a conventional Caribbean tourist bar. There was a huge central bar made of dark chocolate wood that had been pitted by insects and the salty sea air. It backed up to the kitchen and storage area. A third of the surrounding floor was open for dancing. The rest consisted of old tables and rickety chairs. The music and dancing brought the tourists in, the beer and food made the money.

Wanda saw Bruce come in and hurried over. She was late forties with long strawberry blonde hair and beautiful bow shaped lips. She was missing her left foot and wore a strange wooden peg as a replacement. There was no attempt to use a prosthetic foot.

"Hey, B Man. Who are your friends?"

"This is Jenny, Caron and DC. Guys, this is Wanda. Wicked Wanda."

Wanda smiled a mischievous smile and made a small bow. It may have been the most mischievous smile in the history of mischievous smiles. It spoke of secrets and mysterious pleasures only Wanda knew. "Pleased to meet you."

The group all nodded and returned mumbled greetings.

"You got a good table for us, Wanda? I want to turn my friends onto some authentic Bahamian rake n' scrape music."

"Anything for you, baby. Come this way. Wanda clomped off. Her cropped shirt displayed a large tramp-stamp tattoo over her buttocks. It was a broken heart with tribal swirls around it. They took their seats and Wanda added. "I will get someone over to take care of you. You need anything special you just tell them to get me."

"I will, Wanda. Thanks."

As soon as Wanda was out of hearing the talk began.

"She is Wicked Wanda?" DC asked.

"Yeah. She was a wild child in her day. Or so they say."

"What is with the foot?"

"Don't mention it to her, Caron. No one knows how she lost it, and she is touchy about it. Her temper is legendary on Cat Island"

"Come on, no one knows how she lost it?"

"There are stories, but no one knows the truth."

"What kind of stories?" Jenny asked.

"Crazy stuff. A shark bit it off. She lost it a motorcycle wreck. One story is that she was in love with this guy who kept her as like a sex slave or something. He had her shackled to a metal ring. One night he is passed out and she gets her hands on a hand saw."

"Gross. She cut off her own foot?"

"They say she had to be silent as she did it so he wouldn't wake up."

"What happened to the guy?"

"According to the story, she sawed his head off and buried him somewhere."

"That has to be a lie."

Bruce shrugged. "Probably. I don't know. It would explain her back tattoo. She is touchy about that too. Don't mention it either."

"Weird," DC said. "But a great story. What's the deal with this scratch bang stuff?"

"Not scratch bang. Rake and scrape. It originated here. Kind of like reggae in Jamaica or jazz in the states. It was invented by slaves. They didn't have access to traditional instruments so they improvised. The principal instrument is a saw."

"A saw. Is that a joke because of Wicked Wanda?" Jenny asked.

"No. I'm serious. They use a bent saw and a knife blade. It's amazing. They add drums and an accordion, and maybe a dude playing the bottles. They are very proud of it and it's pretty cool stuff. Just wait. When you go home you will be trying to buy rake and scrape CDs."

"They have CDs?"

"Tony McKay, George Symonette, Thomas Cartwright, Ophie and the Websites, the Britlanders. The Britlanders even toured with Jimmy Buffett. You'll see. I had never heard of it either, but now I am full into it."

Helen's group came in to Wicked Wanda's a few minutes later. The waitress hurried to seat them near the music. They all ordered drinks, gin and tonics.

"This is pretty cool," Johanna said.

"It's a little too earthy for me. It smells."

"Oh, don't be such a snob, Meredith. It's nice to see a real bar instead of all those chrome and fern places we always go."

Meredith sniffed her distaste. "If you like body odor."

"I hope Ronnie's going to be alright."

"Forget about the guido, Ash. He'll be fine. He's probably tough as a mule. You can tuck him in when we get back. We are here to have fun."

"And to dance," Johanna added.

"And to get drunk," Helen said.

"Very drunk," Ashley added.

They all clinked glasses and started down that road with sobriety in the rear view mirror.

Johanna nudged Helen. "Those are the kids from last night. The ones who came in with the big guy."

Helen turned as if mildly interested. She had already noticed everyone in the bar. She did not miss much. "Where is the big guy? I don't see him."

"Maybe he's in the can," Ashley said. "You'll recognize him when you see him. He is huge and scary."

"Yeah, he has all these tattoos on his arm."

"Looks like he would kill you as soon as look at you. Really dangerous type. But a total stud."

"If you like that kind. He reminded me of someone who might work on my Mercedes."

Johanna and Helen laughed. "You are such a snob, Meredith."

The band came out and took their seats on the small stage. A murmur swept over the crowd. They were excited. Helen watched for Frank as the music started. He might be outside checking the perimeter. It was the kind of thing he would do.

Frank strolled down the beach to meet Natalie. He could have taken a cab, but he liked walking the beach. There was something about walking a beach at night that relaxed him. He felt it put his demons into a trance. They slept locked within their shackles in his soul. There was no twittering or moaning to be set free. There were no chains rattled or doors beat upon. The dungeon walls held firm. Everything was calm. He felt at peace.

He thought a little about Natalie. She was a beautiful woman. She was scarred by her betrayal. But weren't we all? Wasn't that one of the costs of betrayal? She would always carry that pain, but she was young and beautiful. She would find another man, hopefully a good man, and forget some of her pain. Learn to bury it inside her like Frank did with his own demons. Frank held no illusions that he was that man for her. He was an experiment. He was both dangerous and safe. She would never need to see him again after this weekend. He was a stepping stone to a new life. And he was fine with that. She was interesting in a lot of ways. And she looked a little like Helen. Not just in a general way because she was young and blonde and attractive. There were other similarities. The way her mouth crinkled when she laughed. She had eyes that didn't seem to miss anything. Even her attitude, making choices, not letting them be made for you. They all reminded Frank of Helen. He smiled. It was a genuine smile. She was not Helen. Pretending she was, was a fool's game. Frank was not a fool.

Frank walked down the beach to Natalie's hotel. He stood staring at the ocean. He breathed in the salt rich air. His checked his watch. The numbers glowed brightly. It was a sweet gift. He was early by a dozen minutes yet.

He heard the soft approach of feet, but didn't turn.

"Are you reconsidering our date?" Natalie asked.

"No. Just enjoying the ocean at night."

Natalie linked her thin arm into his. "It is scary and beautiful."

"I am trying to enjoy the little things more. A friend once told me we only have so many good summers left and to enjoy them."

"What does that mean?"

"We get old. We die. We regret not enjoying life more. We don't know how many summers we have left so we should enjoy each one."

"Why only the summers? Why not all our time?"

"I think it is a metaphor or something. Most people have straight jobs and get their vacations in the summer. Or kids are in school until summer. Something like that."

"Oh, I see. That's what I am trying to do. Enjoy life more. Be less afraid."

"Sometimes it is good to be afraid."

"Are you ever afraid? You don't strike me as the type."

"Sure, I'm like everybody else. Nothing special here at all."

Natalie laughed. He liked the sound of her laugh. It wasn't practiced. She covered her mouth with one hand. Her nails were freshly painted Spartan red. It was a good omen, he thought.

"You are not like other men. You have to know that."

Frank shrugged. "I can take a compliment as well as the next guy. By the way, you do look beautiful tonight."

She blushed. Frank smiled. He hoped his smile didn't give her nightmares. He really was practicing.

"Thank you. It takes a lot of effort to look like you haven't put a lot of effort into getting fixed up."

"Well, it worked. You look perfect."

"Thank you for noticing."

"What's the plan? You said you had a special dinner planned for us. Where are we going?"

Natalie's smile was mischievous. She looked up at him from beneath her soft blonde hair. There was something he couldn't read in her eyes.

"That is kind of up to you, Frank. We can go to dinner or I have a special desert planned for us."

"What's for dessert?"

"Me. I had worked out this elaborate plan for us to eat and drink and then lure you back to my room and seduce you."

"You think I am that easy? I could have said no."

"Not a chance. You can have your dessert now or you can wait until after dinner. You choose."

Frank pretended to ponder the question. He pulled her against him. "What if I want dessert now and then again after dinner?"

"Fuck dinner. We can always order room service. And dessert is nice for breakfast too."

"We only have so many good summers left," Frank said.

"We would be fools to waste one."

She turned her face up toward his and they kissed. The kiss was so hot Frank thought it might have burned his lips. She pressed herself hard against his body. She seemed to mold herself to him. He crushed her in his arms. When she came up for air she whispered.

"We better hurry or you're going to have dessert on the beach."

She took him by the hand and led him toward the hotel. She was giggling. Frank felt a twinge of fear. Three times. Had he really implied that he was up for three times in one night? Who did he think he was kidding? He was getting older. He felt the stirrings in his shorts. Somebody was up for the challenge. In more ways than one.

35

The scene at Wicked Wanda's was rocking. The band was wailing. The crowd was dancing. People were drinking. The weather was warm with just a hint of a breeze. It was a perfect party night. Helen's group all took turns dancing, sometimes with the men who approached, sometimes with each other. No one cared. Bruce and DC spent as much time on the dance floor as they did at their table. Finally, the band took a break.

"That music is amazing," Jenny said.

"I try to be a good host and show you a good time. Give you some local flavor."

"Jenny fanned her tee shirt away from her body. I am sweating like a pig."

"Me too," Caron added.

"Ladies don't sweat," DC said. "They glisten."

Caron gave him a peck kiss.

"You can be so sweet."

"I try. God knows I try,"

"I know I must look like a hot assed mess too," Jenny said.

No one responded. Jenny stared at Bruce.

"Well? Any comment?"

"Oh, sorry. You look great."

"That's the best you can do?"

"Sorry. I am not good at this stuff. I'll have to try harder."

Jenny patted his arm. "I forgive you. Just a little faster on the confirmation stuff would be great."

Bruce nodded. He waved a waitress over. "One more round."

The girl hurried away.

"Last round, then we head back to my place. It is getting late."

Jenny gave him the doe eyes.

"What is at your place that we don't have here?"

Bruce smiled. "Privacy."

"I'm in," Caron said.

"Me too," DC said. "You know what would be great."

"What."

"If we could score a little herb for the after party."

"I don't want to get busted," Jenny said.

"I didn't say let's run drugs. Just a little something something for Bruce's place. You got anything at your crib?"

"Sorry. I use to run the stuff, but I got burned out on it. I haven't caught a buzz in over a year."

"See, he doesn't want to," Jenny said.

"I didn't say that. Only I'm not holding. There's a guy I know over there who could hook us up. Just a couple of joints. I'll go talk to him."

"I'll go with you," DC said. "Strength in numbers."

"I hear you. Come on. We will be right back."

Bruce and DC moved off through the crowd. They stopped at a table of locals and talked for a minute working out the details. Bruce's connection nodded and moved off with Bruce and DC in tow. Better to do their deal in the privacy of the bathroom. They were barely out of site when John Keown approached the table. He was dressed in white linen shorts and a dark shirt with the sleeves rolled up. The rolled up long sleeve shirt was his style. He was carrying a bottle of champagne and three glasses. The yellow color told them it was Crystal.

"Good evening, ladies. I am John Keown. Are you having a good time?"

"Yeah, great," Caron said.

"And you, pretty lady? Are you having a good time?"

"Listen, we are with somebody," Jenny said.

"I know. But what kind of fool leaves such a rare beauty alone. Here drink champagne with me." He began pouring the champagne into the empty glasses he carried.

"No thank you," Jenny said.

"Just one drink. That is all. One drink and I will go if you want me to."

"We want you to," Caron said. She glanced around hoping to see DC coming back. Nothing.

"There is no need for such rudeness. I am the Prime Minister's nephew. You are safe with me."

"We know who you are," Jenny said. "We would appreciate it if you left us alone."

"What if I do not wish to leave you alone? On Cat Island I tend to get whatever I want. Expensive champagne. The finest blow. The most beautiful women."

"Not this time," Caron said. "We told you, we have dates."

John made a tsking noise. "They are nothing." He grabbed Jenny's arm and pulled her to her feet. "Come for a walk with me in the moonlight. Let me show you the stars."

"Really. That's your best line. That's what you got?"

John tightened his grip on her arm. Jenny grimaced and tried to pull away.

"Let go."

"I do not need a line to pick up tourists. They swarm to me. They beg for my touch."

"I said let go. You're hurting me."

Caron grabbed his arm and tried to pull it away from Jenny.

"She said no. No, means no, asshole."

The backhand blow was unexpected. One minute Caron was looking in his dark, handsome face trying to decide if he was drunk or high or both, the next instant he struck her hard across the face. She stumbled back against the table.

"Do not dare touch me you white whore."

The word whore sparked something deep in Caron's soul. She had been many things in her past. She had performed many dark deeds to survive. But she was not that terrorized little girl any longer. She was not a whore. She would never be a whore again. No man could call her that.

Her vision narrowed. The borders grew red and closed in around her. John was bigger than her. He was stronger. She grabbed the champagne bottle and struck at him. The blow caught him in his left eye and he fell screaming. The heavy bottle didn't break like they do in the movies. The glass was too thick. It acted like a club. It shattered his eye socket. Blood poured from the tear in the cheek below. John rolled on the ground clutching his shattered face. He screamed like an animal caught in a trap. His legs kicked out, knocking over the table. The champagne glasses fell and shattered.

DC and Bruce raced up. Wanda hobbled over.

"What happened?"

"He grabbed Jenny. He was hurting her. I tried to make him stop, but he hit me."

Two police officers ran up and grabbed Caron's arms.

"Let me go. He was assaulting us."

The policemen looked terrified. They knew who John was.

"She attacked me. The crazy bitch hit me for no reason. Get me to hospital."

One of the policemen helped John to his feet. "Come, we must get you medical attention. Let me see your injury."

John lowered his hand. The eye bulged. The cornea was crimson. A jagged piece of bone protruded from beneath the eye. The policeman was stunned, but tried to appear calm.

"We will get you stabilized and then airlift you to Grand Bahamas Island for treatment."

"Hurry you idiot. And arrest that cunt."

Caron blanched, but the second word held not the power of the first word.

The second policeman tightened his grip on her arm.

"You will pay for this I swear. I will see you spend the rest of your life rotting in a cell."

"Come with me. We must sort this out."

"It wasn't her fault. He started it. He attacked me. She was just trying to protect me."

The policeman shook his head. His job hung in the balance.

"She must come to the station with me."

Wanda moved up. "Come on, Desmond. I will vouch for the girl. Where is she going to go on this island?"

"No. She has to go to the station. John has ordered it."

"He's not your boss."

"His Uncle is. The rest of you wait here until I return. I will need to question you all."

"Tell Frank." Caron called as he pulled her away.

Wanda turned back to Bruce as Desmond dragged Caron away. "I don't need to tell you, but don't be here when he gets back. I will cover for you as much as I can. I will tell them you came in separately and picked up the girls."

"Why not stay?" Jenny asked.

"Because this is the Bahamas. John carries a lot of weight. The facts won't matter. You will only get yourself arrested alongside your friend. Go on now while you still can."

"What about our friend?"

"Get a solicitor tomorrow and try to bail her out. If you do, get the hell out of the Bahamas. John is a vindictive spoiled brat. He will get her locked up for good once he gets out of the hospital."

"Come on," Bruce said. "We got to go."

Jenny grabbed her purse. "Take us back to the hotel. Frank will know what to do."

Helen saw the altercation. She watched it unfold in slow motion. She knew the dark haired girl was going to strike probably before the girl knew herself. She saw that feral look sweep over her face. She had seen the same look in her own mirror many times. What was the saying, "Hide the lion, show the clown?" That was it. The girl was too young to have the will power. The girl didn't have the emotional control it would have taken. Something in her reached out to the girl. She was special in some way to Frank. That made her special to Helen. She would do what she could to help the girl. She just didn't have a clue what she could do to help her.

As the other three young people were hustled out, the bar returned to normalcy. Chairs were righted. The table was straightened. The broken shards of glass were swept up and removed. Drinks were ordered. Food was ordered. The band returned to playing. People started dancing again. Conversations resumed. The sparks of romance were ignited in the warm night. For the others in the bar, the incident was forgotten. It did not concern them.

Helen hid any interest she had in the fight. She feigned amusement at their young antics. She nursed her drink and her plans. Something needed to be done for the girl. Something needed to be done about Frank. Time was running out.

36

Frank walked outside onto the beach. Natalie had convinced him that brunch was the only civilized meal of the day. He smiled at the sight of the ocean. He felt fantastic. Natalie came up behind him and wrapped her arms around his waist. She pressed her face against his back.

"Will I see you tonight?"

"I think it can be arranged."

"It's our last night on the island, we would be fools to waste it."

"Yes, we would. I hope you had a good time."

"Last night was wonderful. And that thing you did with your tongue. Oh, my God, that was incredible. Where did you learn to do that? Wait. Don't tell me. I don't want to know. I don't want to think about it. But it was something else."

"I am glad you approve."

Natalie leaned in and gave him a small bite on his neck. "I could eat you up."

"Sounds like a plan."

"Come over at the same time as last night."

Frank nodded. "What do you have planned for today?"

"Sleep. Lots of sleep. I was up very late last night."

Frank smiled. "Yes, we were. I may catch a nap myself. You wore me out."

"You had better get that nap if you know what's good for you. I took it easy on you last night."

"You call that easy?"

"I got a lot to catch up on. Tonight I am taking the governor off. Wide open. There are some things I've read about that I want to try."

"I better take my vitamins."

He turned around and she kissed him fully.

"I really did have a wonderful time."

"I did too."

"You better get back to your friends. They might be worried."

Frank tried an amused chuckle. He wasn't good at it. It sounded a little like a case of indigestion. But it was getting better. He had the smile about perfect.

"What could happen in paradise?"

Natalie kissed him again. "I met you."

Frank turned her around and gave her a playful pop on her backside.

"All part of my master plan. I will see you tonight."

Natalie smiled and turned back toward her hotel. She was too old to have skipped, but he would have sworn he had seen her do it.

Frank remembered the feeling of eyes on him from the day before. He turned and looked at the nearby hotels where he had felt someone watching him. He stared at the roof, trying to detect something out of the ordinary. He didn't see anything. He didn't feel anything. Maybe he was paranoid. Hell, he knew he was paranoid. If you spent every moment on hyper alert expecting someone to try to kill you, you got a little paranoid.

Frank walked back to his hotel with his sandals off. He liked the feel of the wet sand and sea foam on his feet. If he had known what was waiting for him, he might have run. Or he might have walked slower, savoring the good feelings he had.

Helen's knock was light. She knew Ronnie was awake, but she knew he would probably stay in his room until summoned. The knock was still an outward display of respect. The knock once more.

"Ronnie, it's me, Helen."

The door swung open. "What do you need?"

The tone was both supplicant and outlaw. He was still struggling with his new role. Helen smiled her irresistible smile.

"The girls are still asleep. I am going to run out and pick up something for Cyrus."

"Okay. Do you want me to come with you?"

"No. I want it to be a surprise. You stay here with the girls. If they ask, say I went for a walk on the beach."

If Ronnie had stuck out his lower lip he could not have pouted more. "What do I tell Cyrus?"

"Tell him you went with me, silly. I will give you the details when I get back."

Ronnie nodded.

"I am counting on you, Ronnie. If you get all twitchy and call Cyrus, you know what he will do. You can try to kid yourself that he won't, but he will put you in the dirt."

"I know. Just hurry, please."

Helen leaned in and gave him a kiss on the cheek. "I will. Don't worry. I will be back before you know it."

Ronnie smiled.

She had that effect on men. She couldn't be denied. Helen hurried to the front door. "I will take the limo."

Frank was still opening his door when Jenny came bursting out of her room. DC was close behind.

"Caron is in trouble."

Frank opened his door. "Come inside and fill me in."

Jenny slipped passed him. She gave him a little look. To her credit, she didn't say 'where were you?' or 'what have you been doing all night?' or 'I can't believe you slept with that woman?' or anything else petty and cruel. There would have been no point.

DC followed and gave Frank a little nod and a smile. Guys never asked questions. It wasn't because they didn't have them, it was more that the answers didn't really matter to them. Frank followed them inside. Frank sat on his bed and DC and Jenny stood. Jenny told the story straight through. Occasionally, DC would throw in an observation, but for the most part, he stayed silent. When Jenny had finished, she put her hands on her hips and said, "What do we do now?"

"It is tricky. She's got no passport and no other documentation that shows she entered legally."

"She's in jail. This prick is going to get her put away."

"I got that. We need to move fast on this."

"So what are you going to do?"

"Maybe the simplest way is the easiest."

"Meaning?"

"Bribe. This is the Bahamas. Money talks. The cops have had the night to think about it. They don't want trouble from tourists either. Maybe a bribe gets Caron out. She is released into our care. She disappears and they plead innocence. The prick gets patched up and in a few months all is forgotten."

"Okay. We can pool our cash," DC said.

"I got this," Frank said. "You guys call Bruce, have him bring any stuff you left at his place. Then pack your stuff. We get her out, stay close to the hotel, and then get out of here first thing tomorrow as planned."

"You don't want Bruce to try to help? He knows the people."

"And they know him. I don't want to fuck up his life down here by associating with us."

Jenny nodded. DC nodded.

"I will change and head down to the police station. Meet you back here as quick as I can."

37

The limo pulled to a stop in front of the police station. Helen wanted the police to see that it was a limo. She wanted them to know she was a woman of wealth. Wealth implied power and authority. She was dressed in a conservative outfit with oversized dark sunglasses. She went inside. She was pleased to see that it was air conditioned.

The police station was small. There was only a pair of cells in the back. One cell was large and empty except for a metal bench attached to one wall. There were no beds or blankets or chairs. The other cell was smaller and directly across from it. She could see the feet of the girl sticking out as she sat on the concrete floor. There was a pair of desks and a large wooden counter at the front of the station.

One of the policemen sat at the desk on the left. The other immediately met her at the desk.

"How may I be of service?"

"My name is Helen. I am here about the young girl you have locked up."

The police officer stood straight. Not a good sign. He was trying to look authoritarian. "That is a local matter."

"I am aware of that, officer. I was present at Wicked Wanda's tavern and saw what happened. I thought I should come down here and give a statement."

"Mr. Keown said she assaulted him without provocation. He is currently being treated in Nassau for extensive injuries to his face and eye."

Helen smiled. "Does that seem likely to you, officer? A young girl without provocation attacks a much larger man? It sounds unlikely."

"What do you say happened?"

"The same as anyone else who witnessed it. The young man was being rude and trying to force himself on the young women. When he was rebuffed, he became angry and struck the girl you have locked up. She struck back. Unfortunately, she grabbed his bottle of champagne."

"He may lose his eye. This is serious business. Do you know who he is?"

"It shouldn't make any difference to the law. He was in the wrong. Everything stems from his actions."

The policeman shook his head. He did not want to hear this.

"What you say may be true. It is not for me to say. There will be a trial."

Helen sighed. "I understand. Justice must be served. It seems unfair that she is locked in that cell while a judge is appointed and a jury called. Perhaps I could pay her bail. At least then she would be free to move about the island."

"Bail has not been set."

Helen smiled again. "I know. But what would be fair for such an offense?"

The policeman rubbed his chin. He was calculating his share of the skim. "I don't know. What would you propose?"

It was perfect. There were unsaid agreements being drawn up.

"I was thinking five thousand would cover her bail."

The police officer's eyes sparkled. That was a lot of money. He would be willing to take some heat for that amount. He could always arrest her again later. It wasn't like there was anywhere she could go. That was when things went bad.

"No."

It was the second police officer. He strode up to the counter. His chest was puffed out. He had a very thin moustache that he waxed to make look darker.

"There can be no arbitrary setting of bail."

The police officer turned an imploring look at his friend. "She is talking about five thousand dollars."

"We cannot just make up bail in a case like this."

Helen smiled. He was a toad, she thought. Very well. Time to get serious.

"Then let us say ten thousand. That should cover things."

The first police officer gasped. Unfortunately, the second officer shook his head stubbornly.

"Not at any price. We have strict orders to hold this young woman. And that is exactly what we shall do until told otherwise."

"This is preposterous. She is an American citizen. You can't just hold her without bail, indefinitely."

"It has been made clear to us that she is to stay here until the extent of Mr. Keown's injuries are determined. That is exactly what we shall do."

The other officer shrugged. He had seen his fortunes rise and fall in the space of a few seconds. "I am sorry, Ma'am," he said. "We should hear something soon."

"I am leaving tomorrow. It won't be soon enough to help this girl."

He handed her a piece of form paper. "If you would fill out what you saw on this form and return it before you depart, it will help her case. And be sure to list where you can be contacted."

Helen took the paper. She knew she would never fill it out. Never tell them where she could be reached later. She smiled. The girl was looking at her through the bars. She was confused but hopeful. Helen spoke to her.

"I am sorry. Tell Frank I tried to help."

The girl looked shocked. Helen was shocked herself. She hadn't meant to let the girl know she knew Frank. Helen paused. She didn't make mistakes. Something inside her wanted Frank to know she was alive. Wanted Frank to know she was nearby. Wanted Frank to know she was trying to help. She turned on her high heels and left the police station. She balled up the form and dropped it into a garbage can outside the front door.

When she got into the limo, she spoke to the driver.

"Do you have a high end watch store on the island?"

"Yes, of course. Many."

"Good. Take me to the best one."

Watches were easy. Men liked watches. Cyrus liked watches. As long as she kept it simple and manly looking he would be pleased. Maybe the Swiss made Zenith Captain Winsor would be a good choice. It was a nice little watch. It was a reasonable choice. She was confident she could pick one up for ten thousand dollars. He might never wear it, but he would be pleased she had bought it for him. He would like that she hadn't gone crazy and bought him a super expensive watch. She wanted to keep Cyrus happy. It was the only way she would stay alive.

38

Frank had changed into what he considered proper boat attire. Boat attire for a worker on a boat that was. He had put on his older shorts, a long sleeve pullover thermal to hide his tats, and a pair of sandals. He put on his sunglasses. They probably didn't have cameras at the police station, but it was better to disguise himself when he could.

The cab parked out front and agreed to wait for Frank. He went inside. No cameras. That was a good omen. He slipped his sunglasses up on his forehead. The thin policeman was still at the counter.

"How can I be of service?"

"I would like to speak to your prisoner."

"Sharon?"

"Yes."

"Do you know her last name? She would not tell it to us."

"I am sorry. On the boat she was just Sharon."

"Which boat is that?"

"Neptune's Dream. It is docked in Royal Harbor."

The policeman made a note of it.

"And she works on Neptune's Dream?"

"Yes. She did until this happened. I don't know if they will keep her on or fire her."

"Are the owners onboard? I would like to speak with them."

"The owners don't know what happened last night and I would appreciate it if we could keep it on the quiet for now."

"They will know when she does not return to the boat."

"I know. But the boat is docked here all week and I was hoping we might get this resolved before that."

"I don't know. We will see when they appoint a judge to hear her case."

"Can I see her?"

"Follow me."

Frank did. He gave the policeman several paces between them to feign respect. They stopped outside the cell. The policeman stood there waiting.

"Can I speak to Sharon in private?'

The policeman opened the top drawer of the nearest desk and removed the cell key ring. There were only two keys on it. It was something out of an Andy Griffith TV show. The policeman unlocked the door and stepped back out of the way. Frank went inside. The policeman closed the door, and for an instant, Frank felt like an animal that had stumbled into a trap. The feeling passed. Caron ran to his arms. She clung to him. Frank patted her on the back. He wasn't practiced in consoling anyone. After a minute she broke their hug. She seemed a little embarrassed.

"I am so sorry."

"Don't worry about it."

"He was all over us…"

"And he hit you."

"Yeah. He called me a whore, and I snapped.'

"Words can carry a lot of power."

"I wish I could take it back, but I can't. They say he might lose his eye. They said his face is broken."

"Good," Frank said. "When you hit, hit hard. What did you tell the police?"

Caron lowered her voice. "Nothing except about the attack and that my name was Sharon. It was all I could think of on the spot. Then I just quit answering their questions."

"It's fine. I told them you were on a boat as a deckhand. You probably heard."

"Yeah. It explains why I don't have any ID on me."

"Listen, I got a couple of moves I am going to try, but I will get you out of here. I promise."

"I don't know. The police are scared of the jerk I hit. I mean really scared. I'm afraid they're going to put me away."

"That is not going to happen. I am going to see if they will let me prepay your bail, then we can slip out of here tomorrow morning and never come back."

"It won't work. There was a woman in here earlier. She tried to bribe the cops but they wouldn't have it. She offered like ten thousand dollars."

"What woman?"

"I don't know. I had never seen her before. She was a really beautiful looking blonde. She said to tell you that she had tried to help."

"Was her name Natalie?"

"No. I heard her tell the cops her name was Helen."

For an instant the world seemed to freeze in time. Helen was alive. Helen was here. Helen was on the island. A thousand questions raised their hands in his mind to be considered next. Frank ignored them all. He kept his face blank as he had trained himself to do. Helen was a distraction now. His first concern was Caron. He had to help her.

"Okay. I will get things in motion. You sit tight."

"You don't know who the woman is?"

"No. I don't have a clue. Stay strong." Caron nodded. Frank gave her a squeeze on her shoulder. "Officer, I am done here."

The policeman returned and let Frank out of the cell.

"Can you get her a blanket and pillow? If you are going to keep her locked up, the least you can do is make her comfortable."

"This is not a hotel. We do not have blankets or pillows for prisoners."

"Come on. Help her out. She's just a kid."

The policeman shrugged. "I will see what I can do. But I cannot make any promises."

"Good enough."

"Since you know this girl, I will count on you to search her room and bring me her passport. We will hold it until this matter is decided."

"Absolutely. I will bring it back this afternoon sometime. But let me get it so the owners don't know what is going on. If they hear about this they will probably cut her loose and take off."

"This afternoon. No later."

"Absolutely."

Frank walked outside and got back into the taxi. He rode back to his hotel. His mind was racing.

39

Helen knocked on Ronnie's door again. He opened it immediately. Relief showed in his face.

"You alright? No problems?"

Helen patted his arm. "Of course. I tried to be quick like you asked." Helen knew he had not made a request but he would think he had now.

"You were. Your friends are still asleep."

"Perfect. You have been such a dear about this. I know it has been hard. I know you have struggled with it. So I bought you a little thank you present when I was shopping for Cyrus' watch."

Helen reached into her bag and removed a small watch box. She handed it to Ronnie. He looked stunned. He opened it. Inside was a watch with a chrome band and a blue face. He smiled as he tried it on his wrist.

"It's a Nixon Tide. Nixon makes really nice watches, and when I saw the name I thought it would remind you of our trip."

"Thank you. It was really thoughtful."

"You like it?"

"I love it. It looks really cool."

"Good. I want us to be friends, Ronnie. I want you to know you can trust me and I can trust you."

"For sure."

"Now, just to be safe, I am going to describe everything I can remember about the watch store so you can tell Cyrus you were with me until you went outside to wait for me."

"Yeah, that's a good idea. Just in case he asks."

"He won't, but I want you to be able to see it in your head just in case."

"That's cool. What's up for the rest of the day?"

"More shopping of course. I didn't want them to know what I got Cyrus. They might slip up and spoil my surprise."

"Can I see his watch?" Ronnie asked.

"Of course." Helen removed the other watch box and showed the watch to him like they were partners in the surprise.

"That is awesome, but I like mine better."

"Good." Helen gave him a hug. It appeared spontaneous, but she had planned the interaction on the way back in the limo. She smiled. She had always been good at manipulating men.

"Now I am going to wake the girls. We are burning daylight."

"Let me know when you guys are ready."

Frank found DC and Jenny sitting by the pool.

"Anything?" Jenny asked.

"It's not good. They wouldn't go for a bribe"

"What's our next move?"

"I'm going to meet up with Bruce, see what he thinks."

"He just left a few minutes ago. I think he was heading back to his place."

"How is Caron holding up?" DC asked.

"She's a tough girl. She's doing fine."

"But we have to get her out."

"We will. You guys be ready to go in the morning. Our plane leaves at eight. Bullington said we can't be late."

"We are almost packed now."

"Good. Pack Caron's stuff too. I will do my stuff and then go find Bruce."

"You go ahead. DC and I will pack up your stuff for you."

Frank hesitated only a second before agreeing. "Good plan. I got to get a few things and then I will go find Bruce."

DC looked stricken. "We're counting on you, big man."

"I got this. Don't worry. But no matter what, you be on that plane tomorrow."

"What if you haven't gotten Caron out?"

"You go. It may take more time than I hope. With you guys gone there is one less thing for me to worry about."

"We aren't going without you. Either of you."

"Listen, Jenny. I get it. But I will get her out. I won't leave her behind. No matter what."

Jenny nodded. So did DC.

"Alright, if you say so."

"Trust me."

"We do. It's just hard."

"I know. Just chill here today. Stay out of trouble."

They both nodded. Frank hurried upstairs to his room. He had five thousand dollars on him. If he was forced to stay, it would be good to have extra money. He took another ten thousand out of his stash. Packing light didn't include cash. Always bring lots of cash. He put on his tennis shoes and some low cut, white socks. There wasn't much more he needed. On a whim he grabbed a few cigars and stuck them in the pocket of his cargo shorts along with the old cigar cutter and the cheap lighter. He might have to kill some time and a cigar was a good way to do it.

Downstairs, he had Gabriella call him a cab. It was a beat up old Chevrolet Impala. The word 'CAB' was painted on the side. Nice. Stay classy.

"Where to, my brother?"

"You know where Bruce lives? The guy who runs Beaman's jet skis?"

"No. I know this fella' but not where he lives. What is the address?"

Frank gave it to him. They had been riding less than a minute when the driver asked, "You looking for something special?"

Frank didn't answer.

"I know where to find the best ladies. Very young, very clean."

"No thanks."

"Got good coke, good smoke."

"No. Just this address."

The cabbie tried to engage Frank in conversation, but Frank's glare silenced him for the ride to Bruce's home. The cab pulled up and stopped. There was no sign of Bruce's SUV or Thor.

"You want me to wait?"

"Just hang for a minute while I check this out."

Frank jumped out and went up to the house. It was dark. Silent. He went onto the porch to knock anyway. There was a note stuck to the door with duct tape. The outside said 'Frank'. He pulled it down and read it: "I figure you will show up here sooner or later. I got a lead on something that may spring Caron. I have a lawyer friend, actually he is a retired judge, who might be able to help us, but he is out fishing. Thor and I will wait for him at the dock where he keeps his boat. Wait for me at the jet ski place. I will meet you there. Brothers in arms."

Bruce was a good man. He would have made a good Spartan back in the days when Frank had thought The Spartans MC was more than another one-percenter club. The best Spartans did not wait to be led. They were proactive. They acted.

Frank stuffed the note in his pocket. He didn't have any choice. He went back to the cab and told the driver where he wanted to go. The cabbie started to reply, but thought better of it and just drove. There was a chain stretched across the driveway. There was no padlock. Frank unhooked it and the cab took him down to the office. He let Frank out at the side of the building. Frank paid him and watched him go. He turned and walked down the gravel driveway toward the dock. He pulled out a cigar and cut the tip.

40

Tonello's phone chirped. He answered.

"Yes?"

"I am on de SAT phone. We will be der soon."

"I am ready."

"De place I are bringing de boat, is it deep?"

"Yes, a deep drop up to the shoreline."

"Good. Do you know where de Frank Kane is now?"

"No. But he is still on the island. My boss will know where he is."

"Good. This is you day of rebirth, Crab. We must find dis man quickly."

"My boss will lead us."

"I no doubt dis thing. De Red Hand can be very persuasive. You boss may not survive de questioning. Will dis be a problem?"

"No. There is only the Red Hand. Nothing else matters."

"Good. You have left I a vehicle?"

"As planned. The directions on the seat will bring you to the place I work. We will go together and find my boss and then this man, Kane."

"Dis is a great day. A great day, brudder."

And the phone went dead.

Tonello smiled. Unlimited power was hours away for him. Unlimited wealth and prestige were waiting for him. Unlimited women too. All he had to do was find Frank Kane. Nothing would deter him now.

Frank walked out onto the worn dock at Beaman's Jet Ski rentals. There was no one around. The parking lot was empty. The gravel pile was still untouched. Jet skis bobbed near the end of the dock. He lit the cigar with the lighter and walked out farther onto the dock. The salt seasoned wood creaked and moaned under his weight. He sat on the lone bench and looked out at the quiet cove. He tried to relax, to let his mind go free. There were so many questions. He needed time to think. He needed a plan. Frank wanted to find a way to finesse the situation, but he couldn't. Old habits die hard.

Caron called out to the guard.

"Hey. I need to go to the bathroom."

The guard put down his magazine. He looked bored and a little angry. He got up and retrieved the key from the drawer. He walked up to the cell.

"Do not try anything. It would not be good for you."

"I'm not going to do anything except mess my pants if you don't let me out."

He unlocked the door and pushed it open for her.

"Thank you."

He pointed to the bathroom and she went inside. He wasn't worried she would escape. It had no windows. He wasn't worried she would lock herself inside. There was no lock on the inside, or the outside for that matter. He waited. After a few minutes, he heard the sound of the toilet flushing and running water. She came out drying her hands. He led her back to her cell. She made no attempt to resist. He locked the door behind her.

"Your dinner will be here soon."

Caron nodded blankly.

The guard turned to leave and then paused. He turned back toward the cell.

"You are in a bad place little girl. You need a friend."

Caron didn't answer.

"I could be that friend," he said. "I am Desmond."

"Why would you help me, Desmond?" she asked.

The guard smiled. "Perhaps you could do something for me. Something to make me be your friend."

"Like what?'

The guard put his hand on his zipper and started to lower it.

The door to the station banged open. A woman entered carrying a huge tray. The second policeman followed her. The woman placed the tray on one of the desks and uncovered it. There were three plates of food and bottles of water.

The woman passed a plate through the opening in the door of the cell to Caron. She placed the other trays on the desks. She smiled at Desmond. When she turned to leave he patted her on her buttocks. She squealed in obvious delight and swished her way out of the police station. Desmond and the other policeman ate in silence. When they were finished, they stacked their plates behind the front counter. They took Caron's plate and tossed the garbage into the can. Desmond watched Caron for a moment and then smiled.

"Benny, you can go if you want. I will watch the prisoner."

Benny looked surprised. "Are you sure?"

"Yeah. Go home and see that pretty wife of yours."

"Thanks, Des. If you are sure."

"Yeah. Go ahead. I got this now. See you tomorrow."

When Benny had left, Desmond returned his stare to Caron. He didn't speak. He had already told her what he wanted. Let her think about it.

41

The halogen lights had come on over the dock. Frank figured they were on a timer, but they might have been activated by the dark like those solar powered lights you put in your yard. The bugs were starting to swarm the lights. Frank liked the sounds of night. Frank was on his second cigar when he saw the headlights of Bruce's SUV. He kept his seat and waited. Frank liked to stay in control.

Bruce parked the car and let Thor out. The dog hopped out and looked around. He must have smelled Frank's scent because he took off toward him. Frank rubbed the dog's big head and waited for Bruce. Bruce was smiling as he approached. It was a good sign. It wasn't necessarily an omen like the Spartans liked, but a smile was always a good sign.

"Sorry I took so long. I'm glad you waited.'

"Not a problem. What you got?"

"I have a friend. He's an attorney and a former judge. He's a local. He's been out fishing all day, but I hooked up with him when he came in. Damn fishermen always stay until dark hoping for that big hit."

"And?"

"Yeah. I told him what was going on. He said that since Caron was taken into custody last night, but never charged, we might have a play. He figures they are waiting to hear about this John Keown's condition and to be told what to charge her with."

"What did he suggest?"

"He says he will go in the morning first thing and file a writ of something like habeas corpus. It means surrender the body, which, in this case, is Caron. They can only hold her for twenty-four hours without charging her. They have to release her on the spot."

"Can't they just charge her on the spot?'

"He thinks not. He thinks they are afraid to do anything without authorization from their boss. He hopes they will release her while they try to find out what to do."

"Will they go for it?"

"He thinks they will be afraid of messing up the case if they hold her. The writ is for immediate release. If they don't do it, it could be the technicality that lets her walk later. He says they won't take the chance."

Frank thought about it. It was a better plan than he had.

"We need to insulate you from any blowback from this. Call your guy and tell him that he was approached from someone who said they were the owners of Neptune's Dream about representing Caron. I told the cops that was where she crewed."

"Then he is in the clear too if she disappears."

"Exactly."

Bruce pulled out his cell phone and made the call. Frank couldn't hear the discussion, but he knew Bruce could handle it.

He noticed Tonello walking down the driveway. He briefly wondered where his car was. He waved and Tonello smiled and waved back. Tonello stood for a few seconds watching them on the dock and then went into the office. It struck Frank as odd that Tonello was here so late, but maybe he had stuff to do. Hell, maybe he would finally get hold of the shovel and start moving that big gravel pile.

Bruce came back over. "It's done. He said that was good. Keeps everybody safe just in case Caron isn't available later to be arrested and charged. He says they will get things squared away pretty quick. It being Sunday will slow them down, but he says you got a day at best. Probably only a few hours after he springs her."

"We got a flight at eight."

"I know. He is going to the station before seven. It will be quiet. There is always someone on duty even when the station is closed. And it is a hard time of day to find someone to tell you what to do. He will bring her here, then I will run her out to the airport."

"Us. I will wait here."

"What about Jenny and DC?"

"They know what to do. I will feel better if I'm on site."

"Do you want me to tell them the plan?"

"No. They don't need to know. They have enough to worry about."

Bruce seemed to drift into thought. He smiled at Frank.

"I really liked her, man."

"I could tell."

"Think you guys will ever be back?'

"I doubt it. But maybe we can set something up somewhere else."

"I would like that."

They stopped talking as Tonello approached. Thor ran over to see him. Tonello patted the dog and advanced on them. Frank didn't like the way he was walking. Something was wrong. He was stiff. In the twilight Frank hadn't seen the spear gun Tonello was carrying until he was ten yards away.

"What's up, man?" Bruce asked.

Tonello raised the weapon to his shoulder and sighted on the center of Frank's chest.

42

Little Bird guided the boat with practiced skill. The island was small and ringed with deep water. She drove slowly now, afraid she would ground the boat on the reef or something else. Dawg hurried to the front of the boat and removed the flag showing the red hand with spread fingers. Now was not the time to be noticed. They circled outside the marina and drove toward the place Tonello had described. His car would be waiting for them. Tonight, Dawg would have his revenge. Tonight, his cowardice would be forgotten.

"What are you doing?" Bruce asked Tonello.

Frank didn't speak. He was judging the distance. Tonello was too far away. He could never reach him before he squeezed the trigger. He had to close the distance. Sometimes the best way to do that was to move farther away. Frank started backing up on the dock. Tonello moved forward.

"I am sorry B Man. This is a thing that must be done."

"What are you talking about? What thing?"

"The Red Hand is coming. Lord Tosh is coming. I have promised this man to Dawg."

"Tonello, you are talking crazy, man. Maybe you got some bad dope or something. Put the spear gun down and let's talk."

Tonello swung the gun toward Bruce and then back toward Frank.

"I am warning you. I will shoot you if you do not do as I say."

Bruce held his hands up like he was surrendering.

"Okay. Okay."

Thor sensed the change in Tonello. His short golden hair stood up, mohawking along his back. He started snarling. His black lips drew back revealing his long canine teeth.

"Tie the dog up or I will shoot you."

Bruce moved toward Thor. The dog was tense. Its thick muscles seemed to vibrate along its back. Bruce took it by the collar and drew it toward the dog run. The run consisted of a long line with metal tether hanging from it. Thor barked twice in protest.

Frank moved out farther onto the dock. Tonello's head swung back and forth from Kane to Bruce and Thor. The speargun's sweep returned to point at Frank's chest.

"Stay where you are or I will shoot."

Frank took another step back. Tonello advanced onto the pier toward him.

"I will not tell you again."

The situation was almost out of control. The stalemate couldn't last. Tonello could not control them both and the dog. He had only one bolt in the weapon. He could kill one of them, but only one, and then what? Frank knew the smart play would be to put the bolt square into his chest and then take on Bruce using the empty gun as a club. The trouble was Thor. Would the dog attack? Would it just bark? Maybe if Bruce went down the dog would back off. Tonello was in over his head, and he was starting to realize it.

Thor broke free and ran toward the pier. He was barking wildly now. Tonello swung his head toward the charging dog. Frank and Tonello were about six or seven yards apart. Spanish Johnny called it killing distance. A man with a blade could reach you in one and a half seconds from this distance. It was faster then most men could draw and fire. But Tonello's weapon was already drawn and aimed. It was now or never.

Frank took two quick steps and leaped for Tonello. Tonello swung the spear gun back onto Frank. His finger tightened on the trigger. He was too slow. It had taken barely more than a second. Frank caught him and took him off his feet into the shallow water. Tonello dropped the spear gun and fought to rise from the water. Frank smashed his head under, grinding his face into the sand. Tonello fought with all the panicked strength a drowning man has. It wasn't going to be enough.

"No, Frank, don't kill him," Bruce screamed.

Frank never took his eyes off the back of Tonello's head in the dark water. He forced Tonello's face deeper into the sand. Thor stopped barking and walked around a few feet away in the shallow water.

"For God's sake, Frank, let him go."

Frank didn't flinch. He held Tonello beneath the water with his knee pressing into the young man's back. Tonello struggled. He faltered, and then went limp. He was dead.

Frank held him underwater for another minute. Bruce and Thor stared at him from the shore, neither moved. When Frank was positive that Tonello was dead, he released him. He let the body bob in the water. Frank trudged to shore.

Bruce looked shocked.

"Damn, Frank. He was my friend."

"No. He wasn't. He would have killed you."

Bruce stared at the body and shook his head. "I don't get it. What happened to him? What was that crazy shit he was talking about? Red Hand? Promised who?"

Frank gave a shrug. "We need to get rid of the body."

Bruce didn't answer right away. He looked at Tonello's body and then at Frank. He rubbed his hands over his head. He turned in a circle. He made some kind of decision. He nodded more to himself than to Frank.

"I'll take him out and drop him off in the ocean. The currents should carry him away. If someone finds his body, it will look like he drowned. Maybe got caught in a rip current swimming and didn't make it."

"You want me to go with you? I could take one of the jet skis and we could leave it out there too. Like he was on a ride and fell off."

"No. Thanks. If the jet ski is missing, it will make me need to report it. Get people looking for him. This way he just disappears. It happens." Bruce smiled. "Plus, one of those the damn things costs like twelve K."

"I would pay you for it."

"No. It's better this way. Simpler. I need to do it alone. It will give me a chance to say goodbye to him. Try to get my head around this."

"You going to be alright?"

"Yeah. I thought we were buds. This is so messed up."

"When you get back we will try to figure all this out."

"I better get to it. Let me tie up Thor. I know this freaked him out too. Dogs are sensitive."

Bruce led Thor to his outside run and hooked the leader to his collar. He patted his big head and knelt beside the dog. He pressed his face to the dog's ear and whispered.

"Good boy, Thor. Good boy. You did real good. You saved my ass."

Frank waded back into the water. He took the spear gun and put it on the dock. He drug Tonello's limp body out to one of the jet skis. Bruce looked forlorn.

"I guess we could tie his hand to the back and I could pull him."

Frank shook his head. "It will leave marks on his wrists. If you take him, you got to sit him in front of you."

"Shit."

"I know. I can do it. You wait here. I'll run him out for an hour and dump him. I can get back on my own. Straight out and straight back."

Bruce smiled and shook his head. "No. I'll do it. You would probably get lost. I know the spot. Help me get him into place."

Frank helped place Tonello in front of Bruce on the jet ski. Without power, the jet ski was ungainly and bobbed and tipped. Finally, Bruce got the body positioned.

"When I get back I am going to burn these damn clothes."

"Good idea. I will wait for you in the office."

Bruce pressed the ignition and the engine jumped to life. He revved it a couple of times and then disappeared into the night.

43

DC and Jenny decided to stay in Frank's room. They had all their clothes packed and their bags stacked near the door. The TV was on some old horror movie. It was Rob Zombie's Halloween. No matter where the kids in the movie ran, Michael Myers always showed up to threaten them.

"That's the way I feel," DC said. "Like we are surrounded and the bad guys are closing in."

"Don't give up."

"I'm not. It's just I would feel better if Frank had come back. I hope nothing has happened to him."

"What could happen to him? Hell, he's like the killer in this movie, unstoppable. He is probably just trying to work this stuff out with Bruce."

"Do you think we should go find them?"

"I do. But Frank said to stay here and that is what we need to do."

"She's my girl. I hate just sitting here, doing nothing."

"Me too…"

There was a loud knock on the door. They looked at each other. Couldn't be Frank. Cops? Jenny moved to the door and used the peep hole. There was a man standing outside. He looked like a tourist. He seemed nervous. He knocked again. Jenny slipped the chain on the door and opened it part way.

"Can I help you?"

"Yeah. Sorry. Is Mark here?"

"No, he stepped out."

The man looked around, unsure of what to do next. He wiped his moustache with his right hand. "Can you do me a favor?"

"If I can."

The man stretched his left hand out. There was bottle of Crown Royal in it.

"Mark looked after my kid today when I was… I was… Well, just tell him thanks. The bottle is my way of showing it."

He passed Jenny the bottle.

"I will do better. I promise," the man mumbled and shuffled down the hall.

DC straightened up when he saw the bottle.

"Sweet."

"We can't get drunk."

"I agree, but we can have a damn drink. I know I need one."

Jenny smiled and grabbed two of the hotel glasses. She gave one to DC. "It has to be an omen, right? It would be wrong not to have at least one drink."

"I agree. Only one. But make it a good one."

Jenny poured each glass half full.

Frank rummaged around in Bruce's office. There were several large bins marked 'Lost and Found'. Inside he found tee shirts, hats, sunglasses, and towels. He even found a tiger-striped thong bikini. Who forgets their bikini?

He dried himself off with one of the towels. He took a bottle of water out of the refrigerator and drank it down. He tossed the empty bottle into the plastic garbage can. He took out a second bottle. He sat on the old sofa that filled one side of the room. It didn't seem right to sit at Bruce's desk. The damp sofa smelled like sea water and sweat.

His mind drifted back, back to Hades and the Kryptea.

Cyrus had called him to come to the Asheville compound. Frank had gone. Cyrus was seated at his ornate desk. He was dressed like any other rich businessman would be, in gray chinos and a white long sleeve shirt. It had cuff links. Frank knew the shirt was Italian silk or Egyptian cotton or some hand woven organic fiber flown in on the wings of hummingbirds from the upper Hebrides. Cyrus wanted people to know he was rich. He wanted them to be covetous of what he possessed and fear what he had done to possess them himself. Cyrus looked at his Rolex watch. It was a big expensive thing.

Frank took the chair opposite him. It was after Helen, when her sacrifice had saved them and destroyed his friendship with Cyrus. Part of him hoped he wouldn't see Helen here. Part of him hoped for just a glimpse.

"Thanks for coming, Frank. I know it wasn't easy. I will keep this brief."

"I always come when you call. What's up? You said it was important."

"We got a serious problem."

"We like you and me, or we like the royal we?"

"The Spartans. All of us. Do you know what a nemesis is?"

"It is a Greek word for an enemy."

"Nemesis is the spirit of divine retribution for those who succumb to hubris."

"She is the bad shit that happens to people who start to believe their own lies."

"Well, simplified. She was also the daughter, according to some accounts, of Oceanus the ancient God of rivers. Do you know what the Nemesis of the Spartans is, Frank?"

"Feds."

"No, I think it is our reputation. As we grow, we garner more and more attention from law enforcement in its many forms. We try to insulate ourselves from direct criminal activity. We transfer funds off shore. We avoid collateral damage of civilians. We pay cops and judges and politicians for protection. We keep a low profile."

"Within reason."

"Of course. Of course. A great deal of our influence stems from the fear with which others hold us. That was one reason we formed the Spartan Kryptea."

"I thought it was to kill people."

"It is on its most basic level. Not everyone can do the hard things that need to be done. In ancient Sparta, only the most elite of the Spartan warriors were chosen from the agoge. They were chosen in secret. They were given carte blanche to execute Helots or anyone in Sparta that was a threat to her safety. The elite of the elite."

"Like the Navy Seals."

"Exactly. Better trained. Better equipped. The best of the best." Cyrus templed his fingers in front of his face as he was prone to do when searching for the right words. "Do you now the story of Cleomenes the Spartan King?"

"The basics maybe. Wasn't he Leonidas' half brother?"

"Excellent. He never attended the agoge. Did you know that?"

"I thought all Spartan males went through it as a right of passage."

"Not when you are to become king. Some youths die in the agoge. It was a brutal training ground. They didn't want to take the chance with their future king."

"Didn't Leonidas go?"

"He was not suppose to become king, so he got no deferment. Cleomenes was a ruthless king. He hated the enemies of Sparta, specifically Argos and Persia. He did whatever he felt was necessary for Sparta. He bribed the Delphic oracles. He slaughtered thousands of Argives, he took hostages from Aegina, one of Sparta's allies, because they signed a treaty with Persia. He fostered a lot of enemies. Late in his career, he took to drinking his wine straight..."

"I remember that," Frank said. He smiled at the history lesson. "The Spartans prided themselves on being in control. They always cut their wine with water. They even brought in Helots and made them drink uncut wine so the younger Spartans could see how the Helots acted like fools when they were drunk."

"Cleomenes supposedly went mad from this. He started poking people in the face with his staff of office. He deposed the other Spartan king with someone he could control. He became an embarrassment to the point that the Spartans had him put in chains and locked up in prison. He was found one morning dead in his cell."

"Who killed him? He was still king."

"There are a lot of theories. He may have talked a guard into giving him a knife with which he killed himself. The god Apollo may have caused him to kill himself because he had corrupted his oracles at Delphi. There is also a little known theory that the Kryptea came to see him in the night."

Frank nodded. "They did what had to be done for Sparta. Even to the king."

Cyrus caught and held his gaze. "We have a problem with Neil. Hades has to be stopped."

Frank set up straighter. "Whoa. What do you mean stopped? He is one of the Spartan founders. He is untouchable. He is a god. And he is my friend."

"Even the gods can suffer from hubris."

"What did he do? What could he have done for you to be talking this shit? Hell, we are criminals. We do lots of bad stuff."

"He is selling children," Cyrus said.

Frank didn't speak. The silence lasted for ten seconds before Frank could respond.

"What are you talking about? How can he be selling children?"

"You know I give the Gods a great deal of latitude in how they make money. There are very few taboos. But this is different. It has the potential to bring a lot of heat when he gets caught. And believe me he will get caught. Sooner or later everyone gets caught, and let's face it he's not that smart."

"Are you sure?"

"Yes. When I heard, I brought him in and had a talk with him."

"What did he say?"

"He said that as one of the Gods he could do whatever he wanted. That was what we had promised him. I tried to explain, but he wouldn't listen to reason. He can be stubborn."

Frank got to his feet. "Fuck, Cyrus. What you are asking me to do isn't right."

"You jumped him in. I told you he was your responsibility."

"There has to be another way. Let me talk to him."

"Sure. Talk all you want. The little bastard has his heels dug in on this. He was proud of the scheme. Told me it was brilliant."

"Lay it out for me."

"He got hooked up with this woman who runs a dozen orphanages for the state. She had a little drug problem. They got together and hatched this scheme. There are so many lost kids in the system no one looks for them. Paperwork is lost or misfiled or forged. They slip kids out of the orphanage and then sell them overseas using some of our Spartan contacts."

Frank ran his hands through his hair. "Fuck me. That's crazy. What is he thinking? He's already got plenty of money. This thing will blow up big on him."

"On all of us. Now he won't even take my calls."

"Maybe I can reason with him? He listens to me."

"He doesn't listen to anyone anymore. But you go ahead and try. If he won't come around, then you have to do what has to be done."

Frank didn't speak. He struggled with his emotions. He loved Neil, but this was sick stuff. It was so twisted Frank couldn't even have imagined it.

"Okay. I'll go see him. See what I can do."

"Frank, take Spanish Johnny with you. Hades has his own bodyguards. If you have to end him, you might need the backup."

Frank nodded.

"And one more thing. If it has to go down it needs to look like an accident. The other Spartans can't ever know. No one can, except the three of us."

"I hear you."

"I got a fifty gallon drum of ether on a truck in the garage. Masnick rigged a timer. It's untraceable. It will look like he was cooking meth again and got careless. Spanish is downstairs waiting for you."

"He on board with this?"

"He knows that this is what the Kryptea does."

Frank shook his head. "This is some hard stuff, brother."

"Taking a man's life always is. Go see him for yourself, then decide. But I am telling you he is gone. He is smoking meth again and he is as mad as Cleomenes ever was. It is just a matter of time before he brings the heat on us. The public will wake up and scream for our heads."

Frank remembered just walking out. There was nothing else to say. He was walking a dark path. What Cyrus was asking him to do was crazy. Maybe it was a test. Cyrus loved testing people on their loyalty.

Spanish Johnny was seated in the front seat of the silver Ford 250. The truck bed was covered with a heavy black tarp that disguised their cargo. Spanish Johnny had been one of his closest friends until he had met Helen. Spanish had wanted her eliminated as a witness. Frank had objected. They had fallen to words and Frank had almost killed him. Frank had taken Helen with him. Spanish had reported the treasonous act. Frank and Helen had been called to the compound in Asheville for judgment.

The meeting was an opportunity for Frank to redress the wrong he had done to Spanish Johnny. All he had to do was kill Helen. He could not. He had chosen trial by combat. He was wounded and weak, but Cyrus had placed him against three other of the Spartan Gods, Spanish Johnny, Ares, and Atlas. It was to be a fight to the death with ancient Spartan lacunas, a type of Greek short sword used by the ancient Spartans. It was an obvious death sentence. There seemed no way out. In a brilliant and unbearably cruel moment of clarity, Helen had realized how to save them both. She had become Cyrus' woman and the first of the Spartan Goddesses.

He had not spoken to Spanish Johnny since.

They rode in silence for the first four hours. Finally, Spanish spoke.

"I would like a word, Frank."

Frank kept his eyes on the road.

"What do you need to say to me now?"

"About what happened. The stuff with Helen. I was angry. I felt betrayed and dishonored."

Frank did not respond.

"I can't turn back the clock any more than I can move the sun across the sky. I was wrong," Spanish Johnny said. "Maybe I was jealous that she could come between us. We were brothers."

Frank only nodded to acknowledge his words.

"I overreacted."

"And the physical trial? Was that your idea? Three against one?"

"No. No, that was all Cyrus. I was willing to fight. Hell, I was willing to kill you if I could. Man to man. One on one."

"You wouldn't have made it. Even on one leg I would have taken you."

"I know. But honor demanded it."

Frank nodded. He understood about honor and its requirements. "We could have worked it out without taking it to the council."

"I realize that now. But I didn't then. It all went to shit anyway. You lost the girl and I lost my best friend. Vanity."

"You were always vane."

"And you were always an asshole."

Frank smiled and turned toward him. "It was painful for us all. We all lost."

"Except fucking Cyrus. He always wins. He lives in the eye of the storm while chaos swirls all around. He never gets touched. The prick."

"The perks of his position."

"For now," Spanish Johnny said. "For now."

"What does that mean?"

"Things change. No man lives forever. Cyrus might not always lead us. That's all I am saying."

Frank thought about his words. He made no reply about them except to add, "Why tell me this?"

"I want it behind us. I want our brotherhood restored. If that is possible?"

Frank thought about it. It had not been personal for Spanish Johnny. It had been a matter of honor. Maybe he could get past it. Frank nodded.

"It is done. What happened is forgotten. And for you, has your honor been restored?"

"Yes. I would have us brothers again."

Frank extended his left hand and Spanish Johnny clasped it in a firm handshake.

"Good. Now let's take care of this business with Hades."

"If it's true, it's a mess."

A few minutes later Spanish Johnny said, "Helen is a remarkable woman. It would have been a shame if she were taken from this world."

Looking back at it now, Frank new it had all been a lie, all except maybe the last part about Helen. Spanish had been trying to placate a potential lethal enemy. He had lulled Frank into a sense of safety all the while planning his revenge. Spanish Johnny had shown his true colors when he had driven his knife into Frank after the Spartans had fallen. His final words to Frank still haunted him. 'For Aphrodite.' Frank still wasn't sure what he had meant.

44

Thor's deep bark snapped him back. He heard a car glide to a stop outside. Thor was still tied up and after the first warning bark fell silent.

Now what, he wondered. He stayed sitting where he was. He heard a door open and close. The footsteps were light and quick. They came up onto the porch. The knock was delicate. The voice was feminine.

"Hello. Is anyone in der?"

Frank didn't bother opening the door. He just shouted. "We are closed. Come back tomorrow."

"Is de boss here? I need to see de boss."

"He's not here. Come back tomorrow. If you want a job, you got to talk to him."

Thor was barking again. He seemed agitated.

"Where is he?"

"I don't know. Come back tomorrow."

The voice stopped. He heard movement on the porch. She was leaving. Then the sound of creaking boards again.

"Excuse me. Can I leave him a note? I need to leave de boss man a note."

Frank was tired of her whining. He went to the door and opened it. The girl standing on the porch was very pretty. She was small and muscular. Her breasts were huge on her tiny doll frame. They strained against the confines of her white tee shirt. She wasn't wearing a bra. Frank was only a man, and couldn't help but steal a quick glance before moving to her pretty face. Her smile was broad. Her teeth were white. The fact that her head was shaven didn't lessen her beauty. It made it more exotic.

"Hi," she said in a voice that suddenly dripped sexual honey.

It did its magic. Frank was distracted. He was frozen by her beauty. He didn't even see Dawg step from the side of the doorway swinging the shovel.

The first blow caught him in the face and staggered Frank backward. His front teeth were broken off at the gingiva. Blood poured from his ruined face. Frank tried to regain control of his legs and battle through the pain. Dawg stepped into the room after him. Years of his private shame drove his next blow. Dawg wound up like a baseball player and the shovel swung again.

Frank tried to raise a hand to deflect it, but it was useless. The blow was higher and struck his forehead, driving him to the floor of the office. Frank rolled to his knees and tried to rise. Dawg struck him again across his back and shoulders. Frank hesitated. Dawg hit him again and he fell. Dawg raised the shovel over his head. He would crush Frank's skull with his next blow.

Helen and her friends spent their last night ordering room service. After the trays had been carried away, the liquor had started to flow in earnest. Exquisite glasses of wine were replaced with liquor. They had decided to spend their last night together enjoying each other's company.

Everyone was relaxing on the private deck with a drink in their hand. Ronnie was leaning back on one of the couches, smiling like a king surrounded by his harem. He was wearing his new watch. Johanna was playing bartender and inventing new drinks. Ashley was sitting at the bar sampling each new concoction before trying it on the others. Meredith was quiet for the first time on the trip. Helen thought she was either being introspective or working out a plan of some kind. Helen herself thought about Frank. She fantasized that he somehow had tracked her to her hotel and would come to take her away with him. She wondered what it would be like to make love to him again. The thought sent a tremble of electricity through her body.

Dawg raised the shovel over his head. Frank rolled onto his back. He tried to raise a hand to deflect the killing blow. It was a useless gesture. Little Bird stepped between Dawg and Frank.

"No, me bruder. No."

Dawg's eyes saw only red. The killing fever was on him. Little Bird placed a tiny hand on his arm.

"Dawg, you can no do dis ting. Dreadmon has you in he grip. Free youself."

He stared into her almond shaped eyes. Her delicate fingers tightened on his arm. Her beauty won through the killing fever. The madness seemed to fade.

"Dreadmon," Dawg said from far away. "Dreadmon."

"He has brought de killing madness. Do not succumb."

Dawg lowered the shovel. "They say de Frank Kane can na be killed."

"Then let us discover it ourselves as I peel his flesh from his body."

Dawg stared at Frank who lay semiconscious on the floor.

"One more lick."

Little Bird shook her head. She smiled her seductive smile. "You can na. If he were to die, what den? Lord Tosh would place you upon de altar. He would flay you flesh as punishment and tribute."

Dawg shivered at the thought.

Little Bird stepped in closer pressing her body against his. "He is meant as tribute."

Dawg dropped the shovel. The blade was wet with thick red blood.

"As you say, Little Bird. I will spare him. For now."

Little Bird pressed her body against him. Her voice was thick with lust.

"I have never seen you like dis, Dawg. It wakens I own desires. I would have you inside me."

Dawg smiled. He leaned down and kissed her fiercely. He ran a hand over her breasts and she arched her back like a cat being petted.

"There is time for dat?"

"Who can say how long it took to find him. We can take all de time we like."

Little Bird pulled his mouth to hers. Their kissing grew feverish and she started to remove her tee shirt. Dawg stopped her.

"Wait. First we must secure our prize."

Little Bird looked crestfallen. She was not used to being rejected. It flamed her passion even more.

"We must bind him."

They looked around the office until they found the roll of silver duct tape.

"You do de feet. I will do de hands."

They wrapped the loops of thick duct tape around Frank, securing him. When they were done, Dawg rewrapped him again. He was taking no chances with Frank Kane.

"Now?" Little Bird said in a voice that creaked with its own hunger.

Dawg liked the feeling of power. It seemed to surge through his veins.

"Back de car up to de porch and open de trunk. Let him wait for us dere."

"Like a steel coffin. A fitting resting place."

Dawg smacked her on her round buttocks as she started to leave. She turned back and leapt into his arms kissing him roughly.

"You will pay for makin' me wait for you snake."

"Good," Dawg smiled.

When she left, Dawg knelt beside Frank and whispered in his ear.

"Dreadmon, come for you, Spartan. He come from de world of fires. From de place of no hope. Lord Tosh will lead you to him through you pain. Soon Dreadmon will walk dis world again. And I shall walk beside him."

Dawg reached into his pants pocket. He withdrew a small vial of black powder. He forced Frank's bloody lips open and poured the powder inside.

"Bat give dis to me. It will make you dreams you nightmares. You will feel de terror in you soul as we skin you alive. Now sleep and await you death. And know dis ting. It is Dawg dat has brought you here to dis place of doom. Its is Dawg."

Little Bird threw the door open. She seemed shocked to see Dawg leaning over Frank's body. Dawg looked embarrassed.

"I be telling him goodbye."

Little Bird smiled. "Can we lift him?"

Dawg shook his head. "He be made of stone. We must drag him outside."

Working together, they drug Frank outside onto the porch. The trunk of Tonello's car was open. The trunk was full of PFDs and clothing and trash. Dawg and Little Bird scooped it out and left it on the porch deck and the ground. Roughly, they manhandled Frank into the trunk. Dawg slammed the trunk. He smiled at the closed trunk. Little Bird stood beside him. She traced a long finger up his thigh. His manhood rose and strained against his pants. She grasped him through the fabric.

"Dere is a nice couch inside."

Dawg kissed her and drew her tee shirt over her head. Her large breasts swung free. He gently rubbed them and then pinched the nipples hard. She moaned. And sought his mouth. Their kiss broke and she forced his mouth onto her breast. She howled as he bit at her stiff nipple. She pushed his head away and took his hand. She backed up onto the porch and pulled him through the door.

"I want you to fuck me long and hard."

Dawg kicked the door closed behind him. That was exactly what he had planned.

45

Bruce drove Tonello's body out into the Judas night. The Yamaha jet ski cut through the calm waters like a shark's fin. Darkness circled him in the black water. He checked his watch. It had been an hour. He slowed the throttle. Without power, the jet ski resumed bobbing awkwardly.

Bruce spoke to Tonello's body. "What happened to you? We were friends."

Tonello did not answer.

The jet ski bobbed.

"I never mistreated you. I never wronged you. I never talked shit about you. I treated you straight up like a man. Yet you could do something like this? Man, this is so fucked up."

Bruce started to cry. He hugged Tonello's lifeless body.

"It's not right. It's just not right."

Frank loved the ocean as much as Bruce did. It was a level of connection they had always shared. Frank had told him in prison that the ocean swallowed your mistakes. It swept away evidence better than anything else. It had shocked Bruce at the time because he had never thought of the need to dispose of a body before then. He was a criminal. He was not a killer. Frank was a killer. Seeing him kill Tonello shook something in his core. There was a darkness in Frank. It was that darkness that had protected Frank from the other killers in prison. It was a darkness that had kept Bruce safe in prison too. It wasn't all myth and lies. Frank Kane was a man killer. He was a man to be feared.

Bruce gently pushed Tonello's body off the jet ski into the sea. The body floated on the waves. The body would never be found. If it were, there was no way to tie it to Bruce. Bruce restarted the engine. A cool breeze caused him to shiver in his wet clothes.

Bruce had made his choice. Frank was still his friend. He had to help him. He had to help Caron. He thought of Jenny and her tender kisses. He felt a deep sadness as he turned the jet ski back toward shore. It felt like something inside of him had broken.

Jenny couldn't stop crying. DC patted her back trying to sooth her.

"I thought the booze would make it better."

"Sometimes it just amplifies your feelings."

"I feel like I am dying inside."

"I know. I know."

"We have to get her back."

"We will. Frank won't let us down. He never has."

Jenny popped her head up. She stared with red eyes at DC. "Do you really believe that? Do you really believe he can rescue her?"

DC took her face in his hands. His voice was firm.

"Yes, I do. If anyone can pull this off it is Frank fucking Kane."

Jenny wiped her running nose on her shirt. She grabbed the box of tissues off the bed and wiped her eyes. Her breathing was ragged. She took deep breaths until it calmed.

"I do too."

"Good."

"I mean it. It is time I quit acting like a little girl about this. I have to believe everything will really work out."

"I hear you."

Jenny leaned forward and kissed DC on the top of his head. She smiled. "You are a good man. She is lucky to have you. We all are."

"I don't know about that."

"It's true. I'm going to try to get some sleep."

She lay back on the bed. She closed her eyes for a dozen seconds before bolting back up.

"Remember to set the alarm."

"I will."

She lay back down. A few seconds later she was up again.

"Leave a wake up call too, just in case."

"I will. I did. I promise."

This time she was still for only a couple of seconds before bolting up again.

"Did we arrange the cab already?"

"It is already done. Now lay back and get some rest."

"You should try to sleep too."

"I will. Once I know you are down."

Jenny lay back down. This time she stayed down. DC sat unmoving on the bed until she started to snore lightly. He got up and went over to the table and got the bottle of Crown Royal. He got his glass and plopped down in one of Frank's chairs on the outdoor balcony. He poured himself another drink. He wasn't sleepy. He took a sip. The Crown was smooth after the first swallow burned away your taste buds, he thought. He took another drink. He stared out at the night wondering what Caron was doing. What she was thinking. Was she afraid? Did she miss him like he missed her? He lifted the bottle and stared at the remains. It was going to be a long night, but the bottle should take him through it. Where in hell was Frank, he wondered.

Dawg hitched his pants back up around his waist. He was smiling. He felt stronger than he had ever felt in his life. He knew it was power from Dreadmon. It was an omen. Little Bird was looking at him differently now. She seemed fascinated by him. She was still nude. She rose from the sofa and approached him.

She ran a hand over his chest. It was still wet with sweat. She wiped it with her finger and drew the finger to her mouth. She sucked the sweat from his finger.

"I taste you power, Dawg."

Dawg chuckled, but did not speak. Little Bird was crazy.

"Dreadmon blesses you. He has made you a ting to be feared."

Dawg pulled her into his arms.

"And fucked?"

"Yes. Dat too. When we return home, I will move into you room."

Dawg nodded. He knew Little Bird was attracted to power, hoping to draw some of it into herself. He pitied Roach. He had lost his woman and didn't even know it.

"Get dressed. We must take our prize to Lord Tosh."

"He will be pleased."

Dawg took out his phone and called his cousin again. Tonello's phone rang unanswered. It was a strange thing. Perhaps he was afraid of the final commitment. Perhaps he was afraid of Frank Kane. Dawg had shown Frank Kane who was to be feared. He smiled to himself as he replayed in his mind the beating he had given his old enemy.

Little Bird, now dressed, paused to give him a delicate kiss on his lips. She went out to the car to wait. Dawg followed.

46

Some time after dinner, Caron was allowed to use the facilities. When she came out, the other policeman who had been there was still gone. She had hoped he would return. Desmond was still there. He was smiling.

"What are you doing still here? I thought you were off tonight."

"I let Benny go home. I told him I would watch over you."

Caron went back to her cell. On the nearest desk was a stack of blankets and a pillow. They looked freshly laundered. She tried to ignore them. She sat on the floor of her cell and did not speak.

Desmond pulled the door closed behind her. He walked to the blankets and lazily drew his hand over them. He turned back to her with a smiled.

"I have your comforts as I promised."

Caron did not answer.

"You still need a friend. We can trade favors."

Caron turned her face toward the wall. The smile left Desmond's face. He walked to the air conditioner and turned it down to the coldest setting. He sat at the other desk and took out a Playboy magazine. He started reading. He smiled as a thought took him. He turned back to the cell.

"I know you are cold. Show me your breasts and I will give you a blanket."

Caron didn't answer. She tried to keep her face passive.

"What would it hurt? One quick flash. That is all I want. Just let me see them."

Caron remained silent.

"It is a little thing. What would it hurt? I can be your friend. I can help you."

Caron was stunned. And yet on some level she wasn't. With men in power it was always about breaking you down. One step at a time. First show your breasts. Then let me touch them. Do this for me and I will do that for you. Each small step drew you closer to the abyss. She wouldn't go there. Never again.

"Fuck you," Caron said.

Desmond laughed. "Very well. Be cold. I don't care." He paused for effect. "It is a long night. I might just decide to take what I want."

Caron made no response. That was the end game for him. He would lie to her to get her to have sex with him. He would barter. He would beg. He would threaten. Maybe he would rape her. Maybe he wouldn't. She would not make it easy for him. For the briefest of seconds she considered allowing him into her cell. She imagined luring him in and then somehow escaping and getting back to her friends. She pictured him doubled over from her knee strike to his groin. She brushed the thought away. It wouldn't work. She would fail. Caron fought the urge to cry.

Dawg and Little Bird pulled the car in near the cove where the boat waited. Lord Tosh and the others milled around. They appeared upset. They did not like to wait.

They all noticed the change in Dawg. They noticed the way Little Bird seemed to defer to him. Dawg did not walk. He strode like a king. He felt like a king.

"You be gone long time," Lord Tosh said.

"Dreadmon has provided a gift," Dawg said.

He opened the trunk and the others moved to peer inside. Frank Kane lay unconscious and secured.

"We have found the man we seek."

"Dawg beat him down like a mon's mon." Little Bird said with obvious pride.

Dawg beamed with the praise. "This is de Frank Kane. De killer of men. De Spartan devil. De undead man."

Lord Tosh spun in a circle clapping his hands. His smile split his face.

"A fine ting. A fine ting. And you cousin?"

"We did not find him."

"Too bad. Too too bad."

"Do you want me to look for him?"

"No. We will seek him afterwards. He will complete us. But we no can wait. We must do dis ting dis night while the signs align."

"Yes, Lord Tosh."

"Put him into de boat."

They pulled Frank Kane from the trunk. His hands and feet were still secured. Hands patted Dawg on the back. More words of praise were whispered into his ears. Little Bird let her hand trail lightly across his back. Her touch promised a world of unspoken pleasures.

"He is made of iron," Bat said. "No man can weigh dis much."

"Help me lift him," Roach said.

They dragged Frank onto the boat and left him lying on the deck.

"Take us to the little rock island, Little Bird," Lord Tosh said.

The motor rumbled to life and Little Bird deftly backed it out of the small inlet. She turned the boat northward. The rock island was not far. It dominated the horizon like the hand of Poseidon reaching for the sky.

Bruce drove the jet ski up onto the sandy beach. Thor barked his excitement at Bruce's return. Bruce called out to Frank. There was no answer. He called again. He wondered where Frank could have gone. He had promised to wait. He didn't have a car. He didn't know anyone else on the island except that blonde woman from the dance. Bruce knew Frank would not have contacted her. Something was wrong.

Bruce went to Thor and rubbed his big head. The dog was agitated. Something had spooked the boxer. Bruce unhooked Thor from the dog run.

Bruce caught a whiff of something, but couldn't place the smell. He saw the litter of trash and debris on the steps of the office. What was going on, he wondered.

He opened the office door. He saw one of Frank's shoes on the floor. He saw the blood. He saw the bloody shovel lying on the floor. There was a small dried pool of it. It left a dark greasy drag trail out the door and onto the porch. The smell in the office was heavier. It was an elemental smell. It was blood and sex.

Bruce closed the office door and went onto the porch. He could tell a car had backed up to the porch. That was where they had put Frank before they had hauled him away. He knelt over the garbage. He recognized the PFD as Tonello's. He also recognized some of the clothes and the beach towel. They had taken Tonello's car. These were the people Tonello had been waiting for. They had taken Frank.

What had Tonello been saying? Bruce tried to remember. It had all sounded like gibberish. There were names. Lord Tosh. Dreadmon. Dawg. He had ignored them. There was something about a sacrifice. Dark magic. Shit. He couldn't remember.

Bruce paced around the porch. He didn't know what to do. How could he find Frank? How could he help his friend? Bruce took a deep breath. He tried to center himself. He slowed his heart rate like he did before trying to catch a big wave. He slipped easily into the familiar zone. He let the night wash over him. He felt for the swell. What would Frank do, he wondered? It came as obviously as the big wave. Something. Do something. Get up. Commit. Let the wave guide you.

Bruce hurried down to his car. He retrieved the spear gun and placed it onto the passenger's seat. He let Thor into the back seat. He would search for Frank. If they were coming by boat, he would find the site and rescue Frank. The how didn't matter. Just like riding the wave. The wave showed you how to ride it. When he found Frank, he would know what to do.

Thor seemed to sense his mood and gave a deep bark of approval. Bruce patted his head and was rewarded with a lick to his hand.

"Let's go."

47

Frank awoke in a barren limestone cavern. He was nude. Blood seeped from his old bullet wounds and the cut across his stomach that Spanish Johnny had made. Thick iron shackles hung from his hands. The heavy chains were black and flecked with rust. He could feel them biting into his flesh. They seemed very old.

The air was heavy with the stench of sulfur and smoke. The smoke smelled like burning flesh. Frank's ears rung with distant screams. The way behind was blocked with wind carved stone. There was only the way forward. Frank moved toward the sounds of torment and the flashes of fire.

His muscles ached as if he had been tortured. His steps were little more than shuffles. The passage widened. The ground was littered with bones. Human bones. The white bones were barren of any flesh and looked like they had been broken by tremendous force. They were dry and brittle under his bare feet and crumbled to dust under his weight. Ahead, the flames flashed brighter and the wails of torment rose. Frank moved forward.

Unseen voices screeched and snarled as he passed. He could almost feel their fetid breath on his skin. The passage spread into a huge cavern. Lava flowed like red rivers around the blackened stone. Steam swirled in macabre patterns that seemed to be living creatures. All about the room, people-- men, women, and even children writhed on hooks. Bodies dangled from chains with their skin flayed from them. Screams rose from the people impaled on wooden stakes. In the midst of the charnel house was an onyx black throne. A monster set upon the throne watching the tableau around him.

Dreadmon rose as Frank moved forward. Dreadmon was a dozen feet tall with skin as red as fresh blood. His fangs clacked hungrily as Frank approached. Huge yellow taloned hands opened and closed in anticipation. No sound issued from the daemon, but its words spoke into Frank's mind.

"Bow before me."

Frank looked around him for a weapon. There was none.

"You are lost. Bow before me, Frank Kane."

Little Bird eased the boat up to the stone dock on Falcon's Aerie. Dawg flipped the thick plastic bumpers over the side. Bat hopped over the side and secured the boat's lines to the rock pilings. Dawg climbed out of the boat. He turned to Lord Tosh.

"I will run ahead and find de best spot for de sacrifice."

Lord Tosh waved him away with a long thin hand. Dawg took one of the flashlights and hurried away. Lord Tosh spoke to the others.

"Unload de boat while we wait."

Roach and Bat began to gather their supplies and place them on the dock. They dragged Frank out of the boat and dropped him onto the sea slick rock. Lord Tosh disappeared into the cabin of the boat. He started searching his music for the appropriate songs to accompany their spiritual journey.

When he saw Lord Tosh go into the cabin, Roach climbed into the boat and moved up to the captain's chair where Little Bird still sat. Roach placed an arm around Little Bird and leaned in to kiss her neck. She shook him away.

"No. Do as Lord Tosh commands."

Roach slunk away. He didn't understand how she could be so hot last night and so cold tonight.

Dawg came running down the path. He was smiling.

"Lord Tosh," he said.

Lord Tosh poked his head out of the cabin. "There be a place?"

"It be perfect. It be at de very top, near a ruined house."

"Good. Dreadmon provides de place. Take de Frank Kane and prepare him."

Bat went to help Dawg lift Frank's body. Frank stirred. A moan slipped from his split lips. They struggled to lift Frank's bulk.

Lord Tosh snapped his fingers and pointed at the two men. "I need to tell you what to do, Roach?"

Roach jumped at the recrimination. He climbed out of the boat and helped lift Frank's body. It was a difficult climb uphill, and they struggled to carry Frank. Little Bird watched them go. She was smiling. She felt more alive than she had ever felt. She could feel the elder gods moving around her.

Lord Tosh began singing as he prepared their implements. It was a song by the Rolling Stones.

"Please allow me to introduce myself," Lord Tosh sang. "I am a man of wealth and taste."

Little Bird knew this song. It was Sympathy for the Devil. She smiled. She started dancing. Lord Tosh smiled at her and they danced together on the dark stone dock. They moved around each other swaying to the music. Lord Tosh took her by one hand and spun her about the stone anchorage. It would have looked foolish if it were not so terrifying.

In the darkness an osprey cried.

48

Frank moved toward Dreadmon. The daemon lord was smiling.

"There is no hope here," the daemon said.

Frank's hands were hindered by the tight chains. He swung a double fisted blow at Dreadmon. The demon easily avoided the blow and struck Frank with a savage backhand blow. Frank tumbled backward. He struggled to his feet.

"There is no hope."

Frank limped forward. Dreadmon hit him with a powerful uppercut. Frank crashed down onto the stone and rolled toward the molten lava that crept like fiery tributaries through the stone. The heat seared his flesh making, it blister and blacken. He screamed in pain.

"No hope. Bow to me."

Frank came forward again. He tried to kick the demon, but Dreadmon caught his leg. Dreadmon crushed the bones in the leg and shoved Frank to the ground.

"Bow to me."

Frank tried to stand. He weaved like a drunken man. Dreadmon struck him across the face shattering his teeth. Frank fell again. He tried to rise. His legs did not seem to be working. The gibbering voices rose in their hunger. The wails of the damned rose with his agony.

"There is no hope."

Frank saw her step from behind the black throne. It was Helen. She was wearing a white gown like the ancient Spartan women wore. It was slit up the sides to give her long legs ease of movement. Her golden hair was piled up high on her head in the ancient style. She was smiling. She moved past Dreadmon. He did not seem to see her.

Helen knelt beside Frank. She placed a cool hand to his head. Her eyes were alive with something Frank took to be love.

"Bow to me," Dreadmon roared.

She leaned in closer. Her perfect lips lightly brushed his ear. It sent shock waves through him. She whispered a single sentence.

"Frank Kane does not kneel."

Frank felt new strength He pictured the old Popeye cartoons when Popeye finally ate spinach. The imagery made him laugh out loud.

The sound of laughter seemed to strike Dreadmon like a blow. He took a step back. Frank rose. With a gentle twist of his wrists, the chains shattered and fell away. Dreadmon's eyes grew wider. A roar like storm-wind burst from Dreadmon. The demon charged.

Frank stepped aside and struck the demon lord. It sounded like a sledge hammer striking a side of beef. Dreadmon staggered. Frank struck again and again. Each blow seemed to build in force. Dreadmon screamed. A savage kick from the once broken leg hurled Dreadmon back into the flames.

Frank stood watching the liquid flames, waiting for Dreadmon to reappear. They always came back in the movies. Helen stepped up beside him. She was smiling.

"There isn't much time. Find your way out before it is too late."

She shimmered and disappeared. Frank looked around. On the other side of the cavern, Frank saw a dark opening. He walked toward it.

They laid Frank out on the ground near the ruins of Falcon's home. The ground was flat and covered in the thin covering of fertile earth that Falcon had imported. Old metal cages were scattered about, broken and empty. The salt air had eaten away the bars. The once well kept gardens were overgrown and neglected. Twisted trees rose belligerently from the once thick orchards. The charred remains of a once great house rested against the stone pinnacle bracing its rear.

Dawg took a clasp knife from his pocket and cut the duct tape binding Frank's hands and feet.

"Cut his clothes off," Roach said.

Dawg shook his head.

"After he is secured to the stakes. I do not trust this one."

Roach did not protest. He sensed the changes in Dawg. He was afraid to contradict him. Dawg handed the flashlight to Roach.

Dawg and Bat spread Frank out spread eagle on the ground. Roach held the big light. Bat tied the leather strip to Frank's left wrist. He stretched the arm out and tied it to the wooden stake. Once the stake was secured, he held it upright for Dawg. Dawg took the heavy wooden mallet and drove it deep into the earth. Once it was fast in the ground, Bat moved to the right wrist. He tied the leather band to the arm and then to the stake. He extended the arm and held the stake for Dawg. Dawg struck it, but the ground was too rocky. Roach swung the light around the ground. Bat moved the arm closer to Frank where the dirt was deeper. Dawg tapped it a couple of times to be sure he was not over rock, and then drove the stake into the ground.

Between the pain and the hallucinations, Frank clawed himself awake. He did not open his eyes. He took stock of his situation. He mentally scanned his body. He flexed his legs slightly. Although the muscles ached, nothing was broken. His right arm was tied to something. He gave it a slight tug, but it seemed locked into place. The left arm was similarly bound, but he was able to stretch his hand and feel a wooden stake that was holding it down. He wrapped his fingers around the stake and started trying to move it.

His face hurt. He touched his teeth with his tongue and was rewarded with an electric shock of severe pain. The pain was more intense than when he had been shot. He moaned, unable to ignore the pain. His front teeth were broken shards. His lips were busted and his head swam with pain.

He felt the tremors of the mallet driving the stake into the ground that secured his right leg. He heard the voices around him. He felt the stake at his left arm give slightly. He exerted more strength. He could not allow himself to be immobilized. He would not kneel. He raised his left leg slightly. The men saw it immediately.

"He is waking up, Dawg."

"Hurry. Hold his leg down. We are almost finished."

Frank felt rough hands trying to stretch his left leg outward. He resisted just enough to inhibit them without angering them. He wanted them to think he was still unconscious. It was now or never. He had a plan. Frank Kane always had a plan.

"Dawg," Frank whispered. "Dawg."

They stopped working on his leg.

"He knows your name," Roach said. "How does he know your name?"

"He comes. He comes through me," Frank said.

He knew they were looking at him. He had their attention. His right hand pulled harder on the stake. He arched his body upward and moaned like he was in the throes of a spiritual possession.

"Dreadmon comes. There is no hope. There is no hope."

"Dreadmon," a voice said. "He sees Dreadmon."

"From the caverns of fire. From the black throne. He comes with warning."

The one whose voice he recognized from Bruce's office spoke clearly. This was the one called Dawg. He arched his body again and moaned.

"What is de warning?"

"For Lord Tosh. The warning is for Lord Tosh."

"What is the warning?" Dawg asked.

"Only for Dawg's ears. His alone. There is no hope. There is fire."

"He knows of de Cavern of Lost Hope, where Dreadmon lives. He can see him."

"What is the warning?" Dawg asked again.

Frank whispered the words as he seemed to slip into unconsciousness again.

"Dawg must be the vessel. Dawg must carry the warning to Lord Tosh. Only Dawg. Tell him...tell him...."

Dawg leaned in closer. "What? Tell him what?"

Frank let his eyes flutter open like he was in a trance. He felt the stake move. He arched again to hide his efforts.

"He must...he must."

Dawg moved until his ear was almost touching Frank's broken mouth. "What is de warning? What must I do?"

Frank took a deep breath as if preparing himself to speak the warning. He paused. The stake pulled nearly free.

"Dreadmon says," Frank paused. "Fear the Spartans."

Frank's right hand pulled the stake the last inch and locked his freed hand around

Dawg's throat. He pulled Dawg down against his chest as he crushed his throat. Dawg dropped the wooden mallet and clawed at Frank's hand.

Roach shone the light on the scene. His brother, his rival, was caught in the death grip of their sacrifice. Part of him screamed for him to save Dawg. Part of him urged him to let Dawg die before he acted. Bat was not so conflicted. He jumped on top of Frank and Dawg. Dawg's body prevented Bat from having easy access to a target for his wildly thrown blows. Dawg shuddered in Frank's vice-like grip. Bat stood over Dawg and tried to pull him free of Frank's grip. Roach shown the light still unmoving. Dawg no longer offered any resistance. His throat was crushed.

Bat pulled Dawg free. He tried to pull Dawg farther out of Frank's reach when he felt the wooden stake stab deeply into his leg. Bat screamed and fell. Frank rolled toward him and stabbed him twice more deep in the right leg and once in the left. Roach was frozen in terror.

Frank sat upright and using both hands broke the leather thong that held his other wrist. Bat started trying to crawl away to safety. He was weeping. Frank started to pull on the thong that held his right leg. The effort had reopened the wounds in his head and blood flowed down his face in thick rivulets. Roach stumbled backward.

"Help me," Bat screamed. "Get de gun. Get de gun."

Roach ran toward the dock, abandoning Bat.

Frank pulled the stake up that held his leg. He looked around him. They were going for a gun. He had to run or hide. But there was nowhere to go. He lifted the wooden mallet from the ground. He kicked Dawg. He was dead. Bat had dragged himself a dozen yards on his ruined legs. Frank walked up behind him. He raised the mallet and crashed it down onto Bat's skull. Bat died without a sound.

Frank needed a better weapon. There was nothing. He stumbled to the edge of the precipice and looked down. White caps lapped on the jagged rocks that protruded skyward like a shark's broken teeth. It was too far. A jump would kill him. It was no escape.

Maybe he could hide among the ruins until he could slip down to the water. Even with the moonlight, it was a shambles of dark twisted shadow. Nothing looked like a promising hide. His head still pounded and he watched as the ruined house seemed to melt away and reform as it once had stood.

Frank knew they must have slipped him some hallucinogenic drug. He was rational enough to know what he was seeing was not real. Yet, he did not fight against the vision. The house was white and wide. It spread across one side of the pinnacle. There were huge wrap-around porches. On the top of the two-storied mansion was a widow's walk. Many chimneys-like fingers stood straight, stretching toward the sky.

The house melted again into a clutter of burned and broken timbers. There were a few chimneys still standing along the back. He saw the huge central chimney resting against the stone outcropping. Ghostly shapes seemed to move around the stone. Ghosts? More demons? It had to be fog or sea mist, Frank assured himself. Yet a chill crept up his spine. Maybe he could climb up into the main chimney and hide. It was worth a look, Frank thought. He would not kneel to these men.

49

Bruce drove around the island searching for Frank and the boat. He didn't find it, but he did spot Tonello's car. He eased in beside it. The trunk was open. There was blood inside. Frank had been here. There was no sign of the boat or where it had gone. Had they taken Frank back with them to wherever they came from? No, that would be too dangerous. Frank was formidable. Bruce sat down on the beach. Thor hurried around the edge of the water. He didn't bark. Bruce closed his eyes. He had to think. Where would he go if he didn't know the island? Where would he go for privacy to kill a man? He knew instantly.

He called Thor back to the car and drove for his jet ski rental business.

They had to be going to Falcon's retreat, to the aerie. It was the only choice.

Desmond was watching Caron. She could almost see the gears in his head working. She half expected to see sparks as his brain worked. She was freezing. It felt like it was below zero in the jail. The blankets and pillow rested just outside the cell.

"I know it is cold," Desmond said. "I know you do not care. I know you do not want the blankets enough to give me what I want."

Caron tried her best glare to shut him up. It didn't work.

"I know what you do want." Desmond paused for added effect.

Caron glared.

"You want your freedom. I can give it to you."

Caron's façade must have cracked a little because he continued.

"If you let me lay with you, I will let you escape. After we are finished, I will turn my back and you can slip away."

"I don't believe you," Caron said before she could stop herself.

Desmond smiled.

"I will let you lock me in the cell and run. I cannot guarantee they will not catch you. But you will have until Benny shows up in the morning to make your escape."

Caron thought about it. She couldn't trust him. But she was desperate. He could see her desperation. He shifted in his seat in anticipation of her invitation.

Caron turned back toward the wall. Frank would save her. He had to.

Roach was out of breath when he reached the dock. He bent over with his hands on his knees. He gasped for air.

"Hurry. Get de gun."

"Where is Dawg?" Little Bird asked.

"Dead. And Bat too."

Lord Tosh seemed unfazed. He leaned against the side of the boat. His hands moved through the air as if moving pieces of a puzzle. His face held its serene expression.

"Gather youself, child. Tell what has happened."

Roach repeated the events as accurately as he could. He may have slightly exaggerated Frank Kane's escape. He may have described his strength and speed as supernatural. He may have overemphasized his own heroics in trying to overpower Frank and save his friends. He could even be accused of distorting the cryptic message Frank had used to lure Dawg into his grasp. But no one challenged his version of the events. There was no one who could.

Little Bird felt white hot rage burn in her heart. Who was Frank Kane? Who was this man who had taken Dawg from her? How dare he? She got the shotgun and checked the breach to be sure it was loaded. He would pay for what he did. She would kill him. She would shoot him in his legs so that he could not fight them and then she would peel the skin from him and offer it to Dreadmon. But not before she scooped his eyes out.

Lord Tosh seemed unhurried. He got out the skinning knives and gave one to Roach and one to Little Bird. He took the sacrificial knife for himself. He rolled the other blades up again and replaced them on the boat. He took his boom box out onto the bow of the boat.

"Come. We must hurry before he escapes."

Lord Tosh looked quizzically at Roach before answering. He cocked his head from side to side. "Dere is no place for him to go. Dawg's cousin described dis place. Dere is no place to go."

"We aren't going to just wait here?"

"No. But know dis. Dreadmon tests us with dis mon. We must be worthy."

Roach nodded his agreement. Lord Tosh punched in the music. It was a band called Traffic. The sound was a hallucinogenic techno mix from the seventies. The band was singing about someone called 'Mr. Fantasy'. Lord Tosh bobbed his head to the music. He started smiling. He turned his smile onto Roach and Little Bird.

"Do not fear dis mon. Dreadmon walks with I and I."

Lord Tosh took another of the large flashlights. He turned it on and off, checking the power.

"Roach, stay here. Little Bird and I will find dis mon."

"No. I want to go with you."

Lord Tosh just smiled, but he did not answer. It was Little Bird who spoke.

"Lord Tosh says stay here. Stay here. Guard de boat. It is our only means of escape. Protect it."

Lord Tosh cocked his head from side to side like a shore bird searching for food in shallow water. There was something terrifying in the movement. Roach shivered.

"I am sorry, Lord Tosh. I should na have spoken."

"No. You should na have."

Lord Tosh patted Roach on the shoulder to reassure him. He turned to Little Bird.

"Come. Stay close to I."

Lord Tosh and Little Bird moved methodically up the path. Lord Tosh swept the area before them with the light and Little Bird tracked it with the shotgun. There was no place to hide. There was no place to launch an ambush. It was all killing ground. It was only a matter of time before they found Frank.

50

Frank walked toward the old house. A troop of small monkeys sat quietly on the ruins of the upper floor. They considered his approach, but made no sound. Frank did not like monkeys. Never had. For some reason, their little skinny fingers creeped him out.

He moved through the wreckage. He busted his shins on the pieces of stone and wood. He scraped his arms on the bits of ruin that jutted out from odd angles. He made his way to the chimney. It was the broadest chimney he had ever seen. It dwarfed the tiny fireplace in his study at home. The front had to be four feet wide. Frank crouched and peered up into the chimney. It was as dark and black as a politician's heart. He needed a light. He felt his pocket where he had kept his cigars. They were gone and so was the lighter he was hoping for. He patted his pockets. Maybe he had brought his cell phone. He could use the light on it. Even as he searched, he knew it was in his gear back in his hotel room.

He reached upward. He felt nothing but the wide opening for the chimney. Frank stood up in the fireplace. He reached upward trying to find a hold to pull himself up. The chimney was blocked. He felt around the blockage. It felt like rough stone. What in hell was it?

Frank smiled. It was an omen. The gods provided. He pressed the button on his new watch. The light was startling in the tight space.

The chimney's flue was blocked by a huge wedge of stone. It fit so perfectly that Frank wondered if it had been cut to fit the opening. Why would you do that? Why have a chimney that didn't function? Who would do such a bizarre thing? He remembered that the pirate had been an architect, so that answered the who, but not the why. Frank turned around in the opening of the chimney.

On the wall closest to the main room was an odd arch shaped stone. It protruded out from the stone face. Frank ran his hands over the shape. It was like a crude half-moon. Thin lines were traced across the face of the arch. With no better idea, Frank tried to twist the stone emblem like a turn knob. It didn't budge. He pulled down on it like a lever. Finally, he pushed it inward and felt it give. The movement took Frank by surprise. He pushed harder and felt the emblem slide effortlessly into the fireplace façade.

The back of the fireplace moved inward a foot. Frank turned at the movement. It was a secret passage. God bless pirates, he thought. He knelt and pushed on the back of the fireplace. It didn't budge. He braced his back against the chimney and used his legs to push against the intruded stone. It didn't budge.

Frank knelt and examined the stone. It was void of any markings or releases that Frank could find. On the ground before the stone was another emblem now visible. The wall sliding backward had allowed it to rise up. It was arch-shaped like the emblem on the inside of the chimney. The lines were scored deeper on this emblem, separating it into distinct sections. Metal rods protruded upward from each section in a straight line down through the center of the arch.

Frank sat down in the dirt and debris.

"What the fuck," he said.

He thought he heard the sound of approaching feet. He looked around but saw nothing.

He had to think. What was the trick? What was the code? What did the old pirate do?

Again, Frank had that spark of intuition. It wasn't a half-moon. It was a rainbow. It had to be. That was on the crest of his personal flag. The emblem in the chimney was another rainbow. This had to be a rainbow. Now that he saw what it was meant to be, it was crystal clear. It was a rainbow. The metal rods were the combination. Press the rods in the right order and the wall would open. If you pressed them in the wrong order, then what? The function of the stone in the chimney became evident. It was a dead fall. Press the wrong combination and the stone would crush whoever was in the fireplace and seal off the passage. There was no way to press them from outside. There was probably a lever outside somewhere that reset the stone.

There had to be a key. The old pirate was arrogant. He used the rainbow symbol as a private taunt. It was the secret key to his treasure displayed in plain sight. What was the code? He remembered the story of the pirate telling someone that Giby had the key. Every child knew the colors of the rainbow and the anagram that accompanied it. ROYGBIV. Red, orange, yellow, green, blue, indigo, and violet. That had to be it.

Giby was another anagram for the order of the colors. Frank reached forward to push the first rod, but hesitated. Was it really Giby? Could it have been Givy? Or even Bivy. Fuck. He knew how stories changed over time and with the telling. What about a single word? Had the original word been misheard? Had time distorted it? Maybe because it was thought to be the key to a treasure it had been remembered intact. Passed down through generations.

Frank caught the sliver of flashlight off to his distant right. They were coming. He had to decide. The kill stone crouched overhead. He thought he heard laughter. The fog seemed to swirl around him. It chilled his skin. He felt ancient forms in the fog. Death was watching.

Frank cupped his hand over the light on his watch to hide its glow. No man lived forever. He pushed the appropriate rods. Green. Indigo. Blue. Yellow. Time stopped. Hidden gears turned. Levers shifted. Braces retracted. The back wall withdrew and turned inward on unseen hinges. The black space opened before him.

Frank paused. Was there another trap waiting for him? Voices approached. The harsh touch of a light brushed past him. Go or stay? It was now or never. Frank moved into the darkness. The stone wall swung closed behind him.

51

Little Bird hurried forward. She had the shotgun raised to firing position.

"Dere, Shine de light dere. I saw him."

Lord Tosh swept the light back into the ruins.

"Near de fireplace."

Lord Tosh locked the light onto the empty fireplace.

"I did. I saw him."

"De shadows play."

"No, it was a man. De big man."

Lord Tosh shrugged. He followed Little Bird into the ruins. Frank was not there. Little Bird pointed to the smears in the dirt. "He was here."

"But no more."

Little Bird directed Lord Tosh to shine the light up into the chimney. She shook her head.

"He is here somewhere."

Lord Tosh did not answer. They moved back into the open and continued their search. They quickly found the bodies of Dawg and Bat.

"No one must know of de failure of de Red Hand."

Little Bird and Lord Tosh dragged the body of Bat to the far side of the pinnacle and pushed it off. They then returned for Dawg's body. They dragged it to the edge where they had tossed Bat. Little Bird leaned in and kissed Dawg on his bearded lips.

"Goodbye," she whispered. "You were mine for a little while."

Frank crouched on the other side of the trip plate that had closed the door behind him. He rested in the darkness for a moment, gathering his strength. He thought he could still hear laughter.

Frank activated the light on his watch again. He was in a large cavern. It had been a lava tube before it had been reshaped. Frank slowly swept the light over the area. There were casks and chests. There were clay amphoras still tightly sealed with thick wax sheaths. In the far corner was a site which shocked him even as he had expected it.

Sprawled before him was a body. It was more skeleton than body. The sea air had desiccated and mummified the form. It had to be Falcon the pirate captain.

The body rested against one of the chests. The legs were splayed outward, the right leg slightly bent. There was a tattered leather bandolier of pistols across the chest. The right hand still clutched at a rusted cutlass. The blade was notched and stained.

Suddenly Frank could see the pirate's last stand. He stood beside Falcon as he noticed the approach of the long boats. The big cannons had been on the windward side of the pinnacle, but the leeward side was not undefended. He could see Falcon running from cannon post to cannon post lighting the wicks on the cannon.

Longboats burst apart in the bombardment. But there were many boats. He switched to the six pound cannons, firing cast iron cannon balls. Still they came onward. Eventually, boats made landfall.

Falcon met them with strategically placed deck guns that cut them apart with chain and grape shot. Pirates screamed under the rain of hot metal. Falcon fell back to his next position and continued the battle. More boats landed beyond the sweep of the deck guns. The pirates returned fire with muskets and pistols.

Falcon continued his fighting retreat. He must have known he could not win. The knowing was probably freeing to him. He wanted to make a grand fall that would be spoken of for ages. At the end of the climb he would have stockpiled muskets. He would have fired one and then another and then another. Never pausing to reload. There wouldn't have been time to reload. He had grenades of gunpowder and metal that he threw at his pursuers.

He would have had a series of traps at the head of the path. Boulders would have been restrained by easily released levers. They would have crushed his pursuers, giving him a few precious minutes to fall back to the house. The doors and windows would have been sealed with barricades.

The pirates would have been blood mad by now. The treasure would have grown to epic proportions in their minds to justify the death all around them. They would have been unstoppable.

Barricaded in the house, Falcon had continued the battle until he was on the verge of being overrun. He would have started the fire in the manor himself to buy himself time to escape into the hidden passage, thus assuring his legend.

Frank could see the holes from bullets in the body. Falcon knew he was a dead man. Hidden away in the darkness, Frank could imagine him laughing as he bled out. There was a huge medallion shaped like a trident around his neck just like in the painting. It was another of Falcon's symbols. The outside of the medallion was formed by the shapes of two identical tiger sharks touching nose to tail in a perfect circle. The twins. Inside the medallion was a trident. Frank hesitated and then took it from the neck of the corpse and placed it around his own neck. Trident was the symbol for Poseidon. The twin tigers were a symbol from his own past too. It was a good omen. It was the best omen.

Frank took off his shirt and tore it into strips. He wrapped the strips around his head to control the bleeding. He even wrapped a strip over his left eye that was now swollen shut. The pressure of the bandage made the eye feel slightly better.

Old weapons were stacked about the room. A brace of muskets rested against one wall. He assumed some of the casks held gunpowder and shot. It would be nice to have a gun. Any gun. But even if the gunpowder was still useable, Frank didn't know anything about loading a musket. He knew guns. He knew ammunition. He could guess. Gunpowder first, followed by wadding and then the ball. All of it would be packed tightly. Frank smiled. He would probably blow himself up.

He thought about trying to make a bomb of some kind, but it wasn't his forte. He wasn't Masnick. He could imagine himself jumping out of hiding and lighting a bomb that sputtered and went out. He hated dying, but he didn't want to look like a fool doing it.

He fumbled through the swords. A decent blade was better than nothing. The blades were all rusted and dulled from salt corrosion. He found an eight inch curved dagger. The handle felt good in his hand. Under the corrosion it might have once been ornate. The blade was dull, but with his arm behind it, it could do serious damage. He tucked it into his pants pocket.

Near the secret wall was a stack of torches with a gummy substance coating them. There was a piece of stone tethered to the nearby wall. It had to be flint. Frank struck it against the stone and got sparks. He used the sparks to shower the torch. Miraculously, it lit. The fire was smoky and thick. It smelled oily, like tar.

Frank swept the torch over the secret door. He couldn't see a release for the stone wall. There had to be one and it would be obvious. The trick was getting in, not getting out. But he couldn't spot it. He shifted a barrel, and a huge spider scuttled out.

The spider could not have been native to the island. It was thick and hairy like a tarantula. It bobbed before him, unafraid.

It reminded him of his time with Apollo. Once, when Frank had been in Costa Rica with Apollo, he had almost stepped on a snake. It was a Fer-de-lance, the most venomous snake in CR. The snake had taken up residence near the koi pond. Frank had wanted to kill the snake, but Apollo had stopped him. He had said that the snake had a right to life. Like them, it was a predator. He explained that they should show it some professional courtesy. One predator to another. Frank had let the snake live. He smiled at the memory of his best friend and their time in CR.

Frank smashed his foot with the shoe on it down onto the spider. Frank hated spiders. Apollo wasn't here. And this wasn't Costa Rica.

52

Helen's friends were drunk. It was their last night on the island and they were ending it with a bang. Music was playing. Cigarettes were burning. Everyone was laughing. Ashley approached Helen. She had the look of a little girl seeking permission.

"Helen,"

"What's up girl? Are you having fun?"

"It is the best trip ever."

"I am glad."

"I was wondering something.'

"What?"

"I was wondering if it is alright for me to dance with Ronnie. I know he is only supposed to be acting as bodyguard, but he is so cute and..."

Helen put her hand on her arm. "Of course you can. Here you can do whatever you want. You don't need my permission to have fun. Go for it."

Ashley actually squealed with delight. "Thank you."

Helen smiled, she was surprised Ashley had resisted as long as she had. James had taken over bartending duties from Johanna. The black concierge was mixing more margaritas. Meredith had insisted he come up. He worked to stay in the background. Johanna's head bobbed slightly. She was on the way out. She would be in bed soon.

Ashley and Ronnie started dancing. He was actually a pretty good dancer. He was laughing. Helen felt unusually good. Everyone was having a good time. She imagined that Frank was spending his last night on the island with that blonde whore she had seen him with, but she didn't care. It didn't mean anything. It was only sex. She hoped he had figured a way to rescue the girl at the jail. It wasn't her problem now.

Johanna rose unsteadily to her feet. She raised her glass toward Helen and mimed waving goodbye. Helen raised her glass in response. Johanna slipped off to bed without a word. Meredith was dancing by herself. She was trying to do a popular dance move. Helen thought it was called twerking. It looked like just shaking your ass up and down.

Ashley leaned in and kissed Ronnie. It was a quick little kiss. Helen watched her pull back waiting for his response. To no one's surprise he pulled her into his arms and kissed her. Ashley beamed. They started dancing closer. Their bodies moved in a synchronized rhythm. Ronnie really was a very good dancer. She never would have guessed. Ronnie had one hand around her waist as they danced. Ashley stopped dancing and took him by the hand. She led him toward his room.

Well, well, well, Helen thought. It was indeed a night of surprises.

"Looks like somebody is getting fucked tonight," Meredith said.

Helen laughed. "I think she thought it was now or never."

"Maybe it was."

Helen took a drag on her cigarette. "Probably was the best chance she had to get what she wanted. More power to her."

Meredith leaned forward and took Helen's wrist in her hand. She pulled Helen's cigarette toward her own mouth and took a deep drag. She released her hand and blew the cigarette smoke out.

"No rules. No regrets. That's my motto," Meredith said.

"The anthem of a true hedonist."

Meredith moved closer to Helen. Helen did not move. Meredith slipped closer until she was only inches away from Helen. Helen knew where this was going. She had expected it.

"Do you know what I want to do?"

Helen did not answer. She smiled. Meredith was so predictable.

"I want to kiss you," Meredith said as she moved still closer.

Helen did not respond.

She leaned forward and kissed Helen on the mouth. The kiss was gentle at first and then became more passionate. Helen returned the kiss equally matching its growing passion. Meredith raised a hand to the back of Helen's head to pull her in tightly and hold her in place. The kiss became more passionate. When Meredith finally ended it she sighed deeply.

"I have wanted to do that forever. What do you say we go to our room and continue this in more privacy?"

Helen smiled. "Meredith, you are a beautiful, sexy woman. But I am married. I love my husband. This can't happen."

Meredith moved seductively in front of her.

"Of course it can. You liked kissing me didn't you?"

"Yes, but…."

Meredith placed a long nailed finger against Helen's lips. "No, buts. Not tonight. It will be our secret."

"It won't be happening."

Meredith did a practiced pursing of her lips. "Have you ever experimented before? Have you ever been curious?"

Helen took a sip of her drink. "Go to bed, Meredith. This never happened."

Meredith was shocked. She was insulted. She was embarrassed.

"Are you serious? For real? I can't believe you. You kissed me back. You fucking kissed me back. And it was hot."

"It was only a kiss."

Meredith took a step backward. "It is our last night. I want to do something wild. I want to be crazy. I want to break loose before I have to go home."

"There's always James," Helen said.

Meredith turned to look at the concierge standing quietly in the bar area. She looked back at Helen.

"Is that a dare? You think I won't? I will fuck him if I want to. And it will be the best fuck of his life."

Helen did not answer. She took another pull on her cigarette. Meredith turned and stomped off. She walked up to James and grabbed his face in her hands. She kissed him savagely, shoving her tongue into his mouth. James responded like men are hardwired to respond. Meredith ran her hands all over his back and she ground her perfect body against him. James ran his hands over her butt. This time when Meredith broke the kiss, she had a willing partner. She led him to their bedroom. She glared at Helen as she passed. James lowered his head. He was embarrassed, but Meredith was a beautiful woman. He had been told to make their stay memorable.

Helen watched them disappear into the bedroom. She shook out another cigarette and lit it. She stared out across the wine dark sea and thought about her next move. She went to her bag and opened it. She took her private cell phone out of her bag and punched in Claudia's private cell phone number.

"This is Claudia."

"He returns tomorrow?"

"Around eleven."

"Call Erika and Shawnda. I trust them to handle this. I need two teams of three."

"Did you find out what is going on with Frank?"

"Tell Erika to put both teams on Frank. The others are unimportant. They can't lose Frank. Do you understand?"

"Of course."

"Tell Erika to be in place by eight o'clock. I don't trust Frank not to alter his ETA. And Shawnda is not to engage Frank under any circumstances. If she does he will end her. Is that clear? You got that?"

"Got it."

"I am counting on you, Claudia. Do not let me down. Remember, tell Shawnda not to engage. Just track him."

"I won't let you down."

"And one more thing."

53

Frank smiled at himself. He was amazed that the torch's flickering light did so much to bolster his mood. He looked around the secret door again. The trip had to be right before him. The trick to trap doors was getting to this side, he repeated to himself. Getting to the other side should be easy. Right? So, why wasn't it?

There was no point in looking any longer. He would have to find another way out. He turned toward where the tunnel headed downward. The torch flame flickered. He could feel a breeze. He felt weak. He had lost a lot of blood, and his body was battered. He needed sleep. He squatted down and waited for the weakness to pass. When it finally did, he moved slowly down the old lava tube.

The tube narrowed the farther down it he went. Frank crab-walked forward. He went slowly. He didn't trust Falcon not to have booby trapped this path. Frank was reduced to crawling on all fours before the tube came to abrupt stop at the ocean's edge. The cavern here was broader and much taller. Moonlight streamed in from overhead. Movement caught his eye. The troop of monkeys sat watching him. This was their home now. Maybe they weren't even real. Maybe they were part of his hallucinations sent to mock him.

Frank examined the stone wall before him. He couldn't climb out. He would never make it. He could hear the ocean calling to him like a lover from the other side. The smell of brine was strong. He stepped out into the shallow ocean pool. Brightly colored crabs scuttled away before him. Just ahead was a small opening in the rocks. The limestone was broken here and wedged together by the sea. He jammed the torch into the rocks and started pulling on the stones.

The rocks cut his fingers, but he kept at it until he felt movement. His hands were bloody before the first rock tumbled away. He felt a wave of nausea sweep over him. He rested. He focused on his will. He reached into his heart and drew it forward like drawing a blade.

He returned to the rocks. Another gave way and tumbled to the side. It was still too small of an opening. The ocean swell surged through the widening grip. Frank grabbed a huge chunk of rock and braced his legs against the wall of stone. He strained with all he had to pull it free. The muscles in his back sang with pain. He pulled harder. The stone slipped forward and stuck. In rage, Frank kicked at it. The stone fell out the other way. The way was open.

Frank did not hesitate. He wedged his body through the hole and into the open sea beyond. The waves crashed against him, forcing him back against the rocks, trying to smash him or drag him under. Frank pushed off from the wall. The current was powerful. He had a vague idea where he should be on the island. The boat was on the other side. He would have to swim to it.

Frank swam out from the pinnacle. He knew he was weak. He knew he was bleeding and the blood would lure ocean predators. He also knew in his bones that he was Poseidon. The creatures of the sea would not harm him. He swam unafraid through the night black waters. The twins were out here somewhere. They would protect him.

Lord Tosh and Little Bird returned to the boat.

"Did you find him?" Roach asked.

"No yet," Little Bird said. "But we will. We wanted to be sure he had na circled us."

"He has not been here," Roach said. He brandished his knife. "If he comes, I will kill him."

Lord Tosh smiled at his bravado. Without a word he turned, and he and Little Bird returned for another sweep of the pinnacle.

Frank wasn't sure if he was going to make it. He was beyond the point of exhaustion. He heard ancient voices calling to him from the surrounding ocean. He knew it had to still be the effects of the drugs they had fed him. He swam on with all the strength he could manage. The strips of shirt he had tied around his head were pulled away by the ocean. His head wound reopened. The blood began to flow again. He swam on. At last he rounded the side of the island.

The current was weaker here, blocked by the stone pinnacle. There were no waves. He inched along next to the pinnacle toward the boat's resting place. A few minutes more swimming and he saw the boat. The boat was tied to the stone landing. He moved silently through the water. There was music playing. It was coming from the boat. Frank liked it. It would distract anyone on guard and cover his approach.

He reached the boat unobserved. He floated behind it. There was only one person there. He didn't know if they were armed with a gun. He moved silently to the stone dock. He never took his eyes off the man. He was one of the ones who had taken him to the pinnacle.

The man was looking up at the path to the top of the pinnacle. Maybe he was waiting for others. Maybe he was waiting for Frank. Frank pulled himself from the water. He crept up behind the man. Roach never heard his approach.

Frank took the old dagger from his pants. He lunged at Roach and caught his shoulder, pulling him backward toward Frank. Frank drove the dagger up into the base of his skull. It was an instant killing stroke.

Roach jerked forward and the old blade snapped off. He was already dead. Frank had seen the knife in Roach's hand and picked it up off the deck. There had been no sound in his attack. He dragged the body back to the boat and rolled it inside. The keys were not in the boat. He searched Roach's body. The keys were not there either.

Frank hadn't expected them to be. He could hot-wire a boat as easily as a car. He could take the boat and return to the main island. He could lay low until the plane came tomorrow. He could escape.

Frank remembered the ancient Spartans' philosophy of war. The ancient Spartans were renowned for their battle prowess. But unlike all the other Greek city states, they did not pursue and slay their defeated enemies. The Spartans knew that if a man knew he had to fight to live, he would fight on long after a battle was lost. The Spartans let their enemies flee to safety. This apparent kindness ensured their enemies would give up the fight sooner.

Frank differed from his ancient namesakes in this regard. Frank did not want to leave enemies on the battlefield still alive. They needed retribution. Frank took the unopened cans of gas that were lashed inside the boat. They were probably intended for the trip back to wherever they came from. Probably Jamaica by the accents. He threw them out into the ocean and watched them disappear. He took Roach's knife and punctured the gas cans in the hold. He started cutting the fuel lines. That was when he heard the voices.

He was out of time. They were returning. They would have the gun. One fuel line was cut through. He sawed quickly at the other. The light approached down the path. Frank cursed under his breath. He was out of time. He lowered himself back into the water over the side of the boat. He hoped his handiwork would be enough to maroon them on the island.

Lord Tosh and Little Bird reached the boat as Frank disappeared beneath the water.

"Roach," Little Bird called.

She stepped up to the boat. She saw Roach's body inside, a look of horror twisting his features. Lord Tosh stepped up to the boat. He climbed inside and turned off the music. He stared at the body.

"Dis is an evil place. We have failed Dreadmon in dis ting."

"What do we do now?"

"We must go. Der is noting here but death."

Little Bird climbed into the cockpit and took out the boat key. She fired the engine and put the boat in gear. Lord Tosh struggled to lift Roach's body. He caught Little Bird's eye.

"We will leave him in the ocean."

Little Bird nodded.

"We must return home and re-form de Red Hand."

Little Bird nodded again. She noticed there were tears on her cheeks. She had not thought she cared for Roach anymore.

54

Frank watched them pull away in the boat. He strained his ears, hoping to hear the motor sputter and stop. But it didn't. He watched its lights as it drew farther and farther away.

Frank pulled himself back out of the water. He still had the long bladed knife. But he was stranded on the rock pinnacle. Idiot, he thought. If I had cut the tie lines for the boat it would have drifted away and still been available for him to take back to shore. It was not like him to miss something so obvious. It must be the injury to his head. He wasn't thinking clearly. He squatted on the dock and tried to plan his next move. He thought he might pass out.

The bright light swept over Frank. He hadn't heard anyone approaching. Frank shielded his eyes.

"Christ. What happened to you?" Bruce asked. He was sitting on one of his jet skis.

Frank realized he was probably horrific to look at.

"I'm fine. We have to go after them. Do you have a weapon?"

Bruce lifted up the spear gun from his lap.

"I got this."

"Good enough." Frank showed him the thin bladed knife. "Better than what I brought to the party."

Frank dropped back into the water and swam to the jet ski.

"How did you find me?"

"I saw the scene at the office and went looking for you. I found Tonello's car at a little deep water cove. Their boat was gone, but I figured out where they had taken you. When I got close I could see lights on the island."

Frank pulled himself onto the jet ski. He patted Bruce on the back.

"Nice work." He pointed across Bruce's shoulder. "They went that way. They don't have much fuel."

The jet ski reared like a horse and they rode off into the darkness.

The boat's engine died within fifteen minutes as the fuel line tried to heroically siphon the final sips of gas from the punctured can. Little Bird tried to restart the engine. She went to check the fuel lines and discovered Frank's handiwork. They were adrift. Before she could ask Lord Tosh for instructions, she heard the roar of the jet ski as it approached. She knew enough about coincidences to know this was not one. She lifted the shotgun to her shoulder. The sound seemed to come from everywhere at once. She had to be patient. They would show themselves. Then she would kill these evil men. She would avenge her friends.

55

Bruce could see the lights of the boat in the distance. He headed straight toward it like an arrow. Bruce passed the spear gun back to Frank. The lights seemed to grow long before they could make out the shape of the boat.

"Paint them with the light," Frank said. "Let's see what they are up to."

Bruce nodded. When he thought they were close enough, he switched on the big light. The light bathed Little Bird in its brilliance. She didn't flinch. She swung the shotgun up to her shoulder. Bruce recognized the danger as quickly as she had recognized the opportunity. He turned the jet ski hard left away from the boat. The jet ski spun as smoothly as a racing motorcycle and roared away. It was too slow.

Frank heard the big twin booms of the double-barreled shotgun. Pain flashed from his back and right leg. He thought he was dead. But the pain was minimal. He felt no significant injury.

"You get any of that?" Bruce asked.

"A little. You?"

"Nothing. A few pellets hit the ski. What kind of shotgun was that?"

"Don't know. The load was weak. Like birdshot or rock salt or something. It's not a load for man killing."

"Why have a gun like that?"

"No reason. They fucked up."

Bruce turned the jet ski back in the direction of the boat.

"What now?"

"Take us back in like before. Hit them with the light when we get close. I'll try to get off a shot before they can reload."

Bruce didn't question Frank. There was no reason to. He was on autopilot.

The jet ski raced in close like before. Bruce hit the light. Little Bird had opened the shotgun's breach and was removing the spent shells. She looked up as the jet ski turned away. Her face was twisted in rage.

Frank shot her in the middle of her chest. The force knocked her backward, but she kept on her feet. The shotgun clattered over the side into the ocean. The force of the fleeing jet ski pulled Little Bird from the boat. She skipped along the surface of the ocean as they sped away. It almost looked to Frank like she was chasing them through the water.

Bruce stopped the jet ski. Frank reeled Little Bird in. He had recognized her on their first pass as the girl who had distracted him so that he could be taken prisoner. He pulled her lifeless body to the jet ski. Bruce shown the light on her. Her white tee shirt was plastered to her breasts.

"Jesus, it's a girl."

Frank pulled her up to the jet ski. The spear had struck her through the center of her chest. It hadn't had enough power to penetrate all the way out her back. The barbs had gotten twisted in her ribs. Frank tugged at the spear. It would not come free. He cut the line that tied it to the gun. Her eyes were wide open as she sank. Frank watched her disappear and tossed the empty spear gun away.

"Did you know it was a girl?" Bruce asked.

"It didn't matter. Her or us."

Bruce felt a wave of nausea, but forced it down. He turned the light on Frank. He was covered in blood from the shotgun pellets. The dark blood leaked unchecked into the ocean.

"Fuck, Frank. You're hit."

"It's not a problem. Take me in close. I'll slip off into the water. You take the jet ski around to be facing the bow of the boat. Turn your light on a couple of times to attract their attention. I will swim up and finish this."

"You can't. You don't even know how many more there are."

"There is only one guy left. The leader of these twisted fucks."

"What about the blood. You can't go into the water bleeding like that. It will attract them."

Frank smiled. Bruce was afraid to even say the word shark. Frank patted him on the shoulder.

"I will be fine." He patted Bruce on his forearm where the twins shark tattoo swam. "Just take me in close."

Bruce turned the jet ski toward the boat. As he passed he felt Frank slide off the back. He took the jet ski past and let it bob in the ocean. He turned the light on a couple of times like he was checking something. From a distance no one would be able to tell there was only one person on the jet ski.

Lord Tosh knew his god had abandoned him. Dreadmon was gone. He had returned to his dark fire swept lair to wait for new apostles to free him. Lord Tosh felt his absence. He had failed him in some way he did not understand. He was not saddened by the fact. It simply was. His time had come. He turned on his boom box and let the music swirl around him. Edwin Starr growled out the lyrics to War. And the Prophet sang along with him.

"War, huh, good God ya'll. What is it good for? Absolutely nothing, just say it again. War, whoa Lord what is it good for? Absolutely nothing. Listen to me. War, it ain't nothin' but a heartbreak. War, friend only to the undertaker."

Lord Tosh saw the light of their jet ski off the bow.

"War, huh yeah. What is it good for?"

56

Frank swam silently toward the boat. He moved behind the motor. The tall, bald man was staring toward the front of the boat. There was a small ladder on the back of the boat. Frank unlatched it and lowered it into the water. He opened the door in the transom. Frank pulled himself up onto the deck. The tall man noticed and spun toward him. He carried a long ornate knife in his hand. He was smiling. Frank waited.

Lord Tosh sprang toward him. Frank dodged the strike. Lord Tosh moved to his right and feinted left before slashing with the raven black blade. Frank jumped out of the way. Carving out a bound man's heart was easier than fighting a freely moving one. A hint of concern settled in Lord Tosh's brow.

Lord Tosh charged forward with the blade held low. He struck upward, hoping to disembowel Frank. Frank caught the thin wrist and checked the attack. Once was enough for any man. He stared into the Prophet's eyes. He let him see his own death in the deep blue of Frank's eyes. Frank drove his own blade up beneath the old man's ribs. The thin blade slid in easily. Frank twisted the blade as he pulled it out to make sure the wound couldn't close. Lord Tosh stood frozen in place.

Frank stabbed him three more times in quick succession. Each strike to his bird-like neck. Just that fast, and it was over. Lord Tosh slumped toward him. He held the body upright as Lord Tosh's life spilled out onto the deck. Frank guided his dead body toward the rail. Frank pushed Lord Tosh over the side. The boom box sang on. He picked up the boom box and threw it over the side after its owner.

Blood splattered the deck of the boat. Frank lifted the boat brush from its rack and dipped it over the side into the ocean. He did a quick scrub that diluted the red stains. He tossed it over the side when he was finished. With any luck, the approaching hurricane would sink the cursed boat. There was nothing that tied him or Bruce to the vessel.

He called out and Bruce brought the jet ski back. Frank jumped into the water and climbed on board. He did not fear the sharks or the sea or his own injuries. He was Poseidon. He feared nothing. He could not be killed.

"Hold on tight. It's going to be a wild ride back."

Frank gripped Bruce's waist, and they sped off. As the adrenaline burned itself out, he began to feel very tired. The heaviness of fatigue seemed to slowly engulf him. He was spent. He tried to rouse himself. He still had to rescue Caron. He still had to get to the plane.

57

Bruce ran the jet ski onto the shore at his business. Frank fell into the shallow water. He could barely rise to his feet. He threw up into the water. Bruce helped Frank inside the office. He led him over to the sofa and sat him down. Frank seemed barely conscious. Bruce took out a Leatherman from his desk and set about to remove the pellets that were still under the skin on Frank's back and right leg. He slabbed antibiotic cream onto the wounds. He put bandages on the largest cuts and wrapped the other wounds on his head with a ACE elastic bandage. Frank felt like an Indian prince with a turban when Bruce finished. He dug an extra large shirt from the Lost and Found box. Frank put on the dry shirt and leaned back on the sofa. He closed his eyes for a second and fell asleep.

Frank started to dream. He was standing on a long strand of pink sand. There was a couple standing together looking seaward. He walked toward them. He noticed they were staring out at the rock pinnacle. It was Captain Falcon and his woman, Marlin. They were dressed exactly like the picture at the hotel. They turned to smile at his approach. They seemed very nice, although Falcon's smile had a hint of a sneer to it. Frank understood. Smiling was hard business for men like them.

"You did well, boyo," Falcon said.

"I survived," Frank answered.

Marlin smiled. She was more beautiful than the painting.

"Are you sure?" Marlin asked. She had a soothing voice.

Frank looked around. He didn't understand for several seconds.

"Yes."

Marlin was still smiling. "Then you have to leave."

Falcon extended his ring encrusted hand and Frank shook it. Falcon pointed to the necklace that was around Frank's neck. The one Falcon had worn in life.

"You know what you need to do, boyo. Go home. Make me famous again."

Frank noticed someone farther up the beach. He knew it was Helen. She was wearing the same clothes she had worn when he had fought Dreadmon. She was walking away from him with long slow strides. She looked back over her shoulder at him. Her smile called to him. She was too far away to hear her words, yet, he heard them as clearly as if she stood beside him.

"You must hurry. You must find the way."

Frank woke with Bruce shaking him.

"Frank, you got to wake up."

"I'm awake. I'm awake," Frank said.

"You keep saying that and then you black out again. I was afraid a couple of times you had died."

Frank swung his legs off the sofa and sat upright. "I can't be killed, remember?"

"So you keep telling me."

Frank lightly touched his throbbing face. "You woke me up before?"

"Like ten times."

Frank rubbed his eyes, even the one that was closed shut. "Man, I can't seem to wake up. What time is it?"

"It's seven thirty. You got to get to the airport."

"What about Caron? Did the judge spring her?"

"No. It was a bust. The cops wouldn't release her. They are too scared of the Prime Minister."

Frank lurched to his feet. The room swayed a little. He steadied himself. He braced a hand against the wall.

"I need a car."

"I got a car. I can drive you."

"I need Tonello's car. Can you take me to it?"

"Sure, no problem. But why do you need his car?"

"I got things to do before I leave."

"There isn't time."

"I will have to make time."

"Get to the airport. I will keep you updated on Caron. We can figure something out after you are clear."

Frank shielded his eyes. "The light is killing me."

Bruce handed him a pair of cheap sunglasses from the Lost and Found box.

"Try these."

Frank put them on. It helped.

"I could use a hat too."

Bruce retrieved a worn green baseball cap that advertised a feed store in Arkansas. Frank wiggled it to place over his bandaged head. He stumbled out onto the porch. Bruce helped Frank to the SUV, and they sped off to Tonello's car.

Bruce found the car again. He pulled up tight to it. The keys were gone. Frank didn't seem surprised. He pulled the console down and separated the wires. He wrapped the red wire and the green wire. The car jumped to life. He pushed the seat all the way back and set the rearview mirror. Bruce appeared at the car's window.

"Get off the island, Frank. It's not safe for you here. I'll look after Caron."

Frank smiled. "You're a good man, Bruce. And a good friend. Can you keep a secret?"

"You have to ask after what we just went through?"

"Another secret. A good secret."

"Yeah. What are you talking about?"

"I got a story to tell you, but you have to do exactly what I tell you to do. You got to keep it secret for three or four months until I tell you the time is right. Can you do that for me?"

"Sure. Sure."

Frank took the medallion off his neck and handed it to Bruce. Bruce studied it. "What is this? Are these the twins?"

"It's your providence. The proof that the story I am telling you is true."

And then Frank told him about the treasure. Bruce listened with his mouth open. At the completion, Frank told him what he wanted him to do.

58

Frank pulled away from the cove. He was down to about fifteen minutes. He was running out of time. He made a split second decision. He would make one more stop. He skidded the car to a stop in the parking area in front of the Royal Caribbean Dream hotel. He knew Helen was on the island. He had no reason to believe Helen was here. But he had felt something when he was on the beach. Maybe he was crazy, but he had to know.

He rushed into the lobby and jogged to the front desk. The manager watched him suspiciously. Frank got to the desk without crushing any tourists.

"What happened to you?" the manager asked.

"It was a car accident. I am looking for the lady who was involved."

"One of our guests?"

"She was tall, blonde, incredibly beautiful. Her name was Helen..."

"Yes. She booked the presidential suite on the top floor."

Frank's heart swelled. It was an omen. "I have to see her."

"That's not possible."

"You don't understand. It is an emergency."

"I am sorry she has already checked out. Her party flew out this morning just after six o'clock."

Frank felt an almost physical shock to his body. "You're positive?"

"Yes, sir. She's gone."

"Damn."

"Are you Frank?"

Frank's head snapped up. "Yeah. How did you know?"

"She left something for you. She said to give it to you if showed up."

The manager reached behind the counter and handed Frank one of the hotel's envelopes. Frank tore it open. Inside was a short message written on hotel stationery. He read it and placed the note into his front pocket.

Frank hurried back to the car. It was only minutes until eight o'clock. He couldn't afford to be late or he would miss the plane. But he had made a promise. He drove to the police station. He parked out front. He went to the door. It was locked, but Frank could see two police officers inside. He knocked on the door, but they ignored him. He continued pounding on the door until one of them opened it.

"The station is officially closed until nine. What happened to you?"

"I had an accident on a quad bike."

"You should see a doctor."

"I will. I'm sorry to come so early. I was by yesterday to check on Sharon."

"I remember you. What do you want?"

"We are setting sail this morning. I just wanted to tell her goodbye. See if she had any messages she wanted to give me."

"So your boss learned the truth? Now he abandons her."

"Something like that. Can I see her? I promise to be quick."

The policeman sighed like Frank was asking the impossible. He waved him inside.

"She is still in the back cell."

Frank walked to the cell the policeman followed him. A second policeman lounged in one of the chairs. He had a blanket around his shoulders. It was very cold in the jail. Another blanket and pillow lay just out of reach of the cell. Caron jumped to her feet when she saw him. She put her fingers through the bars. Frank took her freezing cold hands in his.

"What happened?"

"Doesn't matter. I just came to tell you I couldn't get you out."

"Did you bring her passport?" the policeman asked.

"Yeah. Just a second. Let me tell her goodbye."

DC and Jenny sat in the plane, nervously looking out the tiny door for Frank and Caron. There was no one.

"Hey, we got to motor," Bullington said.

"Just a few minutes more. They are coming, I swear."

"We can't just keep sitting here. Somebody is going to notice."

"Just chill. Frank is your friend too."

"I know, baby, but I got product on board. You know what I'm saying. Getting busted down here doesn't do anyone any good. Frank would understand that. It's not personal. It's straight up business."

Jenny went into the cockpit. "What bullshit. You're getting paid. Earn your fucking money."

Bullington held his hands up. "Ease up girl. I can give him five more minutes and then we got to go, Frank or no Frank."

"Okay. Five more minutes."

Jenny wished she had brought her knife. She would make the jerk stay all day if she had her blade.

"Shit," Bullington said. "We might be fucked."

"What are you talking about?"

"We aren't supposed to be here, you dig. That custom cop isn't supposed to be her either. He's checking us out. If he gets curious. Shit. He's coming this way."

59

Caron smiled at Frank.

"You did your best. This is on me," Caron said.

Frank smiled. She was a sweet girl. She had no idea what lay waiting for her in a Bahamian prison.

"I got to go," Frank said and squeezed her hand.

"I need that passport," the policeman said.

Frank turned and reached for his back pocket for the passport that didn't exist. He spun back around and punched Desmond just above his jaw line with a straight hard right hand. The policeman fell unconscious. Frank turned toward the second policeman. He was trying to get to his feet. Frank caught him with a savage left hook that sprawled him across the desk. He tried to rise, and Frank punched him with a short left jab behind his ear. He slumped back and fell into the floor on his back. It had taken less than two seconds.

"Where are the keys?" Frank asked.

"In that desk. In the top drawer."

Frank pulled the drawer open. The keys were secured on a round metal ring. He unlocked the cell door and swung it open. Caron jumped into his arms and hugged him.

"Thank you."

"We don't have time for this. Help me drag them into the cell."

They quickly put the two policemen into the cell. Caron paused long enough to kick Desmond in his groin. Twice. She started to leave the cell, turned back, and gave him a third savage kick to his groin. Frank stared at her quizzically.

"Don't ask," she said.

Frank locked the cell and broke the key off in the lock. Caron turned the temperature down on the air conditioner as far as it would go. Frank had no way to lock the jail. He turned off the light and they climbed into Tonello's beat up car. It was well past eight. They were fucked.

"Here he comes the customs guy," Bullington said. "We are screwed."

Jenny watched the customs guy approach. He was walking slowly. She could tell that he was curious, not suspicious. She unbuttoned her shirt and took it off.

"What are you doing?" Bullington asked.

Jenny straddled his lap in the pilot's seat. It was cramped. She pulled the straps to her bra down exposing her shoulders. She put her hands on Bullington's shoulders.

"Rub your hands up and down my back."

"Are you nuts? There isn't time for this."

"Just do it."

Bullington started rubbing her back. Jenny was arching her back and bouncing up and down on his lap. She was moaning loudly. She was thrashing her hair around in the apparent throes of ecstasy. Bullington realized she was trying to make it look like they were having sex in the airplane. He grabbed a handful of her hair to mimic her passion. The plane was rocking violently.

The ruse seemed to work. He could see the customs guy over her bare shoulder. He watched the customs man stop, then start smiling. The man watched for a minute and listened to the mock sounds of passion. It was all it took to satisfy his curiosity. Just a couple of kids getting it on. He turned and walked away. Bullington could tell he was laughing. He had a great story to tell his friends.

"Did it work? Is he gone?"

"Not yet. Keep doing what you are doing," Bullington said.

Something in Bullington's voice alerted her. She twisted in his lap and looked behind to see the customs agent leaving. She turned back to Bullington.

"You are a pig."

"Well, duh. I was only playing along."

"Uh huh. And what is that sticking up in your pants?"

Bullington laughed as she got off his lap. "I was just getting into the part."

Jenny put her shirt back on and buttoned it. "That's all you're getting into today."

"Pretty slick. It should buy us some time. I can't say how much. We are really pushing it."

Tonello's old car skidded to a stop by the gate in the side fence. Caron and Frank pushed the gate open and ran across the tarmac to the plane. They scrambled inside and took seats. DC rushed up to hug Caron. Jenny was hugging her and Frank. Questions started flying about what had happened to Frank and how had he gotten Caron out. The plane started to taxi down the runway. They bounced along as it gained speed. The engine roared. The plane lifted off. They were safe.

"Glad you could make it," Bullington shouted back.

"Sorry I was late. I had business to attend to."

"Just kidding, Frank. I told them there was no way I would leave you behind."

If looks could kill, the one from Jenny would have stopped Bullington's black heart.

60

The Gulfstream 650 landed as smooth as a goose on a lake. There was already a car waiting for them. The flight attendant extended the stairs and opened the doorway. She and the pilots went out first. They stood at the bottom of the stairs to assist their guests' departure.

Ronnie deplaned first. He surveyed the area has he had been trained to do. It made an impressive site that he enjoyed. Although no one emerged from the Bentley, he knew Cyrus was watching from inside.

Ashley was next. She was all smiles. She let her hand brush Ronnie's arm as she walked past. Cyrus would notice the affection. Cyrus tended to notice everything. It would not disturb him. He would immediately decide how best to use it to his advantage. Having one of his men in a relationship with one of Helen's closest friends could pay dividends. He would encourage the relationship. Having one of his men break the heart of one of his wife's closest friends would also reap certain unpleasantness. He felt a little sorry for Ronnie. He was caught between Scylla and Charybdis.

Meredith was next. Her flawless face was twisted into a frown. Her perfect vacation had taken some unexpected turns. Her ego would force her to atone.

Johanna was happy too. She looked like the classic tourist returned from vacation. She was beautiful. She was tan. She was still hung over. She still clutched a Bloody Mary in her hand.

Helen was last, and made a more grand entrance. She was perfection. Even as the breeze tousled her hair, it seemed perfect. Her smile was genuine. She went to each of them separately. She hugged Ashley.

"I hope you had a good time."

"It was the best. I out-drank Johanna. I played great tennis. And I got to spend time with Ronnie."

"I am glad you had a good time."

"I did. Do you think he will get in trouble with your husband?"

"I will make sure he doesn't."

She hugged Johanna, and Johanna gave her a kiss on the cheek. "Thank you so much for having me. It was wonderful even if you did change our departure time to dawn thirty."

"I am sorry about that. I just wanted to get home. I am so glad you came. We will do this again. I promise."

Meredith was scowling as Helen approached her. Helen held out her arms. Meredith hesitated before stepping in to hug her.

"Do you hate me?" Meredith said.

"No. I love you. There is nothing between us."

"Are you sure? I got drunk and acted like such a fool."

"You were having a good time. That's all that was. It is forgotten."

Meredith squeezed her tightly. "I bet it would have been incredible."

"I am sure it would have been."

Meredith giggled and went to the other girls who were all chatting and hugging each other. Ronnie had gone to gather their luggage. Helen approached the pilot.

"Thank you so much for coming to pick us up early."

"Whatever you need. Whenever you need it."

She shook his hand and walked to Ronnie. He didn't turn around. She stood for a five count before finally speaking.

"Ronnie."

He turned around his face was a mask.

"Did you have a good time?"

He shrugged.

"I am sorry if I put you in a compromising position. It wasn't fair to you. You did a good job watching over us."

A small smile tugged at the corner of his mouth.

"I will make sure Cyrus knows what a fine job you did."

"Thank you."

"I think we are friends again. I think we have an understanding. Am I right?"

Ronnie nodded his head. His eyes caught Ashley and he smiled wider. Helen noticed.

"I do have one piece of advice. When Cyrus debriefs you, he will ask about Ashley."

There was panic in Ronnie's eyes. "How would he know?"

"He won't. But he always gives the impression that he knows everything. Tell him that there was only flirtation, but that you think she is into you. Do not tell him you slept with her while you were on protection detail. That will lead to unpleasantness. Do you understand?"

"Yes. And the other stuff? I'm good with what we talked about."

She patted him on the cheek. "Excellent. I will ask him to put you on my private security team."

Ronnie beamed. "Wow. That would be great."

"You deserve it. You did a great job."

Cyrus finally exited the Bentley. He approached them. He greeted the pilot and crew first, then turned to his wife. He gave her a welcome home hug and kiss that could have come from any popular chick flick. He greeted her friends and guided them toward the Bentley. He shook Ronnie's hand as if they were somehow equals, something so ludicrous that Ronnie could only assume it was sincere. He walked Helen to the car and closed the door before she could get in, and waved to the driver, who pulled away.

Helen's heart started to pound in her chest.

"Come with me. I have a special surprise for you."

His arm was around her slender shoulders guiding her as they walked. She wondered if he could feel her heart pounding. He led her toward an open airplane hanger. The questions raced through her mind even as she held her smile. Had he found out? Was there a second watcher she had not seen? Was he going to kill her? She ran a million scenarios in her head on how to escape before they reached the privacy of the hanger. Once they were inside she would be trapped.

She realized there was no way out. She remembered her own words to Ronnie. He always pretends to know everything.

She wrapped her arm around his waist as they walked.

"What surprise do you have for me darling?"

"Just wait. You'll see."

"Aren't you the mysterious one."

Cyrus laughed. It sounded genuine, but with him it was always hard to tell. They were both such perfect liars. They reached the wide door of the hanger. Cyrus stepped back like a chivalrous knight and waved her inside. Helen went in without hesitation. Cyrus stepped in behind her and turned on the light.

61

Once they were airborne and the questions had slowed and DC had stopped kissing Caron and Jenny had stopped thanking Frank, he went up to the cockpit. Bullington was focused on the controls.

"We heading to CLT?"

"As planned. Weather looks perfect."

"Will they have watchers waiting for us?"

Bullington turned and studied Frank for a few seconds. "Look, I'm just the pilot. Claudia looks after me and turns a blind eye for me. I don't know anything about any watchers. But what do you think?"

Frank smiled his jagged-tooth shark smile. He handed Phil a piece of paper he had taken from his gear. It contained the call sign for a different airport.

"Change of plans. Here is the new airport we will be using. It is a small private field in Tennessee. Is that going to be a problem?"

Bullington smiled. "Not at all. I am under duress, right? I mean what other choice did I have? It will add a little flight time."

Frank pulled a roll of money from his pocket and started to peel off hundreds. Bullington looked at it. He was almost drooling. He shook his head.

"Sorry can't take any cash. It's not that I have an ethical objection, but when I get back, Claudia will have me turn out my pockets. If I am carrying more than a couple hundred bucks she will think I was in on it. I like my job."

"Good reasoning, Phil. Might be why I like you."

"Listen," Bullington said and pulled a card out of his shirt pocket. "I had planned to slip you this anyway. It's my private cell. If you ever need me, you can reach me. No middle man or middle woman."

"Are you expensive?"

"Hell, yeah. But I am discreet."

Frank laughed.

"Dude. Go take a snooze. Your face is literally freaking me out."

Frank patted him on the shoulder as he went toward the back. "I want to be woken up when we are an hour out."

"So you can decide if you need to kick my ass."

"Exactly."

In the center of the hanger there were two brand new Harley Davidson Road Kings. Cyrus had ordered the high output Project Rushmore Twin Cam 103 motor and six speed transmission. His was black. Hers was tricked out. It had LED lights, chrome laced wheels and lots and lots of chrome using all available parts from the new Diamond Ice line. The bike had been lowered to better fit Helen and had only a solo seat on it. Frank didn't want anyone riding with her. It was painted pearl white with sparkly ghost flames. He hadn't liked Harley's color choices for 2017. He also had Iron Braid chrome levers installed with black and white leather streamers.

She turned to look at Cyrus.

"There is one for each of us. It's time you learned to ride your own bike. I got you an open line of credit at the Harley dealership in town so you can choose your own leathers and riding gear."

Helen was genuinely excited. She hugged him hard and kissed him harder.

"Why now?"

"When you started planning this trip it reminded me how much I love you. I wanted to do something special. It was long overdue."

"You spoil me, darling."

"And you spoil me. We need to ride together more. Like the old days."

"Can we ride them now?"

"Unless you want to walk home."

Helen grabbed her white helmet from the seat and strapped it on. She smiled and thanked him with her eyes. Helen moved around the bike. It was glorious. If a falcon came in white and chrome, this was what it would have looked like.

"I love you," Helen said, even as she thought about Frank.

62

Frank leaned back in the tiny uncomfortable airplane seat. He was beyond exhausted, and sleep came easy. But it was not an easy sleep. He dreamed of Hades. He dreamed of Neil Lutins.

Frank and Spanish Johnny had driven to Neil's isolated property. The property was ringed by a huge metal fence topped with thick strands of razor wire. There was a call box at the entrance and a video monitor. Frank leaned out the window, spoke into the audio box, and smiled for the camera. The iron gates buzzed open, and they drove through.

Frank parked before the mansion. They were met by three Spartan guards. They were Hades' own version of Cerberus, the three headed hound that guarded the mythical Hades underworld. A Spartan in black jeans and a brown barn jacket stood out front to greet them. He carried a Benelli pump in one hand. The second and third Spartans flanked the truck. They were both carrying M-16s. Frank and Spanish Johnny got out and greeted their brother Spartans.

Everything was cavalier. Barn coat Spartan was Bob and automatic rifle Spartans were David and Billy. Spanish Johnny asked to check out one of the M-16s and David let him. Spanish Johnny examined it intently and then passed it back saying how impressed he was with the modifications. Bob led them inside. Neil hurried into the room to meet them. He was wearing a baggy green shirt and gray slacks. The expensive clothes looked out of place on him. He had trimmed his whiskers to a normal beard length instead of the usual Duck Dynasty style.

"It is great to see you," Neil said as he hugged them. "I don't get a lot of visitors anymore. Guess it goes with being a god." He laughed.

"We need to talk."

"Sure, brother. I got a sweet deal going. Really sweet. You are going to love it. It's classic."

"What you drinking, Neil?" Spanish Johnny asked.

Neil looked at the half full glass in his hand like it belonged to someone else. He stared, and then smiled as if remembering. "Absinthe from Slovakia. Damn good stuff."

"Awesome. Can I score a drink, man? I have a serious case of Sahara mouth."

"Bob, show Spanish Johnny where the booze is. Help yourself to whatever you want."

"You guys go on. I will catch up. You want anything, Frank?'

"No. I'm good."

"Pussy," Neil joked.

"Okay. Rum."

"Done."

A thin woman came into the room. She had blonde hair that was cut short. Not butch lesbian short, more like school teacher short. She was very pretty with an air of culture and breeding. But she wore a sour expression. Her lips were hard and remorseless.

"This is Marilynn Gideon. She's my business partner."

Marilynn wrapped her thin arms around Neil and kissed him on the cheek.

"I am a lot more than just his business partner."

Neil's laugh was a cackle. "Yes, she is. She is one hot momma. Guess you would say she is my woman."

"How did you two meet?"

"At a hotel bar. She was doing a conference thing. We struck a conversation. I found out she had a wild side." Hades mimicked smoking a crack pipe.

Marilynn giggled like a schoolgirl. It was a surreal sound coming from her. Frank thought he might have stepped into the Twilight Zone.

"Cyrus told me you run an orphanage or something."

"Fuck Cyrus in the ass. He's an old woman. Marilynn runs the entire state system, man."

"This new money making idea. I want to hear about it."

"Cyrus send you?"

"Yeah. Convince me he's wrong."

"Follow me."

Marilynn walked holding Neil's hand. They acted like teenagers. It was disconcerting to Frank. Greek history told the story of a lonely Hades who had fallen in love with a Greek girl named Persephone. He had kidnapped her and held her against her will. Maybe Marilyn was his Persephone.

Neil shouted in the direction Spanish Johnny had disappeared. "We are heading to the basement. Meet us there. Bob can show you the way."

Neil led the way down a large set of stairs. The basement was huge. Numerous doors were closed as Frank followed him down. Neil led them to a large heavy door and punched in the digital code. Frank noted the numbers. Inside was another large room that was divided in half by a set of iron bars just like in a prison. Three children were behind the bars watching television. They were all about four years old and identical, small and blonde.

Neil was beaming. He was so proud. "What do you think?"

"About what?"

"This. I thought you of all people would dig it. Slaves. Get it? Just like the ancient Spartans."

"I don't get it, Neil. You're selling kids. Do you have any idea of the ramifications?"

"Sure I do. I got that covered. We sell them overseas. The Asians and Saudis are wild about it. Marilynn doctors the books so it looks like the kids have all been adopted. No one is the wiser."

Frank walked over to the cell and looked at the kids. They all looked back, but none of them spoke. Frank noticed the wrist tattoo on each child. It was a yellow smiley face.

Neil noticed. "That is just a tat that shows they have been processed through the system."

"Do you have any idea what happens to them once they are sold?"

"No, who cares? It's not like getting adopted is a safe bet for them anyway. When my foster dad wasn't beating my ass he was raping it. And that bitch he was married to knew all about it. She never said a word. But she cashed the damn checks quick enough."

The Greek legends told of the Spring of Lethe under a stand of dark poplars in the underworld. If you drank from the spring you forgot who you were and what you had done. Maybe Neil and Marilyn had discovered their own spring. They were lost and didn't even realize it.

Frank felt a sickness growing inside. "They are kids, Hades. You can't sell kids."

"Why not? They aren't us. They don't count."

"There are just a product with a set value," Marilyn said.

"Shut the fuck up," Frank said. "They are people."

"At least this way they have value to someone. They're throwaway kids."

Neil laughed. "Listen to yourself, Frank. It isn't like the Spartans got clean hands. We sell drugs. We run whores. We sell weapons. We steal shit. We kill people. This is no different."

"It is different. They are kids," Frank screamed. "It isn't right."

"And I say it is."

"Who the fuck do you think you are?"

"I am a God. I am Hades. I can do as I wish. That's what I was told. That's what I will do. I don't need the Spartans' permission. I don't need Cyrus' permission. I don't need yours either."

Frank punched Neil without thinking. Neil flew across the room and struck the wall. He struggled to his feet. Blood poured from his nose. He was in shock.

"Are you nuts, Frank? We're friends. You can't do this shit to me. We are equals. We are brothers."

Spanish Johnny sauntered into the room. He was wiping the blade of his knife on a linen napkin that had once been white, but was now mostly stained red. He was smiling.

"I explained the situation to Bob and David and Billy. They understand and have agreed not to interfere."

Hades looked stunned. "Cyrus sent you to kill me? You are the Kryptea?"

Frank nodded.

"This is sick, Neil. You know it."

Hades smiled and spat on the floor.

"If that's the way you want it. I claim the right to physical challenge."

Spanish Johnny laughed. He grabbed Marilyn by her hair and pressed her against the wall. He held his knife to her throat.

"Go ahead, Frank. He has rights."

Frank drew his pistol and pointed it at Hades. "This will be quicker, old friend."

Hades reached behind his back and took out his own pistol. He threw it across the room. Next he reached into his front pocket. He withdrew a small lock back knife. The blade was three inches long.

"I choose blades. The ancient way."

Frank put his pistol back into the holster on his back. With Frank's hand behind his back, Hades charged, slashing with the blade. Thirty years earlier, Hades would have still been too slow to match Frank Kane. Frank leaned out of the way and struck him with a savage right that knocked Hades off his feet. Hades struggled to his feet and charged straight in. Frank swept the knife arm away and hit him twice with right hand hooks to the body. Hades fell again. Something was busted inside. Blood poured out of his mouth as he gasped for breath.

"We were brothers," Hades said. "I loved you."

Hades struggled to his feet again. He stepped in and slashed again. Frank paused and hit him with a punch that knocked him unconscious. Frank lifted the knife from Hades' limp hand. He felt down his rib cage, searching for the space above the heart. He slipped the blade through the thin chest and directly into the old man's pirate heart. Frank held it there until Hades died. A deep sadness washed over Frank.

"I loved you like a brother too," Frank whispered.

Frank stood and turned to Spanish Johnny. Marilyn slumped against the wall. Her throat had been cut. The thick red fluid still pumped from the severed arteries. Frank didn't say anything. He hadn't thought about the woman. He was glad he had not ordered it himself. Spanish Johnny saw Frank's distress. He came over and put his hands on his shoulders.

"I know he was your boy. I know this was hard. But he went quick like a warrior."

Frank didn't answer, he just nodded.

"I got the barrel of ether upstairs. I'll bring it down and it's done. Masnick's timer is untraceable, evidence is gone, no witnesses."

"What about the kids?"

"Don't worry. I'll take care of them before I set it off. They won't suffer."

Frank slammed Spanish Johnny against the wall and held him there.

"No. They are kids, goddamnit. We don't kill kids."

Spanish Johnny's eye's flashed rage, but he controlled it. He raised both hands in surrender.

"You tell me. What do you want to do?"

"I'll take the kids with me. Helios can cook up some documents for them. We can place them with someone. I know a couple that can take them in."

"If that is what you want to do, sure. You take the truck back. I know Hades has a bike around here. I'll set the timer and take the bike."

Frank nodded. "We are done here. I don't ever want to talk about this again."

"It's just between us. Cyrus will know, but we won't ever talk about it."

Frank patted Spanish Johnny on the head.

"Thanks. I mean it."

"Hey, that's what we do. I got your back, Frank. You can trust me."

Frank had taken the kids and set them up. Spanish Johnny had set the timer and blown up Neil's house. It looked like a meth explosion. No one asked any questions. No one cared.

"Frank," Jenny said. "The pilot said to wake you up."

Frank thanked her and went to the cockpit again.

"Keep it simple. In and out. After you take off, you can tell them the airport code. But I would appreciate it if you didn't remember to ID the car or follow us. That would be an unwise decision on your part."

"Do I look like an idiot?" Bullington said. "Wait, on second thought, don't answer that. Hey, you need me, just call. The phone is secure."

They landed without incident. Jenny wanted Frank to check into a hospital, but he refused. In the end, they just drove home. Frank found a G.P. named McNeil, and then a plastic surgeon named Best, and finally he went to Doc from the boxing gym. They all seemed happy to take cash. A splint here, a little cosmetic work there, and four implants later...Frank was as good as new. It had turned into the worst vacation of his life.

Four Months Later

"Jenny, it's coming on," Frank yelled.

Jenny came running into the room. Her long hair was still damp. She was getting ready for a date. She and Caron had been hanging around a new coffee shop that had opened near UNCG. It was called The Black Broth. Frank had sneered at the name. Black broth was the barley soup concoction the ancient Spartans ate. The legend was that you had to be born west of the Eurotas River to appreciate it. Of course, the mascot for UNCG was the Spartans. Maybe it was more than irony that had convinced the owner to name his coffee shop Black Broth. Young people seemed to love two things, coffee and cell phones.

Jenny ran into the room.

"Did I make it? Has it started?"

"No sit down. They just did the promo again. Here it comes."

On screen a tall attractive woman was approaching a speaker's podium. She wore her long dark hair parted in the middle. She was dressed in a conservative, blue business suit.

"I am Dee Dee Johnson. I am the paralegal for attorney Charles Foster."

She motioned with her hand toward the three people seated behind her in three chairs. Charles Foster wearing a gray Hugo Boss suit smiled and rose to his feet. He approached the podium. He gave her arm a little squeeze. Foster was a showman. The word was that he would be running for Congress next year. He was using this press conference for the extra publicity.

"Thank you all for coming. I was contacted a few months ago by a young man on Cat Island in the Bahamas. This young surfer had discovered a treasure that had been lost for hundreds of years. Dee Dee."

Dee Dee went to the table in the rear and brought something up to Mr. Foster. He held it up for the camera to see. It was a pendant. The central image was a trident. It was encircled by twin tiger sharks.

"The young man recognized this as the emblem of the notorious pirate Captain Falcon who sailed the Bahamian waters. Captain Falcon bought land and retired there. People had long searched for his treasure to the point that it was deemed a myth. But this amulet proves otherwise."

Dee Dee pulled back the cloth covering the table. It was covered with gold bars, raw silver, and a wild assortment of ancient jewels. There was murmuring from the gathered reporters. Charles Foster motioned for quiet.

"This is just a small sample of what was found. We have been in lengthy negotiations with the family who still own the property and the Bahamian government. To help with these negotiations, I enlisted the counsel of Gerry and Linda Schaffer. They are, in my opinion, the foremost authorities on maritime salvage law in the world."

The Schaffers were seated quietly in the back. Gerry wore his thick black hair combed straight back. He was dressed in a Hart Schaffner Marx suit accented with a bright yellow Ferragamo tie with beagles on it. Linda was also impeccably dressed in a red silk gabardine suit with a fitted waist and enough golden jewelry to rival the pirate's treasure. They each nodded toward the cameras.

"When I conclude my remarks, they will be available to answer any questions you have." On the back wall was a huge blow up of a photo of Bruce and Thor playing on the beach. The family agreed to a three way divination of the treasure. "The Bahamian government will retain a third of the treasure that will be displayed in newly constructed museum sites in Nassau and on Cat Island. The family will rebuild Captain Falcon's home and open it to the public with the support of the Bahamian government. The final third will be kept by the young man who discovered it."

"How much is the treasure worth?" someone yelled.

Foster laughed. "I am not at liberty to say. But let me add that this young man would be unable to spend his portion in his lifetime, even if he spent every waking minute trying."

"Damn," Jenny said. "I am so happy for Bruce. Did you know anything about it?"

"Why would I know anything about it?"

Jenny looked at him studying his face. "It just feels like a Frank Kane sort of deal and I know you know Charles Foster."

"Guilt by association?"

"Uhh huh."

"What kind of person would give up that kind of wealth?"

"What kind indeed?"

The doorbell rang.

"Oh, shit, Jacob's here. Go let him in while I dry my hair. And be nice. Don't scare him away. I like him."

"And this Jacob is the guy from the coffee shop?"

"Yes. You know it is. He owns it. He's older than me, but not too old for me."

"He better not be an asshole."

Jenny kissed Frank on the cheek. "He's not. He is super hot. In fact he kind of reminds me of a younger you."

"That's a poor endorsement."

Jenny punched him in the shoulder.

"Keep him entertained for five minutes. That's all I need. Five minutes more to be beautiful."

She ran up the stairs. Frank trudged to the door. He already hated the guy. If he knew what was good for him, he would not break Jenny's heart. Frank opened the door. He froze. He knew the man standing across the threshold from him.

"The Jake."

"Frank."

The Jake gave Frank a big hug. He was smiling. It had been a long time.

"I guess this isn't by chance?"

"Sort of. I was going to reach out to you. I met Jenny by chance, and I figured it was an omen. You were always fond of omens."

"Is Jenny part of the plan?"

"No. I like her for real. It has nothing to do with anything else."

"Good. I would hate to think you were taking advantage of her. That would be unwise on your part. Tell me what brings The Jake to Greensboro?"

The Jake's cell phone rang. He held up a finger and took it out of his jacket pocket. He slid the screen of the iphone to answer. He listened for a few seconds and passed the phone to Frank.

"It's for you."

Frank took the phone and listened.

"Hello, Frank."

Frank smiled. He knew the voice.

"Hello, Helios. What can I do for you?"

"So blunt after all this time. Not how are you? Not where have you been keeping yourself? Not how did you find me? Just straight to it?"

"How are you? How have you been? What have you been up to? How did you find me?"

Helios laughed.

"We don't have time for chit chat, Frank. I have a serious problem that I need your help with."

Epilogue

The yacht rocked gently at anchor. Keith Masnick, also called Prometheus when he was a god of Sparta, slept quietly. A brunette with a near perfect figure slept beside him. She had been at his side since he had fled Florida for St. Kitts. Masnick awoke suddenly.

He looked around the dark master-cabin of the boat. He could hear the woman breathing gently beside him. He neither felt nor heard anything out of the ordinary. Yet, he sensed some change. Some unseen danger seemed to lurk in the darkness. He reached to the nightstand and turned on the light.

Spanish Johnny sat silently watching him from a chair at the foot of the bed. Two other men stood beside the doorway. All three men had their guns out. The two at the door had their guns hanging low by their sides. Spanish Johnny had his arms crossed. His pistol pointed off to the side. For an instant, Masnick considered trying for the gun beneath his pillow. He knew he would never reach it. He paused.

"May I get my glasses?"

Spanish Johnny smiled. "Of course, Prometheus."

Masnick took the glasses off the nightstand and put them on. He removed them again,wiped the lenses with a Kleenex tissue, and put them back on.

"What do you want, Johnny?"

"Cyrus sent me for you."

Masnick made a harrumphing sound of disdain. "The Kryptea? I never betrayed him or his interests. He has no beef with me. There is no need to kill me. The Spartans are gone in any case."

The brunette awoke and sat up in the bed. She did nothing to hide her nakedness as she inched closer to Masnick.

"That is not for me to say. I am to collect you, brother, not kill you."

"My men?"

Spanish Johnny smiled and shrugged. "They weren't as lucky."

Masnick began to breath hard. He clutched at his chest. His eyes were wide.

"Get my heart meds from the bathroom. Please. They are on the shelf by the sink."

Spanish Johnny smiled. One of the men beside the door ran into the bathroom.

"I can't find the switch," he shouted back.

"It is beside the mirror. Over the sink. Hurry."

Spanish Johnny pointed his pistol at Masnick. There was a small explosion from the bathroom and a blinding flash of light. The man screamed inside the bathroom. He stumbled out, clutching at his burned face. The second man at the door ran to his aid. Spanish Johnny did not take his eyes or his gun off Masnick. He didn't even flinch at the sound of the small explosion. He had expected treachery.

Masnick had started to lean forward so it would be easier to spin and reach his hidden weapon. When Spanish Johnny didn't move, he leaned back in the bed.

A third man burst into the room. Spanish Johnny held up one of his hands.

"Start the boat and take us out to sea. Everything is under control here." He spoke to the men who had been by the doorway. "Is Will alright?"

"Yeah. It was some kind of flashbang. He got burned, but he will be okay."

"Prometheus. Such tricks."

Masnick didn't answer. Spanish Johnny smiled, and shot the woman beside him twice in the chest. Her body jerked with the impact and fell to the side of the bed.

"That was on you," Spanish Johnny said. "Bind him. Tightly. Cyrus is eager to talk with him."

To order additional copies of

SPARTAN KRYPTEA

Contact Savage Press by
visiting our webpage at
www.savpress.com

or see our Savage Press
Facebook page.

Or call
218-391-3070
to place secure credit card orders.

mail@savpress.com

First in the Frank Kane Series

Frank Kane goes to Atlanta and saves Jenny and Caron from a life of white slavery. Available at www.savpress.com and from Amazon as a hardcover and eBook.

SPARTAN NEGOTIATOR

JOHN F. SAUNDERS

Second in the Frank Kane Series

Available at www.savpress.com and from Amazon as a hardcover and eBook.